The Enthusiasms of Robertson Davies

Also by Robertson Davies

FICTION

The Papers of Samuel Marchbanks

Tempest-Tost · Leaven of Malice · A Mixture of Frailties

Fifth Business · The Manticore · World of Wonders

The Rebel Angels · What's Bred in the Bone

The Lyre of Orpheus

PLAYS

Eros at Breakfast, and Other Plays

Fortune My Foe · At My Heart's Core

Hunting Stuart, and Other Plays

A Masque of Aesop · A Jig for the Gypsy

A Masque of Mr. Punch · Question Time

CRITICISM AND ESSAYS

Shakespeare's Boy Actors · A Voice from the Attic

Feast of Stephen: A Study of Stephen Leacock

One Half of Robertson Davies

(in collaboration with Sir Tyrone Guthrie)

Renown at Stratford · Twice Have the Trumpets Sounded

Thrice the Brinded Cat Hath Mew'd

THE

Enthusiasms

OF

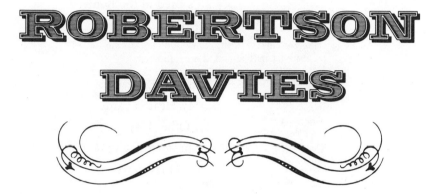

ROBERTSON
DAVIES

EDITED BY

Judith Skelton Grant

VIKING

VIKING
Published by the Penguin Group
Viking Penguin, a division of Penguin Books USA Inc.,
40 West 23rd Street, New York, New York 10010, U.S.A.
Penguin Books Ltd, 27 Wrights Lane, London W8 5TZ, England
Penguin Books Australia Ltd, Ringwood, Victoria, Australia
Penguin Books Canada Ltd, 2801 John Street,
Markham, Ontario, Canada L3R 1B4
Penguin Books (N.Z.) Ltd, 182–190 Wairau Road,
Auckland 10, New Zealand

Penguin Books Ltd, Registered Offices: Harmondsworth, Middlesex, England

First American Edition
Published in 1990 by Viking Penguin, a division of Penguin Books USA Inc.

1 3 5 7 9 10 8 6 4 2

An earlier, different edition of this work was published in Canada
by McClelland and Stewart Limited.

The selections in this book first appeared in *Cuesta*; *Dateline: Canada
1962*; *Globe and Mail*; *Holiday*; *Maclean's*; *Mayfair*; *The New York
Times* (Copyright © 1962, 1987 The New York Times Company); *Opera
Canada*; *Peterborough Examiner*; *Saturday Night*; *Stratford Papers on
Shakespeare* (Gage Publishing); *TV Guide*; *Toronto Daily Star*; *University
of Manitoba Alumni Journal*; *University of Toronto's Varsity Graduate*;
and *The Washington Post*.

LIBRARY OF CONGRESS CATALOGING IN PUBLICATION DATA
Davies, Robertson.
The Enthusiasms of Robertson Davies / edited by Judith Skelton
Grant.
p. cm.
Originally published: Toronto: McClelland and Stewart, 1979.
ISBN 0-670-82994-3
I. Grant, Judith Skelton. II. Title.
PR9199.3.D3E5   1990
814'.54—dc20   89-40342

Printed in the United States of America
Set in Sabon

TABLE *of* CONTENTS

I
CHARACTERS

II
BOOKS

III
ROBERTSON DAVIES

ACKNOWLEDGEMENTS

I would like to thank the E. J. Pratt Library at Victoria College, the Metropolitan Toronto Public Library, the National Library of Canada and the John P. Robarts Research Library at the University of Toronto. All of these institutions bent rules to make it possible for me to read the hundreds of microfilms of newspapers to which Davies contributed.

J.S.G.

INTRODUCTION

*T*he summer of 1977, when I embarked on a reading of Robertson Davies' journalism, was one of surprises. I had imagined myself dutifully ploughing through dated, hastily-written material, kept going only by scholarly thoroughness, before getting on with my main task, a brief introduction to Davies' plays and novels. Instead, I found myself in a state of heady exhilaration as I reeled my way from one microfilm to the next. I found the sensibility and style that inform the "Deptford Trilogy" already evident in the earliest columns in 1940. Always Davies wore his broad learning lightly, beguiling me with civilized discourse and sudden puffs of gusto. He wrote so engagingly that his enthusiasms became mine as I read, and often longer. When the day's "work" was over that summer, I was often enticed into reading the books mentioned in an article or a review. And what an eclectic lot they were—books on circuses, saints, psychology, music, magic, religion, handwriting, book collecting, drama, social history. His taste in literature ranged widely too, from Chaucer to Mervyn Peake, from Shakespeare to Don Marquis. He tried his hand at many forms, liking the challenge of shifting mode, enjoying moving his vocabulary and sentence structure up and down the scale of literary formality. As a journalist he was a man of performances, an actor changing his roles and masks at will. At his most thoughtful, he was a man of deep self-knowledge and of psychological acumen. The subjects he tackled seemed so diverse and marvellous that it was easy to forget that his enthusiasms were not all-inclusive, to forget those areas which had little resonance for him, such as most of science, business, economics. Since he lulled the reader with his enthusiasm, rarely moving to the attack, almost never letting the cloak of civility slip, rarely letting his talent for invective rip, it was also easy to forget that much of his journalism displayed less of his personality than his novels, where his shadow side had more play.

It was startling to discover how much he had written. He made his living from 1942 to 1962 editing the *Peterborough Examiner*. In the evenings and on weekends from 1940 to 1953, he created his one journalistic outlet for his anger and scorn in the columns of his crusty, acerbic, funny alter ego, Samuel Marchbanks. For a year or so before moving to the *Examiner* and for six further years during the fifties, he "conducted" the books page in the Canadian magazine *Saturday Night*. From 1959 to 1962 he wrote "A Writer's Diary" for the Toronto Star Syndicate, a column carried by ten Canadian papers plus the *Philadelphia Bulletin* and the *Providence* [R.I.] *Journal*. At the same time, additional reviews and articles and even the texts of speeches found their way into a wide range of Canadian and American publications, the flood abating only when he moved to the University of Toronto in 1963 to teach and serve as first Master of Massey College.

Yet, few of the delights I savoured that summer were accessible to an ordinary reader. Samuel Marchbanks' lively ventures into the diary and letter forms were, to a certain degree, obtainable, for Davies had created three volumes from the columns. "Created" is the correct word for what he did, however. He was no historian of his own work. Rather, he interacted with it, imposing fresh structures as he collected and reorganized. The weekly rhythm of the column was best caught in *The Diary of Samuel Marchbanks* (1947), which selected half of the columns from two years and presented them as a single year's round. *The Table Talk of Samuel Marchbanks* (1949) imposed the tempo of a formal seven-course meal on Marchbanks' musings, while *Samuel Marchbanks' Almanack* (1967) introduced a whole new whimsical twelve-part structure around selections from several years' columns. Likewise, *A Voice from the Attic* (1960), which was supposed to collect the reviews and essays written for *Saturday Night,* used only about a dozen of the original articles, fitting them into a book whose thrust was very different from that in the magazine pieces.

The huge body of excellent writing that still remained in the files of assorted newspapers and periodicals cried out for collection and republication. In *The Enthusiasms of Robertson Davies* (1979) I drew together three of the major subjects of his journalism, namely, characters, books, and himself. Because Davies tussled with Canada's theatre on so many levels—as playwright, actor, director, commentator, theatre-goer—and because as a writer himself he had discerning things to say about Canada's evolving literature, I gathered his comment on those topics separately in *The Well-Tempered Critic: One Man's View of Theatre and Letters in Canada* (1981). The celebrations of saints' days, holidays, and annual occasions that so flavoured his columns might perhaps be reissued some day as a literary calendar.

In the years since that exhilarating summer of 1977, Davies has gathered his three Marchbanks books into the omnibus *The Papers of Samuel Marchbanks* (1985), imposing yet another organizational device, that of a scholarly edition with its attendant scholarly apparatus. And, in the years just before his retirement in 1981 and in those since, he has produced a fresh spate of journalism, much of it for *The Washington Post.* This new edition of *The Enthusiasms* reprints all but four of the original selections and adds recent pieces to each section.

The profiles in "Characters," usually written upon the deaths of famous people or as reviews of biographies, reflect Davies' delight in strong personality and eccentricity. He writes with equal ease about Lew Fields, the vaudeville performer; Emma Calvé, the opera star; James Agate, the English drama critic; and Arthur Sullivan, the composer. But a larger number of the sketches reveal his fascination with odd quirks in the lives of his subjects. His sketch of the philosopher and essayist Francis Bacon focusses on Bacon's bizarre ideas on health and medication; that on the essayist William Hazlitt, on Hazlitt's unfortunate passion for his landlord's daughter, an uneducated girl less than half his age. He treasures "sturdy idiosyncrasy" of all sorts and presents favourite oddities with gusto. His enjoyment of such individuals is long-lasting, as can be seen in this collection when unusual characters mentioned casually in early columns are examined at length years later.

Davies' eclectic learning enriches many of the reviews in "Books." The most important aspect of this section, however, concerns human psychology. Davies' interest here goes back at least as far as his student years at Queen's University in Kingston, Ontario, where he learned something about Freud's ideas and read Havelock Ellis' four-volume *Studies in the Psychology of Sex*. At Oxford he began to buy and read through the collected works of Freud. When the Kinsey Report appeared in the late forties, he read it with care. And in the mid-fifties he embarked on the thorough study of the works of C. G. Jung which so influenced his later fiction. Along the way he read and reviewed a tremendous array of books that either present theories of psychology directly or draw their organizing ideas from one or another psychological school. His desire to understand human behaviour and his openness to new conjectures about the psyche have resulted in a rare degree of self-knowledge as well as a generous tolerance for the wide range of human variation. These character traits have engendered a fine sense of amplitude and of generosity in his journalism. Consider, for instance, his reflections on three philosophical works in 1943 (p. 126) and his response to Salinger's *Franny and Zooey* in 1961 (p. 206). When he reviews *Lolita* and *The Hotel New Hampshire* (pp. 187, 227), he reveals his broad-mindedness and his psychological acuity concerning authors, readers, and characters alike.

The entries in the third section, "Robertson Davies," are particularly intriguing. Here his character is not just salt adding zest to sketches of others' lives but the moving force—usually the subject—of the articles. When he celebrates significant moments in his life, he reveals the private man, his activities and feelings. Yet, curiously, these pieces do not create a feeling of intimacy. We are always kept at arm's length by the sense that we are witnesses to a performance. Indeed, acting is fundamental to Davies' presentation. We are aware of it; and our consciousness of its variety is what fascinates.

Those who are annoyed by such posturing have missed several essential truths about Davies' performances, I think. These truths can be seen in the most "stagey" pieces in "Robertson Davies": "Mimesis at Massey," "The Three Warning Circles," and "The Table Talk of Robertson Davies." In each one Davies sustains a single attitude—exaggerated imitation of Shaw's and Barrie's copious stage directions in "Mimesis"; the stance of Aged Sage in "The Three Warning Circles"; the role of Wise Pontificator in "Table Talk." All three roles are earned, and real. For instance, Davies knows his Shaw through and through: he began reading him as a schoolboy, has directed and acted in his plays, and chose to teach a graduate course called "Bernard Shaw and His Contemporaries." Davies *is* an aged sage, who gives good advice to the young at convocations; and he *is* a wise pontificator, with sagacious answers to questions that would daunt most of us. We are invited in such pieces to enjoy the mask he wears but also to be aware that it is not the whole man (nor is it easy to maintain). Often the final note of such pieces reminds us of that: "The Three Warning Circles," for example, ends with "the old man of benevolent aspect" hurrying away "as fast as his legs would carry him." The art and the reality of the pose do not conceal the twinkle in Davies' eye; art, reality, and twinkle are all part of the fun, and all essential aspects of the man.

Davies' wit, vitality, and vivacity kept his readers turning to page four of the *Peterborough Examiner* for his editorials and columns, to the books section of *Saturday Night,* to his syndicated "A Writer's Diary" column, and to his many scattered articles. Those who are reading Davies' journalism for the first time will have a pleasure denied earlier aficionados: that of observing the interplay between the journalism and the better-known plays and novels. The fascination with the history, craftsmanship, and theatricality of marionettes which surfaces in the tribute to Tony Sarg written in 1942 (p. 9) also informs the play *Fortune, My Foe* in 1949. The reference to Nellie Melba's singing of Tosti's "Good-Bye" in *A Mixture of Frailties* (1958) is echoed in the profile of Nellie Melba in 1962 (p. 98). The boyhood curiosity about grotesques mentioned in "I Remember Creatore" in 1948 (p. 245) surfaces again in the sideshow characters in *World of Wonders* (1975). The many other instances of anticipation and amplification I leave to you to discover. Much of the pleasure in such connections lies in finding them.

Judith Skelton Grant
Toronto
3 April 1989

I

CHARACTERS

Lew Fields

*T*he death of Lew Fields last week divided what was probably the most famous comedy team to appear on this continent during the great days of vaudeville—Weber and Fields. Vaudeville is dead now, but most of us can remember the days when every movie theatre of any pretension had a few "acts" included in its entertainment. In Canada vaudeville had an individuality of its own, for local taste was divided about evenly between the music-hall entertainment popular in the Old Country, and the distinctively American type of vaudeville which came to us from over the border.

Good vaudeville was remarkably fine entertainment. It had a verve and a hearty, earthy quality which we miss now, for the spirit of vaudeville is not communicable by means of the talking picture, and is even less successful on the radio. I do not mean to say that radio entertainment is not often very good, but it is a thing apart; it is not vaudeville. Only in the theatre was it possible to see the performers and to be warmed by their personal charm, to respond to their efforts and to feel their response to the applause and appreciative laughter of their audience. It had an intimate quality; audience and actors conspired to make a little oasis of happiness and mirth within the walls of the theatre. Try as we will, we cannot be intimate with a shadow on a screen, nor a voice from a box.

And what actors some of the old vaudeville performers were! Theirs was a specialized art; they had to make their impression on the audience in anything from half an hour to ten minutes, and the impression had to be a lasting one. Every second counted, so they worked hard and danced, sang, recited and acted as though for dear life, and gave us some wonderfully stimulating hours. Some of the best modern actors learned their technique in the hard school of vaudeville.

Weber and Fields were both New Yorkers, born in a house on Essex Street in the unfashionable East Side; there was a saloon in the same building and from earliest childhood Lew and Joe took in an atmosphere of lager beer, fights, and strong, rough life. It was this sort of life which they satirized in their later vaudeville acts when they had become America's favourite "Dutch" comedians. Of course, they were both Jews but Jews were not considered funny in the eighties. The stock comic figure then was the Dutchman, because it was the great period of German immigration to the States and the stolid, beer-guzzling Teutons who worked in the mills and the breweries were thought very funny by the more sophisticated Yankees. Why Dutch? Presumably because they came from Deutschland, for few of them were Hollanders. But the "Dumb Dutchman" was the type satirized by Weber and Fields.

A modern audience would probably find Weber and Fields more grotesque than funny. They wore extraordinary costumes, with enormous baggy pants, ill-fitting waistcoats stuffed out with pillows, and vast coats, all these garments being made out of material resembling horse blanketing. They wore low crowned "skimmer" hats, and long chinwhiskers. Dressed thus, they represented the American idea of a German immigrant. Their act consisted of repartee and comic songs. Some of these songs deserve to be reprinted, for they were every bit as silly and meaningless as those which we hear over the radio today. When people yearn for the good old songs of a better era they should be reminded that the majority of them were rubbish such as this:

> I valk dot Broadway down,
> I valk dot Broadway down,
> Der nicest things as neffer vas

Iss valk dot Broadway down.
Der fellers vink der eyes,
Und ven I look around,
There ain't no harm I take his arm
Und valk dot Broadway down.

That is a fair example of "Dumb Dutch" humour, and I cannot see that it is any improvement on "Daddy" or "The Hut-Sut Song."

The most popular act that Weber and Fields ever played was one which was supposed to take place in a pool-room. In this Weber was, as always, the stupid German who knew nothing, and who was induced to play pool by Fields, the slick city man. They rolled on the table, danced on it, did unbelievable things to it, until at last Fields won the game and took all Weber's money from him. One of their great tricks was to carry on a rapid conversation while standing on their heads. Another was to borrow a supposedly valuable violin from a member of the orchestra and then to pull it apart. It doesn't sound very funny now but it seems to have been popular at the time. After they became known all over the States Weber and Fields presented a series of burlesques of famous plays in New York, which crowned their reputation as the finest comedy team of their day. In these they were aided by the famous beauty Lillian Russell; she was not much of an actress, but she had a really beautiful voice, which, with her striking personal magnificence, made her a popular favourite.

Weber and Fields saw the rise of vaudeville and they were its chief glory during its best days. When it declined, owing to the rise of the talking pictures and the growing greed of vaudeville circuit managers, they made a few movies, none of which were strikingly successful, and their greatness became a matter of history while they were still living. No fame is more fleeting than that of the popular entertainer.

Peterborough Examiner, 29 July 1941

Emma Calvé

*L*ast Saturday afternoon the Metropolitan Opera broadcast was of Bizet's popular opera *Carmen*. It was magnificently
conducted by Sir Thomas Beecham, the great British conductor
who has recently been doing so much to show our American
cousins that all the musical talent outside their own land is not
confined to the Axis countries. Listening to the familiar strains,
it was impossible not to be reminded of the recent death (early
this month) of Emma Calvé, the French prima donna who was
accounted the greatest of all Carmens. For many years the singer
had been in retirement in her château in the south of France.
But the possession of a château must not be taken as an indi-
cation that Calvé spent her last years in affluence. She lived in
a castle simply because it never occurred to her that it was
possible to live anywhere else. She was one of those people who
cannot exist without an atmosphere of magnificence. In a small
villa, more in keeping with her circumstances, she would have
stifled; her draughty castle suited her exactly. In it she could
breathe and indulge in the lavish self-dramatization which was
her normal way of life.

Calvé was not born to magnificence; it was a taste which she
acquired in the days of her greatness and which she never lost.
She was at the height of her career during the great days of
the Metropolitan, when she and Melba shared the honours in
the great female roles, and when Caruso and Antonio Scotti, the
de Reszke brothers and Plançon were the golden-voiced heroes

and villains of the day. *Carmen* was then Calvé's special artistic property, and no other prima donna dared challenge her supremacy in it.

She brought to the part a quality of genuine and convincing wickedness and abandon which were rare on the stage in the days of Edward the Peacemaker. Most actresses, and particularly most opera singers, were content then to indicate wickedness by various conventional means, such as mocking laughs and much by-play with feather fans. Not so Calvé. As Carmen she wore upon her lovely face that expression which Shakespeare has called "the leer of invitation," and the effect upon her audiences was electric. She played Carmen for what she was, a gypsy harlot, and some of the reputation which she gained in that role stuck to her in her private life. Oddly enough, she hated the part, but she played it again and again because it brought her the money which she loved. She loved the applause, too. Minnie Maddern Fiske, herself a fine actress, once said: "There are two great actresses in the world today; not as the man in the street might say, 'Duse and Bernhardt,' but Duse and Calvé." Calvé basked in the admiration which she won in the exercise of her great talent.

She made a great deal of money in her time and she spent it lavishly. Speaking of herself and her colleagues at the Metropolitan she said: "We were a race of giants." Quite true, and in case you don't know it, being a giant is a very expensive business. The cost of food and drink, not merely for oneself but for one's fellow-giants and one's scores of attendant gnomes, is a very considerable item. And the cost of jewels for a female giant is really fabulous. It is not surprising, then, that when Calvé's popularity began to wane, she accepted an engagement to appear in vaudeville, at Eddie Darling's New York Palace. The prospect unnerved her so greatly that she was unable to appear at her Monday matinée (Washington's Birthday, 1920) for she had lost her voice. But $4,000 a week is an excellent doctor and she was soon on the job. It was shortly after this that she retired to her native land.

But wherever Macgregor sits is the head of the table, and Calvé soon made her French château a stopping-off place for many of the wealthy and the famous who travelled in that direction on their way to the Riviera. She also took pupils; one of the most distinguished of these was the American singer Peggy Wood, who scored her greatest success in Noël Coward's *Bitter Sweet*. Calvé, who was very fond of money, blamed herself for having put her first earnings into her French castle; her self-accusations were particularly bitter whenever the franc dropped to a new low. Melba, she said, had been more astute; Melba had invested her money, not in her native Australia, but all over the world. Calvé's opinion of her old friend and rival was kindly but patronizing: "the voice of an angel, but no heart," she said. No one could ever accuse Calvé of lacking heart, or temper, either. And she possessed that rarest of qualities in a singer— wit. Her imitations of her friends, and particularly of her ene- mies, were inspired by an accuracy of perception and a kindly malice which made them unforgettable.

The fall of France must have been a bitter pill to Calvé. She had a poor opinion of Germans, both as people and as artists. It is sad to imagine what her last days may have been in her "robber-baron's castle" as Peggy Wood calls it. But one thing is certain; when death came, Calvé met it with spirit. No one who knew so well how to greet life could possibly fail to know how to greet death.

Peterborough Examiner, 31 January 1942

Tony Sarg

When Tony Sarg died a fortnight ago the world lost a master in an art which has few practitioners, the art of making and operating marionettes. Tony Sarg's world of wooden men and women travelled all over this continent, all over Europe, over most of the globe, in fact, and everywhere it went it excited wonder and delight. It was a very old type of entertainment, to which a pleasant American flavour had been added by a man of striking humour and originality. Tony Sarg was a great man of the theatre, even though his proscenium arch was no more than five feet high.

Many of the children who saw his beautifully made wooden people thought that marionettes were an original thought with Tony Sarg. In fact the art is as old as history. There were marionette shows in ancient Egypt; the Romans took great pleasure in them; in the islands of the East Indies there are marionette shows of gods and heroes and devils which are older than any man can calculate; there were marionettes in the Middle Ages, and there were wonderful marionettes, still to be seen in museums, in the eighteenth century; there are still marionettes in England, for is not the Punch and Judy show the greatest of street entertainments in that island? But it was Tony Sarg who first made marionettes really popular in the United States; it was he who brought the old art to the New World.

Sarg's marionettes were often seen in Canada, usually as a part of the Christmas display in a large department store. They drew crowds of happy and excited children, and a very considerable audience of adults as well. The fact of the matter is that marionettes are creatures of infinite fascination, and it is almost impossible for any one who is not a curmudgeon to resist them. Their charm is the charm of the miniature; they are so small, so elegant, and they have such a curious movement; it is strangely human, and yet it has a lightness, a spring, a jauntiness, as it were, which is never seen in mere humanity. They have an infinite range of emotion, but they are never intense or boring, as live actors, and even more, the shadow actors of the screen, are apt to be. Watching them, it is easy to understand why the foremost genius of his time, the mighty Goethe, loved to watch marionette shows, and why he loved to pull the strings himself; the inspiration for the greatest of his works, the tragedy of Faust, came from an old German marionette play which he saw many times.

Tony Sarg made and showed scores of marionettes, but there were two of his creations which were perennially popular: the first, for children, was a donkey which played out a little scene with a clown, finally kicking him about the stage; the second was for adults and it was the figure of a mop-haired pianist who played and thumped upon a concert piano until finally it collapsed on him. Sarg did not often play whole plays with his figures. He specialized in a sort of marionette variety show with many rapidly changing scenes and dozens of marionettes. In Europe, on the other hand, puppets generally perform a drama of some length, and often do shortened versions of such well-known classics as *She Stoops to Conquer;* it cannot be said that these performances are as satisfactory as those by human actors, but they have their own special charm. The famous marionettes of Paul Brand make a specialty of opera, and perform several quite acceptably. Pergolesi's *La Serva Padrona* is one of their best, and they also do the little opera which Mozart composed when he was twelve, *Bastien und Bastienne.* The music and singing is done backstage and the movements of the figures are cleverly co-ordinated with it.

There are never many companies of marionettes in the world because the art of controlling the figures is difficult to acquire, and takes much the same sort of patience as ivory-carving or cutting intaglios; also it requires a great deal of dramatic ability, and most people who have dramatic ability like to display it in person, and not by means of a puppet, while they themselves remain hidden. Generally marionette troupes are made up of families where the art is taught by parents to children, and the skill is regarded as a family possession. But some of the best marionette shows have been made and worked by men who were attracted to it as a miniature art in which a kind of limited perfection was possible. William Simmonds, in England, has made some charming figures, and Harro Siegel of Berlin and Richard Teschner of Vienna have made puppets of breathtaking beauty. Remo Bufano, an American, specializes in enormous marionettes, and some of his which were shown at the New York World's Fair in 1939 stood twelve feet high. Almost every great city has a puppet show, depending principally upon children for audience. New York used to have one, and may still have it, run by a family of Italians. Paris had the charming Luxembourg Puppet Theatre. There are several such theatres in Britain, and every year before the war they exhibited in a gallery on Leicester Square in the heart of the city's theatre district.

Tony Sarg was 61 when he died. In his way he was a predecessor of Walt Disney in the art of the animated cartoon and he was a popular illustrator of children's books. During his life he gave happiness to millions of children and adults, and managed to enjoy himself at the same time. He has left no lasting mark in the world, perhaps, but many people will remember him with affection, and he will always have his place as the man who interested the American public in one of the oldest of the theatre arts.

Peterborough Examiner, 26 March 1942

Richard Harris Barham

A few days ago I happened to pick up a copy of *The Ingoldsby Legends* and was interested to find in it a Preface dated February 1, 1843. The book was a second edition, and not a first, and in any case the *Legends* first saw light in *Blackwood's Magazine* in 1837, but upon this slim excuse I mean to write a column about the book, and anyone who does not like it is under no compulsion to read further. *The Ingoldsby Legends* are first-rate comic verse; they contain some of the most ingenious rhymes to be found in English poetry. They were written by the Rev. Richard Harris Barham, a contemporary of Sydney Smith, that other immensely witty clergyman. What, one might ask oneself, has caused the decline of wit among the clergy? The only witty cleric of our time whose name comes at once to mind is Monsignor Ronald Knox, and he is no match for either Barham or Smith. Let some earnest university researcher look into this matter and give us his views.

Barham came of ancient lineage, his family possessing estates in Kent, near Canterbury; it was his boast—an odd one for a cleric—that a direct ancestor of his was that Reginald Fitzurse who was one of the assassins of Thomas à Becket. As a lad young Barham was in a coach accident which left him lame for life, and may have turned him from the active pursuits of a country gentleman to the more sedentary occupations of a clergyman and a writer. Early in his career he became a minor canon of St. Paul's Cathedral and a priest-in-ordinary of the

Chapels Royal. His cast of mind was not conventionally clerical; he loved burlesque, irony and gay living, and he had a somewhat wry outlook upon the passion for legends and antiquities which possessed so many cultivated persons of his time, and which plunged the novel and the drama into a welter of uncritical romanticism.

Barham had the true burlesquer's gift for turning the grave into the gay with the least possible expense of effort. Consider this stanza from his parody of "The Burial of Sir John Moore"—

> Not a sou had he got, not a guinea or groat;
> And he looked confoundedly flurried,
> As he bolted away without paying his shot,
> And the landlady after him hurried.

In Barham's day parody was more highly esteemed than it is now, and he and Theodore Hook and the brothers James and Horace Smith gave contemporary poets—including Byron and Wordsworth and Southey—an uncomfortable time of it when they set to work.

The best known of *The Ingoldsby Legends* is undoubtedly "The Jackdaw of Rheims," but it is not the best in workmanship or humour. A hundred years ago it was considered permissible and laudable for humorous writers to poke very bitter fun at Catholic legend and belief, and many of the *Legends* travel that easy path. Ideas of good taste differ from age to age, and this must always be borne in mind when reading the works of dead writers; we do not, nowadays, think Barham's burlesques of Shakespearean themes funny, either. The burlesquer and parodist gains his effects by treading hard on somebody's corns, and frequently by exploiting popular prejudice. We can hardly blame Barham for being a man of his time. But the best of his verses have a life which will ensure their popularity for a long time to come. Every reader of the *Legends* has his own favourites; my own happens to be "Nell Cook: The Legend of the Dark Entry," which contains so much of the best of Barham.

It has an excellent story to tell; its form is poetic and its spirit lively; I was frightened by it as a child and have not altogether mastered my dread of the jealous cook who made the poisoned pie. If you have not read it try it some dark night when you are alone; it is a notable bit of grisly fun.

But dispute about tastes is futile, and "The Legend of Bleeding Heart Yard," and "The Legend of Salisbury Plain," and "The Legend of France," all have their partisans. The time to read the *Legends* is at night; that is when they were written; Barham was a night-bird if ever there was one. A story is told of his Oxford days, when he was a commoner at Brasenose; his tutor, a Mr. Hodson, rebuked him for his late hours, and especially for his frequent absence from morning chapel. "The fact is, sir," said Barham, "you are too late for me." "Too late!" said the astonished tutor. "Yes, sir; I cannot sit up till seven in the morning. I am a man of regular habits; and unless I get to bed by four or five at latest, I am really fit for nothing the next day." It was this boon companion spirit which Barham carried through his life. His sermons have not been handed down to posterity, which is not surprising, but his *Legends* have stood the test of a hundred years, and if we may judge from the number of reprints of them which continue to appear, they are good for another century at the very least.

Peterborough Examiner, 29 September 1943

John Martin-Harvey

The death of Sir John Martin-Harvey on the 14th of May breaks the last link between the stage of our time and the great school of acting which reached its peak in the art of Sir Henry Irving. In the nineteenth century traditions of acting were passed from one actor to another in a manner which the different theatrical practice of our day has destroyed. Irving himself got his schooling with a number of fine actors, and was particularly influenced by those who had worked with Edmund Kean: Forbes-Robertson learned his craft from Samuel Phelps, a giant in his day, and also from Irving: Martin-Harvey studied with John Ryder, who passed on to him something of the magnificence of Macready, and later served a long apprenticeship in Irving's Lyceum company. Martin-Harvey always spoke of Irving as "my master," and there was no affectation in the expression; those who have seen Martin-Harvey have seen something of Irving.

Now that he is dead there are no more actors who can show us what Irving was like and what he was able to do. Doubtless actors linger on the stage who played with Irving; Ben Webster, now in Hollywood, who once played Lancelot in Irving's production of Comyns Carr's *King Arthur,* is one; but they cannot recreate anything of the spirit of Irving, any more than ordinary circus clowns can show us why Grimaldi was great. Martin-Harvey acted in the Irving tradition, and he added to it a romantic quality and a sweetness which was peculiarly his own.

Does the Irving tradition matter? someone may ask me. Yes, it does, for if it is lost to the stage now it will be necessary for the actors of the future to rediscover it. The Irving tradition was not merely the personality of Henry Irving; it was the essential spirit of the theatre itself—it was everything which we imply when we use the word "theatrical" in its best sense. There are people nowadays who think that Irving was a ranter and a ham; quite true, he was, but in the sense that Alexander the Great was a martinet and a butcher. Ranting and hamming are very necessary accomplishments for a great actor, and he is able to invest them with a greatness which lesser actors cannot approach. Acting is a positive, and not a negative, art; no man becomes a great actor because he refrains from ranting and hamming: he becomes great by creating greatness on the stage, and pouring it into the eyes and ears of his audience: to do that it may be necessary for him to do many things—ranting and hamming among them—the very existence of which is unsuspected by the self-conscious bourgeois who are now a majority among the acting profession.

Martin-Harvey was an artist of great accomplishment. He played many of the old melodramas which he inherited from Irving, like *The Lyons Mail, The Corsican Brothers* and *The Bells,* and he gave the stage one unforgettable melodrama in *The Only Way.* These plays had no literary value, and were not meant to have any; they were actor's pieces, and the pleasure which they gave was comparable to any other virtuoso performance. But Martin-Harvey also introduced Maeterlinck's work to the English-speaking stage, and lost a lot of money by doing so; he gave a magnificent performance in the *Oedipus Rex* of Sophocles directed by Max Reinhardt; he played several Shakespearean roles greatly; he cannot be dismissed as a merely popular actor because he did much to strengthen and enrich the stage in his time.

Canada has special cause to be grateful to him, for he toured this country on seven different occasions, and brought us great acting and great drama; we supported him whole-heartedly and he did not fail us. His plays were always plays of the fine manners, beauty of speech, beauty of motion and romance of a sort which the movies have never been able to give; Martin-Harvey gave poetic distinction, as Irving did, to some indifferent stuff, but the distinction was genuine. Hollywood, which has never felt that there was a "public" for distinction or beauty, has always been careful to tone down both when an actor has appeared in a film who possesses such graces. In the Irving tradition, Martin-Harvey always insisted that he be the centre of attraction when he was on the stage, and when he was not on it, all the action seemed to lead to his re-appearance. This is contrary to the "ensemble" acting about which we hear so much in these days, but an evening of Martin-Harvey was always worth a dozen ensemble performances. He was a star, and even in his last years—the writer saw him play *Oedipus* at Covent Garden in 1937—he dominated the stage. When he acted he was a most uncommon man, a portent and a phoenix before the eyes of his audience, and the other actors seemed very common indeed, however accomplished they might be; although we are assured that this is the Century of the Common Man, we grow weary of common men on the stage; there we want heroes and demigods, and Martin-Harvey was able to give them to us.

Writing in his autobiography, Martin-Harvey said that he had been happy ever since he was eighteen. He had his ups and downs of fortune; he was idolized by hundreds of thousands of people; he made a great deal of money, and lost much of it; he reckoned his friends by the score; he had at his side all his life a sympathetic and charming lady who was also a versatile actress, although she was not always suited to the roles for which her devoted husband cast her. And his art never declined, even when old age was upon him; in 1932 he toured Canada in a rubbishy play called *The King's Messenger* and although he was 70 at the time he carried the piece far beyond its deserts. It would be foolish to say that we shall not see his like again; we shall do so, for he was of the very best of the company of the theatre and we cannot do without greatness in the theatre. If he has left no one to speak of him as "my master," it will be necessary for the actors of the future to rediscover the secrets of art which he knew.

Peterborough Examiner, 23 May 1944

Osbert Sitwell

The first requisite of a good autobiography is not that the author should have had an interesting life, but that he should be able to write. Any life is interesting in the hands of a writer of genius; no life, however packed with incident, is interesting if recounted by a writer whose abilities are mediocre, or worse. As Aldous Huxley says, "Experience is not a matter of having actually swum the Hellespont, or danced with the dervishes, or slept in a doss-house. It is a matter of sensibility and intuition, of seeing and hearing the significant things, of paying attention at the right moments, of understanding and co-ordinating. Experience is not what happens to a man; it is what a man does with what happens to him." Sir Osbert Sitwell is one of the foremost literary artists of our day, and the first volume of his autobiography, *Left Hand, Right Hand,* is a notable literary event. Three volumes are to follow this one; many readers will be as impatient as I to have them at once.

Sir Osbert's prose, like the creation of a goldsmith of genius, is brilliant, opulent and enduring. He can write in many veins; some of his short stories are as terse as the severest devotee of "starkness" could demand. But of his autobiography he writes: "I should like to emphasize that I want my memories to be old-fashioned and extravagant—as they are;—I want this book to be as full of detail, massed or individual, as my last book of short stories was shorn of it—had to be shorn of it because of its form; I want this to be gothic, complicated in surface and crowned with turrets and pinnacles, for that is its nature." He has achieved his purpose; the book is extravagant and rich, and—of how few books may this be said—a work of conscious but unobtrusive art from start to finish.

Let us establish at once that it is no book for thick-heads. The only autobiography of recent date with which I can compare it is that of George Santayana, which is not for thick-heads either. Both writers are artists and philosophers, but in Santayana the philosopher predominates, and in Sitwell the artist is foremost. But both men, to return to the Huxley quotation, have had experience, and have sifted everything from that experience which it could yield of gold, and both have resolutely thrown away the dross. Both books are of enduring worth, and both have a constant, unifying note—a pedal-point, so to speak—of aristocracy which gives them curious distinction in our age.

The aristocrat, in our Century of the Common Man, is an underestimated creature, driven to be defensive whenever he is not aggressive. Sir Osbert Sitwell, carrying in his veins the blood of a half a dozen old, wealthy and high-born families, is unquestionably an aristocrat. Birth, inclination and education have made him a discoverer and encourager of talent in others; native ability has given him a distinguished place in that aristocracy of the mind which is open to anyone who can establish his claim to a place in it. He, his sister, Edith, and his brother, Sacheverell, have established themselves as writers of unusual grace, erudition, and application; these three aristocrats have slaved over their work, when less highly-born writers have been content to offer the public native woodnotes which have sometimes been very wild indeed.

Let no one imagine that being born in the highest society, of an old and wealthy family, constitutes a passport to literary fame; it is as much a handicap as being born to poverty and obscurity. More of a handicap, possibly, for we are all indulgent to talent which needs a leg-up in the world; few people can descry genius in those more fortunately placed than themselves, as the long struggle for recognition as serious artists of the Sitwells and of Lord Dunsany testifies. In the twenties the Sitwells were smiled at as triflers; we know now that their trifles have an enduring quality which many authors may envy. Sir Osbert's novel *Before the Bombardment* is one of the finest pieces of sustained satire in English; it can take its place beside *The Way of All Flesh* without apology. If it had been written by some struggling author, and not by a man economically at ease in Zion, it would have been acclaimed by the book clubs long ago. But who can forgive an author for being rich?

The first autobiographical volume tells us of the childhood of a rich and aristocratic eldest son at the turn of the century. Grace and *"la douceur de vivre"* which have temporarily deserted this earth were commonplace in that day and in that social sphere. Eccentricity thrived, for two wars had not made conformity to mediocre standards of thought and conduct the virtue which it is esteemed to be today. But there was a thoughtfulness, a sense of responsibility and a concern for the things of the mind among these aristocrats which is uncommon now, and until we replace that class with another, however differently constituted, which is above trifling considerations of what Mr. Shaw calls "middle-class morality," we must expect the arts to suffer accordingly. Aristocrats need not be rich, but they must be free, and in the modern world freedom grows rarer the more we prate about it.

Peterborough Examiner, 18 July 1945

Walt Whitman

The latest addition to the growing and excellent Viking Portable Library is *The Portable Walt Whitman,* edited by Carl Van Doren. When Whitman first published his *Leaves of Grass* in 1855, Emerson called it "the most extraordinary piece of wit and wisdom America has yet contributed." That judgement may still stand, for although the United States has now a considerable literature of its own, containing much that is brilliant, percipient, comprehensive and inimitable, the great books which it has given to the world could be counted on the fingers of one hand. *Leaves of Grass* is certainly one of this small number, and many able critics would name it first.

Those austere souls who maintain that a poet's life has little bearing on his work, and who do not care whether Shakespeare died drunk or sober, must make an exception in the case of Walt Whitman. He died in 1892, and there are people living who remember him well. But he was born in 1819, into an America as fabulous to us as ancient Troy, and unless that America has some shadowy existence in the back of our minds, we shall not be able to read Whitman understandingly. He went to school in the village of Brooklyn, and his childhood memories of a pretty American town were formed in that very place the name of which has now (somewhat unjustly) been made synonymous with sordid urbanity. As a youth his favourite spot for day-dreaming was Coney Island, then a barren waste looking out to the ocean, but now—well, who can define it better than its own historians, who called their book *Sodom by the Sea?*

Himself of English, Dutch and Welsh stock, Whitman moved in a world where Americans of Anglo-Saxon origin were the rule, rather than the exception. A young, fresh country made Whitman—young and fresh as the U.S.A. no longer is. "The United States themselves are essentially the greatest poem. . . . Here at last is something in the doings of man that corresponds with the broadcast doings of the day and night," he said, in his 1855 Preface. It was in this spirit that he sounded his barbaric yawp over the roofs of the world.

But even in a fresh new country a poet's way is the same as it has been in older and devirginated lands. "I had my choice when I commenced; I bid neither for soft eulogies, big money returns, nor the approbation of existing schools and conventions. . . . I have had my say entirely my own way, and put it unerringly on record—the value thereof to be decided by time"; thus he wrote in "A Backward Glance o'er Travel'd Roads" in 1888, when he was sixty-nine. Except for some lines of encouragement from Emerson he got little but silent contempt when he first brought out *Leaves of Grass;* subsequent editions brought such bouquets as "so-called poems which were chiefly remarkable for their absurd extravagances and shameless obscenity"—"Mr. Whitman's muse is at once indecent and ugly, lascivious and gawky, lubricious and coarse"—"You might strike out of existence all he has written, and the world would not be consciously poorer." What Whitman called his "heroic nudity" looked like simple nakedness to his prurient contemporaries, and to many modern readers who are no less prurient.

The reader of Whitman will find his curiosity stirred by two things which are only indirectly connected with his poetry. The first is the late flowering of his genius; a poet who is going to do great things usually shows early promise, but Whitman showed none. A wandering printer, a writer of occasional pieces for the newspapers, a seedy loafer ready to talk to anybody and to dignify bargees and truckmen as "powerful uneducated persons" was not a man to inspire much hope even in a self-consciously democratic society. Nor does he appear to have had great hopes of himself. He became a poet and a new man over-night, as it were, and at first the effect was not entirely happy; he reviewed his own book anonymously at various times and his references to himself are unhampered by elementary mod-esty. What made Walt Whitman a great poet in the course of a year or so? The second point concerns what Hollywood might call his "love-life." There is no record of a love-affair with a woman, though the sensuality of much of his poetry—some of the finest of it—rises from this theme; but he had many intimate friendships with young men, usually powerful uneducated per-sons, and there is an insistence on such friendship in his poetry which raises the second question: Was Whitman sexually in-verted? If so, he dealt with his personal problem in a manner which greatly enriched his poetry.

No poet, however great, can write at the top of his form every time he takes up the pen. In a complete Whitman there is a mass of shoddy. In this new and compact volume the editor has done an admirable job of selection. All the best of the verse is there, and half the book is given over to Whitman's prose which, chaotic and occasionally turgid though it is, must be studied if the full man is to be revealed. To the present reviewer the pas-sages from *Specimen Days* were particularly welcome. Here we have Lincoln, in his habit as he lived, riding into Washington with an escort of cavalry, or driving with Mrs. Lincoln in an open carriage; sometimes his eyes meet those of the burly, bearded government clerk on the pavement, and the President nods gravely. Did he know that it was Whitman? Did he know that the strange man, so hidden in gray hair and beard, was one of the greatest of his contemporaries? Did he know that the man on the pavement was nearer to understanding and com-plementing his soul than the woman by his side, or the ministers with whom he met to plan the course of the war? Immortal though he may be, we cannot hope to comprehend Whitman unless we see him against the background of the America which he loved.

Peterborough Examiner, 26 September 1945

James Agate

James Agate died on the sixth of this month of heart failure; he was 69 years old. To many of my readers this statement will mean little, but it will mean more to their children, and even more to their grandchildren. Literate people know what Hazlitt, Lewes, Max Beerbohm and Bernard Shaw had in common; they were all great drama critics. In the course of time, after his reputation has gone through the usual vicissitudes, Agate's name will be added to that list, for he also was a great drama critic. He was not, I think, a great writer, though he was a distinguished journalist. But he had that flair, that quality of intuition linked with enthusiasm, which makes the great critic, and his judgements on the actors of our time will be read as long as such things are of interest. The death of Agate means nothing in modern Canada, where the theatre does not flourish; but, as our country assumes the amenities of civilization, his name will mean more and will become in its specialized sphere, a great name.

Agate was born in Manchester, where his family was concerned in the cotton weaving business. He was brought up in the mysteries of this trade, but he decided early in life that the theatre was his chief interest, and he hated the calico trade cordially. He broke his connection with it, therefore, and after some rather hard times (during which he kept a small tobacco and paper shop), he managed to make a mark as a critical writer, and in 1923 he became critic on *The Sunday Times,* holding that post until his death. He was also literary critic for *The Daily Express* and film critic for *The Tatler*. He worked very hard, writing about half a million words a year, and he made a great deal of money, which he spent lavishly. He loved show horses, and was president of the Hackney Horse Society in 1945–46. He was accounted one of the four or five wittiest after-dinner speakers in Britain. He was a fine judge of good food and good drink. And he was surely one of the most complete and remarkable egoists of our time.

Because egoism means a deep concern with self, many people think it a discreditable quality. They are right, undoubtedly, in thinking that a commonplace man's concern with himself is detestable, but Agate was far from being commonplace. As Alexander Smith tells us, in *Dreamthorp:* "If the egotist is weak, his egotism is worthless. If the egotist is strong, acute, full of distinctive character, his egotism is precious, and remains a possession of the race." How admirably these words, written before he was born, apply to Agate! His egotism was strong, and he took great pains to see that it remained a possession of the race. His autobiography runs to eight volumes in diary form, and it is appropriately—and indeed inevitably—named *Ego.*

Agate was moved to keep an autobiographical diary by the example of Arnold Bennett's *Journals.* Begun in 1932, and cast in the form of a daily journal, this book is none the less the story of Agate's life from his earliest days; he takes care to let us know everything that there is to know about him. It is an astonishing work of self-revelation, telling of ambitions, fears, regrets and failings which most men take care to keep hidden. If Agate is drinking too much, he notes it down; if he fears madness or death, it is all copy for *Ego;* if he has a foolish quarrel with someone or makes an ass of himself over a girl who has written him a fan letter, he tells his readers about it. And yet there is a self-consciousness about these revelations which to me, at least, is inescapable. Agate seems to be proud even of his follies. He cannot for an instant stop posturing, and in this I detect a failure in his egoism. He was a great egoist, certainly, but surely a supreme egoist would have been indifferent to public opinion? Or is the supreme egoist a madman?

As a critic Agate had many virtues. He had read deeply in the drama and in criticism; he had searched tirelessly for the best estimates of the great actors of the past and was unsurpassed in his ability to relate them to actors of the present. His conception of the stage was noble, his standards high and his critical sense well strengthened by a sense of history. Bernhardt and Irving were the measures which he applied to the great actors of our day, and he was able to make the irreverent feel that Bernhardt and Irving were indeed the appropriate yardsticks. He was perhaps the only critic in London capable of writing an informed criticism of the performances given by the Comédie Française when it made its occasional visits to the British capital. His faults were a tendency toward floweriness in writing and an addiction to quotation which he did not seem able to control. Agate was deeply conscious of the fact that he had not had a university education, and he seemed determined to outdo the most learned of university dons in quotation and literary allusion—and he did so, at the expense of a really good style. But his faults were trifles in comparison with his virtues, and that boundless enthusiasm for the theatre which made him one of its most devoted and brilliant servants.

Peterborough Examiner, 25 June 1947

Bernard Shaw and
Mrs. Patrick Campbell

*I*t is impossible to pour more than a pint into a pint-pot, and it is similarly impossible to love a woman who is merely enchanting as deeply as a woman who is great. Thus the correspondence between Bernard Shaw and Mrs. Patrick Campbell is not as glorious as the correspondence between Shaw and Ellen Terry. Mrs. Campbell had no literary gift whatever, and probably did herself positive injustice when she took up her pen; Ellen Terry might have been a great writer if she had not been a great actress. From these two epistolary loves, which we now have embalmed in print, Ellen Terry emerges as a woman of great spirit and boundless charm; Mrs. Pat appears as a temperamental enchantress, and later as a clumsy blackmailer. *Bernard Shaw & Mrs. Patrick Campbell: Their Correspondence,* which Alan Dent has edited, is absorbingly interesting, but we may be sure that neither correspondent appears to best advantage.

Shaw was attracted by Mrs. Campbell during his period as a theatre critic for the *Saturday Review,* and wrote of her with a mixture of infatuation and harshness which seems to have been a characteristic attitude of his toward women whom he sought to impress. But for a few months in 1912 he appears to have been seriously in love with her, and wrote her several letters which declare his passion with great eloquence and no reserve at all. Mrs. Pat was flattered; Shaw was married, and plainly had no intention of leaving his wife for her; she was engaged, during part of this period, at least, to the man who became her second husband; Shaw was 56 and she was 47.

The nature of his love would have been clear to a more intelligent woman; it had certainly been clear to Ellen Terry. But Mrs. Pat treated Shaw as a spoiled girl of 18 might treat an infatuated lad of 20. She hectored him because he thought he knew how to direct his plays; she nagged him about what she called his "bad taste." She had that unhappy desire to humble her lover which afflicts some women. She appears to have been accustomed to love affairs in which she was the dominant partner. Shaw could not put up with this for long, and although the correspondence continued fitfully until 1939 it ceased to be an exchange of love letters.

We can find it in our hearts to pity Shaw as we read these letters. His love for Mrs. Campbell was what she herself described, in one of her few good phrases, as "sympathy, kindness and the wit and folly of genius." His wife, however, met the situation with suffragette lack of humour and what Freudians call "a flight into illness." Mrs. Pat poked fun at Mrs. Shaw because she would not "leave cards" at her door, and was vexed with Shaw because of his repeated warnings that he would do nothing which would humiliate or grieve his wife. Mrs. Shaw, we learn, made scenes which lasted for days and nights—scenes, which only an angry woman, who was also very intelligent, very well-read, very well-bred and rather plain, could make. Shaw paid dearly for his infatuation with the Rossettian beauty of Stella Campbell.

He did not play fair at all times, of course. He told a friend of Mrs. Pat's that he only made love to her to cheer her up when she was depressed by a long illness. That was certainly untrue. He referred too often to their respective ages, and although this was probably meant as a warning that his love was principally a matter of mind, it was also ungallant. But Mrs. Pat—oh, what Mrs. Pat did!

When he loved her she tried to humble him, and she lectured him on good taste—a concept with which a genius has no concern. When he had ceased to love her she whined, and whined with the exaggeration of an actress of great emotional power. She hounded him for parts in his plays. When poverty overtook her she nagged, entreated, teased and roared for permission to publish his letters to her in order to get money. When at last he gave permission for the letters to be published after his death and his wife's she cadged for money handouts to tide her over the interval.

And all through the letters in which she did these things she rebuked him for conduct which she attributed to his being an Irishman and repeatedly asserted that she had "behaved like a gentleman."

Undoubtedly Mrs. Patrick Campbell possessed a haunting pre-Raphaelite beauty and enchantment. She was not able to convey these qualities in her letters.

The unbridgeable gulf between these two remarkable people, however, was an artistic one. Mrs. Pat declared that she was "an amateur," by which she meant that her approach to acting was that of an artist who depended upon emotion and nerves. She also fancied herself as a lady, in a somewhat narrow social sense, and set great store by certain ill-defined limitations on her creative power which she called "good taste." Shaw was a professional; he demanded the utmost physical and emotional resource from his players, unhampered by trivialities of taste which had no place in the theatre, and he wanted these things under the discipline of an accomplished technique. He wrote *Pygmalion* for Mrs. Pat and she cut his lines, introduced "gags" of her own, and played ducks and drakes with the play.

The reader who wants to find the core of the book need only look at the letter from Shaw dated 15th May, 1920, in which Shaw wrote, "You are not a great actress in a big play or anything disturbing or vulgar of that sort; but you have your heart's desire, and are very charming . . . I enjoyed and appreciated it in its little way. And that was magnanimous of me, considering how I missed the big bones of my play, its fortissimos, its allegros, its precipitous moments, its contrasts, and all its big bits . . . You certainly can boil a scene in bread and milk better than anyone I know. But this, beloved, would be better boiled in brandy." And in a later letter he writes: "You shouldn't talk to me about the theatre: it's my only sore subject; and it is you who made it so."

In the later letters Shaw gives Mrs. Pat lessons in acting which are worth a volume of Stanislavsky. "What with actresses wanting to be amateurs because they think it's ladylike, and amateurs wanting to be actresses because they think it's immoral, the theatre is no place for an honest workman." But Mrs. Pat wanted to be a lady on the stage as much as she yearned to be a gentleman in her conduct of the affair with Shaw. Of her performance as Lady Macbeth he told her that she "pecked at it like a canary trying to eat a cocoa nut."

As a lover's correspondence these letters are not of the first quality; but when love has grown cold and they become a slanging-match between a very witty woman and a man whom nobody has ever called dull, they are very good indeed. Only a heartless reader, however, will miss the pain of irreconcilable temperaments which forced Shaw to write: "I am the greatest playwright in the world, and I have been treated by an actress as no dog was ever treated by the most brutal trainer," and which made Stella Campbell write, at 74, "I hope you will be spared to treat me abominably many years longer."

It is one of those endless quarrels of literary history in which we can all take sides, but in which no final decision is possible.

Saturday Night, 24 January 1953

George Santayana

We now have the third volume of George Santayana's autobiography, *Of Persons and Places*. It is a beautiful and gently illuminating book. Let me confess at once that I find Santayana's major philosophical works forbidding; they are written in language of such beautiful limpidity that I can read several pages at a time with an illusion of understanding them, but afterward I know that I have not really understood anything at all. Yet in his essays and volumes of random reflections he breathes a commoner air, and who then combines clarity and wisdom better than he? Those of us who cannot follow him into the realms of thought where his reputation as a philosopher was made may sense something of his spirit and belief from these lesser works. We do not know what Santayana thought which impressed his brother philosophers, but we know what Santayana *was,* and that may even be a better thing.

Let us not pretend to one another in these book reviews. I know virtually nothing about philosophy, and such people as I have known who were trained in that study have all been objects of puzzlement to me: they knew about philosophy, but they did not seem to be particularly wise men, nor did they lead wise lives. Now Santayana, as we know him through his autobiography and his essays, is unquestionably a wise man. Can it be wholly wrong to suppose that his wisdom and his philosophy were not entirely the same thing? Might they not have been two things, which acted upon one another to their mutual benefit?

There is a Welsh proverb which says "A spoon does not know the taste of soup, nor a learned fool the taste of wisdom." Santayana knew the taste of wisdom. He had firm ideas about the right conduct of life; they are ideas which command our thoughtful respect; he puts ideas into practice in his own life. That is wisdom, surely?

A dominant idea in his life, and apparently in his philosophy, was the idea of non-attachment. Though he had the ordinary human need for friends and for comfort, he was not dominated by the desire to be aggressively a man of his time, or to be what the world calls a success. Bertrand Russell, whom Santayana knew well, is a success—which is to say that he has struggled to impose his ideas upon the world, and has done so in a remarkable measure. Yet in this volume Santayana is critical of Russell for his failure to "shake himself free from his environment and from the miscellaneous currents of opinion in his day," and his judgement is that though Russell is many-sided, he is also "a many-sided fanatic." (How these philosophers claw one another! It makes us lesser mortals tremble as they shake their gnarled fists and tick one another off. In Russell's *History of Western Philosophy* he accords Santayana a scant 19 lines in a book of 836 pages.) Santayana did not care whether the world listened to him or not. He did not care for teaching. He asked only to be permitted to observe and reflect.

> O World, thou choosest not the better part!
> It is not wisdom to be only wise
> And on the inward vision close the eyes,
> But it is wisdom to believe the heart.

Thus wrote Santayana, and it is deeply true of his attitude toward life. But the educated heart, the heart chastened by self-knowledge and knowledge of the world, might alone be safely heeded. The wild, impassioned heart leads only to "adventures in enthusiastic unreason," as he calls the two great wars of this century. The only heart which deserves to be listened to is that which is not too eagerly set upon any of the good things of this world.

Yet, again and again the idea of happiness as the first and greatest good appears in the three volumes of this autobiography, and nowhere more clearly than in the third. "Happiness," wrote Santayana long ago, "is the only sanction of life; where happiness fails, existence remains a mad and lamentable experiment." Twenty pages in *My Host the World* are devoted to the conclusion of the story, begun in *The Middle Span*, of John Francis Stanley, the second Earl Russell, whose existence seems indeed to have been a mad and lamentable experiment, without happiness or serenity, and overshadowed by an uncommonly bothersome pack of sweethearts and wives. To Santayana, the spectator in the stage-box, it was a mingling of farce and tragedy. "There is no cure for birth and death save to enjoy the interval," wrote Santayana, and when we read of Russell's disordered existence, as viewed by Santayana, we know that for the philosopher such sweaty wrestling with life was the farthest thing from enjoyment.

Yet Santayana was no timid shrinker from life. His avoidance of struggle was not the cowardice of the weak man, but the sinewy-minded strategy of a very powerful and egotistical one. He yielded to the world's way in unimportant things, in order that he might have his own way in all that mattered to him. It is significant that in the three volumes of his autobiography we find no instance in which Santayana wanted anything which he did not get. Friends, leisure, travel and freedom from any sort of burdensome attachment were the things he wanted, and they make up a program far more difficult of achievement than a million dollars, three fine homes, and a family. He was set upon the attainment of wisdom and inner serenity; who knows of a more elusive goal? Yet he reached it.

Reached it and enjoyed it. This man, who died last year, gave up his professorship in 1912, and passed the remaining forty years of his life as a traveller and man of letters, retiring at last to be cared for in the convent of the Blue Nuns in Rome. The greater part of his adult life he passed in doing what he liked best, and was able to write, "Never have I enjoyed youth so thoroughly as I have my old age." Is this not success, even as the world judges success? It may be said in passing that he counted his old age as beginning at his fiftieth year, which may be a little hasty, even for a philosopher. But then, Santayana appears to have regarded old age as a stalking-horse, from behind the cover of which he observed the youthful excesses of men much older than himself.

In *Of Persons and Places* we have a record of a life which was in its fashion a work of art, carefully planned and perfectly carried out. The book itself is very much a work of art, from which everything that is excessive or needless has been purged. A materialist in philosophy, Santayana writes like a materialist—but a materialist who is also Latin in race, Catholic in sympathy but not in faith, an artist in feeling and expression. He was certainly an oddity in the philosophical world, as much detested by William James, the radical empiricist, as by the Jesuit who called him "the poetical atheist."

If a layman may venture such a suggestion, many contemporary philosophers appear to have been deceived by the artistic form in which Santayana cast his thought; a philosopher can be, in artistic matters, as big a clod as anyone else, and some of these gentlemen appear to feel that an artist must be weaker, more feminine, than they. But there was a core of gem-like hardness in Santayana; he was no democrat, and he had no regard for what he called "sugary vulgarity"; he did not admit the necessity to believe, abjectly, in anything. His acceptance of Catholicism as a pleasing, poetic, artistic and traditional indulgence was incomprehensible to professors who sought relief from their own austere beliefs in bouts of secret and sentimental Methodism, or in an atheism which he found barbarous and dogmatic. His life and his belief were all of a piece. Such a man is bound to seem strange in a world where, even among great minds, life and belief are likely to be at odds.

Saturday Night, 28 March 1953

P. G. Wodehouse

On June 21, 1939, the University of Oxford bestowed the degree of Doctor Litterarum on Pelham Grenville Wodehouse. The Public Orator, presenting him to the Chancellor in the usual Latin address, spoke of Wodehouse as *festivum caput—Petroniumne dicam an Terentium nostrum?* It was a handsome compliment to the author of more than fifty very popular novels, and it followed the publication of an article in which Hilaire Belloc said that Wodehouse was the best living English writer. Six weeks later war broke out, and shortly afterward Wodehouse was seized by the Germans at his home in Le Touquet, and was interned. In 1941, after being released from his prison camp, and while living under a kind of house arrest in Berlin, Wodehouse made five broadcasts about his experiences over the German radio; he spoke in his usual humorous fashion, for the excellent reasons that he was in German hands, that he had no desire to be political, and because he thought it was expected of him. But these broadcasts released upon his head a torrent of abuse and hatred so serious that since the war he has thought it better to live out of England. Thus, in his fifth decade, his career reached its zenith and its nadir. This is not so strange as it as first appears.

Wodehouse was the victim of his own popularity. The public is very fond of creating idols and then turning upon them savagely when they seem to be most secure. Psychoanalysts call this the ambivalence of emotion; there can be no great love without a corresponding great hatred which can supplant it if something goes wrong; in other words, emotion is a power which retains its strength though it may alter its character. Count no man happy, said Sophocles, until he is dead; and think no man firmly seated in the heart of the public until the public has finally done with him.

This is not to suggest that Wodehouse was at any time a figure of tragic majesty, or that his fall from popularity was abysmal. He was fortunate in some of his friends, who stood by him, and in some critics and people of sober judgement who looked carefully at what he had done and found nothing desperately wrong in it. He was most fortunate of all in his own calm good sense, which enabled him to ride out the worst of the storm without being destroyed and without saying things which made matters worse. But there were great numbers of people who delighted in attacking and reviling him as an irresponsible playboy.

His lifelong friend William Townend has published a volume of letters which he has received from Wodehouse since 1920. It is called *Performing Flea,* for in the excitement of 1941 Sean O'Casey, who should have known better, called Wodehouse "English literature's performing flea." I recommend this book strongly to all writers, and to all those who think that they would like to be writers. With Virginia Woolf's *A Writer's Diary,* it gives the most penetrating insight into a writer's life that I have seen in current literature; indeed, these two books, taken together, would make excellent material for a course in writing. Certainly *Performing Flea* dispels any notion that the writer of more than sixty books, which have sold upward of ten million copies, is an irresponsible playboy. On the contrary he is a man of prodigious industry and, within the limits imposed by his talent, a devoted, honest, painstaking craftsman.

I have not linked the names of Virginia Woolf and P. G. Wodehouse in order to produce a cheap effect of shock, but simply because the similarities between them, in their attitude toward their work, are many and striking. Both show themselves to be victims of that malaise—that dissatisfaction with their work which expresses itself not only mentally but physically—which has marked so many writers; both work to the uttermost limit of physical endurance; both are conscious of their fame, and count it as nothing in comparison with their personal judgement of their work; both slave to do the best that is in them. "I sometimes wonder if I really am a writer . . . I don't know anything and I seem incapable of learning . . . I feel I've been fooling the public for fifty years." Only the last three words reveal that Wodehouse, and not Virginia Woolf, wrote that. This is not the considered judgement of a playboy upon himself.

Of course, nobody who has ever tried it thinks that being funny is play; whether in the circus, on the stage or in writing, being funny is highly skilled work, which demands an individual technique, a fine sense of timing, and a sense of form in addition to the indispensable requisite of a sense of humour. Wodehouse describes his own novels as musical comedies with the music left out. The contrivance of such entertainments is such demanding work that, while hundreds of people can imitate his style, nobody else in the world can write a story just like him. The style is fairly easy to copy, if your ear is good and your acquaintance with Shakespeare, Tennyson and the Bible and Prayer Book is equal to his. But the marshalling of the incidents of the plot, the compression, the masterly placing of the big farcical moments—it is here that Wodehouse shows his dearly-bought mastery.

Wodehouse has always been a good writer; his early school stories *Mike at Wrykyn* and *Mike and Psmith* prove it. But how he has improved upon his natural talent! In the letters which he wrote to Townend, who is himself a writer, Wodehouse discusses matters of technique at length and in detail, and there are few writers who cannot learn something from him. Virtually everyone might learn to cut what he has written. Wodehouse, it appears, is a ruthless cutter. It has been my opinion for years—not simply as a hastening critic, anxious to finish a book, but as an ordinary reader—that most books suffer from being too long; there is a *right* length for every book, whether it is 900 pages or 90, but most writers overshoot the mark because they will not tighten their work. I am happy to have this private opinion corroborated by so able a craftsman as Wodehouse.

Perhaps what has gone before reads as though it had been written by yet one more besotted Wodehouse fan, who seeks respite from a hard world in the Never-Never Land of Jeeves, Ukridge, Mr. Mulliner, Chuffy Chuffnell and the rest, and who quotes Wodehouse (inaccurately and embarrassingly) after the second cocktail. Let me say at once that while I admire Wodehouse very much as a craftsman, I read his work infrequently and with well-controlled delight; of the fifty-odd books listed in the front of *Performing Flea* I have read a modest twenty. I like farce well enough, but I like it spiced with indecency, and Wodehouse is never anything but family reading; his complete rejection of sex except as a reason for some non-sexual antics is part of the boyishness, the Edwardian Good Chapmanship, which lies at the root of his work. Farce as it is known to, for instance, Gabriel Chevallier, is outside his range. And this, to me, limits the appeal of his work; it is not the artificiality of his world, but the rejection of a vital element in human experience and thus in humour, which makes it brittle and oddly wistful. When Wodehouse began to write, this sexlessness was an element of all successful popular fiction; but times have changed since 1902, and he continues to hug his chains—successfully and with the approval, I am sure, of hundreds of thousands of devoted readers.

Performing Flea is called "a self-portrait in letters." It is admirable as comment upon a very successful career, and as a revelation of a mind which, without being in any way adventurous or uncommon, commands admiration for its integrity and self-knowledge.

Saturday Night, 30 January 1954

Sigmund Freud

So many odd tricks have been played of late years with the art of biography that it is a happy hour when a critic is able to recommend to his readers a biography in the classical manner, on a great subject, admirably begun by a writer in every way capable of completing his design. Dr. Sigmund Freud's life and work are worthy of biography on the grand scale; Dr. Ernest Jones, who was Freud's personal friend and devoted pupil, and who is a writer of sober excellence, is the very man above all others whom we would have chosen to write such a biography. The first volume, called *The Young Freud, 1856–1900,* is an admirable beginning, and there seems to be no reason why Dr. Jones should not finish this work, which will occupy three volumes, as well as he has begun it.

Dr. Jones' first words in his Introduction are: "This is not intended to be a popular biography of Freud." We would not have expected or desired a popular biography from such a source. Any book about Freud which attempts to simplify his work, or to give a factitious air of romance to it, will certainly be a falsification of everything that Freud was, and a denial of every principle to which he devoted his life. Dr. Jones has spared us no detail of Freud's early training, of his medical and neurological studies, of those phases of his medical life which were unrelated to psychoanalysis. He has set out to give us Freud's life in full, and despite his literary skill there are long passages which must be heavy and wearisome work for the non-medical reader. But the total impact of this first volume is strong and fine. This is Freud as we have wanted to know about him.

Brief and popular accounts of Freud and his work are misleading, and his own *Autobiographical Study* is a disappointment. The popular works dwell upon Freud as he was at the end of his life—the controversial but commanding figure, austere and withdrawn toward all but a very few people; he had learned by experience how unwise it was to put ammunition into the hands of his enemies by revealing anything that was intimate about himself, and the *Autobiographical Study* seems to conceal more than it reveals. But Dr. Jones' book is revealing without being intrusive, and sympathetic without being hotly partisan. Furthermore, this first volume gives us the young Freud, about whom we have never been told anything.

Although I think that I may say that I have read all of Freud's principal works, and many comments upon them, I have never read anything before Dr. Jones' book which suggested how great his early struggles had been, how stifling the poverty of his family, how stultifying the anti-Semitism of the Vienna in which he grew up, and how passionate and proud his own nature. Freud at the end of his life appeared to have developed the magnificent calm of the triumphant genius; he spoke with authority, and his prestige was a bulwark against his detractors. Although the point is not insisted upon, it is suggested that his family were a drag on his progress; they were Jews of fairly strict orthodoxy, and in Vienna in the seventies that meant that they belonged almost to another world from that of the hospitals and medical schools in which he had to make his way. Their philosophy was passive, and his was aggressive. They lacked ambition, and he was filled with a burning desire to excel.

But he did not know precisely how he was to excel, and even the choice of medicine as a career was not a whole-hearted decision with him. He was perpetually casting about, looking for some channel in which his ambition and intellectual curiosity could find bounds and a direction. He was not a thorough or zealous man in his own interests, and on two or three occasions he allowed discoveries which would have quickly made his reputation as a scientist to slip through his fingers because he had not examined them thoroughly. He was somewhat fanatical, and Dr. Jones' account of his early enthusiasm for cocaine, and his lavish gifts of this drug to his friends, and even his fiancée, before he discovered that it was extremely dangerous, has overtones of farce. Freud, in his very young manhood, was a man without direction.

He was also, of course, a man who had not been submitted to the purgative and chastening discipline of psychoanalysis, and we may be sure that the latter Freud shook his head over some of the extravagances of emotion of the younger Freud. His letters to his fiancée, Martha Bernays, his insistence upon her complete submission to his will, and his quarrels with her family, are nothing new in the history of passionate love, but they are surprises in a life of Sigmund Freud. We learn with surprise, also, of his indigestion, of his prostrating migraines, of his twenty cigars a day, of his trouble with his heart, and his frequent worry and even despair as a physician.

Perhaps it is stupid to be surprised that Freud, as a young man, had the troubles which afflict many young men of unusual powers, but I must confess my own surprise, and probably stupidity; for to me, as to hundreds of thousands of others who have in various ways been influenced by his thought and work, Freud has always seemed a man above human frailty.

Yet these revelations do nothing to diminish his stature. Rather, they increase it, for it was in the midst of a welter of daily tasks and worries that Freud moved, cautiously and often indirectly, toward the discoveries which were the foundations of his great explorations in the human mind. It was when his duties had been done as the good father, the loving husband, and the physician who worked from ten o'clock in the morning until nine o'clock at night with his neurotic patients—a kind of medical work which imposes heavy drains upon the spirit of the physician—that he performed upon himself the self-analysis which was the prototype of all future analyses. For the first time in the history of mankind, he examined, slowly and systematically, the structure of his mind, and established those doctrines of infantile sexuality and its far-reaching effects which are embodied in his book *The Interpretation of Dreams.*

Dr. Jones comments with restraint upon the pity which Thomas Mann has twice expressed for Freud in public lectures, because Freud did not know the ancient and modern literary works which have also plumbed the depths of the mind, and foreshadowed some of his own findings. We can understand what Mann meant, without agreeing with him, for a poet's intuition is not a scientific theory, and Freud was wholly a scientist. He wanted a theory of the mind which would hold together, and be applicable to mankind as a whole; the insights of literary men, great though they are, can only reach those minds which are of a quality to grasp and understand them, and they reach the world disguised as myth and fable.

At the end of this first volume we take leave of Freud just as he is about to move into that dark period when so much of the scientific world set upon him as hysterical peasants might set upon a witch, and when so many of the world's philosophers and moralists cast him for the role of anti-Christ. And it is a compliment to the restrained power with which Dr. Jones has written that we tremble for his hero, even though we know what the outcome of the story will be. Many readers, I am convinced, will share my own impatience to get at the second volume of this remarkable book.

Before ending this appreciation it may not be amiss to say that Dr. Ernest Jones was at one time Professor of Psychiatry at the University of Toronto, and Director of the Ontario Clinic for Nervous Diseases. His decision to return to England robbed this country not only of one of the greatest living psychiatrists, but also of a man of letters of uncommon quality.

Saturday Night, 20 February 1954

Sydney Smith

*I*t was Bishop Monk of Gloucester who said that Sydney Smith was given his appointment as a resident canon of St. Paul's Cathedral for being "a scoffer and a jester"; the Bishop was not concerned with the fact that this valuable piece of preferment did not come to Smith until he was sixty, and that it was not very much for a man who had at least ten times as much character, intelligence and wit as Monk or any other Bishop of the day. Smith was often in hot water with Bishops, and when we consider the letters he wrote to them, and the articles which he published of disagreement with their opinions, we cannot be surprised. He was a man to whom principle was very dear, and he had the courage of a lion in controversy. But he was also a scoffer and a jester, and it is this fact which has given his reputation the colour which it still wears; his wit was in equal proportions his making and his undoing.

The publication, in two stout volumes, of *The Letters of Sydney Smith* gives us an opportunity to re-examine this extraordinary clergyman's career. The letters themselves are like all collections of letters from great men—they are full of trivialities, and they grow wearisome when we read them straight through, but taken as a whole they give depth to our notion of Smith, and illuminate some corners of his mind and his career with a warm and pleasant light. For he was certainly one of the most thoroughly good and delightful men of his time, and it must have been an unfailing pleasure to be on his list of correspondents. When reading his letters we must bear in mind that they were not meant to be taken at a gulp, but were distributed among many people over the course of fifty years. These two volumes are for dipping and bedtime reading, and treated thus they offer riches which will last for many years.

This new collection must be regarded as definitive, for it contains 1,038 letters, of which more than half appear in print for the first time; those which are already familiar have been corrected from the earlier and less careful publication by Smith's daughter and her friend Mrs. Austin. The present editor is Nowell C. Smith, who has provided footnotes, an index and other necessary scholarly apparatus; he has also included a few letters written to Smith himself, which throw light on the main course of the work.

Is there anyone who does not know something of the life and career of Sydney Smith? If there is, he can get Hesketh Pearson's excellent *The Smith of Smiths* very cheaply in the Penguin books, and settle down for an enlarging experience. Simply to read about Smith is to breathe a finer air, to pass into a world where scholarship, common sense and liberal humanism are mingled with so much wit that we find ourselves guffawing two or three times on every page, and smiling till our facial muscles ache. Ah, but there it is again—that fatal wit which both made and unmade its possessor.

If Sydney Smith had not been so witty we should think him now, perhaps, a greater man. A great many people are suspicious of wit, and cannot believe that what makes them laugh is worth further serious thought. In the popular imagination a wise man is solemn and a merry man a trifler. Sydney Smith and the late Dean Inge held very similar views on religion and related matters, but which is remembered as the wise man? The Gloomy Dean, and not the Comic Canon.

He was born in 1771, and was ordained a priest of the Church of England in 1794. He would have preferred to be a lawyer, but his father would spare no money for the necessary training, so he was pushed into holy orders. He found himself an advanced and voluble Whig in a profession which was almost wholly Tory, and where the path to advancement was the Tory path. He was one of the founders of the *Edinburgh Review* and he was a noted exponent of "moral philosophy," as the psychology of that day was called. Early in his career he came out strongly in favour of Catholic Emancipation, and though he wrote the *Peter Plymley Letters* on that subject anonymously, it was noised about that he was their author. His preaching was of a character which packed churches, but no church wanted to keep him. He was too disturbing. He gained influential Whig friends, and was one of the ornaments of Holland House, but it was long before the Whigs could do anything for him, and even when that time came they did not offer him a bishopric. And so, until he was sixty, Smith spent much of his time in obscure country parsonages, where he discharged his duties very well.

It is perhaps indiscreet to enquire why wit, zeal for reform, and common sense should stand in the way of a man's career as a churchman, when these same qualities would have carried him into the first rank in so many other professions. Let us, instead, examine this dangerous wit, and find out what it was like.

Much of it has passed into the language. "It requires a surgical operation to get a joke well into a Scotch understanding; their only idea of wit . . . is laughing immoderately at stated intervals." Smith first said that, and it was he who called Scotland "that knuckle-end of England—that land of Calvin, oat-cakes and sulphur." It was he who divided humanity into three sexes— men, women and clergymen—and it was he who said of a stupid man that "he deserved to be preached to death by wild curates." He said that minorities were almost always in the right, long before Ibsen, and it was he who said of the chatter-box Macaulay, "He has occasional flashes of silence, which make his conversation perfectly delightful." It was probably indiscreet for a clergyman to say that "We have no amusements in England but vice and religion," and that "My idea of heaven is eating *pâté de foie gras* to the sound of trumpets." He it was who wrote to his daughter that he was so hot that he yearned to take off his flesh and sit coolly in his bones, and for a country clergyman there is wistfulness in his remark that "I have no relish for the country—it is a kind of healthy grave." These are a few sparks from his anvil. He could talk in that strain for a full evening, and often did so.

He was so witty indeed that the ultimate fate of the wit overtook him—people began to laugh before he spoke, and nothing that he said was taken as seriously as it deserved. When Smith spoke everybody listened for the joke, but only the wisest listened for the sense. His was not a cutting wit, and he hated to give pain. He did not shoot arrows to kill, but only to tickle with their feathers. He could, and did, write brilliantly cogent pamphlets on political and social topics, and they are among the best things in our language, in their kind. I have read several of his sermons, and even they are terse, witty and comprehensive. He despised the Methodists, and he abominated the Anglo-Catholics. Mysticism was abhorrent to him. His religion was simple goodness, informed and refined by education and good manners. It was essentially eighteenth-century religion, purged of eighteenth-century pomposity and sloth.

Like all men whose creed is common sense he could be wrongheaded and he could be shallow. But this did not happen very often. And, as even the highest spirits must sometimes sink, we find letters in the new collection which show him as a man who has been hurt, who feels that life is passing him by unnoticed, and who wonders quite honestly why people of less merit than himself get on in the world better than he. But these moments of sadness only show him as human, and throw his great courage and his great high spirits into sharper relief. We know him now as a great Whig force, and a great reformer within the Church in his day. We see him not as a dangerous radical, but as a man to whom empty radicalism was abhorrent, and necessary reform a mere matter of common sense. The wit which was his glory and his bane flashes again and again in these letters—a wit, unforced, original and without malice. Sydney Smith was a great prose writer in the tradition which stems from Swift, and which we know in the works of Shaw—clean, persuasive and eloquent without being in any way fancy. His letters are a treasure and a delight, not only for themselves but for the constant reminder which they bring us of the great man, the man of great spirit, whose usually unconsidered trifles they were.

Saturday Night, 27 March 1954

Madame de Pompadour

The light touch is not a gift common among historical writers, nor is an understanding of the subtle relationships between men and women in love. Let us do honour, then, to Nancy Mitford, who brings both of these unusual qualities to her biography of Madame de Pompadour. She throws light upon a chapter of history which many of us have found complex, and she repairs the reputation of a woman who has sometimes been unfairly aspersed by historians who also set up in business as moralists.

Jeanne-Antoinette Poisson Le Normant d'Etoiles was born in 1721 and died in 1764 at the age of forty-two; for almost twenty years of her life she was the mistress of Louis XV. She was not beautiful, in the strict sense, but from the many portraits of her, and particularly those by Boucher, we see that she was a wonderfully pretty woman, beautifully framed and with particularly lovely eyes. To these natural gifts she added a splendid sense of dress, and a great many accomplishments; she was intelligent, witty and high-spirited. Though not an aristocrat she was not vulgar, like Madame Du Barry, who followed her in the King's affections. Pompadour was, rather, a woman of the educated and cultivated middle class, and the story of her life persuades us that she held her place because of her brains and charm, rather than by the most obvious means. It is her skill in recreating this charm of character which makes Miss Mitford's book a delight to read. I felt, while engrossed in its pages, that I was myself enjoying the society of this wonderful woman, and I was sorry when the book was finished. That is a sensation which a reviewer, who is by trade a gobbler of books, rarely enjoys.

It is a waste of time to dissipate one's moral zeal in disapproving of royal persons who have mistresses. The conditions under which a king lived in the eighteenth century made some provision of the kind a necessity. His queen was chosen for him, on political and eugenic grounds; he might be betrothed while still a child to another child whom he had never seen; he would certainly be married before he was twenty, and Louis XV was married when he was fifteen. The astonishing thing was that such marriages often developed into true friendships. But is a man who is raised to regard himself as the superior of all others going to be content with that? Certainly not. The surprise is not that kings and princes kept women as their companions, but that they were so often faithful to the same woman for many years, and that in many cases they chose women of unusual character and intellect.

What is even more surprising is that, in the case of Louis XV, moral disapproval seemed to count for so much with him. On more than one occasion, when he was ill, he confessed the wickedness of his adulterous relationship with Pompadour, apologized publicly to his Queen and his daughters for the scandal he had given them, and prepared to die in the odour of sanctity. Everybody at Versailles knew of these repentances, for the King could not rise or go to bed, dress or undress, die or recover, without a room filled with people watching him do it. Even his supposedly final confessions to his priest were listened to with keen interest. Of course, when Louis felt better he skipped up the stairs again to Pompadour's apartments. It must have been a discouraging life for his confessor.

When the time came for Pompadour herself to die, she confessed, was given her viaticum, and was from that time forth forbidden to see her lover. And when her body was borne away from Versailles, Louis was thought to have behaved rather badly because he watched the sad procession from a balcony. Let no one suppose that these people lived lives that were any more free from religious and neighbourly censure than the adulterers in our smallest Canadian villages. Even wealth and privilege could not wholly insulate them from that frost.

The constant burden of eighteenth-century kings was the pressure of other people's ambitions. Consider the lot of Louis XV: everyone deferred to him, and his lightest wish had to be obeyed. But, being a man of considerable sensitivity and intelligence, this was as much of a nuisance as it was joy to him. He was obliged constantly to think of others, and if he did not, he had to endure the reproach which only very powerful people can be made to feel by their inferiors. He was endlessly teased and plagued for favours; everybody wanted a job, or a pension, either for himself or for some supposedly deserving hanger-on. The King had every privilege except that of being at ease. Pompadour provided the atmosphere in which that final luxury was possible.

She did not do this, as anyone who thinks about the matter for twenty seconds will know, by twenty years of rapt contemplation of the ceilings of Versailles. Indeed, Pompadour was not a physically ardent woman, and love-making tired her. After about eight years of their association Louis XV did not sleep with her; a few pretty girls, some of whom did not even know who he was, lived in a pleasant pavilion in the Parc aux Cerfs and took care of his needs in that respect. But it was to Pompadour that he talked, and it was to Pompadour that he listened; it was for her that he built some of the most beautiful houses of the time, and it was guided by her taste that he continually rebuilt, redecorated and tinkered with all the royal residences. Indeed, these two resemble many happily married and wealthy couples in this way; they had a passion for bricks and mortar, for pots of paint and troughs of plaster. Pompadour had exquisite taste, and it was her delight to plan, and order, and oversee the execution of beautiful things, great and small.

She was herself a beautiful thing, and she imposed upon her life such a pattern of delicate and amusing fantasy that when she died Voltaire (who was not a man to be moved by impostors or triflers) said, "It is the end of a dream."

She was not successful in every field, and she was too human to confine herself at all times to the fields in which she was successful. She meddled in politics, though not as disastrously as some historians have asserted. And she was, let it be remembered, fully as able as most of the male diplomats at Versailles in her time; they were chosen less for ability than for birth, or their luck in getting the ear of the King, or for the fact that they had been around for a long time and needed a job. Pompadour meddled, and for this she has been roundly condemned by such historians as Carlyle and Macaulay—neither of them men who would have liked Pompadour personally, and who took the Puritan historian's revenge of confusing her morals with her political opinions. Carlyle, of course, took Frederick the Great as his hero, and Frederick named one of his bitches "Pompadour"; that was the kind of joke even Carlyle could understand, after a little puzzling.

Pompadour's adventures in religion, too, were unsuccessful. As her health declined she was moved by an ambition to impress the world by her piety. She lacked talent in this direction; also the Queen, Maria Leczinska, and the Dauphin had, so to speak, a corner in piety at Versailles.

Miss Mitford's book is clear and straight-ahead in its form, and the ornamentation of anecdote and speculation embellishes without obscuring the main theme. The book is elegantly and amusingly written, and it shows an understanding of love and pleasure which is rare in books of history. Pleasure is, after all, what most of us live for, whether we are willing to admit it or not. Further, Miss Mitford spares us any moralizing on the nature of the Court at Versailles, which was an odd place, though no more odd, perhaps, than other seats of government.

She looks at her subject through twentieth-century eyes, but she is not so foolish as to forget that the eighteenth century was, as history goes, yesterday. I cannot conclude without suggesting that her book will add immeasurably to the existing number of the Pompadour's fans.

Saturday Night, 22 May 1954

Sean O'Casey

As he closed the sixth volume of Sean O'Casey's auto-biography Davies caught himself in the treacherous act of wondering whether this might not be the last; hadn't the old fella said everything he had to say by this time? A matter of half a million words, maybe, beltin' the Papists every inch o' the way and knockin' the stuffin' outa the lordly critics and ecclesiastical censors who had schemed to break the heart of poor Sean? And hadn't Sean got the best of 'em, every one, at last? Wasn't it time to call it a day, now, and lay down the shovel an' the hoe, not to speak of the shillelagh of Brian Boru and the dainty poisoned kiss of Cathleen na Houlihan? But as he pondered, Davies felt the shadow of shame darken his Welsh brow, and he knew that if another volume came out next year he would seize it with eagerness to see who Sean was thumpin' now.

And didn't he know that his own style would forever be marked by Sean? And why not, after six volumes? Hadn't he caught Sean's modest trick of referring to himself in the third person—although, having two surnames and no romantic, warmly Celtic given-name, the effect was but a poverty-stricken echo in his case? Ah, no! Back in the guilty days, maybe, when he finished *Inishfallen, Fare Thee Well,* he might have yearned for Sean to shove a sock in his gob and get back to writing the darlin' plays which are his true-begotten daughters o' joy; but now he could go on with Sean forever. Dancin' through his mind was the lovely song that his brave mother used to sing to him, as she lulled him into a hungry sleep in his dark Canadian slum—

> The Big Bear played on the pom-pom-pom
>   In a very musical kind of way;
> The Pig and the Bunny they danced for joy;
>   We could listen to this all day
>   Said they;
>   We could listen to this all day.

Davies knew he was in the same boat with the Pig and the Bunny; Sean is a great man, even if he doesn't know when to shut up, and Davies could listen to him all day.

Still an' all, six volumes is a weary weight o' books, and even Davies admitted that Sean wasn't at his best every inch o' the way. It's a long, long trail a-winding into the land of Sean's dreams, and the nightingales and the white moon don't glorify it all. Davies was glad for the fine long looks at Yeats, and understood the meaning of Sean's reverence for the poet's genius, even when Yeats behaved like a fretful old woman. He was happy, too, that Sean valued the greatness of C. B. Cochran, which the blackened souls of London theatre folk sought to darken to their own pitchy night. And Davies rejoiced at the intimate stories of the domestic life of the Shaws, and the dictatorial manners of the kindly but imperious Charlotte. But to reach these oases of refreshment in the journey through the six books, Davies had to toil through every fight Sean ever had with an Irish parish priest, and listen to Sean's imprecations on all the brotherhoods and orders and sodalities till his poor head throbbed with the tunes o' "The Protestant Boys" and "The Red Flag" in an unholy counterpoint that would madden Sean himself, unmusical though he sorrowfully admits that he is.

The Middle Class, too, came in for many a clout from Sean's fist, and Davies reflected that the Middle Class couldn't be all that bad if they forked out four gleaming American and Canadian bucks for every one o' Sean's ought-to-buy-o-graphical volumes. A decent lot o' poor slobs, the Middle Class, and ready with a smile to support any Communist author who writes good prose, even if he doesn't do it more than half o' the time.

Should Sean have cut his manuscript to half, or even a third, Davies pondered inside his poor whitened head, as he speared another spud at that humble table, away below the salt, to which the *Times Literary Supplement* has recently banished all Canadian critics. Wasn't there too much of this class o' thing in it:

"Shaded lamps, turned low, softened this room of delicate azure with their steady lights; besides were pots of fine, large, spreading palms and ferns here and there throughout the room, refreshing the eye of the weary traveller with their cooling greenness. There sat, also, in gorgeous bronze and mirrored pots, some elegantly-blossomed plants, whose rich hues blended beautifully with dainty covers of the dainty tables on which they rested. Different inlaid vases of hothouse flowers graced them, perfuming the air with their varied odours. A low fire burned beyond a rug of horny beauty, whilst appetizing dishes of healthy grapes peeped temptingly above their choice surface."

Aw, but wait a minute, Davies cried to himself; that's not Sean, that's Amanda M. Ros, quite a different Irish writer, and one so like a caricature of Sean that it's no wonder Sean writes like Amanda when he's off his tracks. Shouldn't he have cut all the Ros stuff, now, and left us only the purest and best of Sean?

There's a matter, now, for Dom Anselm Hughes and the Blessed John Feeney and Cardinal O'Rory to collogue over in their marble presbyteries! There's a question to vex the Vatican! Lookit the Welshman there, Dylan Thomas; in two golden little books—*Portrait of the Artist as a Young Dog* and *Quite Early One Morning*—he has given us the distilled essence of a poet's life. And he has shown Sean that a Celt can say all he has to say in a hatful o' choice words, without belly-achin' and payin' off old scores. But can't Sean point in confutation at the haughty English aristocrat Sir Osbert Sitwell, lolling at ease on his golden throne and extrudin' the five marvellous volumes of his rich and splendid life? Every craftsman must have his own tools, and work in his own way. Sean's way is the six-volume way, and you sink or swim in the ocean of his variegated eloquence.

Davies may find his ear tiring of the monotonous cadence of Sean's lyric indignation, but isn't that a small price to pay for Sean's superb deflation of the G. K. Chesterton puffball? For two hundred pages or more it may seem as if Sean never met anybody but fools, and left them weltering in the envenomed blood of their own folly. But isn't it worth that to get to his summing-up of a much admired novelist—"With Graham Greene life is a precious, perpetual, snot-sodden whinge"? And if he transcribes too many of the stupid clerical attacks made on him and his work, isn't it worth it to come to his understanding estimate of Bernard Shaw as a poet and playwright? And if Davies gets punch-drunk from the puzzle of Sean's O-let-us-be-Joyceful prose, whose fault is it but his own?

Davies will never bring himself to believe, however, that this uproarious, resentful, cantankerous old wind-instrument of a Sean is any kind of a Communist. Sean's Communism is a poet's dream. It isn't the Communism of Marx or Lenin or Joe Stalin, and it isn't the communism of Jesus Christ. It is Sean's powerful desire to be free, and to be loved and approved by mankind, and to see all his enemies flat on their backs with the stones o' Rome holding them down. And that's not Communism. It is the age-old hankering of poets of Sean's stamp and it has no name in English, though the Welsh call it *hiraeth*. It makes men ridiculous and it makes them bores and it makes them write six-volume autobiographies and it gives them rewarding glimpses of the glory of God and the greatness of Man. And that, thinks Davies as he moseys down to the oculist to get his reading lenses strengthened, is exactly what it has done to Sean.

Saturday Night, 5 February 1955

Dylan Thomas and
Hector Berlioz

*B*elatedly, but with enthusiasm, I call the attention of readers of this department to *Dylan Thomas in America,* by John Malcolm Brinnin; the book was published in November 1955, and would have been reviewed then if I were not continually in arrears with the excellent books which I would like to write about, but lack space to mention. This is a book which grows in recollection, and as another book relating to another great romantic, Hector Berlioz, has come to hand, I want to write about them both and make some comments on the romantic temperament as I do so.

Brinnin is an American poet who, when he became director of the YM–YWHA Poetry Center in New York in 1950, lost no time in asking Dylan Thomas to visit the U.S.A. and give some readings there. Thus he became Thomas' agent and friend, and was deeply involved in Thomas' four visits to this continent. A more exhausting, alarming, yet life-enhancing experience for a sensitive man could hardly be imagined. Thomas was everything that conventional people sum up in the word "impossible"; he was a drunkard, offensive in his attitude toward women, irresponsible about money and appointments, and even a thief in a minor way. Yet he was also sensitive, lovable, often a glorious companion, and a true poet in the freshness of vision and the splendour of insight which he brought to life.

As we read this hair-raising account of Thomas' descents on American academic settlements we shudder with Mr. Brinnin, yet we admire and envy Thomas. He suffered terrible remorse for his bad behaviour, but while it was going on he appears to have enjoyed it on a plane of delight which few of us ever attain. Is there anyone who has engaged, however humbly, in the speech-making trade, who has not longed to tell the organizers, the sponsors, the eager-beavers, precisely what he thinks of them? Who has not yearned to tell the culture-eager young women what their probable destiny in life will be? Is there an author, however lowly, who has not ached to tell a few professors and critics what he thinks of their necrophagous attitude toward literature?

There is one living Canadian poet known to me who, when plagued by a women's club to reveal his principal enthusiasms in life, replied briefly, "Whisky and dirty stories." But where lesser writers hold their tongues, or break out infrequently, Thomas revelled and rioted his way across the States, saying what he pleased in the language most appropriate to his feelings. And of course he gave superb readings from his own verse and that of other men—readings which brought a whole new glory of poetry to thousands among those who heard him.

If Thomas had been simply an uninhibited poet he would not have been unusually interesting, but he had two elements deep in his nature which marked him as a romantic of the first order. He was a ruthless spiritual exploiter of other people, and he was possessed by a demon of self-destruction. Mr. Brinnin describes, with reserve and yet with utmost conviction, the feeling which stole over him that he was being absorbed into Thomas' life; that he was, beyond any duty as agent and friend, being made responsible for Thomas, forced to act as his keeper and his conscience. Thomas was a man of inordinately strong personality; those who loved him were subsumed in him; his spirit, whether in anguish or in triumph, absorbed them.

He was a man bent on self-destruction. His disregard of medical advice was not the weakness of the drunkard who cannot live without liquor; he could, and did, drink little or nothing when he was at ease with himself. He drank to quiet a horrible nervous exacerbation, a deep despair of the soul, which lured him on toward his death. The years that Brinnin describes were, judged as a whole, years of prolonged suicide from despair.

Why do I call this romance? Because the romantic impulse, when it is strong, is desperately dangerous to those whom it possesses. The romantic attitude toward life—if such demoniacal possession may be called an attitude—is one in which feeling always takes precedence over reason or reflection. The poet of popular fancy—the man of weak nature pursuing pretty fancies and communicating them in verse—is the caricature: the reality is what Dylan Thomas was, a man shaken and destroyed by a bardic fury.

Such creatures are rare, and they are valued more highly by posterity than by the world which knows them and likes its lions comfortably tamed. Hector Berlioz (1803–1869) was a great romantic, and it is pleasant to have a new translation, by Jacques Barzun, of his *Evenings with the Orchestra*. It is a hotch-potch of music criticism, musical anecdote and musical jokes, strung together as the conversation which goes on in the orchestra during the performance of bad operas and oratorios. It has been criticized as a formless, bitty book. I like such books, full of unexpected plums and odd scraps of wisdom, and I do not find it formless; the form is that of the personality of Berlioz himself. This is the table-talk of a man of extraordinary musical genius who was also a very good writer. Berlioz was music critic of the Paris *Journal des Débats* for a quarter of a century. A man of first-rate genius who is also a critic can let us into secrets of the artistic life which nobody else can communicate. This is a rich book for those who know how to read it.

Unquestionably a great romantic, Berlioz possessed a quality not found in Thomas, which helped him to preserve his reason; he is an ironist of high quality. There is a cast of mind, admirably exemplified in Berlioz, which is possessed by the romantic fury and buffeted by it, but which, at unexpected moments, achieves a calm, wry appreciation of itself, a sudden stillness in the storm. Berlioz, too, was an "impossible" person. His love-life was outrageous; his public behaviour was often frantic.

At the conclusion of a public performance of his *Symphonie Funèbre et Triomphale,* which he conducted with a drawn sword, he flung himself upon the kettledrums in a fit of weeping. He was obsessed by a need for musical grandiosity, and effects which he called "Babylonian and Ninevean." And yet this irrational genius also wrote the brilliant satires on musical jealousies and the making of a musical career which give splendid life to the pages of the book which Barzun has re-translated.

Extraordinary demands are made upon the world by men of romantic genius. We can now, without discomfort to ourselves, admire Berlioz. But how should we have responded to Berlioz if we had been his contemporaries? Very much, no doubt, as we responded to Dylan Thomas. The president of a women's club who has been ribaldly insulted, the nubile poetry-lover who has asked to have her mind explored and who has had her bottom pinched instead, the professor of literature who has been told to commit an indecency against his own ultra-respectable person, the kindly host upon whose drawing-room carpet genius has thrown up, the woman abandoned, the friend driven to the edge of endurance: these people have understandable and real complaints. They need not be expected to say, "This is a genius and we must bear with him"; genius in a tantrum has a way of looking much like any egotist in a tantrum. Few people can see genius in someone who has offended them.

Genius is unquestionably a great trial, when it takes the romantic form, and genius and romance are so associated in the public mind that many people recognize no other kind. There are other forms of genius, of course, and though they create their own problems, they are not "impossible" people.

But O, how deeply we should thank God for these impossible people like Berlioz and Dylan Thomas! What a weary, grey, well-ordered, polite, unendurable hell this world would be without them!

Saturday Night, 9 June 1956

Havelock Ellis

When a reader wrote to me recently asking why there was so much about sex in modern novels, I ran over in my mind the many answers that would have to be given to make one reasonably complete answer, and I looked in a few books in which the subject was considered. I found many mentions of the name of Sigmund Freud, whose influence on literature, though great, was oblique. I did not find a single reference to Havelock Ellis, whose influence was direct. As this year marks the centennial of Ellis' birth, some comment on him will not be amiss.

Ellis was a schoolmaster in the back-blocks of Australia when he determined to make the study of sexual behaviour in human beings the principal work of his life. He returned to England, qualified as a physician and set to work on the long process of enquiry which provided material for his *Studies in the Psychology of Sex,* the first volume of which appeared in England in 1897. Action was brought against the book by the Crown on charges of obscenity, and Ellis was grossly abused from the bench. Consequently the remaining volumes were brought out by a highly reputable medical publisher in the U.S.A. To this day the *Studies* are not published complete in England, though they are widely read there. This important pioneering work was completed in 1910.

Two things make the *Studies* influential among writers. The first is that they are finely written themselves; with Burton's

Anatomy of Melancholy they belong at the top of any list of books in English which are at the same time notable works of science and admirable as literature. The second is that the book makes clear that in the sexual realm "normality" is a word of far wider application than had been supposed.

What made the book appear obscene to the law? Primarily, I think, the fact that it contains hundreds of personal histories, most of them from people of education and respectable position, which contradicted popular notions of how respectable people behave. But, the book said gently but firmly, this is not depravity but part of the very wide range of normality. Further, the *Studies* gave offence by saying that pleasure was a normal and necessary concomitant of sex.

It is extraordinary that Ellis, who was a gentle and retiring man, of distinguished courtesy and decency in his personal behaviour, should have been denounced as a pornographer. Olive Schreiner, his devoted friend for many years, said, "In some ways he has the noblest nature of any human being I know." H. L. Mencken called him "the most highly civilized man now living." Yet long after his death in 1939 a Toronto physician assured me that Ellis was "a smut-hound" whose life had been spent in debauch. Poor Ellis! Twenty-five years of his life were passed in coping with the extraordinary behaviour of his wife, Edith Lees, who was sadly unbalanced, but whom he loved and cared for very tenderly. Not debauch, but near-poverty and anxiety were his daily fare.

Recognition came late, but it was generous when it came. In the years between the wars Ellis' reputation as a man of letters and as a philosopher in matters relating to the conduct of life grew very great, though he never lost his power to touch off fireworks in certain minds. I recall Dr. A. D. Lindsay, the Master of Balliol in 1936, condemning Ellis roundly as a fool, with heat surprising in a Quaker.

A friend of mine who knew Ellis personally told me that his insight was so striking as to give the impression of second sight. A young couple known to my friend went to Ellis to ask if they should marry; he talked to them for two hours, and at last said that he would advise against marriage, for reasons which he explained. Within five years they were divorced, and all that Ellis had foreseen had come to pass!

It was only in his later years that Ellis saw many strangers; he was shy, and personal interviews of the kind collected by Dr. Kinsey were impossible for him. He gathered his immense quantity of information by correspondence, and much of his special genius showed itself in the way he sifted the boastful, the lying and the sensational from the true.

Ellis, as much as Freud, may be said to have brought the variety of sex experience, and its importance in the formation of character, into the light. He died at eighty: "Death is the final Master and Lord, but Death must await my good pleasure," he said when mortally ill. I recommend his frank autobiography, *My Life,* as well as the centennial biographies which are shortly to appear.

Toronto Daily Star, 7 March 1959

mehitabel

The first week of this month was International Cat Week, and as the cat is, above all animals, the writer's pet, I suppose I should have written something about it. But I do not care about "weeks," and every week is a cat week with me. Besides, I did not like the I.C.W. publicity; it lacked the truly feline touch which distinguishes, for instance, Baudelaire's reference to his cat:

> *C'est l'esprit familier du lieu;*
> *Il juge, il préside, il inspire*
> *Toutes choses dans mon Empire.*
> *Peut-être est-il fée, est-il dieu.*

That is how cats like to be written about, and anything which falls below the Baudelaire standard makes the writer an object of disdain in the cat world.

Literary cat lovers are many. Dr. Johnson's cat Hodge is famous, of course, and so in their way are the cats which belonged to Heine, Zola, Gautier, Dickens, Swinburne, that writer of exquisite letters Ellen Terry, and the extensive cat menagerie of Mark Twain. Authors like cats because they are such quiet, lovable, wise creatures, and cats like authors for the same reasons. It used to be fashionable for authors to have their pictures taken with dogs, but the dogs always looked like models hired from an advertising agency, and probably were.

Though Hodge was the greatest literary cat in fact, I do not think anyone will deny that there is only one possible candidate for the title of Greatest Literary Cat in Fiction; it is, of course, mehitabel, creation of Donald Robert Perry Marquis. She enlivened his columns in the *New York Sun* and the *Herald Tribune* from 1927 to 1935. Don Marquis wrote plays and novels which have not lived, but it will be long before the charm of mehitabel the cat and archy the cockroach fades. If, by some singular chance, you do not know this remarkable pair, Doubleday publish their *lives and times,* illustrated by George Herriman. (Herriman was a cartoonist who worked in that unmistakable comic style of the twenties; his drawing was crude and messy but expressive, and his people and animals always seemed to be throwing off sweat in huge drops; the last man to work in this convention was Arch Dale, for so many years cartoonist of the *Winnipeg Free Press.*)

When I call mehitabel the Greatest Literary Cat in Fiction I am not being tautologous; she was a fictional creature, but she was also literary, because she wrote verse, which was transcribed by her friend archy. The little cockroach had, literally, the soul of a poet; when Helena Petrovna Halm Blavatsky, the founder of Theosophy, died in 1891, it was asserted by her followers that her soul had passed into a white horse; archy was a reincarnation of a poet. As a cockroach, he had great difficulty in working a typewriter, and could not manage the shift key; that is why he was always archy and never Archy. mehitabel claimed to have been Cleopatra in an earlier incarnation; she also remembered being one of Tutankhamen's queens, and for those who remember the discovery of his tomb, the name of Tutankhamen recalls, not the fourteenth century B.C., but the twenties, when an unwise Egyptian influence manifested itself in house furnishings.

Much of the splendour of a cat's nature was incarnated in mehitabel. She was an alley stray, and thus the sybarite charm of the pet was denied her, but she was in every other way a true cat. "to hell with anything unrefined has always been my motto," she would cry, and her philosophy of life was summed up in "toujours gai, toujours gai," and "cheerio, my deario." After each unwise love affair she would confide in the philosophical archy; after each batch of kittens (which she left in a garbage can that was likely to fill up with rain) she greeted any enquiry with a haughty glance and "what kittens?" She was an artist and could not be tied down by domestic duties; as archy remarked, it takes all kinds of people to make an underworld.

When we read *the lives and times of archy and mehitabel* we must be impressed by the qualities of imagination, intellect and sheer hard work that go into good funny writing. Leo Rosten, creator of H*Y*M*A*N K*A*P*L*A*N, has recently described some of his travail in dealing with his extraordinary brainchild in *The Return of H*y*m*a*n K*a*p*l*a*n*. Almost any industrious dullard can write tragedy—not real tragedy or good tragedy, of course, but the kind of thing that is depressing enough to deceive people who like gloomy reading, and regard misery as a status-mood. But to write comedy with the wit and perception of Don Marquis is a task for an artist.

Such artists linger in the mind. For twenty-two years she has been silent, but during International Cat Week I found myself longing to know what mehitabel would have said about it. She hated mobs and vulgar enthusiasm, so "to hell with anything unrefined," would probably have been her comment. cheerio, my deario.

Toronto Daily Star, 21 November 1959

Casanova de Seingalt

*I*f you were to ask me to recommend a book as a Christmas present for a special friend—one whose fondness for reading goes beyond best-selling novels and the most recent autobiography of an aggrieved field marshal—I would unhesitatingly name the first two volumes of *The Memoirs of Casanova*. They are handsome; they are a compliment to the taste of the receiver; they are engrossing to read, and extraordinarily few people hereabout appear to be acquainted with them.

(Are they expensive, I think I hear somebody murmur. Not at all. The two will cost you about the price of a good dinner for yourself and your friend. I never understand why people expect books to be cheaper than food or clothing.)

Giovanni Giacomo Casanova de Seingalt has long been one of my favourite characters in history. His name is synonymous with adventures in love, and indeed it appears that he was irresistible to women, and by no means anxious to be resisted. But he was vastly more than a woman-chaser; he was a soldier, a scholar, a musician, a gambler, a priest and a thoroughgoing crook who—and this is what marks him off from common crooks—knew precisely what he was doing and watched himself with a gently amused eye. If, when he was down on his luck, he manufactured a tube out of an old riding boot and sold it to a simpleton as the authentic scabbard from which, on a celebrated occasion, St. Peter drew his sword and smote off a servant of the High Priest's ear, he thought it was a great joke; he also thought he had enriched the simpleton by giving him something to venerate. If he cheated at cards, he called it adjusting the carelessness of Fortune; it was immoral for him to lose money to people stupider than himself, because it brought intellect into disrepute. He seduced women, certainly, but he thought it good for them to meet that experience at the hands of a man who could make it a thing to cherish in memory until the day they died.

Do not suppose, however, that I am recommending to you the memoirs of a mere rascal. Casanova was a philosopher, and likewise a very brave man. His escape from the famous Venetian prison called Piombi in 1755 is a classic of adventure, possible only to a man of unique cleverness and daring. And if he had not possessed intellectual quality, he would never have made himself known to the greatest men and women of his day— Voltaire, Cagliostro, Catherine the Great, Madame de Pompadour, Albrecht von Haller and, eventually, Count Waldstein. He spent his last twelve years at Waldstein's castle in Bohemia, as his librarian, and it was there that he wrote his *Memoirs*.

The fate of the *Memoirs* is curious. Casanova wrote in French, but with occasional errors, for he was Italian. When, in 1826, they were published by the famous firm of Brockhaus of Leipzig, the story was shorn of some of its spicier bits, and when translated back into French, cut even more. It was not until a translation was made into English by Arthur Machen, that anything like the full story was told. It is the Machen translation which Longmans have used.

This fact contributes to the worth and charm of the book, for Machen (1863–1947) was a master-stylist. He was a Welshman who won a fine reputation among a limited circle of admirers for his tales of the supernatural. Sometimes, when I see the movies making fools of themselves with cheap tales of horror, I wonder why they do not turn up some of Machen's shuddersome inventions—*The Hill of Dream,* for instance, or *The*

Great God Pan. H. G. Wells said that Machen was the only writer who could make his flesh creep, and Wells was a tough old bird, who devised some notable horrors himself.

Longmans' decision to bring out the *Memoirs* is a welcome one and I hope it will greatly increase the knowledge and admiration of this wonderful adventurer and writer. All the books of reference speak of the splendid picture of life in the eighteenth century which Casanova provides, and I wonder if this has not worked against him. So many people interpret such a recommendation as meaning an endless rustle of lace and brocade, a cloud of snuff and hair-powder. But the vigour and pace of Casanova's writing cannot be bettered. He dashes from adventure to adventure in a fashion which recalls the old Douglas Fairbanks films. Well do I recall the headmaster of my school (the late Dr. W. L. Grant) startling a Sunday night audience of schoolboys by shouting "Live dangerously; sin nobly!" Dr. Grant would have been proud to have Casanova in his Sixth Form.

I recommend this book whole-heartedly, but not indiscriminately. It is not a dirty book, but on the other hand it is not for your old Auntie Bessie, either. It is for the high-hearted, for those who smack their lips over life. And at Christmas it is just as good as a plum-pudding, blazing with brandy.

Toronto Daily Star, 12 December 1959

Father Knox

*I*f you were asked to name a translator of the Bible who was also the author of *The Body in the Silo* you might be excused for hesitating before the correct answer sprang to your lips. It was, of course, the Rt. Rev. Ronald Knox, fellow of Trinity College, Oxford, and Prothonotary Apostolic to His Holiness Pope Pius XII. I think his detective stories much inferior to his serious work, but he was proud of them and if he had not had it in him to produce them, he would not have been the extraordinary man he was—a combination of evergreen Old Etonian and saint.

If you are curious about his career, his friend Evelyn Waugh has recently published a biography which is a model of its kind. Sympathy is balanced by judgement on every page; Father Knox was a hard man to know, and for many people a hard man to like. His shyness was sometimes disguised by a levity which was not far from foolishness; he was insular and narrow in many things; like many shy, clever people, he often made remarks which were wounding, because he did not know how other people would take them. But the other side of the medal from the clerical clown shows us a man of deep humility and melancholy nature, a fine writer whose natural gifts were supported by taste and admirable scholarship.

Waugh brings special sympathy to his portrait of Knox because both were converts to Catholicism who felt that they had experienced losses, as well as gains, by that step. Knox was the son, and grandson, of Anglican bishops, which meant that the Authorized Version and the Prayer Book were part of the fabric of his being; the vernacular prayers of Catholicism, and the Douay Bible were offensive to his taste, and he lived to reform both. His childhood was what one might expect in a bishop's household, and his education at Eton and Oxford made him an Englishman of a special sort; after conversion he found life with seminarians, and under the eye of some members of the hierarchy, unfamiliar and somewhat foreign in tone. Knox did not say so, but Waugh is of the opinion that the Church of Rome never made the best use of Knox (as it failed to make the best use of Newman) because it did not understand his gifts or value them.

One of the greatest of those gifts was his ability to make complex theological and spiritual argument comprehensible to the intelligent but untrained reader. Nowhere, I think, is this shown so well as in his fine book *Enthusiasm,* in which he discusses those movements—Anabaptist, Jansenism, Quietism, Quakerism, Wesleyanism, to name a few—which have arisen when groups of people who feel themselves to be under undeniable instruction from God break away from the high road of Christian thinking. Such a book must have offered great temptations to the worldly side of Knox's character; what chances to score off the heretics, to make fun of the enthusiasts, to write comic descriptions of their uncouth raptures! But although the book is often witty in tone, charity and understanding are always present; we feel for the enthusiasts, but we are left in no doubt as to where they have taken the wrong turning, and split off from the classical balance of the Church. This is a book for which I have felt the strongest admiration and sympathy during the past nine years, and I recommend it seriously to anyone who is concerned with the history of Christian thought.

About Knox's translation of the Bible I can offer no opinion, as I have not seen it, and indeed it seems to be little known on this continent. Nor would my opinion be of any value. It is interesting that after the doubts expressed about it by some members of the English hierarchy, it was a great success with English Catholics, and had earned £50,000 for the Church at the time of Knox's death. Waugh records that Knox was somewhat wry on the subject that no word of thanks was ever offered to him for his substantial and continuing benefaction.

Here we discern an inveterate strain of Protestantism in his nature. He was a devout Catholic, and a priest, but he could not be utterly subsumed in his service to the Church. He expected some recognition of his personal gifts, and when it was not forthcoming, and men of lesser attainment were elevated, he was hurt. He was never at ease in the external world of Catholicism, nor in the Protestant world of scholarship to which he had been bred. Only in his service to God was he able to lose this consciousness.

He took a vow of celibacy when he was seventeen. It seems odd, therefore, that in his detective stories he should have attempted to set down the intimate conversation of married couples. The unconscious humour of these passages often outsoars the wit of his most brilliant conscious flights. This proves nothing, except that celibacy and priesthood lay certain disadvantages upon the novelist. But why did he attempt it? Speculation on such a matter must always be fruitless, leading only to an unedifying ribaldry.

When his translation of the New Testament was to appear, an Oxford friend is reputed to have said: "Ronnie, will the title-page read, 'By the author of *The Body in the Silo*'?"

Toronto Daily Star, 20 February 1960

Hans Christian Andersen

One hundred and fifty-five years ago today Hans Christian Andersen was born. The Andersen legend is well-known—the dreamy child of the poor shoemaker, who became the world's darling and the pride of his native Denmark. Pictures of the statue in Copenhagen, pottery images of the Little Mermaid and the Match Girl must rank among that country's major exports. Every child hears some of the tales (though comparatively few of the 156 are widely known) and the Ugly Duckling and the Emperor's New Clothes have passed into the language of proverb.

The legend is less interesting than the reality. "My life is a beautiful fairy-tale," he says, at the beginning of his *Autobiography*. Unless we are so stupid as to suppose that a fairy-tale is necessarily a simple, charming narrative in which the good are wholly good, and the bad irredeemably wicked, in which virtue triumphs and vice is punished, then we must accept Andersen's judgement. A fairy-tale it was.

Like a fairy-tale hero he was born in poverty, and his father died when the boy was eleven. At fourteen he set out for Copenhagen, to seek his fortune, determined to astonish the world as an actor or a singer; the theatre was his passion, and a toy theatre, made by his father, was the delight of his life. But he was an ugly duckling indeed, tall, shambling and with huge feet and hands; as with Abraham Lincoln, whom he somewhat resembled, the discovery that his face was distinguished and beautiful came when his fame was established. The first Copenhagen years were hard, though not because he lacked patrons; the greatest of these was the King, who sent him to school, and to Andersen, as to many another imaginative boy, that domain where the dullest answer is necessarily the right one was the sorest trial and humiliation of all.

All things considered, his fame came quickly but—again the fairy-tale touch—not for the reasons he desired. His plays were unsuccessful, his novels did not please, but his short tales— "Little Claus and Big Claus," "The Snow Queen," "The Steadfast Tin Soldier"—delighted children the world over. But that was not quite what Andersen had intended; these stories, so full of wit and poetry and insight, were meant only secondarily for children, and were addressed also to adults.

To hold the attention of adults, however, one must at least appear to be an adult oneself, and this was something Andersen never succeeded in doing. He was crippled by a sense that his grandfather, a madman, had been the sport of the Odense streets, and that his illegitimate half-sister was a harlot. He was unable to approach women except as a child; if there is any truth in the story that he once wished to marry Jenny Lind, we can only congratulate them both, posthumously, on a lucky escape. He was neurotically sensitive, and Dickens records that when Andersen was his guest he would burst into offended tears if he were not served first at table.

There is much refreshing comedy in the tale of Dickens' relations with Andersen. In June 1857 the Great Cockney invited the Great Dane to visit him at Gad's Hill for two weeks. Andersen stayed five, at the end of which time his host was referring to him as "a bony bore." Nobody could understand him, in French, Italian or German; Andersen spoke no English, and the Dickenses no Danish.

Andersen's simplicity must have been trying. In a letter Dickens reports: "One day he came home to Tavistock House, apparently suffering from corns that had ripened in two hours. It turned out that a cab driver had brought him back from the

City, by way of the unfinished new thoroughfare through Clerk-enwell. Satisfied that the cabman was bent on robbery, and murder, he put his watch and money into his boots—together with a Bradshaw, a pocket-book, a pair of scissors, a penknife, a book or two, a few letters of introduction, and some other miscellaneous property." No doubt Andersen was tiresome, and Dickens was not the man to brook a rival in the art of capturing attention. When at last Andersen left Gad's Hill, a notice was placed in his bedroom reading "Hans Christian Andersen slept in this room for five weeks which seemed to the family ages."

Andersen, in English, has suffered from bad translators. Most of them are anonymous Victorians, presumably hacks, who translated not from Danish, but from German editions. Their English is pompous and tawdry, and they have altered phrases to suit English standards of nursery propriety. They have even, as in "The Emperor's New Clothes," altered the sense of some stories.

It is almost as though we met a new author, therefore, when we read the selection of Andersen's tales translated by L. W. Kingsland, from the Danish. Through its graceful simplicity we can sense what a masterly prose writer Hans Andersen was. We very quickly discern, also, that he did not write solely, or even primarily, for children. His strength lay in one of the rarest endowments in the whole realm of literature; he was a fabulist, and all his poetry and whimsicality, great though these attributes are, were put at the service of that extraordinary gift.

Toronto Daily Star, 2 April 1960

Francis Bacon

*F*ollowing my comment on April 23 about the notion that Francis Bacon might have written the works usually attributed to Shakespeare, a reader in Regina has sent me a letter in praise of Bacon, putting great emphasis on the worldly wisdom displayed in the famous *Essays*. Certainly Bacon was a man of brilliant attainments and the essays offer us the chilly, mature conclusions of a God-fearing Machiavelli. But the man who wrote that the purpose of poetry was "to give some shadowe of satisfaction to the minde of Man in those points wherein the Nature of things does deny it" does not sound like the man who wrote *A Midsummer Night's Dream*.

Wise, Francis Bacon most certainly was. But no man can be wholly wise, and posterity is sure to uncover his follies. *The Complete Works of Bacon* contain some wonderful, little-known things, including two magnificent prayers, one for scholars and one for writers. But he was an advocate of technical and scientific learning, as opposed to that which is speculative, and like so many men who make a god of science, his god sometimes played tricks on him.

He was interested in longevity, and closely studied whatever the science of his day could tell him about it. Some of his precepts make good sense, such as "Never to keep the body in the same posture above half an hour at a time," and "To shake off spirits ill disposed." But he appears to have taken a horrifying number of medicines to prolong his life, and the wonder of it is that he hung on till the age of sixty-five. He records a recipe for a powder which, when one scruple of it was dissolved in wine, made a drink called Methusalem Water; I cannot give the whole thing, for it is too long, but two of the ingredients are the powdered shells of snails, and crushed pearls, mingled with ambergris and nitre (now more familiar as saltpetre). He took a shot of Methusalem Water every day, and it is no wonder that, as he consumed so much grit, he suffered from stones; he also records a recipe for a broth to deal with this painful trouble. He snuffed up the smoke of burning aloes, bayleaves and rosemary, with a little tobacco added. He drank ale with herbs in it "to beget a robust heat." He records sixty-nine "openers," as he called cathartics, one of which is gun-powder, and some of which cannot be mentioned in the pages of a family journal. He ate pellets of bread soaked in wine, syrup of roses and amber, before he went to bed. He washed his feet once a month in a mixture of lye, herbs and brandy. He took pills of rhubarb and wormwood "for opening the liver." In short, his lordship seems to have been a thorough-going hypochondriac, perpetually dosing himself, and all in the name of the science he so much admired.

If any reader feels disposed to try it, here is a recipe for Bacon's "Grains of Youth": "Take of nitre four grains, of ambergris three grains, of orrice-powder two grains, of white poppy-seed the fourth part of a grain, of saffron half a grain, with water of orange-flowers and a little tragacanth; make them into small grains, four in number. To be taken at four a-clock, or going to bed." Your friendly corner druggist probably has all of these things, but if he is not acquainted with tragacanth, any good household glue will serve the purpose.

Bacon was not eccentric in this respect. The Elizabethans, and most Europeans until well into the eighteenth century, made a hobby of medication. They took quantities of physic which make us shudder, and when a politician did not wish to be available for questioning he did not, as ours do, go on a fishing-trip, but gave out the news that he had taken physic; no humane person could then have expected him to give his attention to anything else. We must assume that if Bacon took one quarter of the medicines he records as conducive to a long life, he was a man of rugged constitution. Probably he recommended them to his acquaintances; pills were just as fashionable in his time as they are now, and when gentlemen met they exchanged pills; ladies exchanged cordials, made by themselves, and as these were strongly alcoholic (the ancestors of the liqueurs of our time) they were undoubtedly tranquillizing in effect.

There is no space even to summarize Bacon's advice to those about to take a purge, for of course a preparatory dose, or pill, was needed to arouse the intestinal tract to a proper sense of the solemnity of what was about to happen. Nor was the purge, and its consequence, enough; after it had had its way with the patient, he must take "abstersive and mundifying clysters" to signal to his tripes that the war was over, and peace-terms were being discussed.

Probably Shakespeare was a hypochondriac; most authors are. But I doubt if he could have competed with Francis Bacon, Lord Verulam. There was a man of scientific mind who grudged nothing to science! Ours, too, is a scientific age, and in three hundred years our descendants will know how much Methusalem Water, however named, we have been drinking.

Toronto Daily Star, 21 May 1960

Arthur Sullivan

*I*n my workroom hangs a caricature of Sir Arthur Sullivan, drawn for the March 14, 1874, issue of the English magazine *Vanity Fair* by Carlo Pellegrini. It is a good portrait, suggesting Sullivan's short stature, his dandyism, and his chronic ill-health with the impersonal malice which is to be found in the work of a master caricaturist. But although whatever was absurd in Sullivan's appearance is deftly hinted at, the picture also shows a man of consequence, of quality, of distinction in his realm. A charming detail is the conductor's baton which Sullivan holds in his hand; it is attached to his wrist with a cord, as was the custom of the day, and from that cord hangs a little silk tassel. I have been looking at the picture with special affection during this past week, while reading *The Music of Arthur Sullivan*, by Gervase Hughes; the more I read, the more I understood how right Pellegrini was to include that tassel.

I do not recommend the book to you unless you are moderately musical, for it is a technical discussion; however, if you know the Gilbert and Sullivan operas, and have some musical skill, you will find it informative and revealing. There are two widespread opinions about Sullivan as a composer: uncritical enthusiasts praise him extravagantly, making a cult of his work similar to that which surrounds the books of Lewis Carroll; stern musicians dismiss him as a trifler. Gervase Hughes holds the balance truly; Sullivan was a man who failed in the highest reaches of music, but he was a fine craftsman and a man of miniature genius in the world of light opera.

The highest reaches of music, to Sullivan, meant church music and grand opera. When he attempted either his evil genius sat at his shoulder, dictating pompous sentimentalities. But when it came to setting the libretti of W. S. Gilbert, he brought all his intimate knowledge of the orchestra, all his taste and feeling for words and all his genius as a melodist to bear upon the task.

A fine melodist, admittedly, but commonplace otherwise, say those musicians who do not like him. Not so, says Gervase Hughes, and proceeds methodically to show that though Sullivan had his limitations and mannerisms, he was masterful in the technicalities of composition. Again and again this author makes comparisons between Sullivan and, first, Mozart and, second, Schubert; Sullivan was not the equal of either, but he must be compared with them if his style is to be explained. What better standard would any composer desire?

There are few of the usual judgements on Sullivan which Mr. Hughes does not contradict. To me the most astonishing is his statement that Sullivan did not write gratefully for the voice; apparently he demanded much, and offered little, to his singers. Perhaps that explains why the voices of the D'Oyly Carte company always seemed to be on the verge of collapse. While reading Mr. Hughes' book I played a number of their recordings, and the general standard of singing is lamentable.

Which was leader in the great combination, Gilbert or Sullivan? The question does not admit of a final answer. Gilbert was a man of dominant character, Sullivan quiet and somewhat effeminate. Yet it appears that Gilbert, who was utterly unmusical, was always ready to provide two quite different sets of verses for every song, so that Sullivan need be under no constraint to set to music anything he did not like. Gilbert, a tyrant in the theatre, was a thoroughly conventional Victorian in his personal life. It was Sullivan who was the Bohemian, the high-flyer, who spent vast sums on race-horses, on roulette, and on hob-nobbing with royalty. Gilbert was stoutly English; Sul-

livan was Irish and Italian. Though business and artistic partners, the men were never really friends. Gilbert had a jeering
quality in his wit which Sullivan did not like, and Sullivan's
silk-tassel side always nettled Gilbert.

The time is at hand for a fresh examination; the copyright of
their works will soon be exhausted, and the D'Oyly Carte dominance, which has been benevolent upon the whole, will be
broken. Sullivan's manuscripts, which Gervase Hughes has studied, will be available to all.

Nobody need fear the outcome. Gilbert was a great craftsman,
and Sullivan had that Mozart-Schubert strain in his work which
has stood the test of time—yea, and of a million murderous
amateur performances. Edward German is little heard, and Victor Herbert is mute, though both were good of their kind and
wrote after Sullivan. The light opera of twenty years ago seems
quaint. But Gilbert and Sullivan is still valid in the theatre. It
looks very much as though the silk tassel were something more
than the foppery of a popular musician; it was a sign of an
aristocrat in his world.

Toronto Daily Star, 16 July 1960

King John

*L*ast week I saw Shakespeare's *King John* performed at the Stratford (Ontario) Shakespearean Festival, and it moved me to wonder what sort of man John really was. Since then I have been doing some reading about John, and he proves to be an interesting and by no means unattractive character.

In popular belief, John was a "bad" king. Contemporary accounts of him stress his wickedness, but we must bear in mind that the chroniclers of John's day were all churchmen; John was always in trouble with the Church, and therefore he received a bad press from the Church. John was the most horrifying thing the twelfth century could conceive of—he was an unbeliever. He went through the religious ceremonies which were required of him as king, but he treated them with levity. He was quite likely to send a message to an archbishop telling him to hustle up his sermon, because the king was hungry; when he advanced to the altar to put the King's Gift in the almsdish, John was likely to jingle the gold and wink at his nobles in a way which made them titter, and gave scandal to the priest. Long stretches of time passed during which the king never took communion; during the period of the interdict on England, which the Pope laid on that kingdom because John would not acknowledge the Pope's choice for the Archbishopric of Canterbury, England prospered, whereas all right-thinking people knew that it should have pined. The Pope at last forced John to make a settlement, but John knew that the settlement was a farce, and undoubtedly the Pope knew it, too. From the Church's point of view, John was a thoroughly unsatisfactory king because he insisted on regarding the Church as a political rival rather than a spiritual superior. In a later time John would have been an agnostic, and a secular opportunist. In one wild moment he proposed to the Sultan of Morocco that England be placed under his protection, on the agreement that England should embrace the Islamic faith. A comparable modern scandal would be if President de Gaulle were to offer to take France into the Communist camp.

The religious climate of the twelfth century cannot be understood in modern terms, for faith lived then with a burning reality which is the exception, and not the rule, today. Men spoke to God with a directness which makes us gape. Consider the vengeance of John's father, Henry II, when he lost the city of Le Mans in battle: "O God," he cried, "since You have today, to heap up confusion on me and increase my shame, so vilely taken from me the city I loved most on earth, in which I was born and reared, where my father is buried and where the body of St. Julian lies hidden, I shall certainly pay You back as best I can, by taking from You that part of me which You love best, my soul." There spoke a man who knew himself to be a king, the nearest thing to God in all creation.

Much that was wrong with John must be blamed on his father. Henry was brilliant and capricious. He reminds us of King Lear, for he turned all his territories over to his sons, Henry, Richard and Geoffrey, making them nominal rulers, while he retained all the power. As a result, his sons were in constant revolt. When John was born on December 24, 1167, there was no inheritance for him, and Henry II jokingly called him Jean Sans Terre, or John Lackland; yet he loved John best, and called him "John, my heart." John did not fancy the name of Lackland, and much of his early bad behaviour and frivolity, and his eventual treachery to his father, undoubtedly sprang from this sense of being odd-man-out.

In the jargon of the sociologists, John came from "a broken home." His mother was that vigorous, extraordinary woman

Eleanor of Aquitaine, but during his childhood she was kept in custody by King Henry, while he devoted himself to his mistress Rosamond Clifford. Later in life John and his mother were firm friends, but it is not surprising that he regarded her as a political rather than a maternal figure. He himself was capricious with women, divorcing his first wife, and doting idolatrously on his second, Isabella of Angouleme, who was twelve at the time of their marriage, and John thirty-two. Anyone who doubts the reality of *Lolita* should read what we are told of John and his Queen.

> King John was not a good man—
>   He had his little ways.
> And sometimes no one spoke to him
>   For days and days and days.
>
>   * * *
>
> And, round about December,
>   The cards upon his shelf
> Which wished him lots of Christmas cheer,
> And fortune in the coming year,
> Were never from his near and dear,
>   But only from himself.

Thus writes A. A. Milne, with complete accuracy. But John was not a monster in a world of saints. If you want to know more about him I can strongly recommend *John, King of England* by John T. Appleby and *Eleanor of Aquitaine and the Four Kings* by Amy Kelly. They are much, much stranger than fiction.

Toronto Daily Star, 30 July 1960

Edward Johnston

*E*arlier in this diary I said that I did not believe that handwriting can be used for character analysis; my correspondents think it can. Perhaps some of my readers will be sufficiently interested in handwriting to read *Edward Johnston* by Priscilla Johnston. It is a biography of the man who, more than any other single person, revived the art of calligraphy in our time, and whose influence extended to the teaching of writing in schools, to the use of calligraphy in advertising and all kinds of public notices, and to the design of type faces. An example of Johnston's writing is so beautiful that it makes the heart leap. I mean that literally. I remember clearly when, as a boy of fourteen, I casually opened Johnston's book *Writing and Illuminating and Lettering* in a public library, I was at once seized with a strong desire to be able to make pages of writing as beautiful as those in the book. It was the beginning of the Easter holidays, and I worked as hard as I could for the whole vacation—without much effect, for I was clumsy, and calligraphers are not made in a hurry—and have toiled at intervals ever since. The quality of Johnston's lettering influenced thousands as it influenced me, and it now influences millions, for it is copied everywhere.

Its beauty was of proportion, not of ornament. When Johnston first tried his hand at lettering in 1896, the art of illumination had sunk very low; illuminated manuscripts were produced, for the usual occasions, in alphabets so grotesque, so contorted and burdened with squiggles and curlicues, that they were unreadable. They were produced with paints and brushes. Johnston went back to ink and a quill pen, and the beauty of legibility. His pupils were many, but the name of Eric Gill is perhaps best known; his influence was profound and what may be called the phoney-fancy style of lettering, whether in printer's type or in manuscript work, is discredited everywhere today.

Has this anything to do with handwriting? Indeed it has. The modern movement which has revived the beautiful Italic hand stems directly from Johnston's work, and some of his pupils have been leaders in it. The ideals of Italic handwriting are legibility first, then beauty; it permits some very fancy flourishes to those who like them, but they are not necessary, and spring from the exuberance of the individual writer. Speed the day when this fine hand will drive the feeble writing which is generally taught on this continent out of our schools.

What did Johnston actually do? He wrote fine manuscripts for people who wanted them. There was enough work of the kind to keep him busy. The last thing to come from his workshop was written in 1944, when he was dying, by his pupil Irene Wellington, under his supervision. It was for Winston Churchill to send to Harry Hopkins, who had lost his son in the war; the plain piece of parchment bore only these words from *Macbeth:* "Your son, my lord, has paid a soldier's debt."

What sort of man was Johnston? His biographer is his daughter, and she has dealt lovingly with a man of great eccentricity. "The truth is the one thing I care most about," said Johnston, and he carried that care into every detail of daily life; he could not compromise, even about the preparation of a cup of tea. He was a fine handicraftsman who liked to make or repair things which could have been more conveniently replaced. He lit his cigarettes with a flint and steel he had made himself; he tied a yard of pink tape on his spectacles so that they could not be lost, and always wore the tape with the glasses; he wrapped a Shetland sweater around his hips, under his trousers, to keep out the cold, and one sleeve usually hung out behind, like a tail.

He was chronically slow in executing commissions, so that people who needed them were kept on tenterhooks till the last possible moment. He constructed an elaborate water-clock which opened the door of his hen-house at dawn. He was vastly innocent of the world, and rather a prig.

He was greatly loved by his pupils and friends, for in his search for the best, the absolutely right, way of doing anything he would spend any amount of time; the designing and preparation of a diploma for the Central School of Arts and Crafts occupied, in all, five years, and his fee was fifteen guineas, or about sixty-five dollars. Understandably Johnston did not grow rich, but he lived by standards which took no account of riches.

A life given to determining the best form for the letters of the alphabet—does it seem extraordinary to you? But no day passes that our eyes do not fall upon something that was influenced, and made better, by this extraordinary, eccentric Scot, and if that is not a life well spent, I should be interested in a better definition.

Toronto Daily Star, 24 September 1960

Theodore Hook

*I*t is most unlikely that anyone who sees this column has recently read anything from the pen of Theodore Hook. Hugely popular as he was in his own day, Hook is now quite unknown; nobody reads him except people like myself, who like to rummage in the rubbish heaps of literature. And indeed, I had forgotten about Hook for years, until yesterday my eye happened to light on a reference to Berners Street.

Berners Street is a short, unremarkable thoroughfare in East London. One morning in 1809 it began to be crowded with people, carriages, vans and messengers, all of them attempting to get to one small, neat but unremarkable house. As the day wore on the crowding became very serious, and celebrities of every sort joined the mob: the Governor of the Bank of England was there, waving a letter which told him that if he called at the house in question, a fraud on the Bank would be revealed; the Chairman of the East India Company came, with a letter of similar import; the Archbishop of Canterbury arrived, summoned by a mysterious message written on excellent paper; the Duke of Gloucester, then Commander-in-Chief, arrived, in answer to a letter purporting to be from a former confidential servant of his mother, who was dying and had something of importance to tell him; finally the Lord Mayor of London appeared. All of these grandees were battling with a crowd of men who were trying to deliver coal, harpsichords, barrels of beer, and merchandise of all kinds. It took hours to untangle the traffic. It was clear that somebody had perpetrated a gigantic hoax.

The hoaxer was Theodore Hook, who was sitting in the window of a house opposite, enjoying the fun. He had made a bet with a friend that he would make Berners Street the most famous street in London for a day, and he won. For a week he had spent all his time writing one thousand letters to tradesmen and important people, summoning them to Berners Street on the day appointed.

Hook (1788–1841) was a brilliant wit, who for many years earned two thousand pounds annually by authorship—a very great sum in those days—but who was chronically hard up. He mixed in aristocratic society, and although he was always a guest, it cost him most of his income to dress fashionably and pay his fares to the great houses in which he was so much admired. He had a neat little house of his own, peopled by his mistress and his children, but his life was passed in the homes of the great.

His attraction for high society was his abounding wit. He was a master of repartee. Nor was table-talk his only accomplishment. He would, on request, sit down at the piano and improvise a song in which he managed to ring in the names of every person present, and make puns on them. Once it was thought that Hook was stumped, for there was a Danish gentleman present with the difficult name of Rosenagen. But Hook left the Dane to the last, and ended his song thus:

> Yet more of my Muse is required:
> Alas! I fear she is done:
> But no! like a fiddler that's tired,
> I'll Rosen-agen and go on.

Once Hook was asked what the light operettas of an earlier day had been like. Sitting at the piano he improvized an overture, and then spun out a short burlesque of the operettas in question, making up plot, characters and solos, duets and choruses as he went on. It has been said that there has never been anyone with so ready a gift of improvisation in musical history.

Coleridge, who was not lavish of his praise, said that Hook was as true a genius as Dante. He must have been an astonishing, glittering and somewhat overpowering companion. But his fame is now a matter of hearsay. Like a few other famous wits, he talked away all his best ideas; his genius was for immediate effects, not for writing. I have tried some of his novels, but they are unreadable now, even by me, and I have more tolerance for the fun of bygone days than most people. Hoaxes, like the Berners Street affair, were only one of his specialties. We have lost our taste for elaborate practical jokes now, and it is no great loss. Mrs. Tottenham, the widow who lived in the house Hook fastened upon, was never quite well after her day of unsought notoriety.

Toronto Daily Star, 8 July 1961

William Hazlitt

The reading public is popularly supposed to like love-stories better than any other fare. What they really like are love-stories that flatter their own feelings; a true love-story can be so painful, so wounding, that most readers find it intolerable.

This week I have been re-reading a true love-story, *Liber Amoris* by William Hazlitt. When he published it in May, 1823, the reviewers dropped on it with the uttermost ferocity: "nauseous and revolting" was the general opinion. Hazlitt's reputation never fully recovered from it while he lived, and many of his warmest admirers skim over it now. It is surely one of the most painful accounts of a love affair ever written.

Hazlitt published it when he was forty-five, and established as the most perceptive critic of literature and painting of his time; he was also known to the more discerning readers of the age as a master of English prose; his friends included most of the great writers of a great period. Now, one of the occupational hazards of criticism is that it tends to shrivel the emotions; judgement takes the place of feeling, and the man is lost in the critic. When Hazlitt published this account of his love for a girl young enough to be his daughter he showed himself to be still a man, and a foolish, jealous, irrational man at that.

Hazlitt was married twice, to ladies of literary inclination. He became estranged from his first wife in 1819, and married the second in 1824, having parted from the first by the expedient of a "Scottish divorce"—the only sort available at the time for people who were not very wealthy. Between these marriages he conceived a passion for his landlord's daughter, a girl named Sarah Walker, the "sweet apparition," the "angel" of *Liber Amoris*.

What happened was what modern psychology would call a "projection." The first Mrs. Hazlitt had proved a disappointment; she had not been whole-hearted in her admiration for her husband's writing, she was a disastrous housekeeper, and she seems to have been rather a fool. Rid of her, all Hazlitt's ideal of womanhood boiled up within him; once again his heart was ready for a great love; he wanted love desperately, with all the fire and determination of his tempestuous heart. And of course he found an Ideal Beloved—which is to say he projected all of his longing and idealism on the first blank screen he encountered. It happened to be Sarah Walker, a commonplace tailor's daughter, rather a flirt and no more capable of understanding him or sustaining his ideal of her than a wax doll.

One must pity Sarah. She liked to sit on his knee, receive little gifts, and listen to extremely high-class admiration. It was flattering to have caught a gentleman, who said he was her slave and really seemed to mean it. When he became jealous, and rather wild, because she had another lover of her own kind, who really meant business as she understood it, she was in a situation far beyond her experience. She escaped, and who is to blame her?

As for Hazlitt, he was neither the first nor the last man of powerful intellect to be deluded by his emotions, and to try to make a silk purse out of a sow's ear—or, more charitably, a princess of romance out of a dull little girl. But he was so frank as to publish a book about it, in which he spares neither himself nor Sarah, and emerges as a middle-aged fool to those who refuse to recognize the desperation and pathos of his story.

It is the nakedness of the emotion of *Liber Amoris* that makes it a great and extremely painful book. His friend Bryan Waller Procter wrote: "To this girl he gave all his valuable time, all his wealthy thoughts, and all the loving frenzy of his heart; for a

time I think that on this one point he was substantially insane."
I disagree; he was in love, with the fervour and the sense of
approaching death which is so often more pronounced in middle
age than it is later. Love is not for youth only, though the young
sometimes have an ability to experience it unscathed which
disappears with time. Hazlitt had learned enough of life to be
able to suffer horribly, and at the same time to know how
ridiculous his suffering appeared. He exposed his feelings, which
was the measure of his greatness or his folly—depending on
how you look at it. I say, greatness.

Toronto Daily Star, 2 September 1961

Baron Corvo

*T*riumph after death is always fascinating, and I can never convince myself that those who are vindicated posthumously do not experience, wherever they may be, something of its peculiar sweetness. I am thinking now of that odd fish among English literary men, Baron Corvo, whose fame grows from year to year. A book of Centenary Essays has just reached me from England.

Frederick William Serafino Austin Lewis Mary Rolfe was born in 1860 and died in 1913; he was a novelist, short-story writer, historian, contributor to the *Yellow Book,* and surely one of the most venomous, cantankerous, ungrateful paranoids in all literary history. He has been the subject of a great biography, *The Quest for Corvo,* by A. J. A. Symons, which appeared in 1929. Symons revealed Corvo as a semi-lunatic, wildly biting whatever hand might feed him. But Corvo has had many defenders, and the quarrel over the rights and wrongs of his complicated vendettas is blowing up into a very pretty literary war.

Who was he? A man of commonplace background (the splendid and unusual names in his impressive list were taken by himself) who seems from his earliest days to have yearned to excel as an artist, a musician, a writer and a priest of the Church of Rome. He was not born a Catholic but, having become one, he desired above all things to be a priest. His cankered nature made him impatient of discipline and bitterly critical of his superiors, so he was soon in trouble. Rolfe was never in ordinary trouble; it was always complex, for he saw personal animosity and persecution in anything and anybody that restrained him. Furthermore, he was without conscience about money, and saw the truth through very special glasses.

Whether he abandoned the Church, or it abandoned him, is still in dispute. He liked to sign himself "Fr. Rolfe," which could be an abbreviation of "Frederick," or of "Father." He wrote a novel of wish-fulfilment, *Hadrian VII,* about a Christ-like English priest, Arthur Rose, who is called through a series of extraordinary events to the Papal chair; a great Pope, he is too good for this world and dies young. In this fantastic book, which has unusual literary merit, Rolfe scores off all his oppressors, sets the Church right on a few vexed matters, and generally enjoys himself thoroughly in the only world that suited him— the world of the imagination.

He was a man of remarkable gifts, but in him that whiff of the charlatan which exists in most artists is a really horrifying stench. He simply could not get on with anybody, and it was always the other person's fault. In his fifty-three years his talents and his undoubted charm won him many friends, some of whom endured much for his sake, but in time he estranged them all. He assumed from 1890 till 1902 the title of Baron Corvo; characteristically, he found a shred of justification for it until he tired of it, and then he said it was merely a "tekhniknym"—his own word for a pen-name. Nothing would have contented Rolfe except the power, wealth and title of a Renaissance cardinal-prince; to be only a struggling English author was unendurable bitterness.

What commands the loyalty of his present admirers is his limited but genuine literary gift, his courage and his integrity; but can we admire integrity when it is put to the service of so much wrong-headedness? Hitler also had a madman's integrity. It was no doubt courageous to quarrel with everybody and to spend at least one bitter Venetian winter with no shelter but a gondola, and no income but the profits from some homosexual pimping; but such courage calls forth pity rather than admi-

ration. It will be seen that I am not one of those who thinks
that Rolfe was a wronged man; I agree rather with the portrait
of him which Pamela Hansford Johnson offers in her amusing
novel *The Unspeakable Skipton.*

If Rolfe had never lived, English literature would be the poorer
for two or three curious books. It is not the vitality of his work
that keeps his reputation on the upward path, but the desire so
many people feel to fight old battles, execrate dead offenders
and posthumously vindicate people who seem to have had a
raw deal from life. As a writer Rolfe has a small but secure
place; as a quarrelling-point he is going on from strength to
strength. How he must exult, if he knows of it!

Toronto Daily Star, 7 October 1961

Nellie Melba

When I had whooping cough at the age of six, I passed many hours playing the family Victrola, and I can recall, in the ear of memory, every record I heard then. From one of them—a Victor Red Seal—emerged a thin, cold voice which uttered the notes, though not in any recognizable form the words, of "Home Sweet Home," a tune I hated then and hate still; on the other side the voice performed, still almost wordlessly, Tosti's "Good-Bye." This was the voice of Dame Nellie Melba.

That memory has coloured my notion of Melba to this day. The voices I liked (which I suppose means the voices that were best suited to the recording apparatus of that time) were the contraltos—Schumann-Heink, Louise Homer and Clara Butt—who sounded like kine lowing in rich pastures. I conceived of Madame Melba as a haughty woman whose eminence as a singer was part of the irrationality of the grown-up world.

It was with some prejudice, then, that I picked up *Red Plush and Black Velvet,* in which Joseph Wechsberg tells the story of Melba and her times. Nor was my prejudice disarmed by Mr. Wechsberg's casual way of dealing with his material; he cannot make up his mind whether Melba's accompanist was Landon Ronald or Ronald Landon, and he does not seem perfectly sure where Melbourne is, to name but two details. But he is very good at recreating the great moments of Melba's career, and he makes it plain why so many people adored her. Better-written biographies have achieved less.

It is Melba's character which commands admiration. She was very much the Scottish-Australian—independent, courageous and direct. There was nothing about her of the Italian opera star, who traditionally fights her way up from ignorance, poverty and a poor inheritance. Nellie Mitchell had an excellent start in life in 1861, and was always on the best of terms with her father, who died a millionaire. Her one great mistake was her marriage to Charles Armstrong, and she resolved that by leaving him to go to England, and subsequently to Paris, to study.

In England, Sir Arthur Sullivan was unimpressed, but thought that if she studied for a year he might be able to give her a small part in one of his operettas. But in Paris Madame Marchesi, one of the greatest teachers of the day, heard Nellie sing, and rushed from the room to tell her husband, "Salvatore, I've found a star!"

After that it was one success after another. Melba retained her voice, almost undimmed, until 1926. Its range was from B flat below middle C to the F above high C, and it was perfectly even throughout its range; her runs were described as "strings of pearls" and her trill (which she could perform even as a child) was like the trilling of a bird.

Obviously the record I recall gave no idea of what Melba sounded like. "Home Sweet Home," however, was her favourite encore. At the end of an opera—*Faust,* for instance—Jean de Reszke as Faust and his brother, Edouard, as Mephistopheles, were not above shoving a piano onto the stage of Covent Garden, or the Metropolitan, and the great Nellie would sit down and sing that dismal air, playing her own accompaniment. The audience was enraptured.

Melba's only defect—if it may be called a defect in an opera singer—was that she could not act. She made a few carefully considered gestures of joy or despair in all her roles; she had a queenly beauty, and was a mistress of theatrical makeup; this was enough, for the glorious voice did all the rest.

Her private life, if not puritanical, was discreet and dignified.

She ate moderately, and drank little. She never smoked. She loved the business details of her profession, and wrung fees from managers which even Caruso did not dare to ask. She died rich. She was generous toward young singers, but had no time for triflers. She was a fighter, loved taking a long chance and making it succeed, and her only relaxation seems to have been a fondness for elaborate practical jokes.

She was, in fact, much more what a great artist is usually like than the popular notion of the tempestuous, amorous, spend-thrift prima donna. Not only a splendid voice but a hard head and great self-control goes into a long career in opera. I am glad to have learned more about Madame Melba, and partly ban-ished an unjust childhood impression.

Toronto Daily Star, 9 June 1962

Edmund Wilson

*H*ow should a reviewer set to work on this book? Edmund Wilson himself gives excellent advice in a letter he wrote to E. B. Blackmur, then editor of *Hound and Horn,* in 1929. He says: "The reader more or less expects the book reviewer to tell him what the book is like—that is to say, how it is written, what sort of temperament the author has, and what sort of effect he produces. There has lately been such a reaction against the impressionistic criticism of the day before yesterday that there is a tendency entirely to eliminate any intimation of what the work under consideration looks, sounds, feels or smells like." So, you see, I have my orders.

How is *Letters on Literature and Politics: 1912–1972* written? As the letters of a busy man tend to be: slap-dash, without striving for any elegance beyond simple clarity. Wilson conducted a large correspondence, and as he disliked dictating he wrote or typed his own letters, which makes for brevity. Not for him the time-wasting lingo of business correspondence, or the expansiveness of the man who seems to be dictating principally to impress his secretary. Of course, as the letters of a first-rate critic, they frequently include passages of great penetration, but these are never calculated or worked up. Every letter is truly personal in the sense that it is aimed at one reader at one time, without any thought that it might eventually appear in a collection like this one.

Of course the letters are full of temperament, and the only

way I can describe the temperament of Edmund Wilson is to say that he was a man of letters. The term is out of favour; when Evelyn Waugh wrote that his father was a man of letters he added that it was "a category, like the maiden aunt's, that is now almost extinct"; in 1969 John Gross wrote a book called *The Rise and Fall of the Man of Letters,* which seems to have been meant as a tombstone for the creature; but the corpse would not lie down. Is there a better term for a man who, like Edmund Wilson, devoted his life to literature as a critic, journalist and author, with occasional brief spells as a special teacher in a university or institute?

What marks the true man of letters, apart from the scholarship and broad range of literary information without which he cannot work, is the extent and quality of his gusto. From childhood, Wilson's gusto knew no bounds, and everything that came his way was grist for his literary mill. When he was a small boy his mother, fearing that he was not getting enough exercise, gave him a baseball uniform; the dutiful child put it on immediately and wore it while sitting under a tree, reading a book. Of course he possessed the restraint, the discretion, of a discriminating critic, but beneath it was a fierce appetite and curiosity about writing, about authors and about everything that pertained to a very broad concept of the literary world. It is the underlying gusto that makes this book delightful to read.

Wilson always knew what he thought and stated it in good set terms. His "russett yeas, and honest kersey noes" were a mark of his reviews, and made him not only one of the best, but one of the most readable, critics of his time. He was sometimes described as Johnsonian, but every opinionated fat man is called Johnsonian; the term was even used of the late Nathan Cohen. But Wilson was not like Johnson for the excellent reason that Johnson was a man of deep religious faith and essential humility. Wilson wrote to Lily Herzog, "I am completely non-religious" and was extremely put out when Allen Tate suggested that he was "a crypto-Christian." But did ever an avowed atheist spend so much time conning the Bible, in English and Hebrew?

His long adventure with the Dead Sea Scrolls, which he did so much to bring to the attention of the ordinary, educated public, seems to have been rooted in a hope that he might uncover something that would blow Christianity up, perhaps by finding that Christ's teaching was no more than a body of accepted belief among the Essenes. Wilson either could not, or would not, understand that Christ's authority was not solely related to an historical teacher. His dissatisfaction with God appears to have rested on the fact that God cannot be argued with, bombarded with human reason and made to give explanations. Much faith is childish, of course; but atheism also has its childish and pompous aspects.

Wilson detested religion, but he seems to have had a hankering after the hieratic and formal side of religion. Like Mencken, he peppers his letters with adjurations to prayer, requests for the prayers of his friends, and the professional vocabulary of theology. But of the noumenous side of religion he appears to have had no experience, and it made him impatient of authors, like Thomas Mann to name but one, whose awareness of the noumenal was at the root of their work. On a lower plane, it was this lack that made him dismiss Tolkien as "awful." His mistrust and dislike of monarchy and aristocracy have their root in the same strong strain of doubt. No, not doubt—aversion.

Nevertheless, it is curious to find the old Stoic flirting with the supernatural and some of what we may call the off-scourings of religion. Late in his life I had some correspondence with him about *The Ingoldsby Legends,* for which we shared a special sort of enthusiasm. He wrote: "I was interested to learn that you, too, had been haunted by *The Ingoldsby Legends* ... almost always when I see W. H. Auden, we express our admiration of the *Legends*. He tells me that he always advises a certain kind of young poet to read them. I've had a letter from another admirer, the Bishop of Arizona. Glad to find that there are at least three others besides myself." I had written to him because he confessed in a *New Yorker* article that he had "a fetishistic feeling" for the book, and "I keep copies in both my winter and summer houses"; he told me that he felt uneasy in a house which did not contain a copy of this talismanic volume. I shared this feeling, but I think I knew the reason better than he cared to admit; the *Legends,* so many of which appear to mock religious belief and all that is supernatural, have extraordinary noumenal force, and they were the work of a clergyman who posed as a jolly good fellow, but who was as fully, and perhaps more truly, haunted, than Poe or E. T. A. Hoffmann. There was an *Ingoldsby* side to Wilson, and from it rose much of his undoubted charm.

Wilson's dislike of creeds was a factor in his falling-out with Communism. Writers rarely make good party men, and when he joined Lewis Mumford, Waldo Frank, John Dos Passos, and Sherwood Anderson in composing a manifesto it contained such naive declarations as: "We recognize the fundamental identity of our interests with those of the workers and farmers of the nation." Would the workers and farmers have seen a comrade in Wilson? In his fiction (in *Memoirs of Hecate County,* for instance) there are characters who are working class, drawn wholly from the outside; the reproduction of their speech is—probably without conscious intention—satiric, and it is plain that the want of intellectual sympathy is what divides the author from his characters. For Wilson to call on "intellectuals of every kind" to identify their cause with that of the workers was futile; he had no hint of the demagogue in him, and his call, if it had ever been heard by a worker (it is odd that he falls for the notion that the real "worker" is a manual worker) would have fallen on uncomprehending ears. No wonder that a few years later he could write "Marxism is the opium of the intellectuals."

There was a patronizing streak in Wilson, which is the shadow of his powerful critical acumen. He very often knew best about literary matters, and when he did not he sometimes said so tactlessly. It was this strain that made his book on Canadian writing, *O Canada,* distasteful to many readers here.

He thought it was because of the emphasis the book put on the writing of French Canada, but in fact it was because of his unconcealed astonishment that a country bedevilled by the remains of monarchy and usually pacific in its political dealings should produce writing as good as that he found. It was naive of him to record, during his investigation into the grievances of the Iroquois, that in Canada, although the courts preserved a robed formality, and the judge was addressed as "my lord," Indians were treated with civility, just like other citizens. But if Wilson had not been extremely sure of himself, he would not have been the useful arbiter of taste he unquestionably was. Nobody appoints a man to such a position unless he first appoints himself.

He had his moments of doubt, of course. He records feeling "for the first time in my life, as if I were a real success" when he sold some of his books for paperback publication; he was already 58. He admits to prejudice, as when he writes that he "can't bear the way [Albert Schweitzer] looks" and therefore is sure that there is "something phony somewhere" about what Schweitzer is doing. He has his unfashionable likes, such as Santayana's neglected novel, *The Last Puritan*. He has an endearing fondness for other people's silly jokes, like Benchley's letter-closing—"Be sure to drop in when you come to Fall River." He can hit very hard, as when he tells one of the editors of the *New Yorker* (Katharine White) that the magazine is pale, empty, silly, insipid and banal, and suffering from hardening of the arteries. This is not the usual tone writers take with magazines upon which they are heavily dependent. His delight in Punch and Judy (he was a good "operator" himself) and in magic makes him a sympathetic character to me, as other enthusiasms will recommend him to other readers.

Have I said enough about the author's temperament, and the effect he produces? Then what about the character of the book? The letters themselves are well edited by Elena Wilson, his widow, but the publishers should have taken more pains with the index. Why is Robert-Houdin called Robert Houdon? Why is Harry Graham's *Ruthless Rhymes for Heartless Homes* attributed to Laurence Housman? Why is the book on Joyce *Our*

Exagmination attributed to Wilson himself; is this a slip for William Carlos Williams, who was one of the authors? These are small matters, but they are just the kind of small matters that Wilson himself would have dropped on like a hawk—these and many others. Indexing is a skilled business, but Alfred Knopf seems to have been the last publisher to acknowledge the fact.

These are trifles in the light of the book's value as an enriching aid to the study of Wilson's age in American and English letters. Such judgements as that in which he sweeps away all the once-praised Edwardians and declares that only Shaw and Max Beerbohm are serious survivors, and the fine page (it is page 367) in which he sorts out Henry James, Joseph Conrad, Tolstoy and Dostoevsky in a letter to Morton D. Zabel, bring Edmund Wilson back to us as vividly as if he had not died. As indeed he has not, in the most serious sense, and this book is proof of it.

Globe and Mail, 21 January 1978

Somerset Maugham

Somerset Maugham wished to be famous and rich, and for at least 60 of his 91 years he had his desire. Few authors before him can have had a wider audience or a larger fortune. Few can have been sought out by so many celebrated people. Few can have been so much envied, so patronized and belittled by literary critics, so imitated by other writers. Fame and wealth followed him all the days of his life.

His career was a triumph over several kinds of bad luck. Maugham was an unhappy child. His much-loved, beautiful mother died of consumption when he was 8, and to the end of his life he thought of this as Fate's worst blow. His guardian was an unsympathetic uncle, a clergyman, and Maugham's life-long atheism had its roots in his dislike of this man. He had a crippling stammer—not simply a hesitation of speech, but a torturing inability to speak whenever he was nervous or at a disadvantage; this affliction made him a butt at school and prevented him from following the law, his family's profession. (One of his brothers became Lord Chancellor.) He was a homosexual in an era when such tastes were inadmissible and dangerous. Nevertheless, at the age of 42, he was co-respondent in a divorce proceeding and married the woman who was carrying his child; this attempt to "do the right thing," like some of his heroes, was a disaster—for to his horror his wife fell in love with him, made great sexual demands on him and resented his long absences with his male lover. He found no happiness in his homosexuality, and was betrayed and used by men he could not resist. He had a three years' struggle with tuberculosis. As he grew old he became eccentric and miserly and at last senile. Which of us would live his life in order to have his fame and his money?

Maugham's life was not a story of unrelieved misery: he had troops of friends, he loved travel and bridge (the two went together), he took keen satisfaction in his service to British Intelligence during wartime, he was a discriminating collector of pictures and seemed to foresee what was about to become valuable, and above all he took unlimited pains with his writing, and seems to have derived deep satisfaction from it.

Literary critics have been grudging toward him, and some have been bitter. Literary critics, however, frequently suffer from a curious belief that every author longs to extend the boundaries of literary art, wants to explore new dimensions of the human spirit, and if he doesn't, he should be ashamed of himself. Maugham had none of these desires, and said so. He called himself "a teller of tales" and took infinite pains with the art of narrative, putting down his story as excitingly and as economically as possible, without pretending to great emotional effects. He politely declined to be ashamed of himself.

He was no lowbrow, of course. He had studied philosophy at Heidelberg, he knew French literature intimately and world literature broadly, and he had qualified as a surgeon. He had seen a good deal of the seamy side of life as a doctor, as a spy and as a member of high society. He was often called a cynic, but that is unjust; he did not doubt the existence of human sincerity and unselfishness, but he thought those qualities exceptional rather than normal. He did not go in for intense psychological probing, though one of his stories, "Rain," was a pioneer work in psychological fiction. Instead, he simply looked at what was before his eyes and recorded it in a long series of plays, novels and short stories. He honestly tried to avoid bitterness, but he refused to sugar the pill.

Maugham was accused of not being a gentleman, which was

absurd, for no author worth his salt is a gentleman. He was accused of taking many of his stories from life, and that is exactly what he did. If they did not please sentimentalists, whose fault was it?

Consider his famous short story, subsequently made into a play and at least two movies, and widely translated, "The Letter." Except for the plot device of the letter itself, it is firmly based on the case of a Mrs. Ethel Mabel Proudlock, who on April 23, 1911, shot her lover in Kuala Lumpur. Maugham's friends the Dickinsons told him about the incident.

What gave offence, apart from the knowledge of the true case held by people in Malaya, was that Maugham did nothing to excuse the behavior of his heroine, Leslie Crosbie, who lies calmly and ingeniously to protect herself. In 1926, when the story appeared, women of Mrs. Crosbie's station in life were supposed to be incapable of lying; was she not English, and a lady? But Maugham wrote of what he knew, and although many people thought him a cad for doing so, they read his stories.

Maugham was thought to be very hard on women, and certainly this was true. It added zest to what he wrote, and nobody was more fascinated than his women readers. His revelation that they could be crooks in love and in social life added a dimension to their nature. Readers were tiring of the sweetly womanly women of J. M. Barrie and the intellectual, honest women of Bernard Shaw. They knew a thing or two that these authors certainly knew but did not like to put in print. Maugham did his bit to free women from the long-standing stereotype of goddess-or-harlot.

Like the rest of us, Maugham was a mass of contradictions; but as he recorded so much of what he thought, we are able to find some opinions that he held throughout his life. Of popular writing, he wrote: "No one can write a best-seller by trying to. He must write with complete sincerity; the hackneyed characters, the well-worn situations, the commonplace story that excites your derision, seem neither hackneyed, well worn nor commonplace to him." Certainly that is true of himself; he wrote with sincerity. Sometimes he was depressed by his limitations, and longed—as what writer does not—for genius. He was of the opinion that his homosexuality prevented him from being a writer of the first rank. He also wrote: "The writer of fiction can only adequately create characters that are aspects of himself . . . By studying the characters with which an author has best succeeded, you should be able to get a more complete idea of his nature than any biography can give you."

In "The Letter," which characters are best presented? Howard Joyce, the lawyer, certainly; there was a fine lawyer and a stern judge concealed within the stammering Maugham. Ong Chi Seng, the ambiguous Oriental who makes the deal for the letter, but keeps his skirts clear; Maugham had a dark, discreet side to his nature. But principally Leslie Crosbie, the woman who leads a double life. If ever a writer lived a double life, it was Somerset Maugham.

TV Guide, 1–7 May 1982

D. H. Lawrence

D. H. Lawrence was a genius. Since his death in 1930, scores of literary critics have assured us that Lawrence was a genius, using the word to mean that he possessed extraordinary powers of creative imagination and original thought. There have been opinions to the contrary, which is not surprising, for no genius persuades everybody to agree with him. What nobody has ever denied is that Lawrence was a man of uncommon courage. He dared greatly.

He was born in 1885, the fourth child of a Nottinghamshire miner. He was not robust, so there was no suggestion that he should follow his father down the mine; he was the favored child of his mother, a woman of some education, ambition for her son, and strongly possessive nature. Lawrence did well at school, for, as his friend Aldous Huxley remarks, he was clever as well as intelligent, and he became a schoolmaster; after the critical attention given to his first novel, *The White Peacock*, in 1911, he devoted all his time to writing. His struggle with tuberculosis made him a lifelong traveller, in search of a perfect climate; he lived much in Italy, Australia and New Mexico. It was *Sons and Lovers,* the autobiographical novel that appeared in 1913, that gave him status as one of the foremost writers of his time. Many critics think it his finest work. He never had much money, for travel and illness are expensive.

In 1914, he married Baroness Frieda von Richthofen, and her

nationality and relationship to the great World War I German air ace—a distant cousin—made that period a difficult one for the Lawrences, and they left England.

Two great scandals affected Lawrence's career, for both good and ill. One was the publication of *Lady Chatterley's Lover*, which appeared expurgated in 1928 but unexpurgated in 1929; no complete edition of it appeared in England till 1960. The other was an exhibition of his paintings in 1929, which was closed: the pictures were judged as obscene.

After two years of deeply distressing illness, he died in Vence, near Nice, in 1930. About his name and his work a fog of scandal still hangs, though his fame is assured.

Now, what was all the fuss about?

Lawrence was a prophet and, like most prophets, he was uncompromising, combative and abusive toward those who opposed him. He was a prophet, not so much about sex, which is what many people supposed, but about the necessity for modern man to cast off the fears and obsessions that made life trivial and pitifully incomplete. Though he was himself of the working class, and romantically attributed special virtues to the poor, he despised their obsession with money and respectability, and their fear of the joys that were to be found in the body. "How I loathe ordinariness!" he wrote. "How from my soul I abhor nice simple people with their eternal price list! It makes my blood boil." But ordinariness is not a monopoly of the working class; it is the common state of man. Lawrence, like a real prophet, wanted to change that and rouse mankind to a new joy in life.

He despised intellectuality. He was constantly at war with what Huxley called the Intellectual Proletariat, meaning the people whose essentially commonplace minds had been stocked with university learning and conventional ideas about art and literature and, of course, sex. They were so dead, he raged. Let them rediscover the real force of life, which was to be found only through submission to the dark gods of the physical life and the spiritual life that was its partner. Stop thinking! Begin feeling! Trust the inspiration of the senses! Above all, cast out fear!

One of the unkind jokes life plays on prophets is that the people who follow them are so often the very people they are seeking to attack. Lawrence was popular with intellectuals, but if the common man heard of him at all, it was as a dirty fellow who was often in trouble with the censor. Osbert Sitwell—who, with his sister, Edith, and his brother, Sacheverell, was representative of everything Lawrence despised: upper class, money and glittering talent—caricatured Lawrence hilariously in his novel *Miracle on Sinai,* where he appears as T. F. Enfelon, the prophet of bodily joys; his disciples are weedy men and charmless women who assemble in the open air to shout dirty words, thereby freeing themselves of fear and guilt. It cannot be denied that in his great crusade, Lawrence frequently made himself ridiculous. A frail man, struggling against tuberculosis, is not the ideal prophet for the life of bodily fulfillment.

Lawrence was lucky, however, in his foremost supporter, admirer and lifelong friend; Aldous Huxley was the only man near Lawrence with whom the prophet did not, at some time, quarrel savagely. There was an ugly, mean streak in Lawrence when he set to work to destroy an enemy. But Huxley avoided quarrels by refraining from contradiction. He was by far the wiser man, and to learn what was great in Lawrence, he held his tongue.

Early in their friendship, Huxley, who had his family's deep concern with science, tried to convince Lawrence of the truth of the theory of evolution. "Lies, lies!" said Lawrence, who detested all science. "But Lawrence," Huxley protested, "consider the evidence." Lawrence shouted: "I don't feel it *here*," and he placed both hands over his solar plexus.

This tells us much about Lawrence. The solar plexus has its place, and a great place, but it is not the final judge of all questions. Lawrence believed only in what we may call psychological truth—that is, whatever he felt in his heart, or his bowels, or his groin—and nothing else had any validity whatever. Genius or not, such a man is headed for trouble.

Lawrence found plenty of trouble when he wrote *Lady Chatterley's Lover,* in which he attempted to restore all the four-letter words that have been banished from ordinary speech—or so they were in 1929. It tells of a frustrated wife, Connie Chatterley, who has a passionate affair with Mellors, her husband's game-keeper. Mellors is a Lawrentian man, living by the laws of the body, and he lifts Connie to a new plane of being. This involved not merely the usual sexual pleasures, but buggery, though Lawrence disguised unwontedly this aspect.

Now that all the scandal is over, it may be said that the book is rather a dull one, and that when the lovers amuse themselves by sticking wildflowers in each other's pubic hair, a mind still unrepentantly intellectual might find it funny. Alas, Lawrence had no sense of humor.

The famous pictures, over which his other scandal arose, are of nudes in landscapes, and they gave offence because they have not merely sexual organs, which might have been overlooked, but pubic hair, which was too much for viewers in 1929. What I have never seen mentioned is that almost all the male figures are idealized portraits of Lawrence himself: a muscular, seminal Lawrence, wholly unblasted by wasting disease. Self-portraits are usually perceptive, not adulatory.

He was a genius, however, and like Huxley we must restrain our doubts if we wish to gain what we can. "Not I, not I, but the wind that blows through me," Lawrence wrote of his inspirations.

A glorious wind, even if sometimes we have a Lawrentian intuition that a good deal of it is hot air.

TV Guide, 5–11 June 1982

Anthony Burgess

*T*here is a danger that *Little Wilson and Big God* may not be received with the seriousness it deserves—though it is far more important than the usual literary autobiography. An author's life is rarely adventurous, and if he has a personal story to tell it is of the inner journey and the struggle with art. This first of a projected two-volume autobiography ends just as we have come to the beginning of Anthony Burgess' story as a writer. He is already 42 and has written seven novels and a novella, but he regards those as byworks thrown off by a man who was really a composer. He has received what appears to be a sentence of death from a physician, and the time has come to get down to business and provide as best he can for the wife who is to be his widow. A serious man, under great stress, and something more—something that makes the story of this provocative English novelist and man of letters turbulent and gripping: he is a man of faith and strong moral conviction.

Not by any means, however, a Holy Joe, clinging to the Old Rugged Cross. He is a rebel Roman Catholic, always in hot water with his superiors. The title of his book comes from an encounter he had with the principal of Xaverian College when he was 17. He was being thoroughly blown up for heresy, because he had said that the sacraments were nothing, and love and right living everything. Father Myerscough would have none of that talk, which sounded (and sounds) like left-wing Protestantism. Later the principal was heard to tell a colleague that it was "a sad business, a matter of 'little Wilson and big God.' "

Why "little Wilson"? He was christened John Burgess Wilson, and later was given the confirmation name of Anthony. It was as Jack Wilson that he met the world until he was well and truly grown up. His beginnings were barren of all distinction. He was born in Manchester and never knew his mother, called "The Beautiful Belle Burgess" in the music halls where she danced and sang. His father was a wholesale dealer in cigarettes, in a small way, with a remarkable gift for playing the piano; his stepmother seems to have been a morose, unloving woman. The musical talent he received from both parents was given no encouragement, and in fact his father's occasional appearances as a pianist in the most dismal sort of silent movie theatres and in pubs (playing for pints) would not have made music more attractive to most sons. He was not born in economic want, but his childhood was lived amid an intellectual poverty that would have dimmed anything but a fierce spirit.

Indeed, a doctrinaire sociologist would have seen a bleak future for little Wilson, handicapped as he was in so many ways, not least of all by being a Catholic. That meant being an outsider in English lower-class life, doomed to inferior education by priests whom he describes as being, in various ways, misfits or sadists, and at a grave social disadvantage among the "proddy dogs" (his term for his Protestant contemporaries). Not that the Catholics fell behind the Protestants in their hatred and contempt for whatever belonged to the intellect. Mr. Burgess grew up in a world where, as he says, education and educated people were the enemies, and later, when he was conscripted into the army, he found that this attitude was not confined to Manchester or to the lower orders. "I remember cleaning out the latrines at Newbattle Abbey and being asked by the visiting general what I had done in civilian life. I told him and he said: 'At last you're doing something useful.' " Mr. Burgess had been a student of English literature at Manchester University. Not useful, and likely to provoke insubordination and embarrassing questions.

There are elements in the human spirit of which sociologists know nothing, for who could have foreseen that little Wilson would teach himself to write music by studying scores, would devour as much of that useless English literature as he could lay hands on and become an expert in the science of English speech? Who would have expected him to emerge from such intellectual and physical squalor without a violent class prejudice of the sort that fueled the Angry Young Men until they themselves achieved a degree of fame and prosperity? Who would have expected him to deplore the lack at Manchester University of those Epicene Exquisites who added so much spice to life at Oxford and Cambridge? This is a man of extraordinarily capacious and generous intellect—except in one area.

That area is the Catholicism against which he rebelled and against which he tirelessly inveighs, but which he insists is the one true faith. Lambaste the Church as he will, he insists that there is no salvation outside it. He declares the Church to be "a bad mother" and sometimes merely "a rough bludgeon for knocking the Protestant Midlands." But the Roman Catholic Church is the only church, and his contempt for the Church of England is total—total as it can be only in one who will not permit a fair crack of the whip to Erasmus and Archbishop Laud.

The nub of the matter seems to be this: the great achievement of the Protestant Reformation was to take the soul of mankind out of the keeping of the Church and deliver each man's soul into his own hands, to be lost or found through his own striving toward God. Anthony Burgess seems to be very much a Protestant in this respect, but he cannot cut the umbilical cord that unites him to the Great Mother, and her promise to make all well in return for perfect obedience. But out of this fierce tension comes the energy that makes him a vastly prolific, adventurous and high-spirited novelist (*A Clockwork Orange, Earthly Powers*), one of the very few whose books, in the present day, one can pick up with the certainty that they will not contain another load of fashionable grief.

The work under review is a good example. It tells of deeply

serious and sometimes tragic things, but it tells of them with an ebullience, a rapidity and an overflowing, joyously deployed vocabulary that make it a delight to read. In his preface, Mr. Burgess calls the book his "Confessions," in the manner of St. Augustine and Rousseau, but there is nothing in it of the minatory gravity of the saint or the self-indulgent egotism of the romancer. Here there are high spirits in abundance, but not a word that could mislead an innocent mind. A truly innocent mind, of course; not the pink vacuity of a ninny.

The life of a man up to the age of 42 must, of course, include most of his sex life. Mr. Burgess's adventures strengthen the impression that sex, which is an imperative in any life, is not an end in itself, the richest of all pursuits and the fountain of spiritual fulfillment. He approached it with all a boy's enthusiasm and romanticism, and it is greatly to his credit that enthusiasm and romanticism remain after a good deal of rough-and-tumble and a first marriage that was at the farthest remove from idyllic. It is a grim moment when a letter to an English doctor, from a colleague in Malaya who had been examining Mr. Burgess and had decided that he was suffering from an inoperable brain tumor, says casually, "His wife is a chronic alcoholic." The disintegrating marriage ended only with his wife's death. It is no wonder that Mr. Burgess speaks of the shallowness of those who do not take the great, grim doctrine of hell seriously.

Autobiography is a remorselessly demanding literary form when it is undertaken seriously. Not the self-justifying blatherings of politicians, not the "as told to" popular works in which a film star's life is invented by a hack with a turn for sensationalism, but the true attempt to come to terms with one's own life is the test for an artist and a man of principle. Nobody succeeds completely, for nobody can be fully objective about himself. Mr. Burgess, weighted with a Catholic conscience of which any Calvinist might be proud, speaks endless ill of himself in his character as a man of principle, but the artist who does the writing gives us constant assurance that these judgements are too severe. Bad men do not give such unfailing literary pleasure, so many hearty guffaws, so many illuminations of wit as Mr. Burgess offers in this first volume of his story. The test is that we await the next volume with high expectation.

New York Times Book Review, 22 February 1987

II

BOOKS

Ghost Stories

*L*overs of detective stories are numbered in millions; surprisingly few people, however, will admit to an interest in ghost stories. Why should this be? If it is mystification you are longing for, a ghost story may be quite as perplexing as a tale of crime; if you want to be thrilled, the claims of the supernatural above the natural cannot be disputed. And yet no magazine thinks of publishing a ghost story, though they crowd their pages with tales of crime and detection. There must be something about the spirit of our age which is uncongenial to belief in ghosts.

Yet few authors of any consequence die without leaving at least one ghost story behind them. And the belief in a survival after death which is the chief article of Christian faith makes a belief in ghosts almost obligatory. Perhaps the real reason for the present lack of interest in ghost stories rises from the fact that they are extremely hard to write; because, to be successful, a ghost story has to be terrifying, and it is much easier to be ingenious than it is to be terrifying. The writer of detective stories must present his readers with a crime and an ingenious solution for it. But the writer of ghost stories must freeze his reader's marrow, and that is anything but easy.

What is more, it is almost impossible to invent a new type of ghost. Almost all the ghosts in fiction derive their characteristics from traditional ghosts which people claim to have seen, and a successful new sort of ghost is almost unheard of. Henry James gave a new twist to the ghost story in his brilliant tale *The Turn of the Screw,* but such inventions are rare. When faced with the task of creating a frightening ghost the average writer is afflicted with paucity of invention, and he falls back upon one of the old stand-bys—a headless lady, or a fiery child, or something equally hackneyed.

Let us consider some of these well-worn ghosts of tradition. The Wild Hunt is known in all Celtic countries; it is a huntsman with a pack of hounds who is seen or heard to rush through the country. Those who see him are doomed to die. The writer heard the Wild Hunt quite distinctly one night in Wales several years ago, but has not suffered any ill effects from it as yet. Upon enquiry, he found that many other people had heard it also at one time or another, and none of them had died as a result. Then there is that tiresome kind of ghost called a "poltergeist" which appears for no good reason and makes the life of a household miserable by breaking the furniture, tumbling people downstairs, frightening them and generally making a nuisance of itself for a week or so, after which it disappears. And a model for many ghosts is the Cauld Lad of Gilsland Castle; he was the ghost of a boy who died of cold because of the cruelty of an uncle, and when any of the family were about to fall ill he would appear at the bedside, his teeth chattering, and would lay an icy hand upon his victim, saying:

> Cauld, cauld, aye cauld.
> And ye'se be cauld for evermair.

Some ghosts appear to be the product of half-remembered legend. In his book *Early Man in Britain,* Professor W. Boyd Dawkins tells us of a mound near the present town of Mold which was called Bryn-yr-Ellylon (meaning the Hill of the Fairy) and which was reputed to be haunted by a soldier in golden armour who was seen to enter it now and again. When the mound was opened in 1832 it was found to contain the skeleton of a man wearing bronze armour overlaid with gold, and of Etruscan workmanship, dating from the Roman occupation of

Britain. There was a memory (or a ghost) which lasted for fourteen hundred years at least. And when Lake Vyrnwy (the Liverpool water reservoir) was made, a rock was blasted open in which, according to tradition, a witch had imprisoned the soul of an outlaw called Robin; inside the rock was found a large live toad!

Ghosts are frequently supposed to return to the scenes where they have wronged someone, or been wronged themselves, in life; they may also return to give warnings, as did the ghost of Hamlet's father, or to foretell the death of another, as Caesar's ghost did to Brutus before the battle of Philippi. Modern belief in ghosts is slight, and many sensible people take pleasure in pooh-poohing the whole ghostly idea. It is difficult, however, to deny the wisdom of the words of John Locke, in his *Essay Concerning Human Understanding,* when he says: "That there should be more species of intelligent creatures above us than there are of sensible and material below us is probable to me from hence, that in all the visible and corporeal world we see no chasms or gaps. All quite down from us the descent is by easy steps, and a continued series of things that in each remove differ very little one from the other. . . ." Surely it is a little conceited of us to suppose that we are the only spiritual inhabitants of this world? But that appears to be the common belief, and one of its lesser evils is that it robs us of a good supply of ghost stories.

Peterborough Examiner, 8 October 1942

The Consolation of Philosophy/The Imitation of Christ/Religio Medici

Recently a small book came my way in which were reprinted three remarkable documents—*The Consolation of Philosophy,* by Boethius, *The Imitation of Christ,* by Thomas à Kempis, and *Religio Medici,* by Sir Thomas Browne. They were printed together, presumably, because all three were confessions of faith, and because all three hovered somewhere in that misty ground between philosophy and religion. Philosophy, considered as pure reason, has nothing to do with religion; and religion, considered as pure faith, has nothing to do with philosophy. But there have been many men who have sought to reconcile the two, and to bolster their faith with philosophy while ameliorating their philosophy with faith. Boethius, Thomas à Kempis and Thomas Browne fared better in this difficult task than most who attempt it, and they have left us books which will always be treasured by those who seek to reconcile the flesh with the spirit.

To many people the word "philosophy" means a sort of wisdom too hard for them to comprehend. None of the works included in this small book is of that sort. And to others philosophy is a matter of clichés—"Every cloud has a silver lining," "It takes a heap o' living to make a house a home," "Care for the pence and the pounds will take care of themselves" and that sort of thing. In the hands of men like Immanuel Kant or Leibniz philosophy does, indeed, become a puzzle too hard for most of us, but Boethius, Thomas à Kempis and Thomas Browne spoke to anyone who had ears to hear. To them, philosophy was a means to an end, and the end was living to the utmost of their abilities. Thomas à Kempis was a monk, and it may be argued that by removing himself from the world he made it easy to live a good life; the argument will not bear too close inspection, for a retired life may easily degenerate into the most useless and selfish sort of existence. But Boethius was a statesman, moving among men as a leader and counsellor, and Thomas Browne was a physician, regularly practising his profession. Their philosophy is derived from the world.

Boethius found himself in prison in the year 524, convicted of treason against the emperor Theodoric; the following year he was executed. The gloomy interval he passed in writing the book with which his name is associated. In it he describes how, as he lay in prison, Philosophy came to him in "a woman's form, whose countenance was full of majesty," and reasoned with him about his fate. Those who seek for Christianity in Boethius will seek in vain, for although it seems probable that he was a Christian in his belief Philosophy does not address him in orthodox Christian manner. She does, however, lead him through a fascinating maze of argument which at last reconciles him to his fate. It must be said that the means which Philosophy uses to argue Evil out of the world are not convincing, but a man at the point of death may be more willing to yield a point than one who has plenty of time before him. What astonishes about this book is the freshness of its thinking, as compared with the admired philosophers of the seventeenth and eighteenth centuries.

The work of Thomas à Kempis is well known to anyone who reads devotional books, however desultorily. It is less philosophy and more devotion than the book of Boethius, but it has the same crystal quality. Its second title is *Musica Ecclesiastica*, and it is music indeed. Its counsel is vigorously compressed. Thomas was a scrivener himself, and knew the weariness of copying prolonged and wordy disquisitions on expensive parchment. In parts the *Imitation* is almost a book of maxims; in others it is a chain of great prayers. It may be that a reader who approached the book with an open mind, and lacking the reverence which the years have attached to it, might think that Thomas was unduly hard on this life (which we have to live) and excessively sanguine of the life to come (which may be anything at all and is scarcely likely to be anything which we expect). But the book has found its readers through the centuries among those who seek guidance along a chosen path, and not among those who have to be persuaded to that path.

Thomas Browne's *Religio Medici* is just what the title implies—a physician's religion. It is an astounding mixture of deep wisdom, religious feeling, wit, thunderous declamation and superstition. Many people read Browne for his style alone, and certainly it is the mirror of a soaring and glorious spirit. If one had to meet one of these philosophers in the flesh, neither the statesman nor the monk would tempt me from Browne; the reason of the former and the sweet faith of the latter are pale beside the courageous humanism of the Norwich doctor. It would be possible to live with Browne, but Boethius would argue any man silly, and Thomas à Kempis would be both too good and too useless for daily company. As each man must choose his own friends, so also he must choose his own philosopher.

Peterborough Examiner, 21 July 1943

A Christmas Carol

*I*n a memoir of his father, Sir Henry Dickens tells of an incident which happened at a Christmas party the winter before the great Charles Dickens died: "He had been ailing very much, and greatly troubled with his leg, which had been giving him much pain; so he was lying on a sofa one evening after dinner, while the rest of the family were playing games." The celebrated author, then so near death, joined in one of the games which was a sort of memory test; the members of the party had to memorize long strings of words which bore no relation to each other, and the first to make a mistake in reciting the string was the loser. When it came Dickens' turn to add a word to the list he said "Warren's Blacking, 30 Strand," an address which conveyed nothing to his hearers, but his son noted that he spoke with "an odd twinkle and a strange inflection in his voice which at once forcibly arrested my attention and left a vivid impression on my mind for some time afterwards. Why, I could not for the life of me understand. . . . At that time, when the stroke which killed him was gradually overpowering him, his mind reverted to the struggles and degradation of his childhood, which caused him such intense agony of mind, and which he had never been able entirely to cast from him." Did Dickens, in the misery of that Christmas of 1869, recall with irony the wretched Christmases of his childhood? Perhaps he did, as his son suggests, for the man who gave our modern Christmas its special character knew little of peace or simple jollity.

No book has done so much to mould our ideas of what Christmas should be as *A Christmas Carol,* which was written, and read by a delighted public, just a hundred years ago at this time. The story of the conversion of Ebenezer Scrooge is familiar to every literate person. Not only in its native English, but in a score of other tongues, it has been read and re-read. A Russian once told me that he had been compelled to memorize the first Stave in its entirety, as part of his English studies, and proved it by setting out "Marley was dead, to begin with. There is no doubt whatever about that." Many people, the writer among them, read *A Christmas Carol* every year as a part of their Christmas ceremonial. Few books written within the past century enjoy such vigorous life.

There is astounding vitality in the story, and that is what saves it from banality. Dickens was never more a genius than when he was writing about Christmas; his amazing ability to wallow waist-deep in sentimentality without ever becoming maudlin or vulgar is one of the surest marks of his greatness. If the story of the Cratchits' Christmas dinner had been written by the late Alexander Woollcott, for instance, it would have been an insufferable and indigestible confection; had the conversion of Scrooge been described by Charles Morgan or John Steinbeck, it would have been a welter of pseudo-mysticism or weepy Marxism; had the theme of *A Christmas Carol* occurred to J. B. Priestley, we should have had a work in the Dickensian mould without a scrap of the Dickens genius. Dickens and only Dickens could write this story and make a little masterpiece of it.

For there can be no dispute but that it is a masterpiece. He did not reproduce its greatness in *The Chimes* or *The Cricket on the Hearth,* though he obviously wished to do so. *A Christmas Carol* is Dickens' greatest short story, and it has no near rival. Like all Dickens' best work it is conceived dramatically, and written in well-shaped and carefully "built-up" scenes. That is why his own readings of this story, and the many subsequent dramatizations of it, have been so successful. Many authors, like many actors, suffer from a fear of overdoing whatever job they may be at, and they restrain themselves constantly and needlessly, as though they feared that their unleashed genius might blind the world; Dickens, who was a very good actor and the greatest dramatic writer, after Shakespeare, in all English literature, had no such groundless fears. When he sat down to write a story about a miser who was converted by the spirit of Christmas, he let things rip, with the most magnificent results.

Dickens drew his great wealth of Christmas enthusiasm from the wells of his amazing personality; he never experienced anything like the Christmas he described in his wretched childhood, nor did he create it in his own home when he became wealthy and famous. A man of violent moods, he was on the heights or in the dumps; he knew no middle ground. "My father was like a madman," wrote the last of his daughters, Mrs. Perugini; "nothing could surpass the misery and unhappiness of our home." This same lady, deeply as she loved her father, did not hesitate to say, "My father was a wicked man—a very wicked man." The benevolence, the loving-kindness which Dickens poured out in his Christmas books, and in *A Christmas Carol* more than any, was a quality which he longed for and idealized, rather than a quality which was richly abundant in his own nature. Happiness, of course, Dickens knew, but he was better acquainted with the bitter suffering of an unruly nature. As we read or re-read *A Christmas Carol* this year it is fitting that we should spare a thought for the fiery and tempestuous genius who first gave it to the world a hundred years ago.

Peterborough Examiner, 15 December 1943

Fairs, Circuses
& Music Halls/
Esme of Paris

*T*oday I want to write about two recent books which discuss the circus, because the subject is admirably appropriate to the season. They are *Fairs, Circuses & Music Halls,* by M. Willson Disher, and *Esme of Paris,* by Esme Davis. Mr. Disher is the greatest living authority on circuses, and it is doubtful if any man who has lived before him ever knew half so much about them; Esme Davis knows something about circus life which Mr. Disher cannot know, for she has had a career as an acrobat, animal-trainer and snake-charmer. Mr. Disher, sitting with his lame foot at the ringside, is the philosopher and scholar of the circus; Miss Davis has been a circus queen and has fallen from a trapeze and almost broken her neck. Between them they know all that there is to know about circuses.

Shakespeare warned us against men who had no music in their souls; I utter a similar warning against those much rarer men who never go to the circus. The war has almost extinguished the travelling circus on this continent, but we hope to see it soon in days of peace. "A good circus," said Oscar Wilde, "is an oasis of Hellenism in a world that reads too much to be wise, and thinks too much to be beautiful." Did anyone ever go to a circus to deepen his understanding of the world's problems, or in any other way to add a cubit to his stature? I think not. In *The Adventures of Jimmy Brown,* a book which I read in childhood, Jimmy's father took him to a circus "Because the elephant is a Bible animal, James, and it cannot help but improve your mind to see him," but it was obvious that the old hypocrite was merely looking for a chance to see the clowns himself. The circus is entertainment, gaudy, unintellectual, stylized and transcendently beautiful. Only those who have stamped out the human desire to be amazed and delighted in their souls can resist the call of a circus. The circus brings everlasting springtime with it.

Willson Disher's book appears in the excellent *Britain in Pictures* series, and it is lavishly illustrated. But Disher's text can rival the pictures in interest. To look at a picture of The Pig-Faced Lady or M. Ducrow's Pet Steeds and Zebras is to wonder at once what he has to say about them. In less than fifty pages he gives an outline of the history of the circus from the days of the Romans until our own time. Stonehenge, says Mr. Disher, with its racetrack, was the first circus in England, and it is clearly his opinion that there will be a circus as long as England retains a shred of its character. Contrary to a popular belief on this continent, America is not the home of the circus; Europe is far better supplied with circuses than we, both of the stationary and the travelling kind. But the appetite for shows of skill and daring, of broad clowning, animal training, of processions and cortèges, is deep in human nature everywhere, and circuses are to be found in every part of the world. And wherever they go they are rapturously received. They change little with the years, and they appeal to that which is unchanging in human nature.

Esme Davis is the daughter of a Canadian banker who was married to Sofia Oswaldo, an opera singer whom many lovers of music will remember. But Esme Davis' grandmother was La Marvilla, a cigar-smoking Spanish gypsy Flamenco dancer who was also one of the great snake-charmers of her day. In this brief account you have the pattern of Esme's life: she has always been torn between conventional respectability (bankers) and the raffish life of the circus ring (grandmamma). Lolita Bazil de Delgado was profoundly jealous of her granddaughter's chastity and professional honour, but she appears to have been somewhat careless of her health; at any rate, she trained little Esme very early to wash and oil her snakes, which were in full possession of their venom. As a result the child acquired a love of snakes which persists until today and she often wears a coral-snake as a necklace; such a necklace, she finds, discourages unwelcome admirers and customs inspectors alike.

Esme Davis, who is now 39, makes perfumes in New York; you may have seen her advertisements in the fashion magazines. But this is merely her latest career. In addition to being a snake-charmer she has been an acrobat, a ballet-dancer and an animal trainer, and has achieved a great measure of success in all these unusual arts. She did it by hard work, determination and single-mindedness; she never wasted time on matters which were of secondary importance. When she was 16 she was married to a young Englishman in the diplomatic service; he sent her to a fashionable girls' school in order to learn how to behave like a lady; a riding-master tried to teach her to ride; she contemptuously showed him a few of the tricks she had learned as a bareback rider in the circus, and the cat was out of the bag; that was the end of the marriage. Her book is full of such tales. Are they true? I think so, because she writes with such complete artlessness that it seems unlikely that she is lying. If the facts of her story are not indisputable, it is probably because the true story is too lurid to recount. The whole spirit of the circus is in the book, and jumbled and formless though it is, it has more vitality than a dozen ordinary autobiographies.

Peterborough Examiner, 21 March 1945

Ouida's Books

Toward the end of last year I was helping to sort and pack several thousand books which had been collected for the amusement of men on active service; they were a mixed lot, ranging from excellent volumes in fine condition to nondescript rubbish which had been contributed only in order to be rid of it. The pleasure of such work lies in recognizing the books which are being packed, and I was particularly pleased to discover a bundle of paperbacks by Ouida; not many men in the services would care to read Ouida, perhaps, but no one who has read a few of her novels ever escapes completely from their spell.

Ouida, if you do not know her work, was Marie Louise de la Ramée, the daughter of a French schoolmaster, who was teaching his native language in the English town of Bury St. Edmunds when she was born on January 7, 1839. Her penname is said to be a childish mispronunciation of Louisa, her own name, and unkind critics have said that childish misrepresentation was her stock-in-trade through life. She began her career as a writer early, for her first novel, *Granville de Vigne,* appeared when she was twenty-one; she wrote copiously from that time until her death at the age of sixty-nine. I do not know how many books she wrote; a partial list in my possession names thirty-one. Ouida wrote easily and her popularity was great; she made a fortune, and at one time she was virtually the only novelist read by thousands of girls on this continent and in Great Britain. The secret of her success lay in the fact that she never permitted common sense or humour to interfere with romance.

Ouida was highly imaginative, and she never descended to writing stories to fit a popular formula. There are certain characteristics, however, which are apparent in all her best-known work. Unlike Jane Austen, she had a passion for describing things of which she had no personal experience; she knew little of men, and there is no evidence to show that she ever had a suitor, much less a lover, but she imagined herself an expert in the psychology of the male and the intricacies of love. Her favourite heroes were British guardsmen who combined lion-like courage and strength with a feminine delicacy of feeling. They are described with loving particularity; the silkiness of their hair (their moustaches in especial), the maiden delicacy of their skins (they always blushed like girls—or as girls are popularly supposed to blush), their delicate, high-arched feet, their long-fingered, white hands, their lustrous and speaking eyes, their red and moist lips—a hero by Ouida is a curious mixture of Sandow and Lillian Russell. They are lady-killers, every one of them: they have but to lean on a mantelpiece, showing their immense chests and tiny waists, and ladies swoon with delirious pleasure. They are poets and essayists, miraculous swordsmen, and paragons of honour. And, in spite of their power to stir female hearts, surprisingly few of them are fortunate lovers. Let psychologists make of this what they will.

Ouida delighted to describe the pleasures of these wasp-waisted gods. She seems to have been unusually ignorant of masculine sports, and her blunders in writing of them have roused the ire of many male readers. "All rowed rapidly, but none rowed faster than stroke," she is alleged to have written, describing a boat-race; I have never found this line in her books (I have not read them all and do not mean to do so) but it sounds like Ouida. Triumphant imagination and her racing pen bore her through difficulties which would have mired a less intrepid and a more reflective woman. Her heroes pay six thousand guineas for a race-horse without winking; when they drive in the park, nothing less than four-in-hand grays, outriders and cream-and-silver liveries will do for them. Does the nation think of acquiring the Duc de Valière's Titians? One of Ouida's heroes is sure to outbid the British Empire, and then present the pictures to the National Gallery. And whatever happens, these heroes greet it with that "melodious laugh, clear and gay as a woman's" which is almost the hall-mark of the product. Did Ouida see herself in these masculine roles? Perhaps she did.

But if Ouida had been nothing more than a female novelist with a lush imagination and an inflated style, she would have been forgotten long ago. In spite of all their extravagance and silliness, her books have quality, and some of her animal stories—*A Dog of Flanders* for instance—are still read, for in them extravagance and silliness have been curbed. Perhaps the truth of the matter is that Ouida had the spirit of a poet, and that spirit can always command a hearing. Her novels are comparable to the melodramas which were popular in her day: *The Corsican Brothers, The Bells* and *The Lyons Mail* are nonsense, too, but they have a poetic spirit which is lacking in the drama of Galsworthy and Shaw. When Ouida created a character such as Cigarette, the "vivandière" in *Under Two Flags,* she conceived her poetically, and thus she is able to invest Cigarette with a charm which is quite lacking, for instance, in Scarlett O'Hara, who is conceived in a vein of shallow realism, and ornamented with quasi-poetic trappings. Cigarette's last ride is still moving, just as the last act of *The Corsican Brothers* is still moving when it is poetically acted. Ouida, eccentric old maid as she was, nevertheless was moved in her creative work by a true poetic inspiration, and that is why the discovery of a bundle of her books can still provoke a Wednesday article, when the works of more recent authors may be passed over without a second glance.

Peterborough Examiner, 16 May 1945

King Jesus

*I*f Robert Graves' new novel *King Jesus* is widely read, it will undoubtedly be the subject of many disputes, for it suggests a number of new and brilliant solutions to some of the problems arising from the life of Christ. People who do not believe that it is possible to shed any new light on this subject, or who prefer not to have their present ideas disturbed, will be wise to avoid the book entirely. Already several book-reviewers have condemned *King Jesus* on religious rather than on literary grounds. *Time* (which has recently become as sensitive on such subjects as it used to be horny-hided about them) calls the book "anti-Christian"; the *Christian Science Monitor* says that it is a relief to turn from *King Jesus* to the Gospels, which arouse echoes of truth in the heart. On the other hand, the Religious Book Club has made *King Jesus* its choice for November.

I am anxious not to involve myself in any disputes with my readers about this book, for nothing is more futile than a religious argument which arises from a literary cause. It is absolutely necessary for me to say, however, that I find nothing in *King Jesus* which I think could suggest blasphemy or irreverence to any reasonably broadminded Christian, even though he might reject much of it. So far as I am able to judge, Graves has done three things which give his book its special flavour, and they are these: he has related Christianity and Hebraism to other ancient religions in a manner which will cause no surprise to scholars, though it will be a revelation to most laymen; he has assumed that Jesus set out deliberately to fulfil the word of the prophets, and thus provoked his own death; he has postulated that Jesus was of noble birth, and that the title on the cross—King of the Jews—was a statement of literal truth and not a mockery.

To the presentation of this point of view Graves brings all the scholarship and literary skill for which he is renowned. Those who take issue with him will have their hands full, for as well as being deeply learned in history, anthropology and ancient tongues, Graves knows the East well, and comes of a family which has long been associated with it. His exposition of the Eastern faiths and mysteries which made their contribution to Judaism is brilliant, though often so compressed that it is hard to follow. But it is plain that the world in which Jesus lived is as thoroughly understood by him as the world in which Shakespeare lived is clear to Sir Edmund Chambers. He is able to relate the affairs of Palestine to the affairs and politics of the rest of the known world, and in this way he removes the story of Christ from the historical isolation in which it is sometimes studied. *King Jesus* is supposed to be the narrative of an imaginary scholar, Agabus the Decapolitan, written about A.D. 89, and its great mass of detail is easily introduced by means of this literary device.

Graves' most interesting hypothesis is that Jesus was the son of a secret marriage between his mother, Mary (whose forebears were heirs of David and thus of aristocratic lineage), and Herod Antipater, the heir of Herod the King. This bold supposition makes credible Herod's enmity toward Jesus when an infant, the mysterious nature of Jesus' birth (after his mother's marriage to the elderly Joseph), and the confusion which later arose between Jesus as spiritual leader and as political leader. In *King Jesus* the hero is not only a great moral exemplar but a royal prince and the rightful occupant of the throne of Herod. This hypothesis also throws new light on the special consideration which Pontius Pilate gave to Jesus' case; the Romans cared little about the religion of the Jews, but they were deeply interested in all matters of legality and title. Graves' hypothesis is a brilliant guess, and like any brilliant guess which supplies the answers to a number of hard questions, it must be treated with respect.

At the beginning of this review some doubt is implied as to whether *King Jesus* will be widely read; certainly it seems unlikely that it will ever achieve the popularity of a bit of pretty *bondieuserie* like *The Robe,* for it is a hard, knotty, unemotional book in which the sentimentally religious will find nothing to delight them. It is written with the fine clarity and literacy which distinguish all the novels of Robert Graves, and it cannot be dismissed as a freak of literature. Many readers will find it an uncomfortable book, for it will make them think again about things which they considered irrevocably settled. But I will venture the prophecy that whatever the fate of *King Jesus* may be during the coming year, it will continue to be in demand long after most of the books published during 1946 have been forgotten.

Peterborough Examiner, 13 November 1946

Ivy Compton-Burnett's Novels

Who is the most remarkable novelist of our day? On the level of farce the name of P. G. Wodehouse at once comes to mind. For comic invention and social satire we turn to Evelyn Waugh. But for comedy—the pure, high essence which Meredith describes in his essay on the Comic Spirit—it is doubtful if any contender can challenge the supremacy of Miss Ivy Compton-Burnett. You have not heard of her? Very possibly not, but you will hear of her, and your children and grandchildren will hear of her. She has written ten novels, all on a very high level of achievement. They have rather curious names: *Pastors and Masters, Brothers and Sisters, Elders and Betters, Manservant and Maidservant* are some of them. If you pick one up in an idle fashion, and begin reading at random, you may find that you have not the book in hand which you were reading the day before. These are strange and idiosyncratic novels, and they do not yield their secrets to careless readers, but they are worth the trouble which it takes to appreciate them.

The comedy which is the foundation of Ivy Compton-Burnett's ten novels is the comedy of life itself. It is not "charming" in the conventional sense, and she does not create eccentric characters who do strange things, like Miss Angela Thirkell. Some readers may find it a bitter type of comedy, but they will look in vain for any bitterness in the writing. Miss Compton-Burnett has one theme only: it is the theme of the complexity

141

and anguish of family life, as it may be found below the surface of family living.

Such books will not appeal to readers who wish to be assured that all is for the best in this best of all possible worlds. Nor are they for people who "like a good laugh," for they are likely to arise from a reading of one of these novels laughing on the wrong side of their faces. Jealousy, hatred, failure, ingratitude, indifference—every element which can invade and rot the family circle—is exposed by this writer, not with glee, and not for cheap laughter, but calmly and with the graces of high comedy. An English critic has said that Ivy Compton-Burnett's characters have more wit than any people created since the comedies of Congreve. That is a considered, defensible and moderate judgement.

The books have some superficial oddities of manner. For one thing, all the characters, young and old, well-educated and ill-educated, talk in the same ornate, involuted Victorian prose. Consider this opening from *More Women Than Men*:

> "It is with an especial feeling that I welcome you back today," said Josephine Napier, rising from her desk and advancing across her study to greet the woman who had entered it. "I do not forget that you are embarking upon your eighth year on my staff. Believe me, I have not been unmindful of my debt. May I say that I think no one has lived a more useful seven years? You will allow me to say just that to you?"
>
> "Indeed I will allow you to say it, Mrs. Napier," she said in a quick deep voice, with a quick, deep laugh. "It definitely smoothes my path toward decrepitude."
>
> "I think that maturity has very few disadvantages in-herent in itself. . . ."

This hardly sounds like the opening of a novel in which a jealous woman will kill another woman's husband, in which a mother will forcibly assist her daughter-in-law to die, in which a schoolmistress and a parson will impose their illegitimate child upon the world as something he is not, in which a young man will callously torture his dying father. Yet the people in *More Women Than Men* do all these things and more. You say, then, that they are monsters, created by a novelist who does not care for resemblance to "real life," as we live it. No, dear reader, the people in the book are just like ourselves, and behave just as we all behave, at times. And they do as we do, or wish to do.

It is Miss Compton-Burnett's special gift as a novelist to show us what melodramatic lives quite ordinary people lead without suspecting it. Once the superficial oddities of her style have become familiar, it is a very special pleasure to read her books. She uses language with the accuracy of an apothecary measuring out expensive drugs. She shares none of the ordinary assumptions: her people, though courteous, never attempt to conceal any dislike which they may feel toward one another; they do not raise their voices, but they speak daggers. And what daggers! Legend tells us of Chinese knives so sharp that a man's throat may be cut with one of them and he will not realize it until he sneezes and his head tumbles to the floor. That is the quality of Ivy Compton-Burnett's prose.

Not to have read at least a few of her books is to be ignorant of one of the major talents in the world of fiction today. These are not children's books, nor are they for people who like to be cosy when they read. But if you want to laugh while your hair is standing on end, she is your writer.

Peterborough Examiner, 18 October 1950

Seeing and Knowing/
The Voices of Silence

*I*t is with considerable misgiving that I set out on the task of reviewing two important books of art criticism which lie before me, one by Bernard Berenson, and the other by André Malraux. Both books present carefully considered and deeply interesting points of view which are, in several respects, contradictory. Am I expected to arbitrate between them? It is as though some mole, struggling painfully into the light from his subterranean gloom, were asked to referee a fight between two eagles, high in the upper air. My artistic friends have made it plain to me that in matters relating to painting and sculpture, I am a dolt. Should I not, then, hand these books over to an art critic, to be dealt with? No: Berenson and Malraux have chosen to write books, and books are my particular province; I think that I may claim to know something about books. So, strapping on my paper wings, and adjusting a few quill pens for tail feathers, I soar heavily from the ground, hoping to find out what the eagles are quarrelling over.

I am prepared to believe anything that Bernard Berenson says about pictures, because he is such a winning writer. His authority rests not only upon his fabulous knowledge of Italian Renaissance art, but upon his cultivation in virtually every sphere; he is surely one of the best-informed and wisest men living; and what he writes has the ring of truth in it. His latest book, *Seeing and Knowing*, consists of forty pages of prose in which he sets upon the painters of our day with a broad-axe, and eighty-eight monochrome reproductions of pictures which have a bearing on his argument.

Because Berenson is eighty-eight years old, there will certainly be people who will attribute his attack upon modern art to the peevishness of one who can no longer keep up with art's progress. Lay not that flattering unction to your soul! Berenson's tone in this book is urbane and reasonable, as always, and it is a continuation of the line of criticism which established him as the most authoritative writer on the art of the Renaissance. He is not an "expert," floundering helplessly as soon as he is out of his own "period"; he is a great critic who has made himself the greatest authority on a particular period. He is not out of sympathy with the ideas and ideals of modern artists, but he is out of sympathy with the means—slipshod and meretricious, in his view—by which they make those ideas and ideals manifest to the world.

Berenson believes that representational art is the only art worthy of the name, and he believes that in that vast field the most important factor is the representation of the human nude, with landscape as a second-best. During the past fifty years he feels that art has dealt in "confusion, struttings, blusterings, solemn puerilities," but he has words of comfort: "in past ages, art has sunk as low, although probably with no such smirking self-adulation, as it has today"; and he thinks that we shall pull through, though we may take a couple of centuries to do so. How? According to Berenson, art is a history of refreshment by genius, derivation and copying of that genius and then refreshment by a new genius. The last genius to appear, in his view, was Cézanne, and there has been no one to refresh and revivify art since his day. Only a succession of brilliant tricksters, of whom Picasso is the most gifted and most perverse. Thus Berenson.

André Malraux writes from a sharply different point of view in *The Voices of Silence*. Here, in 642 pages of the most tempestuous, heaving, voluptuously romantic prose that I have ever read, he sets forth his creed that art is a revolt against man's fate. And what is man's fate? So far as I can descry amid the rich glooms of his exposition, it is simply this: that life is short, often wretched, and ends in death. Art is man's protest, his assertion of what is undying and noble in his nature.

Now it is easy to see why Malraux and Berenson are at odds. To Berenson, painting and sculpture are certainly assertions of the nobility and immortality of the human spirit, but he feels that this work should be limited by the perceptions of the eye. Malraux's appreciation of art is in a great degree subjective, and in the finished product he is often ready to take the will for the deed. And in trying to make plain what these two writers mean I find that I am getting into the difficulty which plagues them both: it is very hard, if not downright impossible, to talk about one art in terms of another, and to describe the effect of painting and sculpture in words.

Let me, greatly daring, attempt a simplification. Let us suppose that Berenson and Malraux are confronted by a picture, the work of an unknown artist. Berenson will form his opinion solely on how well the artist has succeeded in conveying his ideas about the subject, by means of drawing and colour; he will take into account the artist's intention, but it will be his achievement which will fix the final judgement. Malraux, standing before the same picture, will give weight to the artist's intention, to his religion, to the spirit of the age in which he lived, to his politics, to anything and everything which could possibly have had a bearing on the conception and execution of the picture, and in his final judgement the excellence of its execution may not weigh very heavily. Berenson regards art as a means of communication and wants it to be reasonably comprehensible to the world: Malraux regards it principally as the artist's personal statement, for the world to understand if it can. In short, Berenson's view is classical, and Malraux's is romantic.

This cleavage between them is amply clear in their prose. Berenson strips his writing down to the bones. There is no ambiguity anywhere; his Yea is his Yea, and his Nay, his Nay. Wisdom and insight are everywhere to be found in his books, distilled and expressed with economical beauty. Malraux writes a beautiful prose, also, but with what a difference!

Like all romantics, he cannot resist the full palette, and while this makes for passages of great beauty, it also makes for pages of muddle. With hair-raising abandon, he brings literature and music to his aid when he is talking about painting and sculpture, and though this is sometimes illuminating it is just as often like dropping a bottle of ink into a bathtub full of clear water. His book is heavily charged with pity for the fate of man, and pity is a treacherous emotion; it can be noble at one moment and maudlin the next. Nor, it must be said, is everyone so convinced that the life of man is a vale of tears as is André Malraux; to feel greatly is a very fine thing, but it is also part of man's fate to think, and it is often astonishing how a fairly short period of thought can brighten a gloomy prospect.

Yet I would not for the world disparage this book, which has filled me with admiration and provided me with illumination which I sorely need. It is a very important book, in that it contains the deep convictions of a man of great knowledge, sensibility and literary skill. It is the book above all others that I would give to a young man or woman caught up in the greatness and mystery of painting and sculpture; it is not a youthful book, in any sense of being immature or insufficient, but it is addressed to the youthful spirit; it is a book for those who are discovering life, and it is a fine chart for such discovery. Berenson's book is for minds which are harder, clearer, less patient with surges of feeling, romantic aspiration—all that which the nineteenth century implied in the words "poesy and buzzem." Berenson provides you with a glass of a very finely distilled wisdom from which to sip. Malraux provides you with a glorious tank in which you may be submerged and from which, years later, you may never wring yourself dry. As to which is the better, I know my own choice, but as for making a public judgement between them—well, that isn't for the likes of me.

Saturday Night, 20 March 1954

The Magicians/
The Doors of Perception

*T*hough at first glance some readers may find it strange that I should link the names of Aldous Huxley and J. B. Priestley in this article, I hope to show that they have certain important characteristics in common. Both men have lost some of the popularity which they enjoyed in their younger days; both have experienced this loss because they have attempted to probe farther into fundamental matters of experience and belief than their popular following was prepared to go with them; both are now widely misunderstood men.

It is a great temptation for an author to become rigid in the mould of his first great popularity. Huxley and Priestley will both be sixty this year. Huxley reached the peak of his early success with *Point Counter Point* in 1928; Priestley with *The Good Companions* in the year following. They could have stuck there, and for the past twenty-five years they could have turned out work of much that quality, becoming a little slicker and a little more mechanical at each repetition, and they would have increased their number of readers with every book. But they have continued, obstinately, to grow, as real men of letters should. A boxer has probably seen his best days before he is thirty; a writer, if he has anything in him, is probably ready to do his best work by the time he is sixty. (Poets, for excellent but complex reasons, cannot be included in this generality.) Huxley and Priestley have grown a great deal since they became big names, and unless something goes very much astray their finest work has yet to be written.

Characteristic of both men is a discontent with the world of appearances, and the limitations of ordinary human experience. This discontent has made Priestley a wistful and somewhat angry man, and it has made Huxley a student of mysticism and a bit of a crank. But these are superficial aspects of the intellectual pilgrimage which they are making. Two books which lie before me give us a key to what is deeper in their quest.

Priestley's book is a novel, called *The Magicians*. The plot may be summarized briefly: Sir Charles Ravenstreet, an electrical engineer, finds that, in his middle fifties, he has been nosed out of the company which he helped to make, and is at a loose end. He has no talent for leisure, and is soon drawn into association with Lord Mervil, a very powerful entrepreneur who proposes to manufacture for popular sale a drug which provides the taker with a sense of freedom from anxiety and responsibility—cheap as aspirin, no hangover and not creative of addiction. Mervil sees his find as a substitute for alcohol and tobacco, and as a means of reducing the bulk of mankind to amiable obedience. But through an accident Ravenstreet meets three eccentric old men who expose Mervil's plan for a plot against mankind, and introduce Ravenstreet to a wisdom of their own—a change of one's personal attitude toward the passing of time—which restores his zest for life.

Thus summarized, the book does not sound particularly good. But it *is* good, because Priestley is one of the ablest living practitioners of the neglected art of telling a story. He has been much derided by critics who do not like his kind of story-telling—which is of the English rather than the Continental tradition—and who think that because he writes about commonplace people he must himself be commonplace. I dissent sharply from this view; I think that his scope is wide, and his psychological insight keen. He is a true creator of character; I can recall whole scenes from *Festival at Farbridge,* a not very good novel which he wrote in 1950, though I have forgotten completely highly praised books by "brilliant" writers which I read six months ago. Priestley is a man of large and powerful abilities, and in his plays and novels he has given a picture of the externals of his time, and of their internal stresses and longings, which has not been equalled by more than half a dozen of his contemporaries.

In *The Magicians* this sense of longing is particularly poignant, and though the resolution of Ravenstreet's problem is neither complete nor clear, it is honest: man's salvation in a despairing world lies, to a great extent, within his own power; let him exert that power and external help will be vouchsafed to him.

Huxley's latest book, little more than a pamphlet, is called *The Doors of Perception,* and it is a description of his experiences after taking four-tenths of a gramme of mescalin, a drug extracted from a type of cactus. For centuries Indians have eaten mescalin, and it is very like the drug described in Priestley's novel; it brings a state of peaceful contemplation, in which the sense of self is greatly diminished, and the appreciation and understanding of external objects greatly enhanced; it has no after-effect, it does not create addiction, and as the taker is very much withdrawn into himself it does not make him objectionable to other people. Huxley took the dose in order to assist a scientist who wanted to test the effect of the drug on a man of powerful intellect, capable of describing his sensations in detail.

Huxley's account of his experience while under the influence of mescalin is absorbing. Common objects—flowers, a chair, a pattern of light and shadow—assumed an interest and an intensity of being unlike anything in common experience. His sense of personality was much reduced, and he found in its place a remarkable sensation of unity with, and participation in, the existence of objects which came within his range.

Readers who have followed Huxley's work during the past twenty years will bring to this little book much that will enlarge its meaning for them; I seriously doubt if it can mean much to people who have no knowledge of mysticism, which has engaged him for so long. If I am not mistaken, it was in *Ends and Means,* published in 1937, that his attack upon our modern preoccupation with "personality" began. "Personality" means simply the externals of Self, and for many people Self has little existence apart from "personality." But there have always been people who knew that "personality" was a shell, and that Self in the deeper sense was the reality which was capable, in its turn, of participation in the not-Self—which is God, or the Clear Light of the Void, or whatever you choose to call it. I am deeply conscious of my own clumsiness in expressing such ideas; they are commonplaces to many devout and philosophical people, and they are utterly incomprehensible to many others. But if I am not mistaken, Huxley's later work has been a plea to mankind to recognize the perishability, and the essential triviality, of all the externals of daily life and of "personality"; and the infinite preciousness and imperishability of that essential Self which yearns to be united with the not-Self.

The mescalin experiment, by diminishing the insistence of "personality," may have given him some clue as to the delusive nature of our ordinary concept of ourselves, and of the truer nature of the world which we inhabit and which, most of the time, we regard simply as a piece of theatrical scenery in front of which we strut and bellow.

I beg that no one who reads this piece will think that Huxley is advocating that everybody should become a mescalin-eater, or a drug-fiend, or anything of that sort. This is positively a book which you should not discuss until you have read it and thought about it. And if you have any curiosity about the nature of human existence, you should do so, for it is an absorbing contribution to that study by one of the most far-ranging, capacious and powerful intellects of our time.

Have I brought Huxley and Priestley somewhat nearer to one another in your thoughts? I hope so, for though greatly different in external things, they share a discontent with the external world, and with commonplace concepts of man's destiny. Both have refused to be beguiled by an easy popularity. Both have striven to get at a reality which is truer than the delusive evidence of the senses.

Saturday Night, 1 May 1954

Corsets and Crinolines

*T*he number of women who take clothes seriously seems to be on the increase. Of course many women pay some attention to the clothes they put on their backs, but it has always been observable that the best clothes for women are designed by men and made by men, and that all the great philosophers of clothes have been men. But of late some excellent volumes on the history of clothing have been written by women. The name of Doris Langley Moore is justly honoured; Phillis Cunnington has collaborated with her husband in producing the excellent *History of Underclothes;* and I have at hand a handsome volume called *Corsets and Crinolines,* by Norah Waugh. It calls for consideration at length.

Its subject is clear from its title. The book traces the history of the corset from the fifteenth century to the present day, and with it the various means by which women have built out their skirts. The corset seemed to have run its course in the 1920s, but since that time small waists have come back into fashion, and whalebone and steel supports are not unknown; at least one Queen of England has worn an unmistakable crinoline within the past ten years; it would be foolish to assume that these fashions will be seen no more. In any case, it is interesting to study the way in which they have grown.

Miss Waugh is an historian of costume, and she is also a designer for the stage. She states an obvious truth when she says that we cannot expect to understand historical costume unless we know what was worn underneath it; but, like many obvious truths, this one has been overlooked by a great many people. Foundation garments are so called because they give a characteristic shape to the figure, and determine the way in which the wearer shall walk, stand and sit. Anybody who has felt the fascination of historical costume will want to read her valuable book and study its many illustrations.

I have never understood why some elementary study of costume is not part of all courses in history. What knowledge have we of Queen Anne, or Alfred the Great, or Martin Luther, if we do not know what sort of clothes they wore and what they looked like? What people wore in the past decided what they were as plainly as what they ate, or the sort of beds they slept in. It is impossible for every student of history to delve deeply into these matters, but at least they should have a chance to know that Columbus did not wear a wig, but that Captain Cook did so, and that people wore shoes which fitted left or right foot equally well until almost the beginning of the eighteenth century.

I have met several schoolboys who could tell me how Cartier's ships were rigged, and in what important ways his rigging differed from that of Captain Vancouver; knowledge of what these explorers wore, as they conquered the globe, is fully as interesting. Indeed, one of the astounding things about Samuel de Champlain is the extraordinary rig-out in which he walked and canoed through our Canadian wilderness. It is no superficial remark that clothes make the man; clothes show what a man thinks about himself; they are an expression of a philosophy. And as clothes make the woman, too, we must get down to foundations to begin our study.

Miss Waugh reproduces pictures of early sixteenth-century corsets which are simply pieces of armour, for they are made of iron, with uncomfortable-looking holes through which the breasts protruded. She suggests that these were for "difficult" figures—a remarkable understatement. Corsets in England were usually made of linen stiffened with whalebone, iron or ivory; there are records of pasteboard corsets. They were all capable of being laced and strapped tightly, so they would pinch in the waist, and either flatten the breasts, or push them up into prominence, according to the fashion of the moment. The accompaniment of such a corset was a device to give greater fullness to the hips. This might be a bolster of horsehair, tied around the waist, and called a "hausse-cul" in Europe, or a "bum-roll" in England. It could also be a cage of whalebone, or steel, to carry the weight of the skirts. Sometimes these cages were worn only on the sides, and were called "panniers," after the baskets worn by pack-mules, or they were on the sides and back, and were called "farthingales." It was not until the eighteenth century that hoops, which made the skirt stick out all around, came into being.

It must not be supposed that these fashions were accepted without protest. Wits made fun of them; philosophers explained at merciless length that they were foolish; divines roared passionately in condemnation. But for very nearly four hundred years women sought to give the impression, by their dress, that they had tiny waists, unnaturally high breasts, and enormous posteriors. Nobody believed that this was in reality the case; it was merely an ideal of the female figure which was cherished. And who are we, in the fifties of the twentieth century, to laugh at it? What is our ideal of womanhood on this continent? Is it not a girl with a square mouth painted the colour of a postbox, monstrous jutting breasts, and no buttocks at all? And was it not, a quarter of a century ago, a girl with no hair, no bosom and no behind—a mere sausage with legs?

To say that there is no accounting for fashion is to evade a difficult problem. There is a way of accounting for it, as readers of some books on the philosophy of style (Dr. J. C. Flügel's *The Psychology of Clothes,* to name but one) will be aware, but it is too complex a matter for this article, and Miss Waugh does not attempt it in her book. But one point is worth noting: the fact that a fashion is unhealthy has never, of itself, succeeded in destroying that fashion.

The wearing of extremely tight corsets, as was done during most of the nineteenth century, was thought to be bad for the lungs. The best medical opinion of the day said so, and though we know that medical opinion often directly springs from puritanism, rather than science, it seems probable that such squeezing of the lungs and entrails cannot have been good for anybody. Nevertheless several ladies put themselves on record as having laced themselves so tight that they fainted at times, but suffered no other ill effect. Many fashionable girls' schools undertook to reduce the waists of their charges from, for instance, twenty to thirteen inches, by progressively tighter lacing. There was a perpetual outcry against the custom, but it was not discontinued until the fashion changed, and fashion does not change at the dictates of physicians or divines.

Why did women do it? This extract from a letter written by the Duchess of Devonshire in 1778 gives what was probably the usual reason: "My dear Louisa, you will laugh when I tell you, that poor Winifred, who was reduced to my gentlewoman's gentlewoman, broke two laces in endeavoring to draw my new French stays close. You know I am naturally small at bottom but now you might literally span me. You never saw such a doll. Then, they are so intolerably wide across the breast, that my arms are absolutely sore with them; and my sides so pinched!—But it is the 'ton'; and pride feels no pain. It is with these sentiments the ladies of the present age heal their wounds; to be admired is a sufficient balm."

Miss Waugh's book consists of short chapters in which she explains alterations in style, followed by much longer sections in which she reproduces a variety of contemporary comment on each style.

This book is a beautiful curiosity, and deals admirably with its restricted theme. It says little about corsets for men, common though these were at least until the First Great War; a little book could be written about them. But as a work on women's corsets it is unquestionably the best book yet to make its appearance.

Saturday Night, 2 October 1954

Joyce Cary's Novels

Joyce Cary is not a fashionable novelist. He is not in any particular "movement" and he does not build his novels upon any of the fashionable philosophies of our day. But he is a novelist whom we can imagine plying his craft successfully at any time during the past hundred and fifty years. He is in that mainstream of English fiction which begins in the eighteenth century and, in the nineteenth, swells out into a broad river; the river is not so popular now as once it was, and authors who explore its creeks and cut-off meanders are apt to be immoderately praised; but the river is strong, and Cary knows how to navigate it as well as any man living.

His best efforts, since 1941, have been put into two long novels, each of which fills three volumes. The first of these was the tale of the relationship of Sara Monday, Tommy Wilcher and Gulley Jimson; the books are called *Herself Surprised, To Be a Pilgrim,* and *The Horse's Mouth.* Every reader will have his own favourite, and I shall say here that I like the last best of the three, because it seems to me to give one of the best insights into the artist's temperament—the real thing and not the usual fictional fake—of any novel I know. Gulley Jimson is no romantic Bohemian, descended from Murger and with phrases of Puccini sticking to him; he is a jolly old scoundrel, not quite right in the head, but a painter of genius. Others will prefer Sara, that delightful, innocently wicked old kitchen-Venus, and there may be a few whose pity for cracked old

Wilcher will incline them toward him. But I like the books because they provide me with the inexhaustible Gulley—the only fully articulate painter I have ever met.

The other three-decker novel is about Chester Nimmo, the great politician, his wife, Nina, and her second husband, her cousin and her seducer, Captain Jim Latter. Their books are *Prisoner of Grace, Except the Lord* and—recently published— *Not Honour More.* In these books Cary writes about politics better than Disraeli, and as well as Trollope, but politics is not the mainspring of his plot; that is, as always with him, the inexhaustible variety of the human spirit. Nimmo, as an ambitious little clerk, married Nina, who was above him, and rose triumphant over the fact that she never really broke off her relationship with her first love, Jim Latter; when Nina divorced Nimmo and married Latter, they were not rid of him, for the terrible old man settled in their house, and created a situation which the choleric Latter could only solve by killing his wife.

If you truly like novels, and if you like to get your teeth into something really meaty, I recommend these books to you strongly. But do not let me mislead you; if you want something on the Dostoevsky model, with agony and guilt piled high, these are not the books for you. Cary is, in the highest and finest sense, a comic writer. He rejoices in the wild luxuriance of the human spirit; he is stimulated by situations which cause other novelists to pull their solemnest faces. He is always conscious of the farcical element which lies so near to tragedy, and he has a peculiar relish for the manifold ways in which people can deceive and blind themselves to the nature of their own motives and actions. All his characters are the prisoners of their own minds and personalities, and their efforts to communicate with others, similarly imprisoned, are pathetic and comic at once.

This is just the kind of thing I like, because it agrees with my own view of life. There are many people who find it uncongenial; perhaps they are wiser, or it may be that they are simply more tender-minded. But they cannot deny that to read Cary is to get life hot and strong, not as the self-conscious "realist" paints it, but as the man sees it who has a genius for identifying himself with the creatures of his imagination.

Cary is a master of intellectual impersonation. Each of the six books I have named is written in the first person, by one of the characters in his two stories. I have read them with the utmost care, and I have yet to catch him in anything which appeared to me to be a falsity in choice of expression or attitude of thought. The gentle Nina Nimmo, the sensual old Sara Monday, the crotchety Wilcher, uproarious, cracked Gulley, crafty, mystical Nimmo—and in this last book the psychotic, army-trained, anti-democratic Latter—they are all brought before us, stripped naked, complete and terrifyingly human, speaking in their own voices, and writing in cadences which could only belong to them. This is creation of a very high order.

Indeed, I cannot think of anything which comes near it except Browning's great and somewhat neglected poem *The Ring and the Book*. There we have a story told to us by a variety of people, each from his own point of view, each stressing what he thinks important, and each bringing his own understanding of life and his own store of wisdom and egotism to the problem. There are people who find it a bore, and certainly it demands application. I became committed to it when I was sixteen and I have never been able to be objective about it. And only in these novels of Cary's do I find anything comparable in psychological insight, in power to create people and set them up on their own legs, bearing their own faults and their own greatness of spirit.

Saturday Night, 6 August 1955

Confessions of Felix Krull, Confidence Man

The late Thomas Mann was in several respects a singularly fortunate man of letters. Fame came to him early, for he was only twenty-six when *Buddenbrooks* was published and acclaimed; and after this splendid beginning he suffered no serious reverse of reputation, and apparently none of that waxing and waning of creative power which makes wretched the life of so many writers. From being the possessor of a great German reputation to the achievement of a world reputation, and finally to a position of unique authority, was a steady progress; he was a political refugee from Germany by choice and not by compulsion, and thus his exile never brought with it any loss of dignity. His earnings were sufficient to permit him to live in comfort; his marriage was happy and his home life unmarked by scandal or tragedy; during his last years he enjoyed a public regard not too greatly unlike that which surrounded his idol, Goethe. Fortune, it seemed, had lavished her gifts upon him with both hands.

He, in his turn, did all that a man can do to be worthy of Fortune's favour. He cherished his genius, working seriously and methodically, it is said, every day of his life. The honours which came to him gained fully as much lustre from his reputation as they imparted to it. And Fortune, kind to the last, permitted him to live a full eighty years, and to conclude his career as a writer with the first volume of a novel which is worthy of what had gone before. *Confessions of Felix Krull,*

Confidence Man is a happy example of Thomas Mann's work.

I dare not say "of Thomas Mann's best work," for there will be many people whose judgement I respect who will disagree. What, they will say, do I mean by suggesting that this is fit to stand with *Buddenbrooks, The Magic Mountain* and the *Joseph* tetralogy? I do not wish to be involved in argument of that sort, for I am non-Germanic in temperament, and I am certain that much that was greatest in those intimidating novels has passed over my head. Mann was intensely Germanic, and only those temperamentally suited to Germanic thought and the Germanic way of expressing it can know his work fully.

I do not, in saying this, suggest that Germanic thought and utterance is superior to, let us say, English or French or American thought and utterance; I mean only that it takes a different tempo, and reaches us in a copious, detailed, slow-moving form. Thomas Mann shows us life, not by flashes of lightning, but accompanied by prolonged rollings of thunder. In English translation many of his philosophical passages arouse the irreverent thought that he is dealing extensively in hot air.

Yet has not all philosophy this suggestion of hot air? For what is philosophy, at its best, but the detailed and systematic exploration of those magical insights into the nature of life and the universe which poets experience and which poets express, very often, with gem-like clarity and blessed brevity? The poet, having been granted his insight, tries to give it to the world with something of the brilliant compression with which it reached him; the philosopher wants to leave nothing unsaid that will explain and extend his flash of insight, and somewhat too often he wants to transform his fleeting and imperfect vision into a system of thought.

It is amusing to recall that Mann, in a speech delivered in Vienna in 1936, on the occasion of Sigmund Freud's eightieth birthday, gently and humorously rebuked Freud for trying to make a scientific system out of things which poets had known only as an elusive, uncodified collection of insights for centuries. Both Freud and Mann shared in the German passion for thoroughness. I do not think that anyone who lacks some strain of that passion in himself will ever thoroughly comprehend the novels of Thomas Mann. He was a great philosophic novelist; if he had been less thorough, less anxious to explain and explore every ramification of his thought, he might have been something even finer—a great poetic novelist.

When critical books are written about Mann, as they surely will be, much attention will be devoted to the tenacity with which he retained and explored certain ideas which are the foundation of his work. One of these was the division between the Good Citizen and the Artist; another was the kinship of the Artist with the Criminal. The second of these seminal concepts was the source of a remarkable short story which he wrote in 1911, called "Felix Krull"; it told of a young man, the son of a manufacturer of bad champagne, who as a child decided that he was different from other beings—a finer creature with a larger notion of life—and that this difference released him from ordinary considerations of morality. It was a superb story, and Mann could not relinquish it without expansion; in 1954 it appeared in German, with the original story as its first section, and about six times as much new material, which brought it to the length of a novel; it was the author's intention to add another volume to this. Perhaps, had he lived, Mann would have become so engrossed in the story of Felix that he would have turned it into another tetralogy, as absorbing and monumental a work as *Joseph and His Brothers*. That he contemplated a second volume is further proof of the vitality of his creative powers.

Felix writes, he tells us, from retirement; we learn also that he has been in prison. What happened to put him in jail and end his career as a confidence man we shall never know, for this is not the sort of book which anyone will ever dare to complete. *Felix Krull* began as a short story and will remain as half a novel. And for a great number of readers, Felix will always stand as a symbol for a particular type of person.

It is an uncommon type, for Felix is a man who understands himself thoroughly. He always puts his best side forward, even when he is writing his personal memoirs, supposedly for his own amusement; yet, as he lets us know, his memoir *might* some day have a reader, and he sets to work to charm and disarm that reader, just as he charmed and disarmed his victims at the peak of his career. His victims? No, that is the wrong word. Felix is convinced that he never had a victim; he always brought more joy into the lives of those he exploited than sorrow. If he stole from women, did he not leave them with the memory of an exceptionally gifted lover? If he impersonated a man, did he not play the part in a style far beyond the capabilities of the original? Yet, beneath all this elaborate and almost convincing self-justification we sense that Felix knew himself to be a crook, and that he took an artist's delight in his dishonesty, which was his form of creation. Such self-recognition is very rare. Most crooks are whiners, deceived by their own lies. But not Felix. He had the actor's duality of consciousness, giving half of himself to a brilliant performance which was under the intellectual guidance of the other half.

Is *Felix Krull* a great comic novel? I think so. I found it a great farce of the spirit, and read it with entranced delight. But because Mann was a heavyweight philosophical novelist, this is heavyweight comedy; the fun is not broad; it is deep, and yet it is enlivened with those flashes of farce which really happen in life, but which we stupidly think improbable when we see them on the stage. We attract what we are: the tragic spirit finds tragedy in life, and the dull spirit finds dullness; the farcical spirit finds farce at every turn, and when he is a farcical spirit of the stature of Felix Krull, he finds great farce, in which even the vast involvements and pachydermatous sobrieties of German philosophy have a place.

This is also, to my astonishment, an erotic novel of splendid scope. It is not gross, nor does it go in for those details so dear to authors who think that they personally invented sex. But it calls up the atmosphere of sex, and the truth of sex, and the absorbing glory of sex, as only a few novels within my experience have succeeded in doing. Here we have an author, supremely adult, describing one of life's great preoccupations, and the result is superb.

It is pleasant to think that this novel engaged some of Mann's last years, for it is evidence that the man upon whom Fortune smiled with such constancy was her darling to the last, happy and secure in the possession of his great powers.

Saturday Night, 29 October 1955

A Christmas Garland

Last year at this time I confided to my readers my pleasure in E. T. A. Hoffmann's macabre and romantic tales, and recommended them as Christmas reading—an antidote to too much pseudo-Dickens and department-store Gemütlichkeit. This year I hobble out of my library bearing another precious volume, ideally suited to the season; it is *A Christmas Garland* by Sir Max Beerbohm.

The book contains seventeen Christmas stories, written by Beerbohm as parodies of the style of the most eminent writers of his day. The book first appeared in 1912, and again in 1922; it is not easy to get a copy today, and I cannot understand why some enterprising publisher does not reprint it, or prepare a Beerbohm omnibus—if a writer so elegant may be mentioned in connection with an omnibus. Parody has never been brought to such perfection before or since.

Romping parody and vicious parody are common enough; among modern parodists Wolcott Gibbs, Cyril Connolly and S. J. Perelman are specially gifted, but nobody has ever touched Beerbohm in this uncommonly difficult field. We may wonder, perhaps, if his genius in this sphere has not been a limitation on his other writing. But is there an admirer of Beerbohm who would sacrifice *A Christmas Garland* simply in order that *Zuleika Dobson* might be a little more successful? For myself I think that *Around Theatres,* the *Garland* and *Seven Men* are his best books.

I do not wish to fight about this, so if any reader disagrees with me, let him feel free at once to despise me and pity my ignorance. The *Garland* is parody brought to the level of genius; from that point I do not intend to budge.

The book has grown with the years, and that is in itself an astonishing feat for a volume of parody. The authors who are put under the microscope are all dead, and the fluctuation of reputation which follows death is, in the case of most of them, done with. The value of Henry James, Thomas Hardy, Joseph Conrad, George Moore and George Meredith is firmly established. Rudyard Kipling has not met with justice yet, but his reputation is climbing, and the same may be said for H. G. Wells, Arnold Bennett and John Galsworthy. We do not value Chesterton and Belloc as highly as their contemporaries did, and it will be long before the beating of Shaw's bones is finished. It is unlikely that future generations will have much knowledge of A. C. Benson, Frank Harris, Maurice Hewlett or G. S. Street, but Edmund Gosse will long have an honoured place as a critic and as the writer of a great autobiography. These are the seventeen who are anatomized in Beerbohm's book. His genius is shown by the fact that those writers who were great, or worthy, are still great and worthy when he has finished with them, and the lesser fry emerge in all their bedizened vacuity. Such parody is criticism of the most brilliantly perceptive kind.

If the style is the man, how brilliantly Beerbohm captures these men! Consider this opening paragraph from the Belloc piece called "Of Christmas": "There was a man came to an Inn by night, and after he had called three times they should open him the door—though why three times, and not three times three, nor thirty times thirty, which is the number of the little stone devils that make mows at St. Aloesius of Ledera over against the marshes Gué-la-Nuce to this day, nor three hundred times three hundred (which is a bestial number), nor three thousand times three-and-thirty, upon my soul I know not, and nor do you—when, then, this jolly fellow had three times cried out, shouted, yelled, holloa'd, loudly besought, caterwauled, brayed, sung out, and roared, he did by the same token set himself to beat, hammer, bang, pummel, and knock at the door." So also with the Chesterton piece, called "Some Damnable Errors About Christmas"; and so again in "Euphemia Clashthought," in which the involved and often arch manner of Meredith is brilliantly touched off.

There is more to it, however, than putting on literary fancy-dress. Not only the style but the mind of each writer is assumed by the parodist. Does anybody today read Maurice Hewlett? You need not trouble, for in "Fond Hearts Askew" all that romantic silliness, all that fake-archaism of style, is laid before you in miniature. Nor is it only the silly writers that Beerbohm impersonates to perfection.

I greatly admire Edmund Gosse, but who has read his work without being conscious of the fussy, dry, scholarly tone of voice, and the cultured yet innocently eager spirit which lurks behind so much of it? In "A Recollection" Beerbohm (as Gosse) recreates a Christmas in Venice, in which he tried to bring together his two foremost literary admirations, Robert Browning and Henrik Ibsen. The latter had no appetite for the meeting: "He had never heard of this Herr Browning. (It was one of the strengths of his strange, crustacean genius that he never had heard of anybody.)" But at last they meet, and while Browning urges Ibsen (of whose work he knows nothing) to keep away from the theatre, Ibsen tells Browning that no woman ever was capable of writing a fragment of good poetry. "Imagination reels at the effect this would have had on the recipient of *Sonnets from the Portuguese*." Poor Gosse, as interpreter, has to make the best he can of these dreadful failures in *entente* between his heroes. It is superbly funny, and yet it leaves Gosse's real importance and dignity unimpaired. Beerbohm is a mocker, but he is not a belittler; he has nothing of the itch which afflicts common parodists, driving them to drag great men down from the heights they have attained.

This, surely, is his most important quality as a parodist. He is himself a master, and he has no need to spatter other masters.

But he cannot, at all times, take them quite seriously. His mockery is electrifying, but never deadly.

The book is full of splendid things. Consider this from "Endeavour," the Galsworthy piece: "Just at that moment, heralded by a slight fragrance of old lace and of that peculiar, almost unseizable odour that uncut turquoises have, Mrs. Berridge appeared." Or this, which is the remark made by a small boy to his little sister, in the Henry James piece, called "The Mote in the Middle Distance": "Oh, you certainly haven't, my dear, the trick of propinquity!" Or this fine, though slightly off-key, echo from Chesterton: "We do not say of Love that he is short-sighted. We do not say of Love that he is myopic. We do not say of Love that he is astigmatic. We say quite simply, Love is blind. We might go further and say, Love is deaf. That would be a profound and obvious truth. We might go further still and say, Love is dumb. But that would be a profound and obvious lie. For Love is always an extraordinarily fluent talker. Love is a wind-bag, filled with a gusty wind from Heaven." The real Chestertonian note—the note of a sincere, kindly Chadband—is there.

Quotation, however, is dangerous. The splendour of these parodies lies not in isolated snippets, but in the whole impression. One of the funniest, to my mind, is "A Sequelula to The Dynasts," in which the poetry of Thomas Hardy is stood on its head, yet no single lines can be quoted from it. And in "P.C., X, 36" the whole of Kipling's "manlydom," and also his fascist woodnotes wild, are captured with the utmost skill, but no short passage can illustrate how this is done. Nor is it satisfactory to quote from the parody of Conrad, though I cannot resist this sentence: "In his upturned eyes, and along the polished surface of his lean body black and immobile, the stars were reflected, creating an illusion of themselves who are illusions."

Christmas is the noblest and tenderest of the yearly feasts, when we have stripped it of commercialism. Yet even then there is apt to be a certain heaviness about it; our smiles are a little greasy, and our tears contain more sugar than salt. We need a whiff of a keener air, and *A Christmas Garland* never fails to bring it. So, if you can find a copy, and creep away for a couple of hours on the Great Day, there can be no doubt whatever about the merriment of your Christmas.

Saturday Night, 24 December 1955

The Girl with
the Swansdown Seat/
The Abode of Love / 1848

*U*nless we happen to be professional historians, most of us have a careless habit of summing up the moral climate of past ages in a phrase; thus the Middle Ages were "very devout," the Restoration was "very licentious" and the age of Victoria was "very strict." This last piece of nonsense is especially silly, for the Victorian Age has been anatomized during the past thirty years, and if we still think that it was an age of severe sexual morality, we simply have not heard what we were told. Three books are at hand today which still further destroy this Victorian myth.

Of course we must not rush to the other extreme, and assume that all Victorians were frauds and hypocrites. But there are facts (how the Victorians loved facts—our modern passion for statistics is part of their legacy to us) which suggest that Victorian morality, like Victorian clothing, had a far seamier side than the modern article. Figures from *The Lancet* of 1857 tell us that there were more than 6,000 brothels in London at that time, and about 80,000 prostitutes, for a population of two and a half millions: in 1951 there were 10,000 prostitutes and a population exceeding eight millions, with strong laws against keeping brothels. Nor can this difference be bridged by talking about "enthusiastic amateurs" in the modern world; there were plenty of amateurs in the great Queen's heyday, as well.

It is fruitless to try to find a fully satisfactory explanation of the prevalence of prostitution in Victorian England. Economics tells part of the story, for female workers of all kinds, including domestic servants, were ill-paid; but illegitimacy in rural districts was commonplace. The caste system was strong, with its concomitant disregard for the chastity of social inferiors; there were many servants, and servants have always been great debauchers of children. And there was the concept of the Good Woman, an ideal which sorted ill with ordinary human nature.

A Good Woman did not strive to make herself sexually desirable, her conversation was antiseptic and sentimentally religious in tone, and the slightest favour could be gained from her only at an inordinate price—probably marriage. Many Victorians tried very hard to be Good Women, and many of them succeeded. But men of normal temperament, without being in any sense debauchees, like women to be sexually attractive, they like lively conversation which may take a Rabelaisian turn, and they like flirtation. If they wanted these things in Victoria's day, they might find them among the women of their ordinary acquaintance if they were very lucky, but it was more probable that they would have to turn to prostitutes.

These women ranged from the poorest, generally known as Tuppenny Uprights, because of their price and the posture in which they obliged, through ten-shilling, guinea and three-guinea women of superior charms, to extremely expensive courtesans. Of this last group the queen for many years was Catherine Walters, known as "Skittles."

Skittles lived in splendour, owned beautiful horses which she rode to admiration, and entertained many of the greatest men of the day. And let the word "entertained" be understood aright; Skittles did not lie with the whole of the aristocratic, literary and artistic world, but she provided it with gay and charming conversation, and an atmosphere in which it could meet without oppressive fear that a sudden ebullition of unmitigated jollity would be misunderstood and rebuked by a Good Woman. A courtesan, it must be understood, is not a higher-paid version of that former industrious citizen of Toronto, Dirty-Neck Marge; she is a woman who knows how to entertain men, sitting up as well as lying down; we may be sure that W. E. Gladstone did not visit Skittles for anything but jolly conversation.

There will be those among my feminine readers who will declare, with a toss of their curls, that entertaining men merely pampers them. Quite right. And men like to be pampered. Indeed, they insist upon it.

Victorian sexual morality is investigated most amusingly in Cyril Pearl's book *The Girl with the Swansdown Seat,* which I heartily recommend. The girl of the title was Skittles, and the seat in question was on her privy—the comfort-loving puss! The moral of the book seems to be that she who would keep her husband at home should be rather more like Skittles than like a Good Woman. And again, I must insist that it was pleasing feminine character, rather than a flexible morality, which made these women sought-after; they retained their popularity to ages when even modern women have set up in business as sweet old grannies.

Less wide in range, but equally illuminating in its comment on Victorian life, is *The Abode of Love* by Aubrey Menen. This is an account, in the form of a novel, of that extraordinary character Henry James Prince, who, in the middle of the Victorian era, instituted a new religion, with himself as its Messiah, and founded an Agapemone, or Abode of Love, at Charlinch, in the south of England. Here about sixty people joined him, living communally and making over all their wealth to him to be used as he saw fit. Prince also had access to all the ladies in the Abode, a privilege which he took very seriously and discharged with zeal. He had been, in youth, an Anglican church clergyman, suckled at that tumid breast of orthodoxy, Lampeter College; but his weakness for women won him the title of the Kissing Curate, the Established Church would have no more of him, and he was impelled to set up his own establishment.

The extraordinary thing was that the Abode was never troubled by the law. It was probably the handsomest bawdy-house in England, and certainly the only one to have a private chapel. Money talks: the fine clothes, the fine carriages, and the air of well-being which pervaded everything about the Abode discouraged enquiry. Prince had assured his followers that he would never die and upon the whole he did pretty well, living far into his eighties, and a lively old gentleman to the end.

Aubrey Menen is one of the most brilliant writers living, but in his last two or three books he has fallen below his accustomed high standard. In *The Abode of Love* he is firmly in the saddle again, for this is in his wittiest, most agreeably ironic style.

The third of these comments on the past century touches only one year of it. Raymond Postgate has chosen to make a study of the year 1848, which was an especially significant one in the nineteenth century, and he follows the news, domestic and foreign, month by month. He has laced war and revolution shrewdly with social comment.

Those who are shocked by the brutal murders of today should compare them with the killing of John Wall by a gang of toughs headed by a man called Jakeways; they had been hunting and had found nothing, so when they happened on Wall working in his cottage Jakeways said, "Come, let us shoot the old fellow," and they did. The gangs of Victorian London were quite as savage as the gangs of Chicago in the twenties. We also learn such curious facts as that the Duke of Wellington introduced the custom of taking a bath every day into England; he caught the habit in India. It took on, very slowly. When we think of the Victorians we must remember that they were infrequent and reluctant bathers. Skittles, however, washed all over every day, with scented soap. Surely there is a moral in that? Were medieval theologians so far wrong when they called soap "lascivus"?

The Victorians have been immoderately praised, and immoderately blamed, and surely it is time we formed some reasonable picture of them? There was their courageous, intellectually adventurous side, their greedy and inhuman side, their superbly poetic side, their morally pretentious side, their tea and buttered toast side, and their champagne and Skittles side. Much like ourselves, in fact, though rather dirtier.

Saturday Night, 26 May 1956

The Canterbury Tales

Chaucer shares on the literary stock market have been rising during the past ten years, owing chiefly to the enthusiasm, literary gifts and scholarship of an Oxford don, Nevill Coghill, and secondarily to the British Broadcasting Corporation. The fluctuations of the literary market are familiar to everyone; sometimes there is a fierce flutter in a virtually unknown commodity (like the John Donne boom in the twenties); occasionally an almost dead commodity bursts into new life (as in the Trollope boom of the forties); Foreign Moderns (Sartre, de Beauvoir, Camus, Sagan) are eagerly pushed but are apt to collapse suddenly, wiping out those critics who have invested too heavily in them; in the U.S.A. the Deep South and Proletarian Anguish are solid, though all else fluctuates unpredictably. But it has been a long time since there was much movement in Chaucer shares, and I for one am glad to welcome the present bull market; enjoyment of Chaucer has for too long been confined to the scholarly; it is high time the general reader knew more of him.

The reason for the neglect of Chaucer is simply that the language of the fourteenth century is daunting to the modern reader who has not given some time to its study. An untrained person can read it, if he uses some such edition as the famous one by Professor W. W. Skeat, in seven volumes, or the less terrifying, but still formidable, single-volume edition by F. N. Robinson, published in the Cambridge Poets series. But it will scarcely be argued that such reading is pleasant, when every line must be puzzled over, and every second or third word must be looked up in the glossary. Because Skeat and Robinson prepared their editions for scholars and students, they have included variant readings and all the critical apparatus which such people demand, and which the general reader does not want, and very properly resents. He will read Chaucer only if it gives him pleasure—a point of view which Chaucer himself would have understood and approved.

The needs of the general reader have been catered to from time to time by writers who have offered Chaucer in translation; Dryden tried his hand at it, as did Pope and also Wordsworth; in addition many lesser men have provided versions which were not so much translations as tinkerings with the text. But we have now a version of *The Canterbury Tales* by Nevill Coghill which is admirably suited to the needs of the general reader, for it is in good English verse which suggests Chaucer's own without striving for quaintness; it is the work of a lover of Chaucer who is also a scholar; it carries the minimum of notes, and it reads superbly.

Its virtues do not end there. It is also possible to get it, in the Penguin Classics, for eighty cents. If you want a more elaborate book you can, without extreme trouble, get it in two volumes, as published by the Folio Society, with a leather-and-cloth binding, and woodcuts by Edna Whyte (which I personally would be glad to spare, for they are ugly). In whichever form you get the book, you have a splendid experience before you, because it is one of the most entertaining, rich, bottomless books in English.

Mr. Coghill began his version of the *Tales* in 1946, at the request of Stephen Potter, for broadcasting on the BBC's Third Programme; so popular was this first venture that during the next four years more and more Chaucer was called for, and by 1951 the greater part of the work had been offered in this form to radio listeners. There exists a series of four LP gramophone records taken from the broadcasts.

The project of broadcasting *The Canterbury Tales* exactly suited the peculiar genius of the Third Programme; a company of remarkable actors was assembled, chosen for their widely divergent tones of voice and for qualities of poetic intelligence; they all possessed, not the curious bleat called an Oxford accent (though why, since it is rarely heard at Oxford or among really educated people anywhere, I cannot tell), nor yet the fluting, epicene note of the West End actor, but good, clear speech with a country flavour to it. The *Tales* were so arranged that one or two Narrators carried the story, and other actors spoke the lines given to specific characters. In addition there were a few very good sound effects. Thus simply but strongly provided, the broadcasts were given, relying upon the genius of Geoffrey Chaucer first, and upon the capabilities of the BBC very much second. The result is poetic in the highest degree, moving, exciting, uproarious, gripping and vivid.

Only the BBC could have done it, for only the BBC, among the broadcasting organizations of the English-speaking world, is willing to trust an author—in this case Chaucer *cum* Coghill—to know his business. Most broadcasters are nervously doubtful of an author's ability to tell a story, and of the patience of listeners in hearing a story. No doubt they have their reasons, though I think that some of these are unworthy, and are based upon insufficient experiment. But in this instance Chaucer came through magnificently, and the BBC proved the doubters wrong.

Mr. Coghill has given us an excellent modern version of *The Canterbury Tales* which will amuse and enrich everyone who reads it. It may, perhaps, lead a few people to approach the original, braving even such guardian dragons as Skeat and Robinson. In tackling Chaucer in the original, there are well-marked stages of progress; first, mystification; second, a dawning, when the fourteenth-century English seems suddenly to dissolve into great music and good sense; third, a disillusion, when the reader finds that his understanding is not so perfect as he thought it was in the second stage; fourth, fuller understanding, which is always in danger of toppling over into pedantry.

Yet, if the reader does not try to read Chaucer in the original, much that is splendid will be dark to him, for though the *Tales* may be the best of Chaucer they are not by any means the whole of him. Beauties lurk in those crabbed, queer lines which, when we have found the key, speak to us across five centuries with a wonderful, illuminating eloquence. But, for a beginning, here are *The Canterbury Tales,* and of them alone we may say as John Dryden did, "Here is God's plenty."

Saturday Night, 13 April 1957

The Painter's Eye /
The Nude

"*A*rt is one of the necessities of life; but even the critics themselves would probably not assert that criticism is anything more than an agreeable luxury—something like printed talk." The voice is the voice of Henry James, and the sentence quoted is from the conclusion of a short piece which he wrote about the great wrangle between Ruskin and Whistler.

James professes to have a warm admiration for Ruskin, but there is plenty of evidence that he wearied of the portentous judgements of the Master, and sometimes regarded him as an intrusive literary man, seeking to capture in words what is better done with brush and pencil.

"One may read a great many pages of Mr. Ruskin without getting a hint of this delightful truth: a hint of the not unimportant fact that art, after all, is made for us, and not we for art. This idea of the value of a work of art being the amount of entertainment it yields is conspicuous by its absence." These were hard words for a man of thirty-five to direct against the great Panjandrum of British art criticism. But James, while not a particularly exciting critic, was not afraid to say what he thought; he dared even to say—writing of an exhibition of the impressionists in 1876—"the effect of it was to make me think better than ever of all the good old rules which decree that beauty is beauty and ugliness ugliness, and warns us off the sophistications of satiety." And the curious thing about this last-quoted judgement is that it has about it quite the ring of Sir

Kenneth Clark, whose large book *The Nude* I have been reading with the keenest interest.

Let us first finish with James, however. His criticisms of pictures have been gathered into a pleasant book called *The Painter's Eye,* edited by John L. Sweeney. They will please those who will never be content until they have read, and fletcherized, every word that James ever wrote. Others, like myself, will be glad to read how certain famous but now outmoded pictures (*The Blind Girl,* by Millais; *Milton Dictating to His Daughters,* by Johnson; Whistler's *Portrait of My Mother; The Annunciation,* by Burne-Jones; *The Death of Sardanapalus,* by Delacroix) impressed a sensitive critic when they were the latest thing. James' good sense never seems to have failed him, and it is high praise to say that he wrote of pictures at a very sticky period in the history of painting, but not a single one of his judgements seems today to be merely fashionable. He was not a great critic of painting, but he was a remarkably level-headed one. And, of course, his greatness lay in a very different technique of representation.

Sir Kenneth Clark has claims to be regarded as a great critic, and as we read this expansion of the Mellon Lectures which he gave in Washington in 1953, we see very plainly why. Breadth of sympathy is balanced by minute scholarship, and decided preferences are controlled by tolerance; judgements are expressed firmly, but with modesty, and at all times Sir Kenneth remembers what Ruskin forgot—that art is made for us and not we for art. What is more, he writes in a good prose style which is, for an art critic, nothing short of a miracle—for a group of fellows more inclined, as a general thing, to hang themselves in their own rhetorical garters, never set pen to paper. *The Nude: A Study in Ideal Form,* is in every respect a remarkable book.

It is refreshingly free of cant. Sir Kenneth makes short work of the notion that a picture of a naked woman is not indeed a picture of a naked woman, and that anyone who thinks it is so is an unrefined beast.

"No nude, however abstract, should fail to arouse in the

spectator some vestige of erotic feeling, even though it be only the faintest shadow—and if it does not do so it is bad art and false morals," says he. And, later, he presses home the point: commenting on the widely-touted notion that a nude model is simply a form or an arrangement of planes to the artist who paints her, he says, "does this not involve a certain callosity or dimness of response? To scrutinize a naked girl as if she were a loaf of bread or a piece of rustic pottery is surely to exclude one of the human emotions of which a work of art is composed; and as a matter of history, the Victorian moralists who alleged that painting the nude usually ended in fornication were not far from the mark. In some ways nature can always triumph over art."

On the other hand, though a nude may arouse erotic feeling, that is only one of its properties; awe, pity, exaltation and ecstasy may also be expressed through the nude figure as through no other subject possible to painting or sculpture. It is, furthermore, the one mode by means of which artists have been able to give form to the Ideal; nowhere is this more clearly shown than in the innumerable paintings, good and bad, of the Crucifixion; a clothed Christ on the Cross is unthinkable, not for historical reasons, but because the supreme sacrifice of the Son of God is made trivial by draperies.

For the same reason a clothed Venus is hardly a Venus at all; the Ideal Beloved must be shown in the form which centuries of artistic trial and error have shown to be evocative of the highest sensations of awe, admiration and desire.

A full discussion of this brilliant book would require more space than this article affords, and I must be content to mention some of the problems it discusses and clarifies. What it has to say about the medieval approach to the nude through the Gothic concept of art reveals, to me at least, beauty in scores of paintings which had formerly seemed inexplicably ugly and inept. Equally interesting is the change from the tradition of idealizing *the nude*—using the human form as a starting point for a creation dedicated to beauty—to the comparatively modern tradition of commenting upon *the naked*—as in Rouault's and Picasso's pictures of prostitutes.

The nude is an artistic form which was once of supreme value; our age has not yet found a valid means of restoring that value by painting beauty, and seeks its own expression through wry comment and distortion.

This is an odd aspect of recent art history, but Sir Kenneth does not explore it. Indeed, what he does not say in this study provides a table of contents for another big book. All that large field which is explored in Anton Ehrenzweig's *The Psycho-Analysis of Artistic Vision and Hearing,* for instance, is untouched. And just as well, too, for it is the uncluttered quality of Sir Kenneth's book—the adherence to a straight and important line of argument—which gives it special value. This is a work which ought to be in every library in Canada; perhaps, after twenty-five years or so, it might silence the recurrent hubbub about nude paintings which is a feature of our national life. Yes, they are erotic. Yes, madam, the painters are often naughty men, and the models are sometimes bad girls. But there are elements involved in the painting of the nude which draw upon what is highest in art and express what is highest in mankind. Now, may we please look at the pictures?

Saturday Night, 27 April 1957

Tess of the d'Urbervilles

*I*t is twenty years since I read a novel by Thomas Hardy, and I seized with eagerness upon the opportunity which was presented to me by Macmillan's, whose first ten volumes in their new paper-backed reprint library include *Tess of the d'Urbervilles* and *Far from the Madding Crowd*. When I first read Hardy I admired him conventionally, but I do not think he is a young man's novelist; reading him when, in Shakespeare's phrase, "Time hath sowed a grizzle on my case," I see him a master among English novelists. What has made me change my tune?

To the young reader, the first impression of Hardy is that of a contriver of melodramas; his plots are often stagey. What could be more melodramatic, in the most conventional nineteenth-century style, than *Tess*? A simple, beautiful country girl is seduced by a flashy villain complete with silky black moustache, whose first words to her are, "Well, my Beauty, what can I do for you?" and who later gloats, "Ha-ha-ha! . . . what a crumby girl!" She has a child, which she christens Sorrow before it dies. She falls in love with a clergyman's son, and after great inner debate, she writes him a letter in which she tells him of her earlier affair—but by a trick of fate he does not get the letter. Therefore she tells him on her wedding night, and he—with a callousness which makes us detest him—throws her over. When, after she has borne degradation and hardship, her seducer appears again and tempts her back to him, the husband returns and she, betrayed a second time, kills the seducer, and is hanged. If we see only the plot and the stilted conversation, we feel little of the power of the book.

Time, however, teaches us a thing or two. One of its lessons is that the plots of melodrama are shop-worn for the excellent reason that they contain deep truths; they have been rubbed thin by trashy writers, who have understood them superficially, but for the masters they are still the very fabric of life itself. Anybody who has lived forty years in the world and kept his eyes open, knows that girls are very often seduced, not because they are stupid, but because they are trusting, and that the men who seduce them are often, like Alec d'Urberville, less wicked than emotionally unstable. Prigs like Angel Clare are by no means uncommon, though nowadays they have a different line of scruple. And a train of unhappy events, once set in motion, is virtually impossible to check.

Coincidences, like Tess' lost letter, no longer trouble me in fiction; life provides coincidences so startling that no novelist would dare to use them. Not all people, perhaps, but certainly some people, live curiously fated lives, in which they seem doomed to carry out actions which bear no relationship to ordinary probability, and are dictated by necessities which have nothing to do with common sense. *Tess* is melodramatic, sure enough, but so is life. Twaddle as we may about free will, some of us are bound to live lives in a context of farce, some in comedy, some in proletarian realism, and some—unhappy wretches—in tragedy.

It is the sense of tragic inevitability which Hardy brings to his melodramatic story which makes his novel great. We may say, as contemporary critics did, that he often writes clumsily, that his dialogue is often stilted, and that he sometimes piles on the agony to a degree which brings his structure dangerously close to farce. But when we consider the total impact of *Tess*, and the great passages of description, of pastoral beauty, and of tragic splendour, we can put the faults in perspective. We know, when we have finished it, that we have read a great book.

In his admirable book of criticism *Mirror in the Roadway*,

Frank O'Connor is not too generous to Hardy. But O'Connor, a great realist himself, favours the realists, and Hardy is not a realist. It is easy to think him one, especially if the reader is town-bred, for the descriptions of nature, of farm-life and of daily happenings are seemingly as minute as a realist could desire. When we read that the milkmaids at Talbothays Farm often had flecks of cow-dung on their faces, from being swished by cows' tails as they worked, we may think it realism if we do not reflect too clearly about the matter. But the realist, splendid as he is, commits himself to what a reader may be persuaded to decide for himself, whereas the romantic or tragic novelist is determined to tell his reader what to think. It is in this realm, where he presents his own attitude toward Tess' story, that Hardy's great qualities of understanding, irony and compassion are revealed. It is easy for the young reader, through no fault of his own, to miss them, for they are not qualities which have as yet manifested themselves strongly in his own life.

Hardy was fifty-one when *Tess* appeared, and there is something to be said for reading a great novel at an age which is within hailing-distance of the author's age when he wrote it. It gives the reader a better chance of apprehending—no, not the author's thought, for a young reader can do that very well—but his intensity and quality of feeling. For though the young are quick to feel emotion within a limited range, there are intensities of feeling and perception which come later, and which are often demanded by the writings of mature authors. It is certainly true that, where feeling has never been strong, it often dwindles to emotional triviality in middle age; but where feeling has been powerful in youth, and has been cherished and cultivated, it broadens and deepens the pleasure and emotional satisfaction which art can give when youth is past.

Saturday Night, 22 June 1957

Lolita

Vladimir Nabokov's reputedly scandalous novel *Lolita* has at last been published in the U.S.A., and the ban has been removed from its entry into Canada. It has been greeted with laudatory notices, as well it may be, for as this department said of *Pnin* (May 11, 1957) Mr. Nabokov is a writer "elegant, distinguished and profound." Indeed it has been the opinion of the present reviewer since he read some of Nabokov's early sketches in American magazines that Nabokov is among the best writers of English now living.

What is *Lolita* about? Why did so many American publishers refuse to bring it out? Why, when the Olympia Press published it in Paris in 1955, was it banned by the French government, though the French high court later quashed the ban? (There is no need to ask why it was banned in Canada; an American ban on a book brings a prompt me-too from our tremulous Customs.) The secret is out, now; *Lolita* is about a man whose sexual appetite is confined to girls between nine and fourteen. He is not a monster or an indiscriminate ravisher; he is desperately in love with his Lolita; this novel might very well have been called *By Love Possessed,* for Humbert Humbert is a man in the grip of a demon. His obsession, though not rare, is one upon which society frowns, though in the world of fashion and advertising "little-girl" appeal is frankly exploited.

Books about men gripped by sexual mania are common; incest, homosexuality, satyriasis and whatnot are always cropping up in novels which, clumsy though they may be from a literary point of view, are often greeted with solemn commendation. The attitude of the authors of such books reminds me of the story about the little boy who burst into his mother's living-room, eagerly exclaiming—"Hey, Ma! We caught a toad, and we bashed him and squished him and put him through the lawn-mower until"—seeing that the parson had come to tea—"until God called him Home." They are liberal of gaudy incident and sickening clinical detail, but they are careful to abhor what they record. This attitude is called "sincerity" and is immensely valued by critics and readers who want to eat their nasty cake and deplore it too. Nabokov will not play this disingenuous game, and he has written *Lolita* as a comic novel.

Why not? The line between tragedy and comedy is a thin one, as many a bad performance of a stage tragedy has shown. So thin is it that some writers of special insight—Chekhov, Ivy Compton-Burnett, Joyce Cary—have made that borderline their special realm. What tragedy of the first order lacks its comic overtone? What comedy of great stature lacks a root in tragedy? *Othello* and *The Merry Wives of Windsor* have a common theme; *Don Quixote,* the comedy, draws hotter tears than *Faust,* the tragedy. The difference between comedy and tragedy is one of viewpoint, not of subject.

Life is a comedy to those who think, a tragedy to those who feel, says Horace Walpole, but it is not quite true. Nabokov feels for his ridiculous, obsessed pursuer of little girls, and he makes us feel, too. Humbert Humbert is a man of intelligence in the grip of a mania which he knows to be reprehensible, but which he cannot help; he is also the toy of those ridiculous, farcical elements in life to which we are all a prey, but of which we are usually happily unconscious. His plight is comic, and it is as high comedy that it is presented.

If the Lolita whom Humbert Humbert pursues, and for whom he makes a scoundrel, a doormat and a fool of himself had been an innocent child, debauched by a grown man, we might well have shuddered. Before the war the late Stephen Haggard wrote a novel about the reciprocated love of a man for a charming girl-child, and although it was done with skill and tenderness, it made me squirm. But Lolita is not innocent. She is a shrill little gold-digger who has already, at twelve, lost her innocence to a thirteen-year-old tough whose mother runs a girls' camp; it was not a seduction but a co-operation. When Humbert at last gets her to himself, it is she who seduces him. Incredible? Ask any candid magistrate.

Who is the victim in this relationship? Lolita, who grudgingly exchanges what she does not value for unlimited ice-cream, sight-seeing, and travel, or Humbert Humbert, who exchanges money, time, and self-respect for the favours of his darling? Lolita makes him toe the mark by threats of exposure and prison; Humbert keeps her somewhat in check by counter-threats that, if he goes to jail, she goes to reform school.

From one point of view, she is victim, and he a monster: but with equal truth, she is the exploiter, and he the slave. The comedy of their situation lies in the fact that, according to convention (and law is, and must be, conventional) he is grossly culpable and she a legal "infant," unaware of the nature of her actions; but their situation is so unconventional that we must pity Humbert, enthralled to her body and soul, whereas she regards him with neither affection nor distaste.

When she runs away from him, it is not to escape her servitude but to exchange it for a more promising one. And when we last see Lolita, now seventeen and married to a dull young fellow, with a probable fifty-five years of life with her extremely limited self stretching before her, we feel a spark of pity for her, for the first time. Humbert we have pitied from the beginning, for while he is a madman in a sense, his madness is of that unmercifully incomplete kind which creates deep wretchedness, as well as hilarious comedy.

Why so much fuss about this book, which does not contain a single dirty word, or a scene over which the lascivious may gloat? Perhaps the explanation appears in the adjectives applied in these pages to *Pnin*—"elegant, distinguished and profound."

Nabokov writes with style, and style—as distinguished from verbal and syntactical foppery, which is sometimes mistaken for it—gives a dimension to a book which can be disquieting when exercised on such a theme as this. Many authors write like amateur blacksmiths making their first horseshoe; the clank of the anvil, the stench of the scorched leather apron, the sparks and the cursing are palpable, and this appeals to those who rank "sincerity" very high. Nabokov is more like a master sword-smith making a fine blade; nothing is amiss, nothing is too much, there is no fuss, and the finished product must be handled with great care, or it will cut you badly.

Like the late Bernard Shaw, he writes as if every reader were as intelligent as himself, and this is disquieting to some intellects; nevertheless, this is the real sincerity, not to be confused with the fake sincerity which springs from clumsy craftsmanship and simple-mindedness. Virtuosity, so much admired in some other arts, is at present unfashionable in literature. Can it be that those who feared the book and banned it, felt that something really horrifying—something far beyond the anthropoidal sim-plicities of *Peyton Place*—lurked beneath the gleaming surface of *Lolita*?

Saturday Night, 11 October 1958

Origins

*F*rom time to time I receive pamphlets offering to help me enlarge my vocabulary. There is nothing personal about this, I am sure; it is merely that my name seems to be on a lot of strange mailing-lists. I always read the pamphlets, but I have never yet subscribed to the course, or bought the book, because these vocabulary-enlargers want me to memorize lists of big words which I shall then be able to use instead of little words, and that is not what I am looking for. I should greatly like to enlarge my vocabulary; I should like to have a vocabulary as big as Shakespeare's, which somebody has estimated as comprising about a quarter of a million words; but simply memorizing new words will not suffice.

What my vocabulary needs, before it is broadened, is deepening. I need to know more about the words I already use, before I add exotic growths like "adscititious" and "eleemosynary" to it. It is easier to use a word well if you know something about its history and family, and if your education included very little Latin and no Greek at all, as was my case, this can only be done by prayerful searching of the dictionary.

Any good etymological dictionary will do, but I have recently acquired a special one, called *Origins;* it is the work of the English scholar Eric Partridge, to whom I am already deeply indebted for his magnificent *Dictionary of Slang and Unconventional English. Origins* was published last year by Routledge and Kegan Paul in England, and although I have had time only to glance at it, I know that it is up to the high Partridge standard.

An efficiency expert would probably say that it does me no good to know that "polka" comes not from the Polish word *Polka,* meaning a woman of that race, but from the Czech *pulka,* meaning a half-step. But I defy efficiency experts; I have yet to meet one who wrote really good English. I delight in such knowledge. It cheers me to know that "polecat" comes from the Middle English word for a "poultry cat," because the creature was fond of *poules,* or fowls; *poule* is from the Latin *pulla,* which is the feminine of *pullus,* a barnyard fowl.

It is the common words which have the really interesting histories. I rarely need "abyssopelagic" or "galactopoiesis" or "thalassophobia," but I am pleased, as a father myself, to know that the English word "Dad" is linked with the Welsh *tad,* Russian *tata,* the Latin *pater* and its diminutive form *tata,* with Greek *tata,* and that they all stem from the Sanskrit *tatas.* As for "Mama," it has an equally wide connection in Latin, Greek and Celtic, and crops up even in Egyptian and Australian aboriginal dialects. Let Dr. Spock and the contrivers of formulas make of it what they will, the word means "breast."

As for vegetables, "radish" comes from Latin for root, "carrot" from Greek for a head, and "lettuce" from Latin, meaning the milky herb, because of its white juice; "potato" comes by way of Spanish from a now extinct Caribbean language called Taino.

Does anybody look in a dictionary without checking to see if the forbidden four-letter words are included? Partridge, whose excellent work *Shakespeare's Bawdy* has done so much to extend my enjoyment of the Bard, is not a man to shut out these expressive monosyllables. They are all of extremely ancient origin; if weight of ancestry carried as much prestige in language as it does in society, these words would be at the very top of the tree, with Dad and Mum. They trace their family trees back through Old High German, Latin and Egyptian, to Indo-European. *Lady Chatterley's Lover,* instead of calling forth the contemptuous sniffs of the righteous, might serve as an introduction to etymology in our schools.

Words which have a reasonably straight line of descent are exceptional; most of them steer a twisting course. "Rankle," for instance, looks like a simple word with a good sound and a useful meaning, and we do not associate it with dragons. Yet it comes from the Latin *draco*, meaning a dragon; in Middle Latin *dracunculus* meant a little dragon, and the term was applied to fiery sores, abscesses and ulcers; when this word was adopted in medieval French as *raoncle* it was an easy step to the verb *rancler*, meaning to fester or trouble in the mind, and from that comes "rankle." It pleases me, when something rankles in my own mind, to liken it to a small, fiery, poisonous dragon.

Modern prose is full of such little dragons. The other day I was dismayed to see in a newspaper that two highways "junctionized" at a particular point. And last Sunday I saw, cast in immortal bronze, a statement that a property had been "gifted" to the public by a man now dead. Fiery dragons, both of them, and they rankle in my mind still.

This winter I expect to spend many a happy hour with *Origins*, and what I hope from it is not a widening, but a deepening, of my comprehension of the words I use. The effect will probably be to make me a curmudgeon, from the Shetlands dialect word *curmullyit*, a dark, ill-favoured fellow, hence a grumbler.

Toronto Daily Star, 10 October 1959

A Book of Characters

A man of letters who deserves to be better known on this continent is Daniel George. I am constantly meeting people who would be certain to take great pleasure in his work, but who have never heard of him. He does not write novels or essays; his books might be described as miscellanies of entrancing information which he has uncovered in his wide reading. He follows in the footsteps of Isaac D'Israeli (father of the statesman), who wrote several volumes with such names as *Calamities of Authors* and *Quarrels of Authors* which are full of meaty, scandalous reading; but in my opinion Daniel George goes beyond D'Israeli, because his sense of humour is more acute and his gifts as an anthologist are superior. I have had great pleasure from repeated readings of his books, and I suggest that you might like to have a look at them.

Daniel George's real name is D. G. Bunting, and I believe that he was for many years a reader for the publishing firm of Jonathan Cape. (A reader, if you are unfamiliar with the term, is a man who reads and makes reports on manuscripts for a publisher; many distinguished men of letters have done such work, and it can only be entrusted to someone of first-rate critical ability, coupled with a kind of sixth sense which whispers intimations of success.) So far as it is possible to make his acquaintance through his books, Daniel George lacks that air of being too fine for this gross world which is the mannerism of so many men of letters; his taste is sprightly, his humour earthy,

194

his curiosity insatiable. He seems ready to read anything, however unpromising it may appear, and if there is a pearl in a neglected old book, he will find it.

He has just published *A Book of Characters,* the subtitle of which is *Impressions and Portraits in Writing of Famous, Infamous, Remarkable and Eccentric Men and Women with Sidelights upon Them at Various Stages of Their Singular Careers.* It does not lend itself to gobbling, greedy reading, but it is a wonderful bedside book and it is in this way that I have been reading it, savouring a half-dozen characters every night before going to sleep. He has extracted his "characters" from contemporary accounts of them where possible, and from early descriptions when no contemporary record is to be had, but the book is not a mere compilation; it is in the variety of people included, and the way in which their oddities are played off against one another, that Daniel George shows his quality.

What sort of people are they? There is Viscount Sackville (1716–85), who paid great attention to the music in his parish church, and once rebuked a chorister during service by shouting, "Out of tune, Tom Baker!" There is Charles Jervas, the painter (1675–1739), who was so vain that when he copied a picture by Titian he thought he had improved on the original, and "with parental complacency cried, 'Poor little Tit! how he would stare.'" There is Hipparchia, wife of the philosopher Crates, who was so infatuated with her husband that she "made no scruple to pay him the conjugal duty in the middle of the streets." There is the 8th Earl of Bridgewater (1756–1829), who used to send his dogs out for rides in his carriage, and have special boots made for them; he himself never wore a pair of boots twice, and must have been a boon to the trade. There was Sir William Petty, who, though blind, once challenged Sir Aleyn Brodrick to a duel in a dark cellar, with axes. There are misers, usurers, quacks and scoundrels of all sorts, as well as a good sprinkling of noble and worthy men and women, including St. Nicholas, who was so holy that even as an infant he refused to suck at the breast on fast-days.

The book is a splendid survey of human character—not fool-ish eccentricity but sturdy idiosyncrasy. It is refreshing to read it in an age when character is less common than it used to be and when, instead of such monuments of individuality as these, we are offered mere hot-tempered family tyrants like Clarence Day's father, and Egg-and-I cuteness, for our delight. Democracy, which is supposed to set all men free, has in many respects put all men into chains of bourgeois uniformity; we are free to be exactly like everybody else. Where today is there a Parliamentary reporter like Mark Supple, who bawled out from the press gallery, during a silence, "A song from Mr. Speaker!"—causing William Pitt to roll off his chair with laughter? Who, like George Selwyn, would travel any distance to see a hanging? There will be many people who will say that we are better off without such oddities. Yes, certainly, much better off; eggs are healthier if eaten without salt, too.

Toronto Daily Star, 16 January 1960

Clean and Decent

*H*ow often did your grandfather take a bath? How often do you do so yourself? Are you aware that in the city of London, England, one person in five never bathes from birth to death? If these matters, and all that concerns plumbing and the disposal of sewage, are of interest to you, I heartily recommend Lawrence Wright's book *Clean and Decent,* which carries the subtitle *The Fascinating History of the Bathroom and the W.C.* I have read it with keen interest and great amusement.

It has changed some of my notions about plumbing and history. The Middle Ages, it appears, could offer a degree of cleanliness and comfort to the rich which was far ahead of anything known in the sixteenth, seventeenth and eighteenth centuries. Rome, in the fourth century A.D., had eleven public baths and 856 baths in private houses, as well as 144 public conveniences (which last figure puts to shame virtually every city on this continent today). The Roman water supply was based on a use of 300 gallons per head of population daily; what city offers so much now? Did you know that Puritanism went hand in hand with dirt, that Oliver Cromwell put a 100 per cent tax on soap, and that the repeal of the soap-tax was one of the most popular acts of Charles II at his Restoration? Did you know that many of the romantic "declines" and inexplicable deaths from "fever" in the nineteenth century were caused, in actual fact, by bad drains?

Mr. Wright's interest in these matters arises from the fact that he is an architect. He has inspected hundreds of plumbing and water systems, and pored over plans of castles and monasteries to discover the secrets of the past. He is by no means happy with our modern bathrooms, which he says fall short of real practicality, and are sadly lacking in individuality of design and ornament.

It was in ornament that the bathing facilities of the past were rich. Instead of the universal chilly whiteness of today, bathtubs in 1900 offered a bewildering choice of designs. The wash-basin, likewise, was an elegant creation and the W.C. was decorated with patterns of mulberry leaves, acanthus, magnolia, and might be mounted on a classical pillar, a dolphin, or even a crouching lion. Our modern affairs work better, but as ornament they have nothing to recommend them.

The psychology of bathing, as he traces it, is of great interest. The bath, almost until this century, was regarded as a form of "treatment," and the bather was likely to be referred to as "the patient." To bathe the whole of the body was an adventure rarely undertaken; the feet, the hips, the chest and arms, were best bathed separately for fear of weakening the system. Abandoned women were rumoured sometimes to take complete baths, but as they used crystal tubs, or tubs shaped like shells, it was clear that they were up to no good. In the nineteenth century a "slipper bath" with a high back might be lugged to the bather's bedroom, and hot water carried to it, so that he could have his bath in front of the fire; it must have been very pleasant. There were eccentrics like the aged Marquess of Queensberry who bathed in milk and, it was rumoured, sold the milk afterward to unsuspecting lovers of that over-rated drink.

An odd nineteenth-century enthusiasm was the Sitz Bath, which was said to strengthen the hips and their environs, and which could be taken without removing completely any part of the clothing save the coat. Vapour baths and steam baths were taken on the advice of a physician, and the shower-bath, or cold douche, was resorted to only in extremes. It was thought to be capable of killing the patient, as indeed it sometimes does, to this day.

The W.C. took about a century to reach its present state, and the tale of its evolution makes macabre reading. But those who seek its story alone would be well to look at John Pudeney's little book *The Smallest Room*, published in 1954. The philosophy of cleanliness is brilliantly explored also in Reginald Reynolds' fine book *Cleanliness and Godliness*, published in 1946, which ends with an eloquent plea to modern man to stop dumping sewage into his watercourses, and to process it for return to the soil, as is done by the wise people of Milwaukee. Of these three books, Reynolds' is my favourite, but as an exposition of technique and design, Mr. Wright's is its superior.

You don't want to read about sewage? I am grieved but not surprised. One of the shameful incidents in the history of man as a supposedly clean animal is that the W.C. was invented by Sir John Harington, Queen Elizabeth's godson, in 1596, but it did not come into use for three hundred years—all because of people who were too refined to give their minds to such things. But if, on the other hand, the subject interests you, Lawrence Wright's book offers great pleasure.

Toronto Daily Star, 11 June 1960

The Gormenghast Trilogy

Considering that fiction is free to roam where it will, writers are disappointingly fond of well-travelled roads. Most of them shy away from anything that looks like exploration or experiment. They reflect the taste of millions of readers, whose chorus is "Tell me the old, old story." This is not said in contempt of the great, undying themes of all fiction—love, war and death; what I complain of is that love, war and death are written about so often in the old, dull ways.

Readers and critics seem, on the whole, to be unprepared for anything that is unusual in fiction. Since 1946 Mervyn Peake, known chiefly as an artist and poet, has published three volumes of an extraordinary novel; the books are called *Titus Groan* (1946), *Gormenghast* (1950), and *Titus Alone* (1959). Some critics in England have praised it; critics in the U.S. have, so far as I know, neglected it. Very few people I meet have ever heard of it. Yet it is that most unusual thing, a novel conceived entirely as an imaginative creation, owing nothing to contemporary life or history, written by a poet in a brilliant and varied style.

The first volume was described on its title page as *A Gothic Novel,* thus relating it to those tales of horror of the late eighteenth and early nineteenth centuries, of which *Frankenstein* is probably the best known. The description is misleading. There is plenty of horror in the book, but horror is not its staple; it has fine humorous passages, and the tone of the book is a blending of adult fairy-tale with irony. The first of these books, good though it is, is not so good as *Gormenghast,* the second volume; there is a startling and meaty novel, if you happen to have tired of dreary tales of adultery in suburbia, of the despair of illiterates who have never known hope, of pin-heads who fear that they are incapable of love, or any of the other stock themes of modern fiction.

No brief description of Mervyn Peake's books can give a satisfactory idea of their quality. The plot is simple: Gormenghast is a huge and remote earldom ruled by the family of Groan; the Groans are ruled by complex, inherited ritual, and the days of the Earl and his family are lived in strict accordance with the orders of a master of ceremonies; change is unthinkable. To the scholarly seventy-sixth Earl, Sepulchrave, and his bird-loving Countess, is born a son, Titus. In time the child inherits his father's title and rebels against the circumstances of his life. At last he leaves Gormenghast behind him and goes out into the world, which he finds fully as arbitrary, as dominated by irrationality, as packed with eccentrics, as the family domain. In the end young Titus re-visits his home, only to leave it again, knowing that he will never be free of it in his heart.

Such a skeleton of the plot gives no idea of the richness of the books. Gormenghast is peopled with fantastic creations; the castle is a city in itself, riddled with passages that everyone has forgotten, people who are rarely seen, containing even a complete boys' school, with a large staff, as one of its lesser appurtenances. The Earl is its titular head, but the real rulers are Flay, the valet, Swelter, the chef, and Sourdust, the master of ceremonies—succeeded in time by his son Barquentine, a malignant dwarf. The loneliest and most neglected creature is the Lady Fuchsia, the Earl's older child and one of the most interesting heroines in modern fiction. The atmosphere of Gormenghast is that of Fuseli's drawings come to life.

As sometimes happens in novels full of highly coloured characters, the central figure is the one least successfully brought to life. Titus Groan is a minor creation in this army of oddities. Mervyn Peake's best character, in my opinion, is Steerpike, who begins as a kitchen-boy at Gormenghast, and by a hair-raising career of intelligence, craft and ruthlessness, rises at last to be master of ceremonies and real ruler of the castle. Steerpike is a magnificent adventurer, and in the third volume *Titus Alone* we feel the want of him very badly.

This is a long novel, and Mervyn Peake is not able to keep his invention at the highest pitch all through it. He is a painter as well as a writer, and his extended passages of description are masterly—but now and then they are a drag on the action. You must take this long book as you find it; here is no neatly carpentered, simple tale, but a great, walloping gallimaufry of imagination, thrilling adventure (the fight between Flay and Swelter, in which Earl Sepulchrave perishes, is the best fight I know of in modern fiction), poetry, humour and sheer inventive exuberance. It asks for an unusual response in its readers, but it rewards them with riches so strange and wonderful that they are worth twenty times the effort.

Only a handful of men in a century are capable of writing such works. They do not please critics who cannot forget *Madame Bovary,* but they have qualities which we cannot live without, and when the tide of fashionable trash retreats, they are left standing high above the surrounding wastes.

Toronto Daily Star, 17 September 1960

Centuries

*I*n these times of crisis I am astonished that we have heard nothing from the friends of Nostradamus. Though he died in 1566 he has never lacked for interpreters; surely they have been searching his *Centuries* for light on the troubles in Berlin, just as, twenty-two years ago, they sought for prophecies about Hitler?

Nostradamus was the Latin name assumed by Michel de Notredame, a French physician and astrologer who was born in 1503; he seems to have been a good doctor, and showed great bravery during outbreaks of plague at Aix and Lyons. But his fame is based on the *Centuries,* a book of rhymed prophecies he published in 1555; it took the fancy of Catherine de Medici and Charles IX, and gained him a court appointment. The book has been a favourite ever since with that numerous class who "seek unto them that have familiar spirits, and unto wizards that peep and that mutter." There was quite an outbreak of books interpreting the *Centuries* in the early forties.

Certainly his admirers have been able to establish Nostradamus as a prophet. Some of his quatrains contain remarkable forecastings of the changes in government in England from his own day until the Commonwealth; even more remarkable are the allusions to the French Revolution that occur at the proper place in his book. But like so many prophecies, they are easier to understand backward than forward; the *Centuries* work best when we solve them as some people solve crossword puzzles, with the solution ready to hand.

For example, Oliver Cromwell is said to be meant when "Lonole" is written; this name appears to be an anagram of a Greek word meaning "The Destroyer." (I cannot go along with those enthusiasts who say it is an anagram of "Old Noll.") But what if one regards Cromwell not as a Destroyer, but a Preserver? All interpretations of Nostradamus are incorrigibly Tory in tone. Against this sort of dubious stuff we may set the striking line

Senat de Londres mettront a mort leur Roy

which is perfectly plain, and sounded wildly improbable until it came true on January 30, 1649.

During the last war the admirers of Nostradamus were busily at work, and found plenty of "rains of fire," "armies in the sky" and the like to satisfy them. But an unbiased reader must admit that his prophecies became vaguer and more general the farther they extend from his own day. I have been thumbing through the *Centuries* to see if I can find anything about the astronauts Titov and Gagarin, without success. But the interpretation of prophecy has never been my line. Still, one might have expected an astrologer to have a special interest in new appearances in the heavens.

Sixteenth-century French offers special difficulties to most of us, but there are translations of the *Centuries*. A favourite is that of Charles A. Ward, completed in 1891. I cannot find out anything about Ward, though the dedication of the book to his mother is couched in terms that mark him as a very odd fellow; this lady, we learn, was "queen-like" and had already "the heaven-bleached raiment of immortality put on" when the book was finished, and offered to her spirit by her "earth-hampered" son. It is difficult to warm to Ward.

A more appealing book is *Nostradamus or the Future Foretold* by James Laver (1942); he brings intelligence and a moderate scepticism to his task, and concludes that "Nostradamus was a true prophet." Very well, but of what? Mr. Laver writes persuasively of J. W. Dunne's theories, as contained in *An Experiment with Time* and *The Serial Universe,* but these do not help us with such stuff as Century II, verse 43: "During the appearance of the comet, the three great princes shall be made enemies; struck from heaven, peace to the trembling land, Po, Tiber waving, a serpent placed upon the shore."

Only a very bold man would dismiss Nostradamus; his record is impressive, even though we seem fated to understand him retrospectively. Prophecy is out of fashion among intellectuals, but so, we must sometimes feel, is reason. What makes us smile when his name is mentioned is the way in which hopeful people fly to his book in times of crisis and find in it principally what is of comfort to themselves. Has any true prophet ever brought comfort? Are they not, almost by definition, specialists in misery?

Toronto Daily Star, 30 September 1961

Franny and Zooey

Such reviews as I have seen of J. D. Salinger's *Franny and Zooey* have dealt gingerly with the theme of spiritual awakening, which seems to me to be the heart of the book. Reviewers are understandably chary of discussing spiritual matters; as intellectuals of our time they have probably grown up in an atmosphere of agnosticism, and overt spirituality either repels or frightens them; if they show themselves sympathetic to such themes they may find themselves claimed as bedmates by neurotics of all sorts. But what are they to do with Salinger, whose *The Catcher in the Rye* has already found itself on Religious Knowledge reading courses in several universities? The fact cannot be evaded that Salinger writes about religion as unmistakably as George Eliot.

In his latest book Salinger confronts us with Franny Glass, a highly intelligent Irish-Jewish girl who has become obsessed with a prayer which she has found in a Russian book called *The Way of a Pilgrim;* in it a peasant seeks the counsel of a holy man, whom he asks to tell him what the Bible means by its injunction to pray incessantly; the holy man tells him that if he will repeat "the Jesus Prayer" often enough, it will at last become a part of his very being, and bring great blessings with it—not blessings of riches, but of understanding and love. The Jesus Prayer is "Lord Jesus Christ, have mercy on me, a sinner." Franny attempts to follow this advice, becomes ill and unstrung, and is at last persuaded by her brother Zooey that all life, lived in

206

humble striving toward the best we know, is prayer and sacrifice.

Such a novel puts the critics in a difficult spot; some of them must either desert the sceptical position they have so long occupied, or reject Salinger, whose reputation is dear to them. Theirs is the uncomfortable position their fathers were in when Aldous Huxley, the cynic's darling, wrote *Eyeless in Gaza,* a book of unmistakable religious implication, in 1936. We live in an age when strong faith in a literary man can be embarrassing to thousands of his admirers.

There is good reason for it. Older readers and students of literature know how many moistly pious books used to be written by authors whose own spiritual depths could have been plumbed with a foot-rule. Religion can be an intellectual mannerism, practised for gain. But *Franny and Zooey* is anything but trivial in feeling. Its appearance in the same season as Patrick White's fine *Riders in the Chariot* suggests that we may possibly be at the threshold of a new religious manifestation among literary men comparable to that of the thirties, when so many writers embraced Roman Catholicism. The latest movement seems to be toward mysticism and private devotion.

There is little to comfort the conventionally religious in either of these books; they are not in the pink-taffy tradition of the novels of Hall Caine. There is much to discomfit the conventionally irreligious among the intellectuals; nobody is such a bigot as the hard-shell atheist. The intellectually supple reader, however, will find much in both Salinger and White to arrest and challenge him.

I was sorry when Zooey convinced Franny that she should abandon the Jesus Prayer. The whole matter of prayer would make a splendid theme for a fine novel. It is astonishing how widely the idea of prayer is misunderstood, even among practising Christians. Prayer as Petition they know, and prayer as Intercession; but prayer as Contemplation (which I take the Jesus Prayer to be, if carried to its true end) is not widely understood except, presumably, among monks and nuns whose chief task in life is Perpetual Adoration. What Zooey urges on his sister is, in effect, the old dictum that "to work is to pray." Yes, but there are more adventurous modes of praying, and Franny seemed to have seized on one of them.

What do we mean by prayer? Surely the thing that we most desire, with a yearning that is never silent, is our truest prayer— be it money, or power, or something of a more spiritual nature than either of these. If Franny had continued with the Jesus Prayer for several years, what would have happened to her? I wish Salinger had tackled this fascinating theme. He is one of the very few living novelists with the imagination and spiritual insight to attempt such a story. It is a theme that might daunt a Tolstoy or a Dostoevsky, but a writer who succeeded in exploring it, even in part, might give us a very great novel.

Toronto Daily Star, 21 October 1961

Mr. Olim/The Prime of Miss Jean Brodie

I had just finished reading Ernest Raymond's *Mr. Olim* when the October 14 issue of *The New Yorker* arrived containing Muriel Spark's fine long short story *The Prime of Miss Jean Brodie*. These works share a theme—the influence of a teacher of strong and eccentric personality on those taught. They also suggest two lines of thought: first, that Miss Spark is one of the most interesting writers to appear in the past ten years, whereas Mr. Raymond, who has been at the job for at least thirty years, and brings considerable gifts to it, has never really established himself as belonging to the first rank; second, that boys unquestionably respond to education differently from girls, and that perhaps it is a mistake to try to educate them together.

In *Mr. Olim* Ernest Raymond throws a light mantle of fiction over a real person, the Rev. Horace Dixon Elam, of St. Paul's School, London; he was, it appears, a man who felt himself neglected by fate, and who lavished the gifts of his mind and cultivation (which were uncommon) on his classes, accompanying his extravagant embroideries on the curriculum with rich abuse and indiscreet personal confidences.

Miss Jean Brodie, teaching in a girls' school in Edinburgh, also felt herself cramped by the prescribed lessons, and enlarged the minds of her classes by confession of her love affairs, her tastes in art, and her Fascist politics. She created an elite within the school, she demanded unswerving loyalty to herself, she became for a time an ideal to her chosen few.

But mark what happens. When Mr. Olim's pupils have grown to man's estate they give a splendid testimonial dinner to their old master, praise him generously, reduce him to tears, and enshrine him in their hearts as one of the important influences of their early years. Whereas Miss Brodie's girls, at about eighteen or so, outgrow her, drift away from her, and one of them betrays her to the headmistress, so that she is discharged.

Both stories make it clear why Mr. Olim and Miss Brodie came to such different ends. Boys are educable; they are prepared to take ideas and ideals from an older man, which they either swallow whole or transmute into something of their own; when the process is over, they are grateful to their teacher. Girls, after sixteen or so, are ineducable; they learn, but they are their own teachers, or else they learn from men with whom they are in love; they have little gratitude toward the women who set them on their road in life.

Perhaps this explains why scholarships and endowments are usually the work of men, and why women (even when they have plenty of money) so rarely choose to part with any of it for purposes of education. Both sexes learn, unquestionably, but they appear to learn in very different ways. Men can learn from teachers; women seem to prefer to learn from life.

How influential they are, some of them, these men and women who teach! I emphasize the word "some" for when I look back on my schooldays I find years at a stretch which must have been spent under the guidance of teachers whom I do not remember at all. Others—especially three women who taught me before I was twelve—live glowingly in my recollection, though all are dead now. Later, when I was taught by men, I seemed to encounter three principal groups—the Brutes (a few), the Dismals (many) and the Bombshells, for whom I shall carry an unaltered affection to my grave. The Brutes and the Dismals would have been misfits in any profession; they were people crippled or bruised by life. But the Bombshells were the born teachers; I could not always learn from them because I had arid patches in my brain that nobody could cultivate, but I knew how good they were, and sometimes I pitied them as they struggled with my ineptitude, casting their pearls before a sorrowful swine.

There were two or three Mr. Olims in my collection and also a few male counterparts of Miss Jean Brodie. These latter wanted to be not only teachers but god-like lawgivers to their pupils. Unhappy men! Their disciples were so soon grown up and off to work or the university to find new heroes. But the Mr. Olims, who never tried to chain us, never insisted on loyalty, and frequently told us what nuisances we were, won a love which does not perish. It seems to be a paradox of teaching that the teacher must lose his pupil in order to hold him forever.

Toronto Daily Star, 4 November 1961

Sir Aylmer's Heir

*L*ast May, in a London shop, I found a book I had not seen for forty years but which for two or three weeks in my boyhood so dominated my life that I recognized it with a pang, as though I had met an old sweetheart, quite untouched by time.

It was *Sir Aylmer's Heir,* by Evelyn Everett-Green; date of publication, 1890. As I re-read the story I wondered what its magic could have been. Why was I enthralled by it at the age of nine? True, it was about a boy of that age, but as different from me as daylight from dark. Yet I had yearned to be like him. So long as that ambition lasted I was, I am sure, intolerable. What could have possessed me?

The hero of this child's novel was no Huck Finn, no Holden Caulfield. He is little Eyton Desborough, whose mother was dead, and whose soldier father had sent him home from Gibraltar to live with his uncle, Sir Aylmer, in the family mansion. But Sir Aylmer was travelling abroad, the mansion was falling to ruin and apart from a kindly housekeeper the child's only companion was King, a gigantic bloodhound, who immediately recognized in him the Desborough blood.

News comes that Eyton's father has been killed in Egypt, fighting for the Queen. Shortly afterward Sir Aylmer returns, a morose, haggard aristocrat, with a mysterious illness which he quells with a dangerous drug. He is startled by Eyton's appearance, and fights his growing attraction to the child. Soon we know why: Sir Aylmer and little Eyton's father had sought the hand of a beautiful girl, and the younger brother won her; since then Sir Aylmer's life has been but a husk.

Then the magic begins. Eyton is submissive, loyal and loving under all his uncle's rebuffs; in a short time he has brought Sir Aylmer back to the Christian faith, and has launched him on a cold-turkey cure for the dangerous drug. (When flung into the fire it burns blue, and the bottle curls horribly.) At last, to make a fascinating story short, Sir Aylmer regains his health, puts the mansion in order, builds almshouses in memory of Eyton's mother and settles down to be a model country gentleman, radiant in the company of his nephew, whose resemblance to the dead sweetheart grows almost hourly.

The style of the book is remorselessly genteel. Eyton never eats; he "discusses" his food. On the other hand, he "devours" all the works of Sir Walter Scott—sixty-four volumes, excluding works of editorship, by my count. He also finds time to ride his pony, Red Rover, play touchingly on his mother's Cremona violin and teach the groom to read and write. Yet Eyton is no little pedant; he confesses frankly that for a boy of nine he does not know much Greek, though his Latin is adequate. At Christmas he does not receive a single gift, but gains immense spiritual refreshment from the sacred season.

How can I have admired Eyton Desborough? Frank O'Connor has written brilliantly about the influence on his childhood, passed in a Cork slum, of English tales of private-school life, in which boys lived by standards of honour and stoicism impossible to him, and repellent to his companions. Was I moved to reverence this child merely because he was so unlike myself—a normally greedy, rebellious boy who discussed books and devoured food?

Re-reading *Sir Aylmer's Heir* has uncovered the secret, I think. Eyton Desborough is nothing less than the Archetype of the Miraculous Child, as described by C. G. Jung. This archetype transfigures those lives in which it manifests itself. Its appearance heralds changes of character, usually of a favourable kind; it brings hope and redemption. The Miraculous Child has passed out of favour; we expect children in fiction to be like real children.

The Victorians, however, knew thrills beyond the stubby-fingered grasp of realism. Little Lord Fauntleroy is one of these archetypal children. Evangeline St. Clair in *Uncle Tom's Cabin* is another, though her death heralds a decline in the fortunes of those who knew her. Little Nell, who also dies, has completed her work of redemption before she does so. Our forebears understood these creations, so unlike real children, because they were more sensitive to their meaning than we permit ourselves to be. Those critics who make sport of Little Nell have completely missed the point.

There is another strong element in this book, described on the title page as *A Tale for Boys,* which does not appear in fiction recommended for the 8-to-12 of our day, and that is sex. *Sir Aylmer's Heir* boils with it. There is the rivalry of the brothers for the hand of Eyton's mother, a rivalry described with gusto. Eyton himself has recollections of a small sweetheart, Eva Daubenay, whom he wants to kiss; at the end of the story two girl cousins come to live with Sir Aylmer and his heir, and Eyton looks forward to high old times with Cousin Letty, who is fifteen and very pretty. And of course Sir Aylmer, faithful to his dead love, has his heir, who is her living image, except for the small matter of changed sex. Boy readers would not understand all of this—I know I did not—but anyone who thinks that they would not sense its piquancy has forgotten childhood.

Isn't that a dainty dish to set before a boy of nine? No wonder it persisted in my memory as an enriching, if ill-understood, influence.

New York Times Book Review, 14 January 1962

John Cowper Powys'
Novels

*I*s it possible for a writer of genius to be overlooked in our day, when so much critical attention is paid to literature in all its forms?

Indeed it is, and in evidence I bring forward the case of John Cowper Powys.

We have had plenty of time to take notice of him; he will be 90 next October; his most recent book was published in 1959. During the past forty years occasional articles praising him generously have appeared in influential publications. But in what may be called "official criticism"—that which sets the fashion— he has been almost entirely neglected. The most recent important history of English literature, by David Daiches (1961), does not mention him; the last volume of the *Pelican Guide to English Literature,* called *This Modern Age,* ignores him. Yet this is a man of whom an American critic has written, in the *Times Literary Supplement:* "The failure of all but a handful of English readers and critics to perceive that John Cowper Powys stands beside Hardy and D. H. Lawrence among the masters is a scandal."

How do we define a writer of genius? Shall we call him a man of extraordinary intellectual and imaginative power, whose work is strongly marked with individuality? Powys meets this definition as truly as Lawrence and Hardy. He is akin to them, without in any sense copying them. Like Hardy, he writes of the countryside rhapsodically, with a detailed knowledge a naturalist might envy. Like Lawrence, he writes of the uncontrollable torrents of passion that work below the surface of the human spirit. He is not so pessimistic as Hardy; he never scolds or grows weak and shrill, as Lawrence does. He has his own faults; sometimes his prose is so knotted that the reader must struggle with it; he has no spark of humour. But he is worth a struggle, for to read one of his books seriously is to undergo a deeply stirring experience. He must be numbered among those rare authors who add to our range of understanding.

My own favourite among his novels is *Owen Glendower,* which appeared in 1941, but I can see that its concentration on Welsh history makes hard going for many readers. (Powys, in spite of his name, is not a Welshman; his family has been resident in England for 400 years.) The most popular of his novels is *A Glastonbury Romance* (1933); its theme is a Passion Play, presented at Glastonbury in Somersetshire, by a strangely assorted group of local actors; the drama brings to a climax passions which are more pagan than Christian. Recently praise has been heaped on a novel with a similar theme by the Greek writer Kazantzakis; good though it was, Powys' novel seems to me to be greatly superior.

A Glastonbury Romance asks for a serious reader. It sets out with a paragraph which makes clear that what follows will be tough chewing. There are long passages in which the reader can only abandon himself to the author's heaving prose, hoping that in a page or two he will come to safe harbour, or at least get his bearings. But what thus puts the reader at sea is not padding, or incoherent "poetical" writing; it is the intense vitality and scope of the author's feeling. After a few chapters the reader finds his bearings, and unless he is of a rock-like nature, he will begin to experience and understand the story in the same mode of heightened feeling as John Cowper Powys.

One of this writer's finest books is called *In Defence of Sensuality* (1930); it is an appeal for the fuller use of all our senses, in order that we may become aware of the beauty around us; the colour of a stone, the light that falls on the surface of a puddle, the sounds that are to be heard when we seem to be in the midst of silence, the smells which are never absent—Powys calls for recognition of these in order that we may live in a state of real awareness. Inevitably, if we school ourselves to seek beauty everywhere, we shall also find sights and sounds that are ugly, smells and tastes that disgust—but the new treasure of beauty must be bought at this price.

Similarly, as we read his books, we are asked to become imaginatively aware of things we have not considered; at first we may laugh, or feel distaste, or perhaps merely be puzzled. But a great writer makes great demands. If we fail to give what he asks, it is we who are left the poorer.

John Cowper Powys is a writer of our time who has asked extraordinary things of his readers. He is like nobody else, and he has had no imitators. He is snubbed by those critics who love "schools" and "trends" and "influences." He is obstinately great, deeply loved by those readers who know him—and out of fashion.

Toronto Daily Star, 27 January 1962

The Young Visiters

A comment in this "Diary" has brought me a quantity of hopeful correspondence. I said that the letters of Edith Thompson, who was hanged for murder, were the work of a "born writer." How, my correspondents ask, does one spot a "born writer"? Quite undeterred by the fact that it was Mrs. Thompson's literary gift that brought her to the gallows, they are anxious for confirmation of a talent which they suspect in themselves, or in someone dear to them.

One query is from a woman whose son, aged nine, writes unusually pleasing letters. Is he a writer? It is, I am sorry to say, quite impossible to tell.

Literature is an art almost without child prodigies. Most writers are past thirty before they have shown what they are made of, and their compensation is that the gift, once proven, lasts as long as life itself. The work of writers over seventy often shows a decided cooling in passion, but it may gain a compensatory, silver radiance; and of course, like Thomas Mann's, their last work may rank with their finest.

Very young writers are usually freaks. The only one to whose work I return with enthusiasm is Margaret Mary Ashford, better known as Daisy Ashford. Her best-known work is *The Young Visiters, or Mr. Salteena's Plan,* which she wrote when she was nine, and it is an undoubted, if inadvert, comic classic. It is not widely known that she wrote *A Short History of Love and Marriage* when she was eight, *The True History of Leslie Wood-*

cock when she was eleven, and *The Hangman's Daughter* when she was twelve. After that, so far as we know, she wrote nothing. Burned out at twelve, we must assume.

Daisy Ashford offers splendid evidence to support those who think that children should be allowed to read anything and everything. She seems to have been particularly fond of the novels which were popular during her childhood, at the end of the reign of Queen Victoria. Theirs is the form she adopts, theirs the social attitude she accepts as normal, theirs the prose she imitates and improves.

Perhaps her work would never have been known if J. M. Barrie had not been shown the manuscript of *The Young Visiters;* he was entranced by it, and arranged for its publication with a preface by himself, in 1919.

The Young Visiters is about Mr. Salteena, described as "an elderly man of 42," whose gnawing regret is that he is "not quite a gentleman." In the hope of acquiring polish he persuades the Earl of Clincham (who has apartments in the Crystal Palace) to take him as an apprentice; the obliging Earl introduces Mr. Salteena at Court, where he meets the Prince of Wales (later Edward VII), whose royal eye immediately pierces the disguise, and wrings from Mr. Salteena a confession that his father was a butcher, though his mother (a Miss Hyssops) was of grander birth. The Prince approves of Mr. Salteena's ambition, and in the end he gets an appointment at Court, even though the Prince explains that "being royal has many painfull drawbacks."

But this is not all of the Salteena Story. He loses his love, Miss Ethel Monticue, to the younger, handsomer, better-born Bernard Clark. Daisy Ashford's command of the language, and conduct, of lovers, is astonishing in a writer of nine. Because she is innocent of the mechanics of sex, though deeply imbued with its spirit, she throws her lovers into situations which only an adult can fully appreciate. Bernard Clark and Ethel, for instance, share apartments from the time of their engagement, and return from their honeymoon of six weeks with "a son and heir a nice fat baby called Ignatius Bernard."

It is as a stylist and phrasemaker that Daisy Ashford shines. One of Bernard's ancestors is "a Sinister son of Queen Victoria"; when he proposes to Ethel she replies, "I certainly love you madly you are to me like a Heathen god"; he in turn tells her that "no soap could make you fairer." The Earl, who is democratic, says that high birth and breeding are "as piffle before the wind," but Mr. Salteena feels that without them life is "but sour grapes and ashes."

This splendid gift of words disappeared, apparently, at twelve. Perhaps it was just as well; literature has room for only one Shakespeare.

Toronto Daily Star, 17 March 1962

The Tale Bearers

With this volume of collected literary essays V. S. Pritchett throws out another wing on the substantial edifice of critical writing he has built during his long lifetime. It is an excellent house, something of a random house, and a comfortable if rather austere house. Because it is very much an English house it is sometimes cold, but it is spacious and the views it affords are extensive. The wing that preceded it, called *The Myth Makers*, was admirable, and this is just as good, and the two taken together form a pleasing unity.

These are called essays, rather than book reviews, although many of them deal with particular works by writers ranging through Saul Bellow and Mary McCarthy among the moderns, through Kipling and Conrad among those of an earlier day, and extending backward as far as Pepys, Swift and the Lady Murasaki. Among the subjects are no-nonsense—well, *almost* no-nonsense—types like T. E. Lawrence and Edmund Wilson, and there are exotics like Max Beerbohm and Frederick Rolfe. In every instance the opinions are fresh without being eccentric, the writing is beautifully achieved without being obtrusively so, and the judgements classically balanced, by which I mean that all the writers are judged by the same high, necessarily general standards, and there are no obtrusions of enthusiasm.

This is not to say that the critic is cold, but only that he is never carried away. Himself a writer of fine fiction, he does not fall victim to the love-or-hate relationships which sometimes betray less experienced and less widely-read critics. He is an ideal reviewer. His judgements will stand.

To test this quality, I "proved" one of his criticisms by the method arithmeticians use to prove problems. That is to say, I worked backward from the solution to the problem, from the criticism to the book, and found it just and correct in every detail. The book I used was Angus Wilson's *No Laughing Matter,* which I had not read since it appeared in 1967; I re-read it in the light of the criticism in *The Tale Bearers* and found that criticism to be just, perceptive and illuminating. Just, because it puts its finger on a quality of excess in the book which is enjoyable though perhaps artistically self-indulgent; perceptive, because it dwells on Wilson's brotherhood with Dickens and Fielding in the histrionic quality of the novel; illuminating, because it summed up judiciously what a very good novel it is in a way that I, as a reader, could not have done for myself. This is criticism in a fine, often misunderstood tradition.

Every editor knows how hard it is to get good reviews of new books, because the circumstances of modern periodical publishing do not allow editors to pay enough for the work. Publishers and the public want reviews as soon as possible after publication, and the people who rely on reviewing for an addition to their income want to do as many reviews as they can. The result may sometimes be lively journalism, but may also be slapdash, cheaply effective and hard on the authors, though not, in some cases, as hard as a thoughtful, long-pondered review might be. This is especially true of the reviewing of fiction; it is easier to find someone to do an expert's review on a book of fact or opinion than to find a reviewer who is truly sympathetic toward a work of art, which is what serious fiction aspires to be. There have been reviewers like Arnold Bennett and Alexander Woollcott whose exuberant good word could make the fortune of a book and its writer when first it appeared, but it is instructive to inquire where most of those books, so quickly praised, are today. To look at a list of the best sellers of 20 years ago is melancholy work, and we are grateful for a book like the present one which talks of books most of which are 20 years old, more or less, and which are as good as, if not better than, when they were new. Criticism like that of V. S. Pritchett is a fine balance in the hurly-burly of weekly publishing.

Critics like Pritchett belong to the small body of serious lovers of literature who will not compromise with standards that reach beyond the enthusiasms of the immediate present. This is not to say that they are out of sympathy with what is new, and judge all writing, as did a schoolmaster under whom I once suffered, by the yardstick of Addison. But they do attempt to discern a pattern and a reasoned growth in literature—to detect it rather than to impose it on their sole authority. Thus they may sometimes seem a little cold, as is V. S. Pritchett when he writes about Edmund Wilson, who was never cold. But Pritchett helps us to see Wilson better, and Wilson loses nothing of his essential quality under such examination, though he is shorn of some of his testy *ipse dixit* authority. Pritchett sees that the dandyism of Max Beerbohm cloaks a steely nerve and a gimlet eye, that the humanitarianism of E. M. Forster springs from an essentially indecisive spirit and that the mannerist prose of Rolfe is the perfect expression of a unique, one-book talent. All this is achieved with justice; the whip and the butter-tub have no place in his critical equipment, and when he puts on the red robe and the full-bottomed wig of the judge we acknowledge his right to wear those fine critical habiliments.

This is not the sort of criticism that brings a fortune or millions of readers, but it has its recognition and its reward. Since 1975 he has been Sir Victor Sawdon Pritchett, knighted for his services to literature. A proud accolade, and in his 80th year we are happy indeed to salute Sir Victor and thank him for what he has done.

Washington Post, 25 May 1980

Rites of Passage

The deep satisfaction we feel in reading and reflecting on William Golding's novels rises from his power to isolate, describe and make real to us moral problems that concern us all. The notable moralists of our day are novelists and poets. Philosophy is remote from the average intelligent person, and the churches rarely command his allegiance, but for all that he is eager to come to grips with serious problems of morality. Much popular fiction offers him nothing but a reflection of the easy, fashionable despair of those who paddle timidly in the shallows of experience, but William Golding tackles moral problems head on, and wrestles them to the floor.

How does he do it? His mind possesses a coherent, compassionate but unsentimental attitude toward life and mankind, and his scale of values, though not inflexible, is firm. In the broad sense of the term it is a religious mind, because it is engaged with the great themes of our existence and will not be content with easy, pessimistic approaches to them. Too often pessimism is achieved by ignoring whatever cannot be made to fit its needs. His reflections present themselves to him in the form of fiction, and here again he is not satisfied with the bonelessness that contents those contemporary writers whose novels remind us of Edward Lear's flopsican mopsican Bear. He brings a formidable professionalism to his writing, and his novels have the completeness that marks them as works of art.

His latest book, *Rites of Passage,* takes the form of a journal kept by a young man who is traveling to Australia during the early days of the 19th century. Edmund Talbot—a name suggestive of aristocratic family—is writing of his experiences at the behest of his godfather, a nobleman (the Earl of Shrewsbury, perhaps?) who has obtained for him a post on the staff of a colonial governor, and who wants an amusing chronicle of the long voyage as a partial return. Talbot begins in an affected manner, designed to please a man of fashionable but not trivial intellect, but as his voyage progresses, he grows in understanding of himself, because he is engaged in a moral problem. It concerns another passenger, the Rev. Robert James Colley, who also discovers something important about himself during the first 50 days of the journey, and dies—literally wills himself to death—because of it. Colley's wretched end sobers the rest of the ship's company, but this new sobriety serves only to make them even more unmistakably themselves. Contained in Talbot's journal is a long confessional letter written by Colley to his sister; the truth of Colley's destruction is not told there, because Colley was never fully aware of it—only of a portion of it.

Could Talbot have saved Colley by showing him a little more friendliness? There is Golding's moral problem and a fine one it is. Of course it is not a novelty to isolate a group of people on a ship and show them as they are, but every fictional device is new when it is handled with mastery, and that is precisely the quality Golding brings to it.

His splendid professionalism shows in the skill with which he takes the device of the personal journal and the letter, so familiar from the fiction of the period he has chosen for his story, and gives them convincing period quality, while at the same time insinuating into them a kind of insight which is post-Freudian. But these insinuations are never obvious; we never feel that the 20th century is nudging the 19th or that our age is pretending to some absolute superiority in judging human affairs.

One of the marks of the novelist of the first rank is his capacity for what might be called impersonation, the ability to speak through a character in such a way that more is revealed than the character is directly aware of; young Mr. Talbot, who writes of himself as if he were a silly, snobbish young ass, comes off rather better than he could know. Colley, who writes as a man who has removed himself from all that is dark in man's nature, provokes our pity. He is a man who has never seen his Shadow, and who is depending on his clerical rank and his feverish piety to overcome an inborn inferiority. He hopes to attain gentility through sanctity, an idea that could only occur to a fool.

Here is where Golding will rub some of his readers raw, for it is not a fashionable attitude to suppose that some people are naturally inferior, not in birth but in character. But this book anatomizes snobbery, that peculiarly English trait, in a manner that hints that snobbery may sometimes be a response to a genuine intuition, as is the case with Talbot.

Although there is plenty of ambiguity in this novel, there are no loose ends; everything is present that enables the reader to draw extensive and possibly profound conclusions about what happened, and why, and whether or not it was inevitable. The whole book is written with a fine economy. It seems to move easily and, when Talbot is writing, somewhat self-indulgently, but there is nothing unnecessary at any point; every joke, every scrap of flattery addressed by the godson to his noble patron, tells us something we need to know. The minor characters are drawn with a certainty of line and occasional enriching with color that reminds us of the pen and red chalk drawings of the period in which the story is set.

This is very good Golding, and good Golding is among the best fictional currency we have. Its hallmark is a suggestion of hope, and that is a rarity in serious modern novels, so many of which are blighted by what old theologians called "wanhope," by which they meant despair of salvation. But not William Golding: he is not so Graham Greene as all that.

Washington Post, 2 November 1980

The Hotel New Hampshire

There is something of Byron about John Irving. Not only is it that he woke after the publication of *The World According to Garp* to find himself famous, but the extremity of his opinions and the nervous violence of his language recall that intemperate nobleman, and, like Byron, he would certainly say that love is no sinecure. Indeed, nothing in life is easy for Irving's characters, and in his five novels the still, sad music of humanity rises to the orgasmic uproar of a rock band.

Is this the New Romanticism? The acclaim that greeted *Garp* suggests that the author has found the keynote of at least a large portion of our romantic age. When he appeared in my city to give a reading some time ago, he was greeted by an audience of women who threw the keys of their hotel rooms, and in some cases their panties, onto the stage, as they shrieked their admiration. This surely recalls the response to Byron, and the cult for Franz Liszt, whose cigar butts were snatched up in the street, and whose chair seat was on one occasion cut out and preserved as a relic by an admirer who must have been somewhat lacking in humor.

Those who admired *Garp* will find the new novel, *The Hotel New Hampshire*, very much to their taste. Irving has expressed himself strongly on the subject of reviewers, so I shall not commit the reviewer's sin of spilling the beans about his story. It is enough to say that it is in the powerful, reader-coaxing mode of his earlier books, and recounts the adventures of the Berry family, two parents and five children, as they seek some kind of repose in three hotels, two in New Hampshire and one, named for that state, in Vienna. Repose is not, of course, what they find, but they achieve a rueful fatalism, a stoicism that reconciles the four survivors to life.

The Irving bench-marks are all here: body-building, bears, Viennese whores, rape and the pleasures of sexual intercourse. It would be unjust to call this "the mixture as before," because it is fresh and newly invented. Irving is unusual among modern novelists because his mind has a determined color, and he writes of certain themes in all his novels not because he cannot think of anything else, but because these themes seem to him to have overmastering importance. To the present reviewer they seem to boil down to a romantic insistence on the supremacy of passion and a desire for poetic justice.

Passion, of course, is everywhere acknowledged. To desire something is to have it or be broken in the pursuit of it, and those who do not feel this impulse are necessarily secondary characters in the drama of life. This is now, and always has been, a principal ingredient of the romantic attitude.

Poetic justice, however, is much less widely recognized for what it is. As the courts become more lenient in their treatment of evildoers, urged in this direction by the popular humanitarianism of our time, there builds up below the surface of millions of minds a yearning to see evildoers get their lumps, and to get them in the coin in which they themselves traded. The murderer must die by his own weapon, the adulterer must lose his sexual power, and the rapist must himself be raped. This is a romantic attitude, but it has deeper roots; as Irving employs it, poetic justice takes on an unmistakable Old Testament character. Let them suffer as they made others suffer. Not a pretty doctrine, but it gives a warm glow in those dark caves of the spirit to which humanitarianism has not penetrated.

John Irving has obviously not achieved his position by dealing in trivialities. He has said his say about "new fiction" and does not seek to do anything new with language or form. Indeed, in some respects he appears to have retreated, and the wrap-ups which finish *Garp* and the new novel, in which the fate of every character is revealed, are reminiscent of some of the Victorians.

Conventional, also, is his insistence in the new novel on the magic of his heroine, Franny Berry, who becomes a film star and sex-symbol. But where Little Nell and Little Dorrit were extreme in their submissive virtue, Franny is extreme in her self-will and her violence of speech. She uses the bleakest words associated with scatology and sex to address her intimates as well as her enemies; but words grammarians call "intensives" when overused end as "privatives," and the supposedly irresistible Franny becomes a common scold. She must surely be the most foul-mouthed heroine in all of fiction, and as Little Nell and Little Dorrit are incredible in their virtue, so we think that Franny is incredible in her hysterical speech. She seems also to be inordinate in her sexual appetite, and demands of her brother exertions that put Casanova, who thought six orgasms at a session his best work, quite in the shade. Of course, John Berry is an iron-pumper, in the gym as in bed. We reviewers are expected to speak the truth as we see it; therefore it must be said that like Little Nell and Little Dorrit, Franny is interesting as a character in romantic fiction, but as a portrait of a woman she is not a success.

During the time that I was reading the complete works of John Irving, I read Leon Edel's *Henry James* for diversion, and inevitably reflected on the wholly disparate artistic attitudes of the two writers. Just as it is impossible to think of James describing a woman as "the best-looking piece of ass in all Vienna," it is impossible to think of Irving tip-toeing solemnly around a scruple, like James. The one delights in retention: the other lets it all hang out. James' plots proceed by indirection; Irving's tramp stolidly forward, and sometimes his novels seem less novels than chronicles. James used language like a drowsy balm; Irving uses it like a firehose connected with a rather dirty main.

What a lot they could have learned from each other! What splendid heart-to-hearts they may yet have in Elysium!

Washington Post, 6 September 1981

Mantissa

*H*ere is a splendid *jeu d'esprit* by John Fowles, which will give delight to anyone who is truly fond of literature, though it may cause annoyance to readers who have little sense of humor.

The book cannot be called a novel, for it has no story to tell. The title is not fully explanatory, and will baffle those to whom a mantissa is a fraction of a logarithm. But if we go to the greatest dictionary of them all, the Great Oxford, we find that a mantissa is "an addition of comparatively small importance, esp. to a literary effort or discourse"; it is interesting that the illustrative quotations this dictionary offers to show how the word has been used are all from theological works. What Fowles has given us is no trifle, though it is not physically bulky, and not theological in any ordinary sense of the word.

It reaches toward the world of the gods, however, for it is about the relationship of an author with his Muse, in this case Erato, traditionally associated with erotic poetry (and geometry, for these Muses were versatile), whom Fowles thinks most likely to be interested in the modern novel.

Erato appears in several guises, and in all of them her concern for erotic poetry, or anything simply erotic, is amply apparent. Her occasional associate, in the mind of her author, is Persephone, or Kore, who turns up in the book as Nurse Cory, a beautiful Barbadian who is simpler and more generously erotic than Erato, who occasionally appears as the minatory Dr. Delfie.

As you can see, it is a book of some verbal complexity, and you have to be wide awake as you read it.

It will be helpful if you examine the jacket carefully before you begin. It carries an etching by Picasso, named *Sculptor and Model*. A female figure, plainly a goddess, though a lesser one, is looking at herself in what may be a mirror or possibly a portrait; she wears a chaplet of flowers, appears well pleased with what she sees, and although from the waist down she is white, from the waist up she appears to be black. Gazing at her, with slightly weary, proprietorial eyes, is a large naked man, handsomely bearded. When you look at the author's photograph on the back of the jacket, you see that this mythological figure might well be an idealized portrait of John Fowles. But the third element in the Picasso is what may be a head fallen from a broken statue, or it may be another rendering of the head of the sculptor, for its gaze is intent, perplexed and by no means pleased.

As indeed the sculptor, or the author, has every reason to be in the book, for Erato, or Dr. Delfie, is as distracting, capricious, tender, critical, admiring, captious, bossy, yielding, cold, hot and in every way such a mingling of opposites that one might say there was no knowing where to have her if it were not that the author (whose name is Miles Green) seems to manage pretty capably in that respect. The relation between author and Muse is a powerfully erotic one, although that is not all there is to it, and here again Erato is tease, prude, tough expert and untouched virgin in a series of bewildering changes.

What is the book about, you are asking. It is about what I have been describing, it is about how an author—or better say how Miles Green—encounters and is inspired by his Muse, and it is quite the liveliest description of this fairly common encounter that I have ever read.

Muses are usually dealt with respectfully, not to say gingerly, by poets and prose writers who speak of them at all. In the 19th century there were many pictures of the Poet, seated at his desk, preparing to write something (with a quill) dictated by a female figure of asexual aspect who hovered at his shoulder. Muses were to be heard, but not touched.

Not so in *Mantissa;* Erato is touched, and indeed sometimes thumped, and in her turn she lands several shrewd blows on the author whose inspiration she is. Not only do they fight and make love; they talk, splendidly and entertainingly, and Miles Green's attempts to bring Erato up to date on the latest developments in the novel are hilarious, particularly those in which he explains the necessity for the thickest and most impenetrable existentialist gloom.

There is little here to give comfort to academic devotees of the latest fashions in the novel, or to the earnest proponents of Women's Lib. Erato is a partner, and sometimes senior partner, in what Miles Green writes, but she is not herself a writer. She is the Eternal Feminine, who does not need to be freed because she has never been bound, though now and then she is sat on, and for good reasons.

The book is a splendid lark, but no trifle. It is the best possible evidence of the relationship between John Fowles and his own Muse that he can spin a web like this which is so light, and yet so strong.

Washington Post, 19 September 1982 .

The Essential Jung

This is by far the best introduction to the work and thought of Carl Gustav Jung now available. I wish it were possible to require that every teacher and critic, cleric and cocktail-party magus who takes the name of Jung upon his tongue should have read Anthony Storr's admirable compilation at least once, for untold misunderstanding and unwarranted assumption would be saved thereby.

The book takes the form of a chronological anthology of selections from Jung's large body of work—his Collected Works extend to 20 big volumes and are not yet complete—connected by brief explanatory notes contributed by Storr. Thus Jung speaks for himself, but in a single convenient book his extraordinary range of exploration and speculation is given a coherence which is otherwise obtainable only by those who have wrestled with his own writings, through which there is no straight path.

Jung was not a graceful writer like Freud, whose work translates so readily into English; in Jung the full Teutonic tangle confronts the reader, whether in German or English. He has two styles: the first is his formal manner, when he writes academically, and this is not easy; the second is his conversational style, recorded from his lectures and seminars, which were often in English, idiomatic and accomplished in the main but sometimes vague in the way lectures tend to be, when they are amplified by the speaker's intonations or his expression. For all but the most devoted student, a guide is needed, and here it is.

Jung is misunderstood because so many readers judge him as the blind men in the fable misjudged the elephant; they grasp some special part of his enormous bulk and take it for the whole. Often, too, they simply will not take the trouble to understand what he has said (never easy) and throw terms such as "archetype" about carelessly, without having troubled to distinguish an archetype from a stereotype. Still others assume that Jung was really Freudian in his outlook, but had added some woozy, boozy notions to Freudian thinking that can be used to support almost any sort of pseudo-psychiatric nonsense about myth and the world of the unconscious.

These people are mischievous, but perhaps no more mischievous than the devoted Jungians who have solidified Jung's ideas into a system, which they proceed to apply rigidly to several regions of human behaviour. Neither Freud nor Jung devised systems, though Freud was unquestionably dogmatic. Both men knew that only Ulysses can draw the bow of Ulysses, and that to be either a true Freudian or Jungian requires at least some hint of the quality that distinguished the genius of the originator. Nature, said Jung, is unrelentingly aristocratic, and careful study of Jung will not give the mediocre student his scope or daring. Both Freud and Jung have suffered much from their disciples. Jung himself once said: "Thank God I am Jung, and not a Jungian."

Careful study, however, will enable an intelligent person to trace the mazes of Jungian thought, and to see what light it throws on a wide variety of human concerns. At root, Jung's conception of the human mind is broader and less reductive than Freud's, and the two men quarrelled irreparably because Jung would not recognize infantile sexuality as the basis of all later experience. This refusal makes all the difference in the application of the thought of either man to the problems of neurosis. Freud considered that after 45, psychoanalysis could do nothing for a neurotic: Jung was convinced that 45 was roughly the period of life when its immensely important second development began, and that this second period was concerned with matters which were, in the broadest sense, religious.

Many people are put off by this attitude. They want nothing to do with religion and are too lazy or too frightened to accept the notion that religion may mean something very different from orthodoxy. They attach themselves to the notion that Man is the centre of all things, the highest development of life, and that when the individual consciousness is closed by death, that is, as far as they are concerned, the end of the matter. Man as the instrument of some vastly greater Will does not interest them, and they do not see their refusal as a limitation on their understanding.

The anthology and explication under review leads the reader as gently as possible through Jung's ideas about the nature of human consciousness, and the separation of mankind into extraverted and introverted types, varying greatly in their approach to experience. From this the move is to the recognition of the Unconscious as a vital element in experience, and the Collective Unconscious as a definition of what lies beyond the merely personal and distinguishes man—though not entirely—from the animal and inanimate world. The Archetypes are not patterns, but inescapable conditions of experience, not themselves to be defined and manifesting themselves in human destiny. From this, the movement is toward a definition of what Jung means by "integration," the achievement of wholeness in life which is not simply moral betterment but a recognition of whatever can be recognized about individual existence.

Moral betterment is not a Jungian aim; wholeness, rather than goodness as orthodox religion defines it, is man's aim. As another great psychologist puts it, in the mouth of a whole, but not wholly admirable, character:

> This above all: to thine own self be true
> And it must follow, as the night the day
> Thou canst not then be false to any man.

Not false, but not necessarily a Pollyanna or a Helpful Hannah, either.

It is in this realm that Jung falls foul of Christianity, which makes perfection its impossible goal. In his relations both with Catholicism and Protestantism, Jung insists that evil is a reality, and not simply a temporary absence of good. He also urgently asserts that a religious faith which, like Christianity, makes very little room for feminine values is an incomplete faith and cannot last unless it is rigorously amended.

Jung, the most courteous of controversialists, was in hot water all his life with theologians and frequently with physicists, though some of this latter group were his strong supporters. But his concern with alchemy, which he proved to be a forerunner of psychology rather than a foolish pseudo-chemistry, alienated many scientists who had not read him but had heard tell of him, and who mistrusted thought in a realm which they considered "mystical"—a word thrown like a stick at Jung all his life.

The accusation of mysticism has stood in the way of his consideration by physicists, who are peculiarly fitted to cope with some of his most complex thinking. His theory of synchronicity, as an acausal connecting principle in experience, was of intense interest to Wolfgang Pauli, but has not made much headway with physicists of more mechanical bent.

It is not possible for a brief review to deal even fleetingly with the richness and variety of Jung's thought. People who associate themselves with it, and not only read Jung but ponder at length on what he says, reach a philosophy that is enlarging and supportive. The word "philosophy" is used here, of course, in its old sense, as a mode of thinking which encourages fullness of life, rather than as a system that seeks ultimate truth, without touching daily experience. Once again, thanks and praise to Anthony Storr, clinical lecturer in psychiatry in the University of Oxford, for a masterly achievement.

Globe and Mail, 18 June 1983

The Philosopher's Pupil

*I*t is not easy for a reviewer to know where to catch hold
of a novel by Iris Murdoch, when he has to make up his mind
about it. This latest example is the most difficult of all. Has it
a story? Yes. A good one? Yes, but not one of your neat plots:
wambling and discursive, like life itself, rather than smartly
turned by a fabulist's invention. Is the style distinguished, then?
There are several styles, and all are right for what they have to
carry. Is it innovative? (This is the voice of eager youth.) Well,
yes, you might say so. Is it a good read? (This is the voice of
slippered age.) That depends on how alert you are to what is
being said. What influences are apparent in it? (This is a professor, hot for the long chain of succession in what he calls The
Art of the Novel.) Well, sometimes it reminds me of the 19th-
century novel, in its leisurely pace and heaping-up of significant
detail, and its pleasure in description of natural surroundings;
but at other times it is a novel which could only be written now.
Would you know it for a philosopher's novel? (This is someone
who knows that at one time the author plied that demanding
trade.) No, or at least not to the point where it hurts. Do you
recommend it, then? Oh, indeed I do, but don't come whining
to me if it is not your sort of book.

Not an easy book to write about, as you see. There were
moments when I wished that it could be infinitely extended.
There were other moments (such as the 4,000 words that in-
tervened between a character reaching a door and crossing the

threshold) when I found myself mentally shouting, "Get on with it!" The author has a fine profusion of imagination, but her complexities do not always justify themselves; she delights in parentheses and conditions, so that if we are not always alert we may miss something important; she cares nothing about putting the reader at ease, and likes to tease us by calling a woman Alex and a man Emma. She assumes that her reader has a strong visual imagination, and delights in her power of painting with words.

From time to time she astonishes us with splendid passages, like a fine Quaker sermon, uttered by a minor character who exercises a major influence. She says things that bring us up with a start, because of their quality as aphorisms: "The sending of a letter constitutes a magical grasp upon the future." She takes pleasure in the device of the Buried Quotation or Allusion: "Gabriel had undone her corded bales well out in the middle of the sand." She is writing for the clerisy, and people who do not catch the references must be content to be left out.

She has many voices, and to me the most astonishing is the Dialogue Voice; the talk among her characters whips along rapidly, pushing the plot well beyond the speed limit, and giving us insights and illuminations that we must catch on the fly; a dramatist might envy her skill. She cannot wholly discard the Philosophical Voice, and once—just once—she allows herself to set up a clergyman as stooge for her philosopher, who wipes the floor with him in a fashion just a little too easy. As the clergyman has slight faith and the philosopher is a great bulging monster of contention, the victory is too easy, and one longs for a return match when the clergyman knocks the philosopher out of the ring. Or could he? The unfair advantage of philosophers is that they are not obliged to believe anything.

Her philosopher is her principal character, though perhaps she meant the pupil named in the title to have that place. It is difficult to make a philosopher credible in fiction, because to carry complete conviction he would have to talk sometimes in a way that would leave us non-philosophers baffled. But John

Robert Rozanov convinces us because he is clearly a man of powerful intellect, and at the same time a victim of that over-whelming silliness that may overcome a man who has lived most of his life in his mind, and does not know what to do with emotion when it tosses and gores him. One of John Robert's problems is the pupil, a middle-aged man who has little turn for philosophy but a painful longing for the wisdom that philosophy is supposed to engender. We can understand and suffer with the philosopher's problem, faced with this tedious detrimental, who wants to be loved and is violent when he cannot have what he wants.

The philosopher's other dilemma arises because of his grand-daughter, and it would be unfair to the author to spill the complex bag of beans involved here. His difficulty is a terrible one, and by no means so uncommon as some readers might at first suppose. Iris Murdoch's great skill shines forth in the way in which, slowly and steadily, she convinces us of the truth of what she tells.

All the people in her book are in muddles of one sort or another, but they are not the tedious muddles of stupid people of whose fate we soon weary. They are the muddles of people who, either because they think more than they feel, or feel more than they think, cannot gain any serenity, however fleeting. But they all possess some distinction that makes them worth caring about, and they all behave in ways that we believe, even if we do not fully understand. When the philosopher, supposedly a man of wisdom but really just a man of broad knowledge, gets into a fantod about an affront to his granddaughter, we know why he does it, and how truly angry he is, and we feel for him as we wish to shake him into a better frame of mind.

Indeed, this may well be the real power of the book, which has many sources of energy. The author does what old-fashioned novelists did when they could: she makes us gods, observing, weighing, rebuking, forgiving, and happy with our omniscience. To professors who talk about The Art of the Novel this has been abhorrent for many decades, but it is one of the most difficult and rewarding things a novelist can do for us. It is an age-old attribute of the real story-teller, and Iris Murdoch possesses it in high degree.

Washington Post, 26 June 1983

III

ROBERTSON DAVIES

I Remember Creatore

My first clear memory of the Canadian National Exhibition is of seeing Signor Creatore eat his dinner.

Although I cannot have been more than six years old at the time, I had definite ideas about genius, and especially about musical genius. One did not expect a genius to behave like other men in any respect; the divine afflatus, with which geniuses were filled, permitted of nothing that was commonplace. Geniuses were also notably idiosyncratic in the matter of hair. I had heard Creatore draw ravishing music from his concert band during the afternoon, and I looked forward with delight to his evening performance; his hair fell to his shoulders in glistening black ringlets; his manner of eating could only be described as vivacious gormandizing. Plainly the man was a genius, and I watched him with such awe that I was barely able to eat.

Other boys went to the CNE to see automobiles, or to haunt the Midway, or to collect samples of food in the Pure Food exhibits, or to gape at effigies of the Prince of Wales, modelled in creamery butter. I went to hear bands. My father paid occasional visits to the Press Building, and one of my brothers took a queer interest in a dingy little building where paintings were hung; but what real business would a family of Welsh extraction have at such an affair as the CNE except to listen to the bands? In our household music was not a hobby or a pastime; it was one of life's chief preoccupations. My father sang and played the flute and directed a choir; my mother sang and

245

played the piano; one of my brothers sang and wrought manfully with the cornet. I sang myself—a piece which began:

> A little pink rose in my garden grew
> The prettiest rose of them all;
> 'Twas kissed by the sun and caressed
> by the Jew . . .

"By the dew," the voice of authority would say. But next time the Jew would be sure to get into it, and I saw no harm in him. After all, was not Mendelssohn, an effigy of whom sat upon the piano top, a Jew? To a boy reared thus, what could the CNE offer to touch its bands?

At the time of my earliest acquaintance with the CNE my musical taste lacked chastity. It was chastened later by a Scottish music master, and reached a fine peak of virginal austerity when I was about twenty-one. Of late years it has begun to grow a little blowsy, and there are times when I feel that I could relish one of Creatore's band concerts again. He liked richly emotional music, and to it he brought his own fine endowment of sentiment. It is many years since I heard music played as melodramatically as it was played by his band. Rossini, Von Suppé, Auber—these were musicians whose works he played. But it was in Verdi that he showed his strength.

His rendition of the "Miserere" from *Il Trovatore* was a masterly piece of showmanship. Before it was played there would be a short pause while the principal cornet player left the bandstand and removed himself to a considerable distance, in the darkness (for this was inescapably a piece for the evening concert). The dreary howling of the monks was heard, and the plaint of Leonora, and then, magically,

> Ah, I have sighed to rest me,
> Deep in the quiet grave—

It was the principal cornet, personating the imprisoned Manrico, far away in the darkness. It would have drawn tears from a brazen image. When it was over, Signor Creatore was forced to bow again and again.

There were other bands, of course, chiefly English bands from the Guards regiments and a few lay bands, like the Besses O' the Barn. These bands played in a style quite different from that which Creatore displayed so magnificently, and they played different music. I even heard an American band—naval, I think—on one occasion, but did not care for it, as both the vigorous emotionalism of the Italian and what I may call the imperial grandeur of the English bands were lacking.

One of the great tests of a band, of course, was its manner of playing "God Save the King." Creatore sought to astound his hearers by running the emotional gamut in this piece of fourteen bars. He began sadly and very softly, as though His Majesty were on his last legs and prayer unavailing; then he plucked up hope, then he exulted, then he blared in triumph. It was exhausting, glorious, and took twice as much time as the English bands required to play the same piece. The English did it with effortless superiority, as though to say, "We have frequently played this air in the presence of the King-Emperor and have reason to believe that he was perfectly satisfied." The American band gave an impression that every man was treacherously muttering the words of "My Country 'Tis of Thee" into his instrument; which was, of course, intolerable. I have probably misjudged this band, for like most children I was a patriotic bigot.

Music played an important part, also, in the nightly spectacle which was held before the grandstand. Here one was likely to be confronted with a choir of one thousand voices, which sang slowly and carefully, much as one understands the ancient Roman hydraulus, or water organ, to have been played; like the hydraulus, too, its sound could be heard for approximately sixty miles. Nero was fond of the hydraulus, and Nero would have liked the CNE choir. I preferred the clowns who rescued furniture from a burning house and tumbled out of upstairs windows with pianos in their arms. I did not care for the policemen who rode their horses in a seemingly interminable gyration called a Musical Ride, for it did not appear to me to be sufficiently musical, and it was obvious that as a ride it was giving no pleasure to anyone. But the fireworks with which the performance came to an end were superb; they rejoiced the eye as Creatore had feasted the ear.

In the recollections of many of my Canadian contemporaries the Midway plays a prominent part, but it is not so with me. I recall a journey through something which was called a House of Mirth, and I remember that the final mirthful burst consisted of being shot down a chute into the arms of two large, sweaty men, who stood one on one's feet. This was probably very merry for middle-aged women, but I did not like it. Nor did I care for the sad-faced monkeys who were strapped into tiny motor cars and whizzed rapidly round a track. I liked to gape at giants, dwarfs and malformed persons; but this was considered, quite rightly, to be a displeasing characteristic in a child and was not encouraged. My curiosity was in no way cruel. Deviations from the commonplace attracted me strongly, as they still do; and to me the hermaphrodite and the living skeleton were interesting for the same reason as was Creatore, or the resplendent Guardsmen of the bands—because such people did not often come my way, and I hoped that they might impart some great revelation to me, some insight which would help me to a clearer understanding of the world about me. There are people, I know, who refuse to believe that children ever think in this way, but my remembrance on this point is clear and, I believe, honest.

Because the Toronto Saturnalia played so important a part in my early life I did not quickly grasp the possibility, when I was living abroad at a later time, that foreigners might not have heard of it. Every country of any size has, I now believe, some similar jamboree which it solemnly believes to be the finest exhibition of its kind on earth. I have spoken of the CNE to Frenchmen and they have not been impressed; they prefer to talk about occasional Paris expositions which are, they assure me, very large and very gay. Englishmen are unsatisfactory in the same way; they assume that the CNE is an inferior Wembley. Australians seem to think that the CNE must be a mild Canadian version of the Melbourne Show. I have talked eloquently about the great age of the CNE and of its remarkable place in our national life, but I have found that even Westerners do not fully believe me. And here and there I have discovered disaffected and contumacious persons who call it (pretending afterward that it was a slip of the tongue) "the Toronto Fair." I suppose one has to be born and bred in Eastern Canada to understand the true and abiding inwardness, the mystical essence, of the CNE; one must have attended it as a child.

My most recent visit to the CNE was during its last epiphany before it was suspended because of the war. I had hoped for a band, but there was none which could engage my attention. Lily Pons was there, but I have an unreasonable prejudice against listening to singers while standing in a restless crowd. The pageant before the grandstand lacked theme and clowns. The whole show was showing the strain of war. But even in such reduced circumstances it had something of its old magic, and I was not sorry that I had gone. I shall go again. I will never be one of those zealots who sleep on the ground outside the main gates for a week before the Exhibition opens, in order to be the first inside; but I shall go from time to time, and if I ever get my Cloak of Invisibility I shall go quite often.

There are people who maintain that one may achieve invisibility for a time by eating fern seed. I may try it this year, and drop in for a few hours at the CNE. My desire to be invisible is simply explained: I want to watch people closely without attracting their attention, and I have never mastered the trick of doing this, which detectives are said to possess. When I stare at someone, he stiffens, glares about him till he finds me, and stares in return. Sometimes he makes personal remarks. Yet I mean him no harm, and my intent gaze implies no criticism. When I stare at women their necks grow red and they nudge their escorts. When I stare at children they weep. My staring is innocent of evil intention, however. I merely want to see what people are doing, and if possible to divine what they think about it. The CNE is an ideal spot for this pursuit, and when I was a child I could stare to my heart's content and no one noticed me. I long to recover once again this most precious of the gifts of childhood.

If, therefore, I should partially materialize at your side when you are visiting the CNE this year, apparent yet transparent, and staring with the intensity of a hypnotist, you will know that the effect of the fern seed is beginning to wear off.

Mayfair, September 1948

Three Worlds, Three Summers—But Not the Summer Just Past

One might think, to hear some people talk, that this had been a particularly fine summer. From their point of view, I suppose, it has.

They have rushed about the lakes in noisy little boats; they have permitted themselves to be dragged behind other little boats, standing more or less upright on ironing boards; they have immersed themselves in lakes into which countless summer cottage privies drain; they have laboriously pursued summer flirtations, and some of them have achieved gritty conquests on the sands; they have sat in hot little boats waiting to catch fish which they have then had to eat; they have passed many hours changing their skins from pinkish-drab to brown, erroneously believing that they are "storing up sunshine" against the winter months; they have motored penitential distances; they have taken thousands of feet of film of people whose names they will not be able to remember in November. They have amused themselves after their fashion, and I have no quarrel with them. But their ways are not my ways, nor are their thoughts my thoughts. I have not had a particularly good summer.

Every man makes his own summer. The season has no character of its own, unless one is a farmer with a professional concern for the weather. Circumstances have not allowed me to make a good summer for myself this year. For one thing, I have had to work too hard. My colleagues have taken their holidays in a fashion which has made it necessary for me to do double work for weeks on end.

Important alterations are being made in the building in which I work, and the noise of steel construction, carpentry and roofing has penetrated at every moment of every hour into the chamber in which I am supposed to think. I am no Carlyle; I do not get into a frenzy over the scratching of a mouse in the wainscot, but power drills and power planes are quite another matter.

My summer has been overcast by my own heaviness of spirit. I have not had any adventures, and adventures are what make a summer. No man can have adventures while he is working. The thing is out of the question.

I have known good summers and I have had adventures. Make no mistake about that. Because I shall say something about some of my good summers and my adventures in this brief memoir, do not imagine that this is an exercise in nostalgia. I despise nostalgia, the refuge of the feeble and the stock-in-trade of the decaying essayist. I shall have good summers again, and I shall have many more adventures. But before I can go on, I must make it clear that I have no budget of rich experience to present to you from the summer of 1949. Most of this magazine, I believe, is devoted to other people's good summers. If you are to have anything about my good summers, they must be summers past.

How far in the past? Quite a long way, I think. I should like to dredge up three summers: the first was when I was three years old, the second when I was ten and the third when I was fourteen. As I am now thirty-five you can work out the dates, if you choose. Of course, I look so much older than I am that people expect me to recall the death of Queen Victoria, and old ladies with dim vision accept me as a contemporary. But I really cannot go back any farther than 1917 without lying abominably.

My early childhood lay, theoretically, under the shadow of war. In the village where I lived in Western Ontario, we took the war with the utmost seriousness. Any stranger, particularly if he happened to be a tramp, was under suspicion of being a German spy; there was some sort of important electrical gadget nearby, and these creatures were supposed to be intent on sabotaging it; or they may have wanted to poison the village waterworks, which would have been easy, as it consisted of a large open tank, not unlike a Roman bath, with a wire fence around it.

The Germans, and indeed the Kaiser himself, knew very well that our village had sent a good many young men to the front lines, and were eager to revenge themselves upon us; poisoning our waterworks would obviously appeal to their villainous and depraved minds. We were experts in German psychology: was there not a family of German extraction on a farm nearby, and had not the woman of this family, buying nipples for her baby's bottle in Watson's drugstore, been heard to assert brazenly that German nipples were better than the kind that Davey Watson sold? Could arrogance and contumacy go further? Rightly were they called Huns. And it was to defeat the Huns that I, three years old and rising four, was snipping beans on our front verandah one sunny afternoon in the summer of 1917.

Bean-snipping was an authentic form of war service. Our village possessed a canning factory, and goods from it went direct to our boys overseas, so we all did jobs for the cannery as volunteers. One such job was the snipping of the ends off astronomical numbers of string beans; this was done with scissors, and could be trusted to children as young as I; I snipped slowly and laboriously, and from time to time I absent-mindedly ate a bean, forgetting that I was taking it right out of the mouth of a boy at the front. My mother had a washtubful of beans to snip that afternoon, before the cannery cart called at five o'clock. She and a friend snipped as they sat in rocking-chairs; I sat upon the steps, where I could hear all that they said, and snipped too.

They were talking, of course, about the war. It seemed to me that grownups never talked about anything else. Their theme was a favourite one, German atrocities. Yet, my mother said, was it to be wondered at that they did dreadful things? Were they not bred to it? A cousin of hers had been educated at Heidelberg—he had gone there to study music and was anything but a warlike person—and he had told her that the very first toy that a German child was given was a little sword or a little gun. He had been at Heidelberg just before the turn of the century; all the children that he had seen with swords and guns would be just the age to use big swords and guns at the present moment. How were we, peace-loving to the point of simple-mindedness as we knew ourselves to be, to cope with a people who had been educated like that?

I listened, in what I recall as a stealthy manner. I now know that the stealth of children is not so imperceptible as I thought it then, but the grownups paid no attention to me. And as I listened, bean-snipping lost its hold upon me. There I sat, a Canadian child fighting the war with a pair of scissors, and I thought of German children—bullet-headed and scowling, no doubt—playing with sharp little swords and popping at one another with dangerous little guns. After a time the vision was too much for me, and I crept away.

I went to the back of the house, to the woodshed, and I selected several blocks of wood and carried them out into the yard. There I lined them up, and when they were arranged to my satisfaction, I gave them names. Two I christened by the names of the Presbyterian minister and his wife; one I named after the mayor of the village, and one after the magistrate; one I named for our policeman, a harmless creature who had not even a uniform; and one I named for our family doctor. When I had told all the blocks who they were I went to the woodshed and got the axe.

With the axe I chopped the law, religion and science. The axe was heavy, and I suppose anyone who had discovered me would have seen a child pecking ineffectively at a few billets of wood, in some danger of hacking his own toes. But to me it was a German massacre; I was a German—a Hun—and I was enjoying myself thoroughly. I experienced a few moments of pure, un-restrained feeling. When I had exhausted my blood-lust I threw the corpses back in the woodshed (an orderliness the Germans might have admired had been imposed upon me in my earliest days) and replaced the axe. I felt much, much better. I snipped no more beans.

Perhaps this is a shameful confession. Perhaps psychologists see deep below the surface of my action to some dreadful anarchy of the spirit. Perhaps I should have grown up to be a delinquent. I relate this incident only because it was a high point in a good summer, and because I learned something from it. Precisely what I learned I could not put into words, but it was an adventure, and I was never quite the same afterward.

Every summer brought its adventures, but I was to leap now from my fourth year to my tenth. I no longer lived in a village, but in a town; my parents had moved from Western Ontario to Eastern Ontario in the Ottawa Valley, and anyone who thinks that all Canadians are one flesh should try such a change for himself and learn the truth. It was a town big enough to be visited by Chautauqua, and it was at a Chautauqua session that a great revelation was manifested to me.

I am constantly surprised by the number of people who have never experienced a Chautauqua session, and who know only vaguely what the word means. It was one of the many forms of packaged and denatured culture which have always been so popular on this continent. In such a town as the one I tell of a large tent, with seats for perhaps 1,000 people, was set up, and for a week lectures, concerts, demonstrations of crafts and skills, plays and exhortations were given in the tent every afternoon and evening to uplift and divert the subscribers. It was possible for mere dilettantes to go to single performances of their choice; their money was accepted at the door, but they were not of the aristocracy of Chautauqua; the intellectual cream, the Chautauqua people assured us, were those who bought books of tickets and went to everything, stoking themselves with enough variegated cultivation to keep them burning with a hard, gem-like flame for a year.

My parents had subscription tickets, but for reasons which I did not understand at the time they did not take Chautauqua very seriously. Their tickets were complimentary, for my father was the publisher of the local weekly newspaper. Since I have been a newspaperman myself, and have done a little work as a critic, I have often reflected that the system of giving free tickets to the press is a bad one. It too frequently shrinks the critic's attitude to a good-natured tolerance; he responds slowly to the good, and accepts the bad with an easy-going fatalism. Newspapermen should have to pay their way into public entertainments; they would then be bitter in condemnation of whatever is inferior, and standards in all arts would shoot upward like rockets. But this is by the way. As my parents did not seem eager to sit through twelve assorted outbursts of popular culture, I was able to go to whatever failed to attract them.

Why they did not go to the "cabinet opera" I do not know, for they were both uncommonly fond of music. Perhaps they felt that opera as presented by Chautauqua might fall short of the highest standard. I had no such misgiving, for I had no standard at all. I knew what opera was, of course. We had a number of gramophone records which were operatic excerpts, and I identified them easily because they came in a special sort of envelope—the things which radio men now call "shirts." The shirts of the opera records were green, and in the bottom right hand corner was a picture of a gramophone with a large horn, from which issued a sort of cornucopia containing pictures of ladies and gentlemen in costume—Norma with her wreath of unspecified fruit, Marguerite with her prayer book clasped in her hands, an unidentified man with a large limp cap like a pie upon his head, and at the top Mephistopheles, with the unmistakable beard of Pol Plançon. I knew that opera meant a play in which people sang, and that it was imbued with an ineffable magnificence; was it not commonly described as "grand"? But I had no direct experience of it.

What I felt as I set out for the Chautauqua tent that night I do not know; I do not think that I expected anything superior to the performance of *Smilin' Through* which I had seen earlier in the week. Even I, the family defender of Chautauqua, felt that opera was a little out of its sphere; the stage was small, and I was informed that the stage of the Metropolitan was vast; but nothing would have kept me away. When I reached the tent the preliminaries were not encouraging: the audience was smaller than usual, and most of those present wore the dogged look of subscribers. After a time a man in a crumpled summer suit stepped before the curtains, and told us that what we would see would be a condensed version of Verdi's *Rigoletto;* there would be no choruses, no recitative, and a minimum of action. The singers would wear costume, he said, brightening a little, and there would be scenery. He gave us a brief account of the plot which, like all such accounts, was utterly incomprehensible, and he leaped down and began to thump out the Prelude to the opera on an oak-finished upright piano of unromantic appearance which stood in front of the stage.

The curtains parted, and revealed three men and three women seated on bentwood chairs which were arranged in a semicircle; they wore costume; that is to say, the men wore those jerkins which costumiers used to call "shapes," and tights with darns in them. The women wore long dresses, strings of beads and small caps, like doilies. One of the men sang the part of the scapegrace Duke of Mantua; another (a short, blockish man with a scowl and a loud but hollow voice) was Rigoletto; the third man, whose voice was more remarkable for range than tone, sang the parts of the other six male characters of the opera as well as he could. Of the women, one was Gilda, and the other two sang the four other female roles and assisted the man with the Protean voice whenever a concerted number seemed to be getting beyond him.

The scenery represented a wall, upon which roses about the size of cabbages grew in profusion. Its bearing upon the opera was never made clear.

I do know what principle controlled the movements of the singers. They seemed to have made an agreement not to act— or at least not to act with the air of people who were trying to make themselves invisible by some system of muscular tension. Their faces were immovably set, but their haunches contracted and relaxed beneath their tights, and their toes tapped in time. When their turn came to sing they hurled themselves out of their chairs toward the front of the stage, and roared defiance to the world. They gestured violently; they sobbed; they began to drop upon their knees, thought better of it, and leaped up again. Sometimes, forgetting the convention under which they were working, they turned toward one another and made dreadful faces. And in the last act, when Rigoletto's daughter is concealed in a sack, the soprano turned away from the audience, bent her knees and clasped her arms about herself as though she had suddenly been seized with cramp. Not to act was plainly hard work for those six unfortunates, inheritors of a great Italian tradition. I could not have cared less. To me it was all glorious. I did not understand the story, but my heart beat in time with the music, and it seemed to me that I grew a foot in the two hours I passed in the Chautauqua tent that night. This was emotion on a scale undreamed of. This was a reality surpassing anything that had come my way before. This was a distilled essence of life; this was the way people behaved when they took off the masks which all adults seemed to me to wear; this was noble. A veil had been rent between the greatness of mankind and myself, and I knew that I would never be the same again. Nor was I. Since that night I have made some progress in my attempt to understand mankind, but I have never made another such giant leap.

My third adventure that I have chosen to describe is quickly told. It happened when I was fourteen. I was living in a city, for my parents had made another of their frequent moves, and I was at home for a summer holiday from boarding-school. I read a great deal, but not voraciously; I was, and remain, a slow reader who sucks every sentence as a gourmet sucks the buttery leaf of an artichoke. I was not a reader of modern literature; I knew nothing about it. But on this day I had been visiting a friend of my own age whose ambition (since realized) was to become a priest of the Church of England; as I was leaving he handed me a small blue book, saying, "Read this; it's great stuff." I carried the book home, without much curiosity—he had a way of lending me essays by Dean Inge which I could, as the saying is, take or let alone—and lay down to look at it in the sun, behind a barberry hedge in the garden.

The book was *Antic Hay* by Aldous Huxley, an author unknown to me. But I had not read more than a page or two before I knew that this man Huxley stood in a very special relation to me: here he was, saying many things that struck deeply into my mind, about my own time. Not my own country—that would have been too much to expect—but about the present, and about wonderfully amusing people that I wanted to know, and with an easy scholarship, a witty pedantry, a literacy which enthralled me. This was not the world of brutal anarchy, nor the passionate world of *Rigoletto,* but the sunshine world of high comedy which was opening to me, and as I read on and on I experienced once again that wonderful feeling that the world as a whole would never be quite the same again for me. Another veil had been rent, and a new light was striking upon me. This was adventure, casting a summer glory over my life which no conceivable winter could dispel.

I have known other comparable revelations since, but not in the summer of 1949. This has not been one of my great summers.

Mayfair, September 1949

A Chat with a
Great Reader

A few days ago I was introduced to a man whom I had not met before, and after a few preliminaries we had a conversation which I herewith record.

THE MAN: I always read your stuff in *Saturday Night*. I'm a Great Reader, and I've always wanted to meet a Critic.

MYSELF: That's interesting; I've always wanted to meet a Great Reader.

THE MAN: I bet you know lots of Great Readers.

MYSELF: No; I know one or two, and I'm not absolutely sure about them.

THE MAN: You're joking. You're a Great Reader yourself. You must be in your job. I don't know how you get through all the stuff you read.

MYSELF: I can tell you at once that I don't do it by being a Great Reader. I am not even a Fast Reader—just a Persistent Reader.

THE MAN: I think we've got our wires crossed. What do you mean by a Great Reader?

MYSELF: I mean somebody who reads greatly. Somebody who gives his whole attention to what he is reading. Somebody who brings to a book a curiosity and a sympathy which matches the intention of the author. Somebody who gives himself wholly to a book. Isn't that what you mean?

THE MAN: Oh no; I mean somebody who reads critically.

When I sit down with a book I read a few pages to see if the author can hold me. If he can't, I pick up something else.

MYSELF: You mean, you dare the author to interest you?

THE MAN: Yes, you could put it like that.

MYSELF: Do you consider that fair?

THE MAN: Why not? Isn't an author a public entertainer? Haven't I bought the book?

MYSELF: I don't know. Have you?

THE MAN: Well, that's just a way of speaking. Actually, I get almost all my books from the Public Library.

MYSELF: I see. And do you get almost all your meals in soup kitchens?

THE MAN: I don't understand you.

MYSELF: Perhaps that is as well. My remark was rude, though not unjustified. But you see, I become impatient with people who regard literature as something that they should get for nothing, but who criticize it as they would not dream of criticizing any other gift, or charitable donation. Let us get back to this business of being a Great Reader. I agree with you that an author is a public entertainer. But do you give him a chance to entertain you?

THE MAN: How do you mean?

MYSELF: You gave me the impression that you put him on trial for a few pages, and that you prided yourself on being hard to please.

THE MAN: Of course I'm hard to please. I haven't any time for junk.

MYSELF: I wouldn't want you to read junk, but I think that a Great Reader ought to give a book a fair chance. It sounds to me as if you expect the author to do all the work. You want him to amuse you, but you don't want to exert yourself at all.

THE MAN: But I read for relaxation. I don't want to settle down to work when I'm reading. I want to be amused, or thrilled, or told something.

MYSELF: Do you like music?

THE MAN: Very much. I never miss a first-rate concert.

MYSELF: But you don't relax and defy a composer to interest you, I suppose? You concentrate when you are listening, don't you?

THE MAN: Of course. You must, if you expect to get anything out of it.

MYSELF: And you don't think it is necessary to do that when you read?

THE MAN: It's different. The texture of music demands close attention, especially in new and unfamiliar stuff. If you don't concentrate, you'll miss most of what's going on. But books are written in language, and I can comprehend that without too much concentration.

MYSELF: It depends whose books you are reading. It sounds to me as if you were a Good Listener, but not a Good Reader. Let's leave the word Great out of the argument. Do you go much to the theatre?

THE MAN: As much as I can. And I never walk out in the middle, if that's what you are going to ask me.

MYSELF: You are a Good Listener, and a Good Play-goer, but I still don't think you are a Good Reader. You don't do enough for the books you read.

THE MAN: Explain. You interest me strangely, as Mutt and Jeff always used to say.

MYSELF: Well, I think that you should be ready to give as much effort to reading as you do to listening to music, or watching a play. You ought to be alert to every shade of meaning, and you ought to give the book a good mental performance, if I make myself clear.

THE MAN: You don't.

MYSELF: When Emlyn Williams visited Canada, reading the works of Dickens, did you hear him?

THE MAN: I went to hear him four times, and I'd have gone again if it had been possible. And of course I heard Laughton and his group reading *Don Juan in Hell*. Wonderful! I've got that for my gramophone. We play it at least once a month.

MYSELF: Aha, the Good Listener again! But you know, when

you read books yourself, you ought to read them like Williams or Laughton. You ought to give them all that fire and concentration. You ought to bring all that imagination to them, all that rhetorical and histrionic skill, or you are not being fair to your author.

THE MAN: But that would kill me! I read for relaxation.

MYSELF: Does it kill you to give your full attention to two hours of great music? Does it kill you to see, let us say, *Oedipus*? Why should it kill you to give the same attention to what you are reading?

THE MAN: For one thing, I hear music and see plays in complete performances. It sometimes takes me a week to read a book, getting fifteen minutes here and half an hour there. And I read when I'm tired; I usually fall asleep reading at night; a bedside book may last me six or eight weeks.

MYSELF: In other words, you give to literature the fag-ends of your time and the dregs of your intellectual energy. You do not think enough of books to buy them, preferring instead to get them from charitable institutions which were not founded for people who can well afford to buy books. And you call yourself a Great Reader!

THE MAN: Books cost too much.

MYSELF: You are shuffling. The cost of a book is comparable to the price of a concert or theatre ticket. A book costs about as much as a good dinner. And there are many fine books which can be had cheaply. Have you noticed that the Penguin reprints have just brought out their 1,000th volume? No, the real trouble with you is that you are not willing to give a book the same chance that you give gladly to other artistic creations. You treat books badly, and when they do not satisfy you, you talk as if books were at fault. If I had my way books would not be written in English, but in an exceedingly difficult secret language that only skilled professional readers and story-tellers could interpret. Then people like you would have to go to public halls and pay good prices to hear the professionals decode and read the books aloud for you. This plan would have the advantage of scaring off all the amateur authors, retired politicians, country doctors and I-Married-a-Midget writers, who would not have the patience to learn the secret language, and it would exalt literature in the eyes of people like you by making it rare, expensive and delightful. The professional readers would be artists, and through them an author's work would be finely interpreted, instead of being strained through the dirty sock of every incompetent, tired, inattentive pinhead's imagination, who trifles with books and then describes himself as a Great Reader.

THE MAN: Well, well. Shall we go and have a drink?

MYSELF: With pleasure. After you.

Saturday Night, 11 September 1954

The Palest Ink

A great many complimentary things have been said about the faculty of memory, and if you look in a good quotation book you will find them neatly arranged. You may observe, however, that memory was most praised by the Greeks and other races who depended on memory, rather than on written records, for much of their important knowledge. The quotation we like best is a Chinese one which says: "The palest ink is better than the best memory."

What sent us to the quotation book was the news of a memory test which a psychologist, Dr. Charles Winick, gave to eighty students of Queens College, New York. Here are the fifteen questions he asked:

1. What was the name of your third-grade teacher?
2. What did you have for dinner last Tuesday?
3. When did you go on the first train trip you took without a grownup?
4. What was your telephone number before the present one?
5. What did you do on your 21st birthday?
6. What was the first book you read outside of school?
7. What was the name of the first person you went out with alone?
8. What's the name of the person you were introduced to most recently?

9. Who was the first acquaintance you met when you left your home yesterday morning?

10. What was the theme of the last sermon you heard?

11. What was the name of the leading character (not the actor's real name) in the last movie you saw?

12. What was the name of the last novel you read?

13. Do you remember how much income tax you paid last year?

14. What suit or dress did you wear last Thursday?

15. What was your first favourite song?

If you can answer thirteen of these, Dr. Winick thinks you have a remarkable memory; if you answer less than seven, apparently you shouldn't be allowed out without a nurse.

We have taken the test, under extremely unscientific conditions, in our office. Our score was two. Our third-grade teacher was Miss Belle Eady, and a splendid teacher she was; she was also our teacher in grades four and five, which may be why we recall her so clearly. And the first book we read unaided was a taut, thrilling tale of high-life called *Mother Hubbard's House Party;* we forget the plot, except for a sizzling scandal about Jack Horner and Red Riding Hood. Having done so poorly we think little of the test.

In fact, we think Dr. Winick's choice of things to remember shows him to be a man of trivial mind; we cannot remember our first favourite song, or what we wore last week, but we remember the answers to the questions in the Presbyterian Shorter Catechism—which is not short at all, but contains nearly 150 tricky questions. Thus armed, we scorn the doctor's test. And we shall continue to put our faith in ink, like the Chinese.

Peterborough Examiner, 2 April 1956

The Writer's Week

Saturday: I receive a letter which says: "Your column disappoints me. I had expected a real diary, something intimate about a man who presumably differs from his readers in a special way because of his preoccupation with literary expression. But all you are offering is book-reviews. I want to know what a writer thinks, reads and does." Very well, my dear Sir, you shall have what you want. Today I chopped ice and made drains in front of my house. Is this literary? Yes, I think Havelock Ellis would have found ample evidence in it of the character-complex he called Undinism.

Sunday: Lay on my back most of the day, reading, sleeping and day-dreaming. Very literary. Some women, however, resent it, so young writers should choose their wives with care. Many a promising career has been wrecked by marrying the wrong sort of woman. The right sort of woman can distinguish between Creative Lassitude and plain shiftlessness.

Monday: Read quite a lot of *Dear and Glorious Physician*, the new novel by Taylor Caldwell. The critics are making sport of it, and as literary art it has no exalted standing, but it is easy to read, and I find myself going on and on, eager to know what happens next. It is about St. Luke, and thus comes in the category of Semi-Sacred Novels. All the characters are really modern North Americans, gussied up in wigs and beards like a

Sunday School pageant dressed by Malabar. But in spite of its shortcomings it has real narrative movement, and that is something many writers never achieve. No sign of Our Lord yet, but a lot of hints have been dropped.

Tuesday: In a short piece about Scott Fitzgerald his friend George Jean Nathan tells how he rummaged around in the Fitzgeralds' cellar and there found some of Mrs. F.'s diaries tied up in a bundle. So he read them and later offered to edit them; but Fitzgerald would not allow it, as he said he gained a lot of inspiration from them for his own work. The literary world is not conducted according to Marquis of Queensberry rules; if you find somebody's private papers, you immediately rootle through them, looking for raw material. This is something non-literary people never understand. They are apt to confuse it with a vulgar, prying nature. Moral: when you have authors in the house you needn't lock up your spoons or your daughters, but get your diaries into the Safe Deposit.

Wednesday: Heard the Mendelssohn Choir sing Bach's *St. Matthew Passion,* a work which is one of the supporting pillars of whatever critical structure I have been able to assemble. Found myself reflecting on the many ways which are open to those who wish to probe the great mysteries of religion by means of art. There is Bach's way, and there is Taylor Caldwell's way; is there any point in disputing about the validity of the two? If people like their religion with plenty of sugar in it, who is to say that they are wrong? I know where my own tastes lie, and that is with Bach's Baroque grandeur.

Thursday: Visited my own dear and glorious physician for a check-up. Hypochondria is the Author's Neurosis. After the usual all-in wrestling, inspection by radar and unmentionable intimacies which a thorough examination involves in this great age of medical science, he pronounced me hale and hearty, except for a chronic allergy which sorely afflicts my gospel-pipe.

The effect of it is to make me speak like Alec Guinness playing Fagin in the film of *Oliver Twist*. As every practising hypochondriac will understand, this disability became much worse after talking to the doctor about it, so I took my special remedy—two No-Nods dissolved in a wineglassful of gin.

Friday: Which is also Good Friday, and I follow the custom of many years by working hard all day—as good a form of mortification as I can manage. In the evening picked up George Gissing's *New Grub Street*, which is now handily available in World's Classics. As good and as true a picture of the literary life as I know, but not a book to give to the starry-eyed young, who think that the life of an author is a Quest for the Oversoul. Was struck to rediscover, at the beginning of Chapter 8, this sentence: "Of the acquaintances Yule had retained from his early years several were in the well-defined category of men with unpresentable wives." What makes one shudder about Gissing is that he does not mean this as irony, or satire, or anything except the bleak truth. To read him is like looking into one's mirror on these mornings when the white sunshine of spring, unbroken by foliage, strikes upon the irreducible minimum of one's personal beauty, and one realizes that one looks indeed like St. Paul after a gaudy night with the Corinthians.

Toronto Daily Star, 28 March 1959

Haiku and Englyn

Saturday: A correspondent accuses me of frivolousness because I called Taylor Caldwell's *Dear and Glorious Physician* a Sacred Novel last week. Well, what else can I call it? For generations musicians who compose music for use in churches have called their stuff "sacred" and even "semi-sacred" (such ditties as "Because" and "My Task"). The use of the word is no guarantee of quality; it seems to apply to Malotte as much as to Bach. Why shouldn't novels which stifle criticism because they are about the officially uncriticizable be called Sacred Novels? Of course a book like George Moore's *The Brook Kerith* need not be placed in that category; it is quite good enough to be called, simply, a novel.

Sunday: This is the day when I read the English Sunday papers, a few weeks old. *The Sunday Times,* I see, is having a Haiku Contest. Haiku are Japanese poems, of seventeen syllables disposed in three lines, and Aldous Huxley says that they have a quality like "the best of Wordsworth." The examples given are:

> Up the barley rows
>   stitching, stitching them together
>   a butterfly goes.

And another:

Blossoms on the pear—
  and a woman in the moonlight
  reads a letter there.

How very English, to work up so much enthusiasm for an Oriental form, and to try to become Japanese in spirit for seventeen syllables! The English have always loved intellectual fancy dress.

Monday: Still haunted by Haiku, and tried my hand at it, but I fall pitifully short of the Wordsworthian touch. But failure in this realm turned my mind to an old enthusiasm of mine, the Welsh englyn. This verse form was derived by the Welsh from the inscriptions which their Roman conquerors put on tombs, and it has been very popular since at least the sixth century. It makes Haiku look like child's play, for a good englyn must have four lines, of ten, then six, syllables, the last two lines having seven syllables each. In the first line there must be a break after the seventh, eighth, or ninth syllable, and the rhyme with the second line comes at this break; but the tenth syllable of the first line must either rhyme or be in assonance with the middle of the second line. The last two lines must rhyme with the first rhyme in the first line, but the third or fourth line must rhyme on a weak syllable. Got that? I shall try it again.

Tuesday: My englyn is not very good. However, it demonstrates the mechanics of the form, and here it is:

Controversy

A Canadian flag of our own—ah,
  Unity's black tombstone!
Was ever design shown
Did not arouse a cyclone?

The assonance of "ah" and "black" is poor, but in spirit the thing is an englyn.

Wednesday: I have been much troubled by the hubbub about diet in the papers, and I see no hope. If I eat the high-protein diet to grow slim and thwart thrombosis, I am silting up my veins with cholesterol, and may burst like a clogged water-main. If I eat the cholesterol-free diet, I am stuffed with starch, and insurance companies threaten me with rapid transport to the Hereafter by the Fat Route. Only women have the answer, and I sat in a restaurant today watching them eat lettuce and scraps of vegetable with lemon-juice dressing. Yeats' splendid lines flashed through my mind—

> It's certain that fine women eat
> A crazy salad with their meat,
>   Whereby the Horn of Plenty is undone.

I murmured this while emptying a big bottle of cholesterol over my fatty lamb chops.

Thursday: Wrote a somewhat better englyn today. Here it is:

The Old Journalist

> He types his laboured column—weary drudge!
>   Senile fudge and solemn:
> Spare, editor, to condemn
> These dry leaves of his autumn.

That's rather neat, I think, and I shall distribute nicely printed copies among the Press Clubs of Canada, to be hung in the washrooms.

Friday: Met a real Haiku enthusiast today, and told him I thought it silly for Western people to try to write like Orientals. We went on to Oriental religions, and thence to Yoga. "Western people seem to think that they can achieve the spiritual grandeur of the Oriental sages by adopting their extraordinary postures, and their systems of breathing," said I, "but have you ever heard of an Oriental trying to develop Western governmental efficiency, or scientific ingenuity, by sitting or breathing like us?" This was unanswerable, and he resorted to abuse. "You are as complete a donkey as any that ever grazed with King Nebuchadnezzar," said I, in conclusion. This resort to the authority of Holy Writ silenced him.

Toronto Daily Star, 4 April 1959

Love and a Cough

*T*his being the week of the Dominion Drama Festival finals in Toronto, I think it only fair to call attention to a new school of playwriting which is not represented on the program. The success of the Primitive in modern painting has led to some experimentation with the same technique in the theatre. The following brief drama is the first of its kind from the hand of Grandma Moses, who has already won fame as a primitive painter. Both plot and dialogue are old friends, and every line has the virtue of being, not merely quotable, but often quoted, for it consists entirely of proverbs. Ladies and gentlemen, here is—

Granny's First Play

(*The curtain rises to reveal a man and a woman eating breakfast in surroundings of Grandma-Mosaic cosiness and simplicity; they are young, and we know at once that they are lovers.*)

LOVER: He was a smart man that invented eating and drinking.
WIFE: Kisses and bread-and-cheese is a bachelor's breakfast.
LOVER (*kissing her*): It's a poor bachelor that can't make some husband jealous.
WIFE (*kissing him*): Love and eggs are best when they are fresh.
LOVER: When a wife sins her husband is at fault.

WIFE: All husbands are alike, but they have different faces so you can tell them apart.

LOVER: We two agree like bells: we want nothing but hanging.
　　(*They kiss again.*)

WIFE: If the pillow could tell what it knows it would put many to the blush.

LOVER (*taking her on his knee*): There's never so bad a Will, but he'll find as bad a Jill.
　　(*They kiss with ardour; footsteps are heard outside.*)

WIFE: Two things return before we've a mind, a jealous spouse and a spit in the wind.

LOVER (*as he hides in a small trunk*): Good gear goes in small guise.
　　(*The* HUSBAND *enters; he is an elderly farmer of Currier and Ives aspect: he shakes off a great deal of snow.*)

HUSBAND: East, West, home's best.

WIFE: He who comes before his time must be sure of his welcome.

HUSBAND: Wives and purses should keep their mouths shut.

WIFE: Familiarity breeds contempt.

HUSBAND: When I have drunk my fill I turn my back on the well.

WIFE: It takes two to make a quarrel.

HUSBAND: A kindly cat makes a proud mouse.
　　(*The* LOVER *coughs in the trunk.*)

HUSBAND: When the cat's away the mice will play.
　　(*He opens the trunk and drags out the* LOVER.)

LOVER: Love and a cough cannot be hid.

WIFE (*giving* HUSBAND *a piece of pie*): Better cross an angry man than a hungry man.

HUSBAND (*angrily eating the pie*): Sin in the morning is twice sin.

WIFE: He who loves his wife should watch her.

LOVER (*as* HUSBAND *threatens* WIFE *with pie-plate*): Never strike a woman, even with a flower.

HUSBAND: When a man takes a wife he ceases to dread Hell.

WIFE: Where there is love there can be no sin.

HUSBAND: A cheating wife lies as fast as a dog can lick a dish.

WIFE (*to* LOVER): Tell God the truth, but give the judge money.

LOVER (*giving the* HUSBAND *a dollar*): The beginning of love is bad, but the end is worse.

HUSBAND (*mollified*): If you would avoid suspicion, don't lace your shoes in your neighbour's melon-patch.

LOVER: Philandering is reaching into a bag of snakes in hope of catching an eel.

WIFE (*taking the dollar from her* HUSBAND): Love is an egotism of two.

LOVER: To love a woman who robs you is to lick honey from a thorn.

HUSBAND (*kicking the* LOVER *through the door*): Better an empty house than a brawling guest.

LOVER (*popping his head in again*): Beware of soup warmed up, and a wife who repents.

WIFE (*as* HUSBAND *drives him out again*): Experience keeps a dear school, but fools will learn nowhere else.

HUSBAND AND WIFE (*hand in hand*):

> Cold broth hot again, that I loved never,
> But old love renewed again, that loved I ever.

(*Here we lower the curtain, upon which is ornamentally inscribed those ambiguous words*

> It takes a heap o' livin'
> Fer to make a house a Home.)

Toronto Daily Star, 23 May 1959

Elements of Style

The world is over-stocked with people who are ready and eager to teach other people how to write. It seems astonishing that so much bad writing should find its way into print when so much good advice is to be had. I am myself a tireless reader of books about writing, but as the years wear on I become impatient with all but a few of them. The advice they offer is, in most cases, good, but it is rarely good enough.

What is the point of holding up mediocrity as a model? What is gained by urging aspiring writers to be simple and direct, choosing the concrete word in preference to the abstract, and avoiding complexities of structure? Of course real simplicity can be great writing, but few writers achieve it; what they attain to is not simplicity, but flat-footed, drudging simple-mindedness. What about the kinds of writing to which a simple style is unsuited? What if a simple style does not agree with the author's personality? Does anybody seriously wish that Sir Thomas Browne had written like Bunyan? The perusal of many of these guides to writing persuades me that their authors do not really care about simplicity for its own sake, but despair of teaching their readers anything complex. There are better styles; their secret is that a man must teach them to himself. One of the great living masters of a Baroque style is Osbert Sitwell; would anyone wish his six volumes of autobiography re-written in the style of, for example, E. B. White?

Not that Mr. White's style is not a fine one. I am reminded

how fine it is by his re-working of a good little book called *The Elements of Style,* written originally by his master, William Strunk. This is a wonderful book, if you want to write like a White or a Strunk. But do you? I should hate to read a novel written in Strunkese. As for Mr. White, his style is a perfect instrument for what he has to say, but for my taste that sounds too often like a few wise, weary words written by a man who is on the point of retiring to bed with a heavy cold.

Nor do I care much for *Say It with Words* by Charles W. Ferguson. It is a good book as far as it goes, but it does not go far enough. It is inspiring to be urged, as Mr. Ferguson urges his readers, to take delight in words, and to seek ways of making them perform splendid feats. But what feats? The book is short on examples. Mr. Ferguson has feared that he may tire his readers, or discourage them by making writing seem hard. Writing is both tiresome and hard. Mr. Ferguson will cheer some aspirants on their way, but he will not take them as far as it will be necessary for them to go.

The best book on writing that I know is *Style,* by F. L. Lucas, who is himself an admirable writer, and a merciless task-master. He writes his book as though he meant to tell his readers how to write greatly, and he gives numerous and varied examples of what great writing is. He warns of dangers about which most instructors are silent, and one of them is the danger of extreme lucidity; there can be a lack of strength, and a pinched quality, about writing in which clarity has been made the foremost virtue. He warns, also, against a lack of dignity and grace which will appear in writing where the author has been too conscious of his public. If a writer is over-anxious to please, he ends by underestimating the intelligence of his readers; this is not merely a fault of style, but a mortal sin which will corrupt his soul. Much pretended simplicity of writing springs from a dreadful arrogance in the writer. When a writer thinks of his readers, common sense will tell him that a few of them will certainly not be his intellectual equals, but that the majority will be so, and that there will be some who are greatly his superiors; he should comport himself like a gentleman toward all of them.

It is in this matter that I fall foul of so many American writers on writing; they seem to think that writing is a confidence game by means of which the author cajoles a restless, dull-witted, shallow audience into hearing his point of view. Such an attitude is base, and can only beget base prose.

In my enthusiasm for a more ornate and varied style of writing than is generally recommended I know that my readers will not suppose that I am praising what Walter Savage Landor called "the hot and uncontrolled harlotry of a flaunting and dishevelled enthusiasm." In writing, as in architecture, ornament is never an end in itself; it is a splendid and sometimes playful exuberance; it is not stuck on for effect, but is indivisible from the whole. To manage it a man must be at least a fine craftsman.

No book will make a writer a fine craftsman, but some books can point the way. Strunk and White, I fear, lead only to becoming an honest maker of hen houses. Charles W. Ferguson shows you how to make "ranch type" prose of somewhat inferior materials. Only Lucas seems to speak to the writer who hopes that some day, somewhere, he might be the builder of a cathedral.

Toronto Daily Star, 1 August 1959

Gems of Yesteryear

*T*wo things which happened last week sent me to the somewhat inaccessible cupboard in my house where I keep old music. The first was the arrival from a New York bookseller of a catalogue of nineteenth-century music; the second was the appearance in the heap on top of my gramophone of a record of the piano compositions of Louis Moreau Gottschalk (1829–69), made by Eugene List; although Percy Scholes' *Oxford Companion to Music* assures me that his works "belong wholly to a past phase of musical taste" I have always had an affection for the few known to me.

The appearance of the catalogue suggested that nineteenth-century popular music, long neglected, was coming back into favour, and so did the record. So I rootled around in my cupboard to find the album which contained Gottschalk's "The Dying Poet" and in my search I looked through two or three other albums which I cherish, inherited from a great-aunt who played the piano quite well, in the fashion of her day.

One of them particularly pleases me because it exhales so powerful a perfume of its period, which is about 1875. It was the fashion of the time for ladies to have their sheet music bound in albums with morocco backs and corners, and handsome marbled end-papers; this one has a decoration of lyres stamped in gold down the spine. Such collections have no plan; they reflect only the taste of the owner. Whoever assembled the album I write of had a penchant for sentimental songs, such as "The

Maiden's Dream," composed by Julius Benedict; he was a composer of some merit, and a good conductor, but he was known
on this continent chiefly as accompanist to Jenny Lind. Two or
three of the songs have the curious and elaborate title pages of
the day; "Little Sweetheart, Come and Kiss Me," for instance,
is prefaced by a picture of a young man with eyes as soft and
brown as sucked humbugs embracing a girl whose chief beauty
seems to be what was at that time called "a wealth of hair."
But for me the charm of the album lies not in these things, but
in a handful of somewhat special occasional pieces.

One of these is a sacred song, "Just As I Am," published in
St. John, New Brunswick, and composed by Lieutenant Governor Robinson in 1874. On the cover a stout young woman,
again richly endowed with hair, raises her hands in supplication,
while in the background a three-master sets out to sea. The
music is terrible. The song is a reminder, however, that music
has flourished in high places in Canada; Lord Willingdon, when
Governor-General, arranged several performances of his own
compositions, and in this book there is a song from *The Mayor
of Brieux* which was, we learn, "an operetta composed for Her
Excellency the Countess of Dufferin's private theatricals at Government House, Ottawa"; the publisher was A. and S. Nordheimer. To judge by this single example, called "Only a Daisy,"
the operetta must have been very mild fun, and the composer,
Frederick W. Mills, has been gobbled by oblivion.

Music publishing seems to have been less centralized in 1875
than it is now. This album, for instance, contains pieces from
three publishers in Philadelphia, all of them on Chestnut Street
and all extinct. Nordheimer was the leader in Canada; "The
Elephant Mazurka" by a Hamilton, Ontario, composer was
published in Cleveland. I think that my favourite composition
in this album is "The New Premier Galop," composed by J. F.
Davis, and written in honour of the Hon. Alexander Mackenzie;
it was an outburst of triumph following his 1874 campaign,
and I presume that my ancestress, a staunch Grit, played it with
political as well as musical zeal. The Mackenzie theme is a

rattling air, and there is a theme for Lucius Seth Huntington (who prosecuted John A. Macdonald in the C.P.R. proceedings), a theme for Edward Blake and a theme (wonder of wonders) for that glum, ungalloping editor of the *Toronto Globe,* George Brown. How long has it been, I wonder, since a successful politician was accorded musical congratulation in Canada?

How long has it been, indeed, since we had any new patriotic tunes? The U.S.A. produces them occasionally, but not Canada. Nordheimer, in 1875, brought out a stirring march for the pianoforte, called "This Canada of Ours," which crashes along proudly for exactly 100 bars. Mathematically, as well as musically, it is a foursquare piece of work.

If you have any old music of this kind, you should preserve it, or hand it over to a library which will do so, for though most of it is of trivial musical worth, it is a record of the emotion of an age which has gone. We find out what past ages were like not only by the best they produced, but by the second- and third-best; indeed, this lesser art is probably more truly representative of popular feeling. The fat angels, the maudlin lovers and the dashing soldiers on their covers were once charged with emotion for the people who bought them and loved them. We should not laugh at such emotion until we have made sure that we know what it meant in their terms, as well as in our own.

Toronto Daily Star, 7 November 1959

An Author's Pleasure

"*B*ut you never tell us anything about being a writer," says a young woman who addresses me by mail, more in sorrow than in anger; "why call it a Writer's Diary when it is all comment about the writing of other people?"

Well, my dear, I'll tell you a secret; when I write about myself people send me letters telling me not to be vain, and making it clear that they are not a bit interested in me or my affairs; and when I write about books, I get letters like yours. However, you have asked for some comment on what it is like to be a writer, and I shall tell you. I have just finished writing a book. It took me eighteen months to complete it. This included writing; typing of the first draft; revision of first draft; typing of completed book, and revision of that. There had to be six copies of the final piece of work, two of them on heavy paper and four on onion-skin. Four of these had to go to New York. Last week I took them in a briefcase and they weighed exactly fifteen pounds. In all of this the gifted lady who types my MSS made only five errors, all of which were subsequently corrected.

In intervals of writing the book, I wrote a play, took it to Ireland to see the man who will direct it, and revised the draft while staying with him. A play runs to about 40,000 words, but of course they are not just any old words. In addition to these jobs I carried on my normal work, which involves writing a great many words, as well.

"He writes far too much," I hear the wiseacres say. How true:

how poignantly true! But an author is like a horse pulling a coal-cart down an icy hill; he ought to stop, but when he reflects that it would probably kill him to try, he goes right on, neighing and rolling his eyes.

What did I do in New York? I gave the fifteen pounds of typescript to my agent, and then went to lunch with him. This is one of the nicest parts of authorship. He sent the book around to the publisher, who asked me to lunch with him at his house in the country, on Sunday. This, too, was delightful, and I was especially charmed when the publisher's splendid lunch concluded with a figgy pudding, which is my favourite food, and what I strongly suspect the gods eat on Olympus. I was tempted to burst into that Christmas carol, the refrain of which is—

> We all love figgy pudding,
> We All Love Figgy Pudding,
> WE ALL LOVE FIGGY PUDDING,
> So bring some out here!

—but I do not know my host quite well enough for such unbuttoned behaviour, and with difficulty I held in. Very harsh things have been said about publishers, but there can be nothing but good in the heart of a man who regales an author with figgy pudding.

Toronto Daily Star, 19 December 1959

Scraps and Morsels

Since childhood I have been a maker of scrapbooks—not one scrapbook, but many. It is a habit almost as embarrassing as writing diaries (to which I am also sorely addicted), for my outworn enthusiasms keep popping up to embarrass me, and remind me that I am both fickle and foolish in my tastes. As a boy, my scrapbooks were economical and solemn, with column after column of close print crowding every page. In my youth they became more frivolous, and the lay-out was as fancy as I could make it. Then, as I grew busier, the scrapbooks became disorderly, and there were so many scraps which had never been glued into place that the books had to be tied up with string. But this magpie habit has never deserted me. I suppose I shall keep scrapbooks till I die, and may possibly keel over in the very act of sticking a juicy morsel in its place.

What fills the books? Anything that interests me, which covers a lot of ground. I have one with page after page of pictures and descriptions of clocks, and another with a mass of political cartoons. I have long ceased to try to produce any order in the scrapbooks I keep about the theatre, and I have a surprising accumulation of scraps about musicians.

Anything can find a place. I cherish a picture of the chairman of the Chubb Lock and Safe Company, at the age of ninety-five, doing tapestry-work; pictures of the Queen and Princess Margaret, as children, in Christmas theatricals; of a testimonial dinner given to Arthur Machen, a fine writer who seems to be forgotten today; of gypsies in the Balkans; of the new Soviet anthem by A. V. Alexandroff (new, that is, in 1944).

It is not utter chaos. One book, which I made in the early forties, turned up the other day when I was cleaning out a cupboard. Its label is "Clippings Relating to Oddities, Absurdities, Curiosa, Crime and Suicide, and Strange Manifestations of the Holy Ghost," and that is precisely what it contains, neatly compartmented.

"Oddities" leads off with a newspaper article about Newfoundland speech; apparently when a patient tells a doctor "I've got such a pain in me kilcorn I can't glutch," it means he has a sore throat. There is a picture of a group of soldiers dressed as girls, doing an Eastern dance in a hospital revue; they each have one wooden leg, and call themselves the "Amputettes." A clipping from Lucknow, March 25, 1943, tells how an American soldier gave an Indian woman a hundred-rupee note, mistaking it for a ten-rupee one; in her gratitude she threw her infant into his train compartment as it drew away, embarrassing him, as Damon Runyon would say, more than somewhat.

"Absurdities" includes the tale of a best man at a wedding in Belfast who was so rattled that he said "I will" instead of the groom, and the ceremony had to be done again. Also a picture of Rubev, the Scotty chosen to be "bride" of President Roosevelt's famous Fala; Rubev was the daughter of Telek, the Scotty given to General Eisenhower by Winston Churchill. (Will the Great Republic's new First Dog be of this famous line?) And a picture of Miss Bunty Maitland-Makgill-Crichton, who, as bridesmaid at a fashionable London wedding, wore a monocle.

"Curiosa" includes the report of the Ontario farmer who sold his daughter, aged twelve, to her suitor for $75, with an old overcoat accepted as part payment, on August 13, 1942. Another odd fish in this net is a female bigamist, who acquired eight husbands, all living, before she was twenty-six. Bigamy is usually a man's weakness. From Florida comes the tale of a man of seventy who kept the embalmed body of his nineteen-year-old sweetheart in his bedroom for years, hoping to find a way of restoring it to life.

"Crime and Suicide" does not need explanation, though the clipping about the sailor whose pleasure it was to torture his parrot with a poker has a macabre interest. The extraordinary means of suicide form the chief interest here.

"Strange Manifestations of the Holy Ghost" includes an account of the dying contractor who caused all his workmen to file past his bedside, while he thanked them for their services and bade them farewell. And of a Bible Class which "dedicated" a new outdoor fireplace with a wiener roast. And of the British seaman who rowed for two hours in a fire to save some injured companions, till his hands were burnt to the bone; he received the George Cross posthumously. And of the woman in Halifax who had the heel torn from her shoe by a poltergeist while she was running from it.

Strange reading? It is meant to be. The world is full of romantic, macabre, improbable things which would never do in works of fiction. When those that come within one man's notice are gathered together in a scrapbook, they tell of a world which sobersided folk may not choose to recognize as their own. But it is their own; I have the evidence.

Toronto Daily Star, 10 September 1960

Dangerous Jewels

To be apt in quotation is a splendid and dangerous gift. Splendid, because it ornaments a man's speech with other men's jewels; dangerous, for the same reason. A man who quotes too easily risks the loss of any capacity he may have had for personal expression; he has only to dip into the filing cabinet of his memory and—presto!—the witty, or impressive or brilliantly compressed essence of what somebody else has thought is his to utter. Furthermore, many people are so impressed by his ability to quote that they overvalue the sense of what he has so elegantly said.

Few of us are in danger from this facility. We have to use dictionaries of quotations. Perhaps the best known is *Familiar Quotations*, founded on the 1855 volume published by John Bartlett, book-seller to so many Harvard men. It is a generally useful book, arranged according to authors and with a line index. Its English equivalent is *The Oxford Dictionary of Quotations*. Both have their "spheres of influence" because of their countries of origin. Bartlett does not record any quotations from Beatrix Potter, nor the Oxford book anything by Louisa May Alcott, though both are sufficiently quotable. Both assume that if you want to quote, you already have your quotation in mind; this is not the case with that invaluable volume *A New Dictionary of Quotations*, compiled by H. L. Mencken, which lists its riches under subject-headings, and makes no pretence of offering what is familiar.

Indeed, we may wonder as we look through Bartlett precisely

what group of people ever quoted, with easy familiarity, from the works of Mary Mapes Dodge or Edmund Clarence Stedman. Nor is our wonder diminished when we look in *The Oxford Dictionary of Quotations,* though of course we all unconsciously quote Harry Dacre ("Daisy, Daisy, give me your answer, do!") and Henry J. Sayers ("Ta-ra-ra-boom-de-ay!") and Ira David Sankey ("In the sweet by-and-by"). But too much traffic with a quotation book begets a conviction of ignorance in a sensitive reader. Not only is there a mass of quotable stuff he never quotes, but an even vaster realm of which he has never heard. It is depressing thus to be reminded how little one knows.

It is a pleasant hobby to collect quotations which are not in the books for your personal use. You may do it by jotting them down whenever something turns up in your reading that sounds as if it might be useful to you some day. I have a mass of such quotations, and I offer a few for your inspection. "To do great work one must be very idle as well as very industrious"; that is Samuel Butler, and none of the three books named here contains it, though the Oxford book has his admirable "An honest God's the noblest work of man." And here is something from Anton Chekhov: "Drama takes place inside a man, and not in extreme manifestations . . . Shooting is not drama; it is an accident"; the TV people would be ruined if they ever permitted such a thought to cross their minds. Nor would the TV comics like V. S. Pritchett's remark that "Facetiousness gets shriller and lighter; humour sinks deeper and deeper into its ribald and wicked boots."

I am fond of a German comment by the late Albert Einstein: "*Raffiniert ist der Herr Gott, aber boshaft ist Er nicht,*" which means "God is subtle, but he is not malicious." Equally disturbing is Dostoevsky's comment that "To be too conscious is an illness." I do not think our censors would agree with Edmund Burke that "Vice loses half its evil by losing all its grossness," though they might give a judgement of their own to the effect that "What is literature in hard covers at $4.50 may be obscene in a 50-cent paperback."

Sometimes, when I am asked to make speeches, I feel like quoting Cyril Connolly's comment that "Writers should be read and not heard," and when people ask me for advice about writing I often do quote Evelyn Waugh, who says that "The three elements of style are lucidity, elegance and individuality." I am also fond of Middleton Murry's definition of a truly great novel—"A tale to the simple, a parable to the wise, and a direct revelation of reality to the man who has made it a part of his own being."

Van Wyck Brooks wrote, "Earnest people are often people who habitually look on the serious side of things that have no serious side," and Frank O'Connor explores another part of the same philosophy when he says: "Gay people have no need of pride, because gaiety is merely the outward sign of inward integrity, but melancholy people, if they are to exist at all, must have a code, no matter how unreasonable it may appear." There is much meat for reflection in those two remarks and in W. R. Rodgers' saying that "Moral earnestness is the rheumatoid arthritis of poetry."

There you are: a little bundle of quotations which you will not find in the big quotation books, but which I feel deserve a wider circulation. I have culled them from notebooks I have been keeping since 1950. If you do not like them—which is entirely probable—there is nothing to stop you from making an anthology of your own.

Toronto Daily Star, 1 October 1960

Shakespeare over the Port

When Dr. Jackson asked me to speak at this dinner, he did not say that I was to have the honour of replying to a toast to Shakespeare himself. He spoke of "an informal talk over the port," and he even hinted that there might not be any port. God be praised that such an un-Shakespearean austerity has been spared us! But because of the way in which Dr. Jackson phrased his invitation, I have not prepared a very grand speech, and if you find its tone too humble, too personal for the state of afflatus you have reached at this point of the Seminar, apply yourselves to the port, and float my imperfection to a higher level.

I am going to talk about the part Shakespeare has played in my own life. To begin with, I was lucky in being born of parents who loved the theatre, and whose conversation about it was charged with that enthusiasm which immediately catches the ear, even of a very young child. Theatre-going was not easy for them, because we lived far from any large city, but several times each year my parents were absent for two or three days, and I knew why. When they came home, I could count on a full and vivid description of the play. I recall that on the wall of my father's workroom hung pictures of two noble Romans. Only, of course, they were not real Romans. I was not so green as to believe that. They were pictures of William Faversham as Mark Antony, and his wife (a now forgotten, very beautiful actress called Julie Opp) as Portia, in Shakespeare's *Julius Caesar*. To me, they were far more interesting, more awesome and noble, than any genuine Roman could possibly have been.

Shakespeare, it was clear in our home, was the very pinnacle of theatre experience, and theatre experience was one of the half-dozen most splendid things that life had to offer. So I was anxious to get at him, and before I could read I knew all the pictures in the family Shakespeare and I can recall them still. It was one of those volumes illustrated with portraits of actors in their most celebrated roles. They look funny, now, just as the pictures of the actors we see this week will look funny in years to come. But when we laugh at them, we are laughing at our own mortality. If we look more intently, sympathetically, those absurd figures reveal themselves as what they truly are—the Real striving, with very uneven success, to embody the Ideal.

When my brothers, who were older than I, reached that point in school where the study of Shakespearean plays began, I used to sneak their textbooks to see what the plays looked like. Alas! They were the old Copp Clark editions, bound in oilcloth the colour of pond-weed. They had an educational smell of glue and economy. Inside the covers was written additional matter, such as:

> Julius Caesar
> Was an old geezer
> Who froze his feet
> In an ice-cream freezer.

The pages were freckled with tiny numbers, which in their turn led to notes at the bottom of each page, explaining what *bootless* and *gramercy* meant. It was a let-down, I can tell you.

In due course I myself came to study from these unappetizing books. By this time I had discovered that all the gamey bits were cut out of the school texts, because I had a Shakespeare of my own; the Ontario Department of Education was hard at its impossible task of trying to educate the masses without in any permanent way inflaming their minds. The peak of my school experience of Shakespeare came in my senior matriculation year; the set play was *A Midsummer Night's Dream,* and it was taught by a solemn donkey who understood nothing but the political organization of fairyland. I well remember him dictating a long note which began, "The fairies live in fairyland full stop. They have a king comma and a queen." But by that time I was going to the theatre myself as often as I could, and I had outsoared the shadow of the Ontario Educational System.

Or so I thought. But when I went to the university, to study Eng. Lang. & Lit., I learned that escape is not so easy. The professor who lectured on Shakespeare seemed to be entrapped in a grotesque, retrospective love-affair with every one of Shakespeare's heroines. I think he even had a feeling that he could have made a respectable faculty wife out of Lady Macbeth. It was from him I learned that the stage is too coarse a medium for the works of the supreme poet; Shakespeare's depths can only be plumbed in the solitude of the study. So I used to shut myself up and plumb away for hours, and I acquired such aptitude that for a time there was a belief that I might pipe Shakespeare into young minds for the rest of my days, as a full-fledged academic plumber.

To further this end, I was shipped off to Oxford, where I worked with some of the fanciest plumbers of the day—Sir Edmund Chambers, Percy Simpson, Neville Coghill, and principally with the Rev. Roy Ridley, a merry Anglican priest, who was editing the New Temple Shakespeare at that time. What astonished my Canadian soul was the gusto which these men brought to their work. Gusto had never entered into my Shakespeare studies before. They did not believe for an instant that Shakespeare belonged entirely in the study, and I gave a howl of relief and stopped pretending that I believed it, too. The greatest gift that Oxford gives her sons is, I truly believe, a genial irreverence toward learning, and from that irreverence love may spring. Certainly it was so in my case. By this time I knew what *bootless* and *gramercy* meant and was ready to get down to work.

Work involved a certain amount of devilling for my tutor, who was editing Shakespeare's plays at the rate of one a week. In his rooms I met a good many actresses, of whom he was very fond, and learned also that sherry is greatly improved if you put a generous dollop of gin into it, which is something Falstaff never knew. In the course of time I got a degree and began to look for a job.

But I had lost my interest in teaching. It had always been a puny growth, and the gin and the actresses finished it. So I went on the stage, and in no time at all I was a very minor member of the company at the Old Vic, of which Dr. Guthrie was at that time the director. I played modest roles in Shakespeare; I once played the Widow in *The Taming of the Shrew*. This was because my Oxford thesis was a study of the male actors who played women's parts in Shakespeare's theatre, and the director wanted to see what the effect was. Principally I played pedants, idiots, old fathers, and drunkards.

As you see, I had a narrow escape from becoming a professor. It was easier to keep myself from becoming a success as an actor. Critics were careful not to outrage my modesty by their praise, and the public scrupulously refused to debauch me with applause. I have thought about it a good deal since, and my conclusion is that I was ahead of my time. Or behind it. Or something.

But my years in the theatre were by no means lost, for there I heard actors—some of them very good ones—talk about Shakespeare's plays. Actors, I need hardly say, are delightful people, but they are not ungovernably intellectual. They are rich in rhetoric, bankrupt of logic. What is more, they are imperially indifferent to matters of scholarly fact. Thus I found that I had left the black coffee of criticism for the opium-pipe of untrammelled theorizing. It was a surprise for me, I can tell you.

I became in the course of time that ambiguous creature, a literary man, and in a modest way, a playwright. I don't suppose there is a country in the world where a playwright has such a tremendous field for modesty as in Canada.

Not that we Canadian playwrights are wholly without our triumphs. Quite soon the Stratford Shakespearean Festival intends to present a play written by a Canadian on the remarkable stage devised by Dr. Guthrie. Many people, I am sure, will think when that happens that the first Canadian dramatic work is being performed in the Festival Theatre. But no. Not quite. In 1956 the Festival presented *The Merry Wives of Windsor,* and as you all know, there is a scene missing from the text of that play, in Act IV, which explains and completes the horse-stealing plot. But that scene was mysteriously present in the production here, and it was gratifying to hear the audience laugh at it just as if it had been written by Shakespeare himself. Rather louder, it sounded to me. I was listening very carefully because, you see, I wrote it. As I listened to that welcome laughter, I was reminded of the famous lines of archy the cockroach:

> coarse
> jocosity
> catches the crowd
> shakespeare
> and i
> are often
> low browed
>
> the fish wife
> curse
> and the laugh
> of the horse
> shakespeare
> and i
> are frequently
> coarse
>
> aesthetic
> excuses
> in bill s behalf
> are adduced
> to refine
> big bill s
> coarse laugh

but bill
he would chuckle
to hear such guff
he pulled
rough stuff
and he liked
rough stuff*

As you listen to *Romeo and Juliet* tomorrow night I hope you will pay close attention to a scene where Romeo speaks to Juliet on her balcony. I don't want to seem boastful, but I think it's rather neat.

But although I escaped the university, and the stage escaped me, I did not escape Shakespeare. I had been filled full of the Shakespearean Orthodoxy of the universities, and I had experienced the evangelistic, inspired, Nonconformist ravings of the theatre folk. I emerged as a Shakespearean agnostic.

I read him frequently, but I haven't plumbed him for years; in fact, I find that he is plumbing me. This is not egotism, but one of the effects of great art. I have freed myself of the impudence of measuring Shakespeare in relation to myself, and am measuring myself in relation to Shakespeare. I seem to have found my place at last, and it is in the audience. Like my parents before me, I am a bewitched play-goer, and to me Shakespeare is the best that the theatre has to offer. I keep a book in which I make notes about the plays I have seen—I warned you that my first love was pedantry—and I find that, excluding movies and amateur assaults, I have seen 96 Shakespeare productions; there are six of the rare plays which I have never seen—three of them are the three parts of *Henry VI*—but I have hopes of bagging them. It is a happy addiction, and the best of it is that it gets worse as time goes on.

To enjoy Shakespeare most in the theatre does not mean to enjoy him there only. There is not much point in going to the theatre with an empty head or what critics who are seeing a Shakespearean play for the first time insist on calling "an unprejudiced viewpoint." If Shakespeare has become part of your life, you cannot dismiss him until the curtain rises, or the gun is fired. The devotee inevitably takes a great deal to the theatre with him. And what is it that he takes?

A quality of hard-won simplicity is, I think, the best equipment he can have. I do not mean the simplicity of the naive play-goer who wonders during the interval whether Macbeth is going to get away with the murder. It is an excellent thing if, as a play-goer, you possess some knowledge of what the scholars have said about Shakespeare, so long as it does not obsess you. No, I mean rather that calm of mind in which the Shakespearean world is encountered in simplicity—in which one is prepared to accept Shakespeare without inhibiting and irrelevant reservations.

Such reservations, for instance, as those that Bernard Shaw advanced against Shakespeare. The man's intellect, he said, was commonplace, and in order to endure him it was necessary to think of him entirely as a poet.

But if you go to the theatre looking for intellect above all else, you are in the wrong place. It is Shakespeare's breadth of vision which strikes awe into our hearts, not the profundity of his philosophy. To appreciate him we want, not a plumb-line, but a powerful telescope. We can enter into that breadth of vision if we will, though I warn you against the nineteenth-century folly, not quite dead, of trying to see Shakespearean characters as if they were people you might meet in daily life. If you try that game you will find Dogberry in the courtroom, and Holofernes at the university, and Justice Shallow and his Cousin Slender at the cocktail party, but not many of the others. Because Shakespeare was not so much interested in characters—he knew that the actors would look after that—as he was in emotions. He called them passions, and he reveals them more nakedly than anyone else has ever done. Shakespearean characters are not so much remarkable for their subtlety as for their size. For subtlety he could not hold a candle to Henry James, for instance, or George Meredith, but in the weight and force of passion he is like no one else.

How does our simplicity enable us to enter into those passions? Not, I think, by trying to find them in the world outside us. The crimes and the follies which get into the newspapers will teach us nothing about Shakespeare unless we have first of all, sometimes with pain and dismay, found them in ourselves. It is our own jealousy and our own ambition, which we keep so carefully on the chain, that will carry us deep into Othello and Macbeth. Goethe said that he could imagine himself committing any crime, and if we are honest most of us can do so, too. Under the pressure of circumstances, we would all be brought to any enormity. It is this simplicity and this self-knowledge that we must take to the playhouse with us, and when we are there we must so lay ourselves open to the play that passion can speak directly to passion.

Ah, I hear you say, he means identification. Surely that is a little naive? No, I do not mean identification, which is the assumption of a character other than our own. I mean recognition, which is what happens when a work of art wakens what lies deep and unexercised in ourselves, and gives it a splendid voice.

Nor would I have you think that I suggest that we go to the theatre only to revel in secret villainies. It is not easy for us to find Shakespeare's tragic heroes in our own breasts—though they are there, in some degree—but I think it may be even harder for many of us to respond in the kind of simplicity I urge to the exuberant happiness of his comedies.

Consider *A Midsummer Night's Dream* and *The Tempest*. These are, I honestly believe, greater mysteries than *Hamlet* or *Lear*. In them there is a marvellous reconciliation of the supernatural with the explicable, which is in effect a balancing of the Conscious and the Unconscious parts of the mind. This is genius. It is here that we approach the supreme glory, the very godhead, of Shakespeare. These two plays were possible only to a man who had the most uncommon access to the remotest chambers of the Self; to that realm beyond the Ego, at the very heart of being. Here we find the writer who spoke from that vast realm which the depth psychologists and the religious mystics have tried to chart, and which so obstinately resists the approach of anyone but the artist—and only the supreme artist.

It is simplicity which we must bring to Shakespeare in the theatre or even—for my old friend of my university days was not entirely wrong—in the study. Not the simplicity of inertia, but the calm stillness with which we wait for revelation. And again I repeat that it is easier to reach an understanding of Shakespeare's bitterness than it is to know the flavour of his sweetness. There is a danger that we may be satisfied with a half-acquaintance with Shakespeare, nodding our heads darkly over the madness of *Lear* or the misanthropy of *Timon*. But what Shakespeare demands of us is not acquiescence, but experience; he does not want to make us think, he wants to make us feel. And here the comedies are the great test, and the two greatest comedies are the final test. It is with our understanding of them that we measure our success in what Chesterton so revealingly calls "the mysticism of happiness." Any donkey can persuade himself that he feels tragedy, simply by being low-spirited; but comedy on the level of the *Dream* or *The Tempest* is in part for a play-goer who possesses the simplicity of youth, and even for the play-goer who is revelling in the tinsel pleasures of sophistication, but only fully for the play-goer who is within hail of that later simplicity which means wisdom.

Much that is illuminating and valuable has been written about Shakespeare's pessimism. But I have never known anyone to suggest that it would have been impossible without Shakespeare's optimism. It is a matter of psychological balance; no man could look so deeply into the blackness of—no, not anything so trivial as murder—into misanthropy, pride, and jealousy, which poison life at the spring, who had not also compensating experience of a joyous and exuberant serenity.

Why, you ask? Why should there not be an exclusively tragic form of genius? I do not know; I only know that there has never been a tragic writer worth considering who did not have a rich endowment of comedy, and I think it must be because no man can know what loss of fortune means at its worst, who has not a warm understanding of what the fruition of fortune is at its best. There are not two Shakespeares, a comedian and a tragedian; there is but one Shakespeare, and he wrote from one mind.

A speech about Shakespeare ought really to end with a peroration—a gush of splendid words such as "deep-browed," "organ-voiced," "o'er-topping," "England," "All the world's a stage," and so forth—but what I have said has been so personal, so much in the line of an informal talk over the port, that it would be silly to pull out the diapason now, and roar at you. I do not even pretend that what I have been saying is a final opinion, to which I expect to be committed for the next thirty years. It is only a part of what I think now, after a part of a life which has been engaged, in part, with Shakespeare.

As for Shakespeare himself, I have not forgotten that this is a reply to a toast to his memory, and I am certain that he would wish me to thank you very much. So thank you for Shakespeare, and thank you for me.

Stratford Papers on Shakespeare, 1960
Toronto: Gage Publishing, 1961

Forgotten Dialogues

Rummaging through the ten-cent box in a bookshop recently, I came upon a paper-bound volume called *McBride's Temperance Dialogues*. On the cover an angel, her face a mask of scorn, was pouring a jug of water over a devil, who bore in his hand a bottle of unmistakable shape; this devil was also having trouble with a large snake who had coiled round his waist and between his legs in what must have been a ticklish and embarrassing fashion. I bought it at once and read the whole 183 pages.

My interest was not especially in temperance, but in that now forgotten dramatic form, the dialogue. When I was a boy the dialogue was still immensely popular in the rural day and Sunday schools I attended, but I realize now that it was on its last legs. I took part in innumerable dialogues myself. I wonder if there is anybody, anywhere, who recalls my performance as the Editor in a stirring dialogue called "The Christmas Magazine"? In that character I interviewed several authors who read (or rather, recited) Christmas pieces, but at last awarded a bag of gold to a Poor Child (so called in the list of characters) who read the story of the Nativity. But perhaps my best performance was as a comic physician, called Doctor Ipecac, who closed a school because of an epidemic of pink-eye. This piece came from a book called *Twenty Health Dialogues*, and was performed in honour of Health Week.

My knowledge of the dialogue included experience as an auditor as well as an actor. I recall one which took the form of a debate between a Country Boy and a City Boy, as to which enjoyed the greater advantages. In my school, which was a country one, we could cast and costume the farmer's boy to perfection; he wanted to chew tobacco, to lend realism to his role, but the teacher refused, even though he explained that it would only be liquorice. The City Boy was a problem, but he made a fair show in his Sunday suit, a new cap, and a watch-crystal stuck in his eye for a monocle; we sincerely believed that the effete sons of the great municipalities all wore monocles and talked with English accents. This dialogue was unquestionably the dramatic triumph of my time in primary school, and I was sorry not to have a part in it; our teacher, Miss Belle Eady, was an early enthusiast for type-casting, however, and I was her specialist in Professional roles—editors, doctors and, once, a clergyman.

McBride's Temperance Dialogues quickly brought back anything I had forgotten about the nature of these entertainments. They were always jocular in style until just before the end, when they took a sharp turn toward seriousness and pounded home a moral with sledge-hammer blows. In the *Temperance Dialogues* all the comic aspects of drink are exploited fully; drunken men stagger, mix up their words and commit every sort of foolishness, but at the end they are shown to be beasts; indeed, several of them are reduced to vomiting, which the writer delineates by making them fall on their knees, saying "Ook! Ook!" piteously. I cannot imagine any boy of spirit who would not be delighted to play a drunkard—even to vomiting—in front of his Sunday school. Indeed, the vomiting might be the chief attraction of the role.

Why these little dramas were called "dialogues," rather than "plays," I do not know, unless it is because action is very limited in them, and talk is profuse. I have seen dialogues in which nobody moved from start to finish, the players standing in the transfixed positions of those who are waiting for their next turn to utter. Of course when I went to school we did not call them dialogues when out of the teacher's earshot; we called them "skits" or "take-offs," not that they ever took off anything; their intention was moral rather than satirical.

Who wrote them? Men like the mysterious McBride, who may have been teachers, but cannot possibly have known anything about the stage. In the back of my book there are twenty pages of advertisements for collections of dialogues, but they are credited to publishers rather than authors. There are advertisements for other books, too. One is *Blackbridge's Complete Poker Player,* and another is *The Manufacture of Liquors, Wines and Cordials.* The publisher catered to every taste—temperance dialogues for the young; distilling and poker for the unregenerate old.

Toronto Daily Star, 11 November 1961

A Curmudgeon

What should jump out of the mail at me one morning this week but a questionnaire from somebody at a distant university, who says that he is collecting information about "a selected group of authors." After the usual questions as to how old I am and how many divorces I have survived, comes this one: "What do you conceive to be the Public Image of yourself?"

I had never thought about it, but this Tempter put it into my head, and approaching a younger colleague of mine whom I consider a judicious sort of chap, I put it to him. "What would you say the Public Image of me was?" I queried, perhaps a little coyly. After gazing at me for an uncomfortably long time, he replied: "An exacerbated curmudgeon." As I did not reply at once, he continued: "Insofar as there is a Public Image of you, that's to say."

"I don't think I understand you," I said. "Well, let's say the public thinks you're a grouch," said he. "I understood your words well enough," I replied; "it is their application to myself that puzzles me." "Ah, wad some power the giftie gie us . . ." he began, but I was in no mood for dialect comedy. "Spare me Burns; you have made your point," said I, and swept out.

Then, while my Good Angel hovered above me, rubbing her hands and humming a lively Alleluia, I entered the words "Exacerbated curmudgeon" in the appropriate space on the questionnaire.

This problem of the Public Image is not new in the literary

world. Lord Byron, while he lived, was regrettably careless about his P.I. and word quickly got around that he was not only dangerously fascinating to women, a wife-beater and general tough, but also guilty of incest with his half-sister. This bad publicity did not seem to harm his popularity as a poet; indeed, since his time I do not believe that anybody but John Betjeman (a very different kind of man) has sold so many copies of a single poem during the first week of its publication. But after his death his executor, John Cam Hobhouse, set to work to tidy up his friend's reputation. If you want to read about it, the whole story is told in a new book, *The Late Lord Byron*, by Doris Langley Moore.

Hobhouse met with opposition in unexpected quarters. Lady Byron did not want her late husband's reputation cleared: she enjoyed an agreeable celebrity as a wronged wife; furthermore, she had herself written some verses which Byron had not taken seriously, and this, as well as his indifference to her charms, rankled. (Anybody who has had experience of poetesses knows that they may forgive a punch on the jaw, but never a suggestion that they would be wiser to give up versifying.) Nor were Byron's friends always helpful. They wanted to write books about him, and of course they wanted the books to sell. Virtue, alas, does not make such spicy reading as vice. Poor Hobhouse had a rough time of it for many years, and indeed it cannot be said that his determination to establish the facts about Byron has succeeded even yet.

Byron himself made Hobhouse's task a difficult one by leaving his unpublished memoirs to the Irish poet Thomas Moore, to be used as he saw fit. Moore thought it best to burn them, and although enough evidence has been collected to suggest that they were mild stuff compared to what we see in print now, the rumour persists that they were a male version of *Fanny Hill*.

An uproar about a Public Image is going on right now. Sigmund Freud's son and daughter are distressed that a film is being made by John Huston and Universal Pictures about the great doctor's courtship and marriage. Montgomery Clift, not the most intellectual of mimes, is to appear as Freud. Another angry party to this project is the French playwright and philosopher Jean-Paul Sartre, who wrote the script. It ran to 2,000 pages and would have made a ten-hour film. With a kind of logic unknown among writers and philosophers, Sartre saw no objection to this, but Huston thought otherwise. Result: high-class hubbub.

I feel sympathy for the Freud family. To have one's father—especially so austere a father as Sigmund Freud—presented to the world in terms of Hollywood romance would be worse than anything that happened to Byron.

Suppose, improbable though it is, that a film were ever made about me and my Public Image. Who would be chosen for the title-role? Zero Mostel, very likely.

Toronto Daily Star, 25 November 1961

The Pleasures of Love

Let us understand one another at once: I have been asked to discuss the pleasures of love, not its epiphanies, its ecstasies, its disillusionments, its duties, its burdens or its martyrdom—and therefore the sexual aspect of it will get scant attention here. So if you have begun this piece in hope of fanning the flames of your lubricity, be warned in time.

Nor is it my intention to be psychological. I am heartily sick of most of the psychologizing about love that has been going on for the past six hundred years. Everybody wants to say something clever, or profound, about it, and almost everybody has done so. Only look under "Love" in any book of quotations to see how various the opinions are.

Alas, most of this comment is wide of the mark; love, like music and painting, resists analysis in words. It may be described, and some poets and novelists have described it movingly and well; but it does not yield to the theorist. Love is the personal experience of lovers. It must be felt directly.

My own opinion is that it is felt most completely in marriage, or some comparable attachment of long duration. Love takes time. What are called "love affairs" may afford a wide, and in retrospect, illuminating variety of emotions; not only fierce satisfactions and swooning delights, but the horrors of jealousy and the desperation of parting attend them; the hangover from one of these emotional riots may be long and dreadful.

But rarely have the pleasures of love an opportunity to manifest themselves in such riots of passion. Love affairs are for emotional sprinters; the pleasures of love are for the emotional marathoners.

Clearly, then, the pleasures of love are not for the very young. Romeo and Juliet are the accepted pattern of youthful passion. Our hearts go out to their furious abandonment; we are moved to pity by their early death. We do not, unless we are of a saturnine disposition, give a thought to what might have happened if they had been spared for fifty or sixty years together.

Would Juliet have become a worldly nonentity, like her mother? Or would she, egged on by that intolerable old bawd, her Nurse, have planted a thicket of horns on the brow of her Romeo?

And he—well, so much would have depended on whether Mercutio had lived; quarrelsome, dashing and detrimental, Mercutio was a man destined to outlive his wit and spend his old age as the Club Bore. No, no; all that Verona crowd were much better off to die young and beautiful.

Passion, so splendid in the young, wants watching as the years wear on. Othello had it, and in middle life he married a young and beautiful girl. What happened? He believed the first scoundrel who hinted that she was unfaithful, and never once took the elementary step of asking her a direct question about the matter.

Passion is a noble thing; I have no use for a man or woman who lacks it; but if we seek the pleasures of love, passion should be occasional, and common sense continual.

Let us get away from Shakespeare. He is the wrong guide in the exploration we have begun. If we talk of the pleasures of love, the best marriage he affords is that of Macbeth and his Lady. Theirs is not the prettiest, nor the highest-hearted, nor the wittiest match in Shakespeare, but unquestionably they knew the pleasures of love.

"My dearest partner of greatness," writes the Thane of Cawdor to his spouse. That is the clue to their relationship. That explains why Macbeth's noblest and most desolate speech follows the news that his Queen is dead.

But who wants to live a modern equivalent of the life of the Macbeths—continuous scheming to reach the Executive Suite enlivened, one presumes, by an occasional Burns Nicht dinner-party, with the ghosts of discredited vice-presidents as uninvited guests.

The pleasures of love are certainly not for the very young, who find a bittersweet pleasure in trying to reconcile two flowering egotisms, nor yet for those who find satisfaction in "affairs." Not that I say a word against young love, or the questings of uncommitted middle-age; but these notions of love correspond to brandy, and we are concerned with something much more like wine.

The pleasures of love are for those who are hopelessly addicted to another living creature. The reasons for such addiction are so many that I suspect they are never the same in any two cases.

It includes passion but does not survive by passion; it has its whiffs of the agreeable vertigo of young love, but it is stable more often than dizzy; it is a growing, changing thing, and it is tactful enough to give the addicted parties occasional rests from strong and exhausting feeling of any kind.

"Perfect love sometimes does not come until the first grandchild," says a Welsh proverb. Better far if perfect love does not come at all, but hovers just out of reach. Happy are those who never experience the all-dressed-up-and-no-place-to-go sensation of perfection in love.

What do we seek in love? From my own observation among a group of friends and acquaintances that includes a high proportion of happy marriages, most people are seeking a completion of themselves. Each party to the match has several qualities the other cherishes; the marriage as a whole is decidedly more than the sum of its parts.

Nor are these cherished qualities simply the obvious ones; the reclusive man who marries the gregarious woman, the timid woman who marries the courageous man, the idealist who marries the realist—we can all see these unions: the marriages in which tenderness meets loyalty, where generosity sweetens moroseness, where a sense of beauty eases some aridity of the spirit, are not so easy for outsiders to recognize; the parties themselves may not be fully aware of such elements in a good match.

Often, in choosing a mate, people are unconsciously wise and apprehend what they need to make them greater than they are.

Of course the original disposition of the partners to the marriage points the direction it will take. When Robert Browning married Elizabeth Barrett, the odds were strongly on the side of optimism, in spite of superficial difficulties; when Macbeth and his Lady stepped to the altar, surely some second-sighted Highlander must have shuddered.

If the parties to a marriage have chosen one another unconsciously, knowing only that they will be happier united than apart, they had better set to work as soon as possible to discover why they have married, and to nourish the feeling which has drawn them together.

I am constantly astonished by the people, otherwise intelligent, who think that anything so complex and delicate as a marriage can be left to take care of itself. One sees them fussing about all sorts of lesser concerns, apparently unaware that side by side with them—often in the same bed—a human creature is perishing from lack of affection, of emotional malnutrition.

Such people are living in sin far more truly than the loving but unwedded couples whose unions they sometimes scorn. What pleasures are there in these neglected marriages? What pleasure can there be in ramshackle, jerrybuilt, uncultivated love?

A great part of all the pleasure of love begins, continues and sometimes ends with conversation. A real, enduring love-affair, in marriage and out of it, is an extremely exclusive club of which the entire membership is two co-equal Perpetual Presidents.

In French drama there used to be a character, usually a man, who was the intimate friend of husband and wife, capable of resolving quarrels and keeping the union in repair. I do not believe in such a creature anywhere except behind the footlights. Lovers who need a third party to discuss matters with are in a bad way.

Of course there are marriages that are kept in some sort of rickety shape by a psychiatrist—occasionally by two psychiatrists. But I question if pleasure of the sort I am writing about can exist in such circumstances. The club has become too big.

I do not insist on a union of chatter-boxes, but as you can see I do not believe that still waters run deep; too often I have found that still waters are foul and have mud bottoms. People who love each other should talk to each other; they should confide their real thoughts, their honest emotions, their deepest wishes. How else are they to keep their union in repair?

How else, indeed, are they to discover that they are growing older and enjoying it, which is a very great discovery indeed? How else are they to discover that their union is stronger and richer, not simply because they have shared experience (couples who are professionally at odds, like a Prime Minister and a Leader of the Opposition, also share experience, but they are not lovers) but because they are waxing in spirit?

During the last war a cruel epigram was current that Ottawa was full of brilliant men, and the women they had married when they were very young. If the brilliant men had talked more to those women, and the women had replied, the joint impression they made in middle-age might not have been so dismal. It is often asserted that sexual compatibility is the foundation of a good marriage, but this pleasure is doomed to wane, whereas a daily affectionate awareness and a ready tongue last as long as life itself.

It always surprises me, when Prayer Book revision is discussed, that something is not put into the marriage service along these lines—"for the mutual society, help, comfort and unrestricted conversation that one ought to have of the other, both in prosperity and adversity."

Am I then advocating marriages founded on talk? I can hear the puritans, who mistrust conversation as they mistrust all subtle pleasures, tutting their disapproving tuts.

Do I assert that the pleasures of love are no more than the pleasures of conversation? Not at all: I am saying that where the talk is good and copious, love is less likely to wither, or to get out of repair, or to be outgrown, than among the uncommunicative.

For, after all, even lovers live alone much more than we are ready to admit. To keep in constant, sensitive rapport with those we love most, we must open our hearts and our minds. Do this, and the rarest, most delicate pleasures of love will reveal themselves.

Finally, it promotes longevity. Nobody quits a club where the conversation is fascinating, revealing, amusing, various and unexpected until the last possible minute. Love may be snubbed to death: talked to death, never!

Saturday Night, 23 December 1961

Basic Optimism

*L*ast week I became involved in one of those conversations which are inevitable for anybody who writes about books. A lady of determined expression cornered me at a party, and our talk went like this:

DETERMINED LADY: I read your Diary.

MYSELF: That's very kind of you.

D.L.: Not kind at all. I don't always agree, you know.

M.: Shall I commit suicide here, or go into the kitchen?

D.L.: Don't embarrass our host; wait till you get home. I think you're an escapist. You're always recommending books you say "gave you pleasure" or that you "read with delight." Do you think your readers want a diet of cream puffs? Some of us are pretty serious.

M.: So am I pretty serious.

D.L.: You don't show it.

M.: I try to take the advice of that great journalist Bernard Shaw. He said his policy was to discover what needed saying, and to say it with the utmost possible levity.

D.L.: Surely a lot of very serious books must come your way.

M.: A lot of very solemn books. The serious ones are few.

D.L.: Would you like to explain that distinction?

M.: Serious books say important things, often in an amusing way. They give great pleasure, serious as they are. The solemn ones try to give an impression of importance by piling on the agony. They betray themselves in the first few pages as the work of one-eyed writers who see only what is gloomy and dispiriting in life. It is just as stupid to be a narrow pessimist as an idiot optimist.

D.L.: But surely the Human Condition is basically pessimistic?

M.: That is a fashionable attitude.

D.L.: It's a philosophical attitude.

M.: There are others, just as philosophical, that are more hopeful. And of course there is the religious attitude, which is very hopeful. Religion is in fashion nowadays—theology, that is to say, not just hot-gospelling.

D.L.: All right. But in literature, don't you think tragedy is more important than comedy?

M.: No, I think comedy is more difficult to write, and feel, than tragedy. It is easier to fake tragedy than comedy. Be as depressing as you can, and there will be readers who will acclaim your work as clear-eyed, penetrating and tragic. Of course real tragedy is something more than merely gloomy and nasty writing, and it is very rare. So is real comedy.

D.L.: Making people laugh can't be very hard. Look at the people who are able to do it.

M.: Be fair. Look at the equally shallow and silly people who can make an audience cry. But I spoke of real comedy, which goes through laughter to something far beyond it.

D.L.: How?

M.: Tragedy is more than boo-hooing: comedy is more than guffawing. Do you know G. K. Chesterton's essay on *A Midsummer Night's Dream?* In it he speaks of "the mysticism of happiness." A magnificent phrase. Great comedy lifts us to a level of feeling from which we see life stripped of inessentials; its glories and splendours are revealed.

D.L.: But isn't that what tragedy is supposed to do?

M.: Yes, and it does. But so does comedy.

D.L.: But you wouldn't say that comedy and tragedy are the same thing?

M.: They are parts of the same thing. Both leave us with a

sense of the wonder of life and the greatness of man. Comedy that never gets beyond laughter and tragedy that never goes beyond tears leave us stale. Novels like television programs about silly people, and novels about people who have never had a chance and wouldn't know a chance if it bit them, have nothing to do with either comedy or tragedy. So I rarely write about them.

D.L.: And the decision is entirely your own?

M.: How can it be otherwise?

D.L.: Well, anyway, I don't always agree with you.

M.: Madam, that is a privilege you buy with your paper.

D.L.: Because life is a serious business, especially now.

M.: Too serious for foolish indulgence in unnecessary gloom.

D.L.: There you go again!

M.: And there you go again! Have a macaroon.

(We both do: our jaws are glued together: the conversation ends.)

Toronto Daily Star, 3 February 1962

Book Collecting

Some months ago I was visiting friends in Ireland who took me to call on a neighbour, a titled lady who, they told me, was in financial straits. I was surprised to be shown into a library which I knew at once would bring several thousand pounds if she chose to sell it. I therefore assumed that she must prize her books highly, and tried to lead the conversation toward literature and collecting, but with no success. She would talk only about farming, gardening and the difficulties of maintaining a large house with no staff.

At last I asked her point-blank about the library. Her eyes misted. For an instant I felt I had intruded upon a secret sorrow, or shown some sort of North American grossness. But her reply reassured me.

"I suppose it is quite nice," said she. "My husband's father knew quite a lot about it, but we've never troubled ourselves. There's a Shakespeare Fourth Folio somewhere, but I haven't seen it for a long time, and a first edition of *Pride and Prejudice,* though I think it's been lost. Oh, and we have the first printed edition of the Venerable Bede's book"—she waved toward a copy of the *Historia ecclesiastica gentis Anglorum* which I had already spotted, and the cover of which was hanging loose— "and some other things."

Indeed there were some other things. I had made a quick tour of the shelves while the others chatted. The library was suffering painfully from neglect but was still a splendid accumulation, and there was nothing wrong with it that a good book repairer and a lot of love and saddle soap could not put right. As my hostess talked on about how short of money she was, I asked her why she did not sell her library, since she did not appear to attach much importance to it.

"I'd have no idea what to ask," said she. "Several years ago I met a little man at dinner who wanted to know if we had any books. An American—a medical man, I think. I said yes, and asked him to come to see them some time. Do you know, he turned up the very next day! Just at teatime, and we had some people in, so my husband went to the door and said it wouldn't be convenient, and I think they can't have got on, because the little man never came again."

"I don't suppose the American's name could have been Rosenbach, could it?" I asked.

"Yes, that was it," said she. "I thought he was rather pushing."

This encounter must have been one of Doctor Rosenbach's few defeats during his famous tour of Ireland, when he scooped up so many fine things for his clients. Edwin Wolf and John F. Fleming's recent biography of him makes no mention of the incident, which was not important to Rosenbach, but it might have proved a profitable experience for the lady who had mislaid her Shakespeare Folio to have received the most astute and highest-paying book dealer of our time.

I have found this story useful as a means of discovering what interest people have in books. Those who think of them principally as objects of value exclaim at the lost opportunity to do business with Rosenbach. Those who love books for themselves grieve at the neglect of a fine, perhaps a brilliant, library. And of course there are a few who glory in the aristocratic spirit which sets a tea party ahead of a sorely needed business deal.

This last point of view is of immense psychological interest, but has no place in a discussion of book collecting. Members of the first group, who think of books as valuable objects to be bought and sold, are interesting only when they achieve something approaching the proportions of a Rosenbach. If they buy and sell on a lesser scale, they might as well be dealing in rare stamps; like so many collectors of all sorts, they are mere hagglers and swappers, occasionally goaded by an obsession to complete an assemblage of objects to which they have themselves set arbitrary limits. If a man determines, for instance, that he will get together examples of all the books Horace Walpole produced on his private printing press at Strawberry Hill, he has set himself a difficult and expensive task, for this realm is confused by clever forgeries. Such a man may be—or become—a real Walpole enthusiast, but the chances are that it is the difficulty the collection presents and the particular sort of status attached to its assemblage that enchant him.

Is there anything wrong with such an attitude? No; it ranks with collecting pictures by a famous painter, or school of painters, not because you like them but because they are valuable. It is a way of gaining face, and I suppose it is sometimes an evidence of the creative spirit; if you cannot make a work of art yourself, you can at least make a distinguished collection of such works. The galleries and museums, and through them the public, owe an incalculable debt to this spirit. But my real admiration is reserved for people who collect books because they love them.

If you love books, why is any good edition not as dear to you as a first edition, or one which presents some special features? Edmund Wilson attacked Rosenbach and his imitators in 1926, saying, "All this trade is as deeply boring to people who are interested in literature as it seems to be fascinating to those others who, incapable of literary culture, try to buy the distinction of letters by paying unusual prices for bibliographical rarities." That is partly true, but if we visit those great libraries in ancient universities where the collections of book lovers of the past are preserved as unities, we soon know better. In those splendid rooms we feel the presence of something noble, which has played a great part in shaping a man's mind to a noble form. We sense books as things with more character than the commercial productions of a trade. It is splendidly austere to say that Shakespeare is just as much Shakespeare in a paperback edition as he is in the beautiful Nonesuch Press edition of 1929 or the First Folio of 1623, but not all of us are such literary Calvinists. We value beauty and we value associations, and I do not think we should be sneered at because we like our heroes to be appropriately dressed.

It is the snobbery of book collecting that disgusts. Suppose our friend the collector shows us his first edition of Max Beerbohm's *Zuleika Dobson;* we handle the chunky, red-brown book with pleasure, reflecting that it was in this form, and in this pleasant type, that Max first saw his child presented to the world; for a moment we are close to the London of 1911. We think of the author with affection, and seem almost to see him across the void of fifty years. But then our friend the collector begins to boast a little: his copy, he points out, is a Gallatin 8 (b); and furthermore, it has the ornamental frame on the spine stamped in green, instead of in gold. He urges us not to mistake it for a mere Gallatin 8b, which is a much inferior article, printed in 1912 and (from the dizzy eminence attained by the owner of a Gallatin 8 (b)) hardly worth having. Perhaps we begin to sicken of our friend the collector, and tell him that we have only a Modern Library edition, which we read every year, with growing appreciation. This may well be a lie, but we have to put the ass in his place somehow. We are driven into bibliographical Puritanism by his antiliterary nonsense.

This is what can happen, but worse may befall. We may begin to yearn for his treasure. We do not covet his house, nor his wife (who gives dismal evidence of his lack of taste), his ox nor his ass, but with a searing flame we lust intolerably for his book. We know what it cost him, because he has not been able to refrain from telling us; he ordered it from a book seller in England (whom he calls "my book seller," as though he owned the fellow bodily) and so he got it for less than twenty dollars, which is considerably less than he would have had to pay for the same copy in New York.

We have twenty dollars in our pocket this minute. But it is not money that matters, nor our ability, at last, to get a Gallatin 8 (b) of *Zuleika* for our own. It is *his* book we want, and we want it now.

In this fevered state men have stolen. Book collectors are often tempted to steal, and if they are not of iron character, they do so. Rosenbach, in his *Books and Bidders,* admits to the temptation: when in doubt as to whether he could buy the very copy of Johnson's *Prologue* used by Garrick at the opening of Drury Lane in 1747, he wished that he might be weak enough to steal it. If he ever stole, he will answer for his deed in distinguished company. Sir Thomas Bodley, founder of the great Bodleian Library at Oxford, had to be watched by his friends; Pope Innocent X, before he gained the triple tiara, was involved in a scandal over a rare book he stole from the famous collection of Montier; Don Vicente, a monk of the Convent of Pobla in Aragon, murdered several collectors in order to get their best books; and of course men in great political positions, like Cardinal Mazarin and Cardinal Richelieu, stole whole libraries under the guise of dispersing the property of enemies of the state. Frederick Locker-Lampson, the poet, confessed that he very nearly married Lady Tadcaster to get his hands on her Shakespeare Folios and Quartos. This is a lust which cannot be described, and is so terrible that I could not wish anyone to feel it.

Between stealing and what may be called Borrowing with Mental Reservation I do not see any great difference. Conscious of this viciousness in my own bosom (oh, what struggles with the monster, in the dead of night and in the dusky recesses of libraries!), I used for many years a book-plate which bore Doctor Johnson's admonition "To forget, or pretend to do so, to return a borrowed object is the meanest sort of petty theft." I wonder if the scoundrels who stole from me have troubled to steam that label out of my books.

Setting aside all the unworthy creatures who value rare books for the wrong reasons, let us look at the true collectors—

splendid fellows like you and me. Why do we collect books?

There is no single, honest answer. It is not solely the love of beauty, which may be the mainspring of the man who collects pictures, or furniture, or china. The book lover will have some beautiful books on his shelves, but there will be some ugly little articles as well. One of my special favourites is a hideous, ill-printed jest-book of 1686; it is stained and thumbed, managing somehow to suggest that it was carried in the pockets of several generations of veterinarians as they went about their business; but it is a rarity. Yet I can honestly say that it is not its rarity that comes first with me; when I read it, I am transported back nearly three centuries to the reign of James II, and its jokes (fearful jokes they are, blunt and dirty) are more congenial than if I had the same book in a neat modern reprint. To the book collector the historical sense is at least as potent as the love of beauty.

Unique qualities are prized, of course, but only a rich man can hope to possess many books which have no mates anywhere in the world. I have a modest example of this kind, a copy of George Cruikshank's *Punch and Judy* which contains all the proofs which were pulled for the publisher, Prowett, taken from his scrapbook. Great collections, like that of Pierpont Morgan, contain hundreds of unique volumes. The ultimate in this line is, of course, the manuscript of a book. Morgan acquired the exquisite, touching original script of Thackeray's *The Rose and the Ring* with the author's own water-colour illustrations; a facsimile has been made, which is in itself enough of a rarity to be a pleasant possession. These things run high; Rosenbach paid £15,400 for the manuscript of *Alice in Wonderland,* at a time when the pound was worth close to five dollars.

An interesting type of unique book is that which dealers describe as "extra-illustrated." In the early nineteenth century people used to make such books for their own pleasure. A man who acquired a biography of his particular hero might also own a considerable number of portraits, significant landscapes, and even letters written by the hero; he sent these away to the binder with his book, and in time it came back to him, handsomely recased, with all the pictures and letters neatly mounted on extra sheets and bound into the text. Such books can be of great interest and value, or they can be junk; it depends on the taste of the original owner. I have one or two books of this kind relating to the theatre, and the additional matter they contain makes them valuable to me; I am not so foolish as to suppose that they would interest anyone who was not bewitched by the theatre of the early nineteenth century.

Collectors, if they are realists, must make up their minds early in life whether they are getting together a group of books which they hope will grow in value, or simply a collection which gives them pleasure. The man who expects to gain a day's posthumous fame when his library disappears into the maw of a university must never lose sight of his primary aim. The professional bibliophiles will paw over his books, and be quick to despise him if he has bought any fakes, or anything unworthy—and how quick legatees are to spot anything which is not up to their demanding standards. But the man who collects only for his own pleasure may buy anything he pleases, not caring that when he dies he will be called a magpie, and that books he has loved will be bought for ten cents apiece by the dealers. He will have some fine things, of course, but as individual items they are not likely to fetch the prices they would bring if he had controlled his desires, and bought only the ingredients of a coherent collection. The fellow who can leave his alma mater every book and every scrap of manuscript relating to or owned by Button Gwinnett is a greater man, in this realm, than the fellow who troubles the university librarian with attractive odds and ends.

The former will put the Gwinnettologists forever in his debt, and tiny pinches of incense, in the form of footnotes, will be cast into his funerary flame. "The late Enoch Pobjoy, to whom Gwinnett scholars are obliged for the new light his collection has thrown on Gwinnett's sanitary arrangements"—that is what *he* will be. But the collector who has lived only for pleasure— what of him?

Well, so far as I am concerned, he is the only collector who really matters. He is a man who loves books, and reads them. He loves books not only for what they have to say to him—though that is his principal reason—but for their look, their feel, yes, and even their smell. He is a man who may give books away, but who never thinks of buying a musty immortality with his library. His affair with books is a cheerful, life-enhancing passion.

Considering what a nuisance books are, it is astonishing what a number of collectors of this stamp one meets. For books are a desperate nuisance; a library of even a few thousand volumes anchors a man to one house, because it is such a task to shift them.

I face the ordeal of a move myself, and regardless of how much I try to concentrate on the realities of the matter, I catch my mind wandering toward fearful calculations as to the amount of shelf room I can possibly hope for in the new house.

Will it be necessary to sink to the horror of a stack room, a book-hell, in the basement? Or (for cheerfulness will keep breaking in) will it be possible to devise some splendid new arrangement so that in a twinkling of an eye, any book may be found?

The one thing that never occurs to me is to get rid of some books, or to forswear buying any more. And that, I suppose, is what being a collector really means.

Holiday, May 1962

Too Much, Too Fast

Graham Greene makes me feel foolish. I admire his work and read everything he writes, but always with the uncomfortable sense that I am a goggle-eyed youth listening to the wisdom of a being vastly more mature, more penetrating in his view of life, than I can ever be. I think I know his secret: his dogmatic religious belief diminishes those who have small appetite for dogma, and his conviction that life is a dreary swindle makes those of us who have frequent spells of cheerfulness feel naive. I know what it is about his work that makes me feel like a fool, but the trick works every time.

Consider his essay "The Lost Childhood," in which he talks about reading. "Perhaps it is only in childhood that books have any deep influence on our lives," he begins, and goes on to say that the books which had most influenced him were those he read before he was fourteen. This is directly contrary to my own experience and makes me feel that I am rather a hick to enjoy reading so much at my advanced age. But then I do not believe, as Mr. Greene does, that life grows more intolerable the more you know about it. And I recall that Sean O'Casey described Greene's attitude to life as "a snot-sodden whinge."

The books I read before I was fourteen were influential, in some cases. One of them was *Pickwick Papers*, which I read at twelve; it took me about ten weeks, as I remember, and much of it was weary work. But after fourteen I really got into high gear. *The Old Wives' Tale* was a revelation, and so was *Ma-*

demoiselle de Maupin, both of which I read as a schoolboy. At seventeen I discovered *Antic Hay* and rushed on to *Point Counter Point;* they, too, were landmarks for me. I read most of Shaw at school, which won me a quite unmerited reputation as a dangerous thinker; it was the plays and the jokes I liked, not the political argument. *The Way of All Flesh* was another violent explosion in my life. Up to twenty life was certainly not running downhill for me.

Nor did it take a downward turn between twenty and thirty. I had my defeats as a reader. I could never get through all of *War and Peace,* though I hope to have another tussle with it in a few years. I never read a novel by Dostoevsky until I was thirty-five, and then *Crime and Punishment* opened up a new world of sensation and introspection. People who write about what they read in youth rarely fail to put me to shame, because they seem to have read so much, so young. But like most of the world's population, I had a living to earn, and a life to lead, and my reading was eager but spotty.

What I really liked was gnawing my way through all the works of a single author. I am one of the not very large group of people not engaged in psychoanalysis who have read the whole of Sigmund Freud's collected works; it was amply worth while, if only for the astonishment I feel when people attribute ideas to Freud which he never expressed, or categorically dismissed. I am chewing my way now through all of C. G. Jung, whom I find a more congenial thinker, but a less engaging writer, than Freud. I have read all of Dickens—much of his work many times—and am amazed at the people who express extravagant admiration or condemnation without having taken this elementary step.

There is no writer within my experience who responds so well to this treatment as Shakespeare. To read his complete works, in the order in which he wrote them, seems a small tribute to pay to the greatest of dramatists, but many people shrink from it. Reading Shakespeare, of course, is hard work—not because it is difficult to understand, but because it is so emotionally demanding. Not brilliant intellect, but profound feeling, is demanded.

It would grieve me to think that my best reading was already over—not to speak of having lost one's delight in it at fourteen. People who have read enormously in youth do not call forth my envy; I have heard them talk about the masterpiece they gobbled at eighteen, and it is clear that they brought an eighteen-year-old understanding to the work of mature giants. So often they have missed the point. A great book—or just a good book— contains some of the best of a perceptive, sensitive, perhaps inspired writer's life. It cannot be encompassed by a hasty reading.

A truly great book should be read in youth, again in maturity and once more in old age, as a fine building should be seen by morning light, at noon and by moonlight. We all read too much, too fast. I am taking the summer off to work slowly through several books that are due for a second reading.

Peterborough Examiner, 16 June 1962

Confessions of an Editor

You ask me for the story I have always wanted to write. Like most newspapermen I know a lot of stories that it would have been an exquisite pleasure to write—if one had intended to suspend publication the following day. But what is the point of grieving over them now? I have written what had to be written.

Very early in my newspaper experience I was given the job of writing an obituary notice of a priest who had died in a rural community within the circulation range of the paper I was working for; the facts available made one slim paragraph, and I had to piece it out, somehow, to respectable length. Nobody seemed to know anything about Father Blank and so, in despair, I wrote a description of a perfect priest, ascribing all the virtues to him, and tacked it on the end of my story. Within the week after it was published I received several warm commendations on the skill with which I had captured Father Blank's character. I had, it appeared, described him to a T.

I hope this experience did not make me cynical, but it certainly taught me that newspaper writing is not entirely a matter of objective, carefully guarded reporting. Sometimes, when I read those obituary notices in the London *Times,* in which it seems to be obligatory to knock the dead, just to show that the newspaper is above ordinary considerations of tact, I wonder what would happen to a *Times* man who tried that game on a small Ontario daily.

I write the words "small Ontario daily" with reluctance, because so few people seem to understand just what "small" means in such a context. On these small papers we work like beavers, and are also very highly organized. We are small in comparison with the metropolitan papers, but locally we are very big indeed. We cannot hide from people we have traduced or wounded, because we are sure to meet them on the street within a few days after the appearance of the offending story. The harsh light that beats upon a throne is as a tallow candle to the rays which suffuse a mayoral chair in a city of 35,000 to 70,000, and mayors and aldermen are correspondingly sensitive. On the small papers we have to be very sure of our facts, and there are proportionately just as many people anxious to mislead us and make mischief as there are in the big cities.

Therefore we are sensitive when people interpret the word "small" in such a way that it implies also "easy-going" and "folksy." I have friends on metropolitan papers who have never worked anywhere else, and assume that my life is that of the small-town editor of fiction. In the eye of their imagination I sit in the news room in my shirtsleeves, puffing my corncob pipe, waiting for farmer friends to bring in champion big turnips, or potatoes that have grown into a likeness of Winston Churchill. I write with the stub of a pencil (which I lick at every fifth word) in handwriting that only one trusted old compositor can read. I know everybody in town, and offer good, ungrammatical advice to the young folks. I am the master of boundless leisure.

Where this picture of the editor of a small newspaper originated, I don't know. When I was a boy, my father ran a weekly with a circulation of 500, and he never had time for any of this character-part nonsense. He was always as busy as his nerves and physique could stand, and so am I. If there are any flowery beds of ease in the newspaper world, they must be in the offices of the metropolitan dailies; they are unknown to me.

A few years ago a friend from a large city dropped in to see me on a busy morning, and composed himself in my visitor's chair for a long, leisurely chat. "My dream is to buy a little paper like this when I retire," he said, "and just run it for fun. Say exactly what I think, and not have to give a damn. I envy you—do you know that?"

That was several years ago, when I was younger, and of a more passionate nature, and I am sorry now that I killed him. Stabbed him with a file. His paper must have been overstaffed, because so far as I know nobody ever missed him. Probably someone else is drawing his salary to this day, and the management thinks he is in Africa, getting the low-down for a special series. I have repented my hasty action, and every year I send an economical wreath to be placed on the spot where I hid the body. People roundabout imagine I buried a beloved pet there.

But—stories I have always wanted to write, and can't, or daren't? Pretty nearly every story qualifies in some way for that category. There is always something a newspaperman knows that cannot be fitted into the piece he is writing. He knows what he knows, and it is certainly a fact, but he can't prove it. Proving facts is very much harder than professors of mathematics would lead us to believe. So far as a newspaperman is concerned, a fact is not only something that is demonstrably true, and well-known to several other people; it is something that he can persuade a court to believe, and call witnesses to support. That diminishes the store of facts in his possession by roughly two-thirds. Early in life the newspaperman loses his desire to posture as a reformer; a few years' experience teaches him not only that facts are slippery things, but also that his judgement is fallible and his knowledge imperfect, and that the fact of today may be the shameful error of tomorrow.

When I worked on *Saturday Night* there was a legend that in the days of Fred Paul, an early editor, the publication owned nothing but a table and a few chairs, and was therefore not worth suing. Nowadays there is no such thing as a paper that is not worth suing, and everybody knows it. This, more than any other thing, has tamed the press.

Dateline: Canada 1962, Ottawa, 1963

Mimesis at Massey

Some years ago I spoke at the annual dinner of an association of architects, offering a few comments on their art from a layman's point of view. I enjoyed making the speech, but passages from it have risen to haunt me ever since. In particular, many of the architects present remember that I said: "One of your functions is to provide appropriate scenery against which we can act out the drama of our lives." I considered that a compliment, for I think of man's life as a splendid thing and, as a student of the theatre, I know how greatly a fine setting complements a great play. But several of the architects felt that I was reducing them to the level of decorators. I have been called upon frequently to explain myself—a phrase which usually means to retract or fight the battle all over again.

Last autumn the Vitruvian Society met at Massey College, and I discovered that some of the Vitruvians were still vexed with me. One of their number asked if I thought the College was appropriate scenery for the dramas lived within it; the question was couched in terms which demanded the answer "no," so naturally there was nothing for me to do but give the answer "yes." What tactful reporters call "a spirited discussion" followed. So spirited was it that the same night I dreamed a dream of an unusually vivid character.

It was not my pow-wow with the Vitruvians alone that determined the nature of the dream: that morning I had cause to speak of *La Vida Es Sueño* in a lecture on theatre history; that afternoon I had given a tutorial involving a discussion of the Edwardian Stage Direction, especially as evinced in the work of those tireless writers of stage directions G. B. Shaw and J. M. Barrie.

In my dream I was sitting in my study, looking out of the window into the quadrangle of Massey College. The architect has given my window the proportions of the proscenium in an Edwardian theatre, and heavy curtains hang at its sides. My dream demands to be described in the terms of a Stage Direction; to do otherwise is to falsify my impression and mislead the reader. So here it is, in the mixture of technical jargon and self-indulgent prose familiar in the drama of 1900 to 1914.

(BEFORE CURTAIN all lights set for DAWN; light steals up from BLUES at ¼ to FULL STRAWS and PINKS at ½ then BLUES OUT; time fade-in for full Act. Before Curtain fifteen seconds of BIRD CALLS.)

THE SETTING reveals the Quadrangle of a College for Graduate Students in the University of Toronto. In the immediate foreground is a pool in which fountains play gently; their sound is not aggressively audible, but dulls all other noise, especially sounds from the East Gate (R.L.E.). The setting recedes in sharp perspective and the stage is sharply raked, giving the impression of a design by Sebastiano Serlio (1475–1554), who was, as every well-informed dreamer will instantly recall, an architect who chose to become a scene designer. There are seven entrances to the Quadrangle, and the façade of the building reveals three ranks of windows, some of which are lighted, showing that certain eager students have mused over their books the whole night through (or have, more prosaically, gone to bed with their lights on). A Tower rises to a height of five storeys from the Pool; on two faces of the Tower a clock is seen, set at 6 a.m. The Quadrangle has lawns, paths, trees and shrubs; as Act One progresses, leaves appear on trees, flowers on the shrubs, and foliage on the vines.

AT RISE OF CURTAIN A REVELLER lets himself in through the East Gate and, hearing the birds sing, sings himself in a loud, unmusical voice. The COLLEGE CAT enters from the West Gate and views the REVELLER with disdain. From an unlighted window an unseen hand hurls a boot at the RE-VELLER, who dodges it, then picks it up and drops it in the Pool with noisy laughter. As the REVELLER disappears into Entrance Three a youthful MAINTENANCE MAN in overalls enters from the West Gate; he retrieves the boot. The Clock has now advanced to eight a.m., and the PORTER runs from the East Gate to the Tower and rings the bell eight times. The CHEF enters from extreme downstage Left, takes three very deep breaths and goes out. Several GRADUATE STUDENTS appear from all entrances, in varying stages of disarray, and straggle across the Quadrangle; time passes and as the clock moves to Nine, they all return to their rooms, and re-emerge, some smartly dressed and carrying briefcases, others precisely as they arose, except for faint traces of egg about the lips; they leave by the East Gate. The BURSAR crosses the Quad, smoking reflectively; he carries a ledger in either hand; as he heaves them gently up and down we realize that he is balancing his books. Two or three SENIOR FELLOWS enter and go to Entrances Three, Four and Five; they are smiling. Shortly afterward they are followed by groups of GRADUATE STUDENTS, some of them girls who look sourly at the birds, who are still singing. As they pass the Pool one or two stoop to dip their hands in it, and seem astonished that the water is real. The Stage empties, except for a COLLEGE CLEANER, who appears at the door of Entrance Four, shakes a mop, waves to the birds and goes in again, leaving the Stage vacant, which, as every student of Jacobean drama knows, indicates the end of an ACT.

———

(BEFORE ACT TWO all lights set for MIDDAY; FULL STRAWS from overhead, and PINKS on all the shrubs; BLUE FLOODS concealed beneath Pool to give sky reflection Special Effect: lawn-sprinkler at full upstage C. All windows open. Play recording of TRAFFIC NOISE off stage outside East Gate, but keep below splash of fountains.)

AS ACT BEGINS, PORTER marches smartly toward the Tower, and bell rings twenty-one times; a married JUNIOR FELLOW is seen holding a telephone out of the window of the Porter's Lodge, for the bell is celebrating the birth of his son and, in the hospital, his wife is listening. PORTER returns to East Gate, his brisk gait contrasting with that of the REVELLER, who creeps from Entrance Three toward L.L.E., where the entry to Dining-Hall is supposed to be; he thinks better of it and sinks on one of the benches near the pool; finds the sunlight trying to his eyes (check bloodshot makeup) and moves to a bench in the shade. He retches weakly, and addicts of symbolism will realize that this marks him as a poor wretch. GRADUATE STUDENTS come from East Gate and from entrances everywhere in Quadrangle, toward Dining-Hall. Time passes, and they emerge at a slower pace, settle on the benches, and play with the COLLEGE CAT, which disdains all but those who have chosen the fish plate at lunch. The LOVER walks alone; from time to time his lips are seen to move; he is trying to find a rhyme. The CLOCK moves to TWO; the GRADUATE STUDENTS hurry off again through the East Gate, and the REVELLER drags himself back to his room, where the curtains are seen to close. TOURISTS arrive, and the PORTER shows them the Quadrangle; a few, certain that something is being concealed from them, creep into the entrances, and are shooed out again. Several AMATEUR PHOTOGRAPHERS appear and take pictures, squinting, clambering and crouching; one of them offers a SENIOR FELLOW fifty cents to pose in his gown, reading a Greek book. THE MAINTENANCE MAN appears;

he is now in robust middle age (addicts of symbolism will instantly realize that he represents Time, and will whisper their discovery to their friends); he changes the position of the lawn-sprinkler. Stage clears, indicating the end of the ACT.

(BEFORE ACT THREE all lights set for SUNSET; change STRAWS to AMBERS at ½, and bring up PINKS ½ and BLUES to ¼; cut FLOODS under Pool and substitute two INDIGOS. Cut traffic sounds and bring in bird-wings recording slowly. Close windows.)

THE QUADRANGLE is empty, except for birds, gathered in numbers on the branches of the trees, from which leaves are falling; the vines on the walls have turned red. From the door of the Examination Room comes a ragged procession; seven middle-aged and elderly men, THE EXAMINERS, move deliberately across the lawn toward the East Gate, chewing at their pipes and bobbing their heads in the manner of professors talking; one young man, THE EXAMINEE, tries to walk like them, but youth and the consciousness that he has just achieved his Ph.D. cause him to give an involuntary triumphant prance every now and then. The MAINTENANCE MAN, elderly now, enters with a rake and barrow and proceeds to scrape up the fallen leaves. The BURSAR enters, wearing the look of perverted triumph suitable to a businessman who knows he may not think of a profit, but glories in the smallest attainable deficit. The COLLEGE SECRETARY joins him, and they go to the Examination Room, where, in a few minutes, they are joined by a group of SENIOR FELLOWS, for a meeting of the College Corporation. Groups of JUNIOR FELLOWS enter from the East Gate; their step is light, and they have the air of men anticipating the opening of the bar at five o'clock. The REVELLER comes from his entrance, alone and palely loitering. He tries to play with the COLLEGE CAT, but it prefers to scuffle in the leaves. Some friends hail the REVELLER, and after a full five seconds of inward struggle he follows them to the bar. The LOVER is last to come through the East Gate; like the others, he collects his letters from the Porter's Lodge, and hastens to open one of them; he stands by the pool to read it; his shoulders droop and he shakes his fist at the sky, which is darkening. The CHEF appears from extreme downstage left and calls to the COLLEGE CAT, which runs to him with a hypocritical expression of affection on its face. The LOVER, observing it, laughs symbolically, then goes to his room. The Stage is clear, marking the end of the ACT.

(BEFORE ACT FOUR change all jellies; STEELS for accentuated areas and INDIGOS for shadow; small amber spot in each entrance to the Quadrangle; otherwise strike all BABIES and upstage NIGGERS; Pool partly iced over, but fountains continue to play, with icicles clinging to faucets; snow on grass areas but paths are cleared; trees, shrubs and vines bare. Clock set at ten p.m. Snow effect and Wind Machine ready.)

MUSIC from the Christmas Dance is heard offstage. Two JUNIOR FELLOWS, accompanied by girls in evening dress, run across forestage and disappear L.L.E. The LOVER appears from his entry, goes to the Lodge, puts a note in the box for out-going mail, then walks swiftly to the Pool and throws himself into it. Death is apparently not all that he had anticipated for, with a roar, he immediately rises, flounders to the edge and crawls out. As he gains the brink the MAINTENANCE MAN, now old, the CHEF and the PORTER run to the Pool, throw a blanket round the LOVER and hurry him back to his room, where the light goes on. The PORTER and CHEF run the length of the Quadrangle and vanish in the direction of the Hall; after a short interval the PORTER reappears, leading a GIRL who displays all the flustered elation of one who has driven a man to the point of death; following them is a JUNIOR FELLOW in flawless evening attire, except for the socks, which are his own and tragically flawed; he bears a hot drink and the distinction of a successful rival; they disappear toward the LOV-

ER'S room. Re-enter the MAINTENANCE MAN and the PORTER; the latter recovers the suicide note from the Lodge and tears it into small pieces, which he flings into the air; as the paper descends snow begins to fall. Laughter is heard from the Hall, and the sound of "Auld Lang Syne," to hammer home the symbolism for those who are a little slow. The MAINTE-NANCE MAN, now very old, shuffles from the Quadrangle, a scythe over his shoulder. Slow CURTAIN as snow falls faster, and the Wind Machine is accelerated from one-half to full.

Well! *La Vida Es Sueño* indeed. I shall not refer this dream to my psychoanalyst. I think it is plainly a matter for the Vitruvians.

University of Toronto's *Varsity Graduate*, Spring 1965

The Three Warning Circles

Once upon a time, on a spring morning, a group of young men and women were crossing a bridge. They had, for some years past, been inhabitants of a crowded walled city, dominated in part by the dead, in part by living interpreters of the dead, and also by a few ogres, a scattering of gnomes, and seasonally by dragons. These dragons slept in their caves during most of the year, but were apt to become a nuisance in the spring. Now, for these young people, the last dragon had been vanquished, the drawbridge had been let down, and they were escaping into the great world, to seek their fortune. They were in a holiday mood.

On the bridge they met an old man of benevolent aspect, and because they were in a holiday mood they made much of him, and gave him a scarlet cloak to wear and a magnificent hood. The old man was greatly moved by their kindness, and thus he spoke:

"You have been generous to me, and I should be greatly pleased to do something for you. What would you like?"

They talked for a few moments among themselves, and at last one of them said: "How about granting us three wishes? We don't want to seem greedy or ask for the impossible, and if you don't feel up to the work have no hesitation in saying so. But this seems to be a decidedly fairy-tale situation, and you might just happen to be a wizard in disguise, so we thought we'd ask."

"As a matter of fact," said the old man, "that is precisely

what I had in mind. But I know you will understand that a lot has happened since the great days of folktale, when I would have granted your three wishes without a moment's hesitation. Since then there have been a number of new ideas let loose upon the world, one of which is called The Protestant Work Ethic, which makes the granting of wishes more difficult than it was, even for democratically elected governments. So, instead of granting you wishes outright I shall do it the modern way, and tell you how to make your wishes come true. You may get what you want, or you may get into dreadful messes, just as you would have done in Olden Times, but it will all be very up-to-date, which I am sure is what you would like. Tell me what you want, and I'll do my best for you."

The young people, who were all Canadians, immediately formed themselves into a committee of the whole, from which they elected a working committee, which discussed the matter for about an hour, though as it was a committee the time seemed to be a year and a day. When they had brought in their report, the old man said, "What is your first wish?"

"To be Healthy," said the chairman of the committee.

The old man made a sign over his heart, as though he were drawing a circle. "And the next?" said he.

"To be Wealthy," said the co-chairman, who was inevitably a girl, because this was a modern group of young people, who firmly believed that the sexes were not merely equal, but almost indistinguishable.

The old man drew out his pocket-book and made a sign over it, as if he were drawing a circle. "And the third wish?" said he.

"To be Wise," said both chairmen together.

The old man leaned down and with his finger he drew a circle in the dust. Then he bowed gravely to the young people, but said nothing.

"We do not understand," said they. "Is that all there is to it?"

"Remember the circles," said the old man, "and Health, Wealth and Wisdom will be yours."

This immediately threw the young people into another committee, from which they emerged at last, to say: "You are not playing fair; you really must tell us more than that. Your circles mean nothing to us. Explain yourself. After all, we gave you a perfectly real red cloak; surely you aren't going to fob us off with three invisible circles?"

"Very well," said the old man. "I shall explain my circles. I want you to keep them in mind because they will continually remind you of the tendency of everything in this world to run into its opposite. You are all well enough acquainted with bush-lore to know that if people lose their way, they are likely to walk in circles. So it is in life: many of the troubles we encounter come from frantic movement in circles.

"Take Health, for instance. It is a very fine thing, but if you chase it too hard it will turn into ill-health. You see it everywhere about you. The people who live too much for the body suffer because of the body. You all know the hockey-player with his pulled muscles and his charley-horse. Some of you know the dancer with his inflamed tendon, and the singer with his perpetual sore throats and colds. Who is not acquainted with the runner, miserable because of his constipation, and the weight-lifter whose secret weakness is his haemorrhoids? Now, I do not for a moment advise you not to play games, and pursue arts that make heavy demands on your physique. But I do warn you that the cult of the physical, unless you pursue it with reason, is very likely to push you right around the circle into bad health. Be moderate, even in health.

"Perhaps you have observed that athletes and health zealots are not, as a class, any more long-lived than people who treat their bodies gently. For that is the secret; you must make a friend of your body; you must not bully it, and nag it and fuss over it. Keep out of its bad books. For you must always bear in mind that some day your body is fated to become your enemy, and it will kill you. Treat your executioner with loving consideration, therefore, so that it will remain your friend for as long as possible."

The young people looked rather grave, but they could not stop the old man, who was enjoying himself and hurried on.

"As for Wealth," said he, "what is it? Is it a needless superfluity of money? No, it is freedom from care. Now, of course, you cannot be free from care without some money, and I urge you not to fall victim to the modern delusion that just enough money for subsistence is enough for happiness. That may be all right while you are young and strong, but after the age of thirty-five it is misery. You can live on very little money if you can rid yourself of craving, but even if you do that, you may be sure you will be forced to live alone, for your wives, or your husbands, or your children will probably not be free of craving, and your government will never weary of craving, so make up your mind to it. You must have some money, for wealth is having more than you need, and you will be astonished how your needs increase.

"But if you live for wealth, the message of my circle will be terribly clear to you. Wealth has a very ugly way of running into its opposite, which is poverty, and let me assure you that the poverty you endure in the midst of great possessions is even more terrible than the poverty of downright daily need, for it has no bounds and nobody can appease it. You do not think now that you will ever fall victim to Avarice, any more than you worry about gout. These are ailments of later life, but you must watch for their symptoms now, or you will become poor in spirit, and that is the ultimate poverty.

"Be particularly careful that in achieving wealth—even moderate wealth—you do not make a slave of anybody else, because if you do the day will come when your slave will be your master, or the master of your children's children. The tyranny of the industrialists of the nineteenth century has given place to the tyranny of the trades unions of the twentieth century: the slavery of the southern plantations is giving place before our eyes to the slavery of the northern cities. Do not make a slave of anyone, though you will meet many people who are astonishingly eager for slavery, which they mistake for security and freedom from responsibility.

"But the commonest personal slavery is the slavery to money and possessions, and it is a slavery toward which the economy of our civilization increasingly tends. You will be told that you must consume more and more in order that others may work. If you believe that, you will be a fool, and though many fools have had gigantic wealth, no fool in the world's history was ever content. And contentment is wealth."

The young people were looking extremely grave by this time, and some of them would have been glad to get away before the old man finished his advice, but good manners kept them where they were.

"And so we come to Wisdom," said the old man, who by now was thoroughly warmed up. "You have been told that wisdom is to be desired above all things. But the people who told you so were often greatly muddled about what they meant. Some of them thought wisdom was a matter of believing certain things, but a much greater number thought wisdom was a matter of disbelieving as much as possible. 'Cast aside all unfruitful and unworthy belief,' they told you, 'and you will make a new world.' And indeed mankind has been casting aside beliefs as fast as possible for at least one hundred and fifty years.

"With what result? We now live in a world where nobody and nothing says, with complete conviction, THOU SHALT NOT. The old God of the old world—which was, quite simply, this world—is dead, and the new God of the Infinite Galaxies has not yet found his prophet.

"But here we see how the warning of my circle has gone unheeded. Wisdom has run so furiously after what is new, and has discarded so prodigally whatever seemed incapable of proof according to the new ways of thinking, that it has run into its opposite, and is dangerous folly. Because it is belief, vastly more than disbelief, that has been the mainspring of human development, and law quite as much as freedom has made it possible for us to live together without hourly conflict. You are governed by your beliefs, and you will perish by your want of belief, because belief is purpose. So, although you may pay what heed you will to the immensities of unbelief, be sure that you are aware of the daily, hourly beliefs by which you stand and which govern your ordinary concerns. Beginning with good manners in all its forms, those beliefs must extend to the high concept of honour, for without honour there can be no fair dealing between man and man, and no splendour of existence, and man cannot live long without some splendour. These beliefs by which you live must accord with the best you know of yourself. But in your search for wisdom do not go around the circle until you come to the folly of a life which is wholly conditioned by negatives, a life in which unbelief has utterly dispossessed belief."

By this time the young people were growing rather sick of the old man. So much so, indeed, that one of them spoke for all the rest, without even a moment's committee work.

"We think you have cheated us," said this speaker. "Your advice is just the tired old stuff that we have heard since the cradle, and your pretence to grant us our three wishes is nothing but a cheat."

"Not at all," said the old man. "You must encounter my circles, whether you like it or not, for they are part of the common fate of mankind. What I have done is to show you the circles, which you would otherwise have had to find out for yourselves. And, I assure you, your danger is that as you make your journey round the circles, you become quite a different person, as all true travellers do, and if you go so far as to draw near again to the place of your beginning you will not recognize it, because you are coming at it from a new and unfamiliar direction. So you should take great pains to remember the circles.

"What I have given you is certainly very old. It is the warning of Heraclitus, who said: '*Panta rhei; oudon mene:* Everything flows; nothing is constant.' And its secret is that if you can avoid travelling in circles, you will still have to travel somewhere, because nobody can possibly stand still in this travelling world. Therefore your aim will be to travel inward and outward, approaching the world at some times, and retreating from it at others. You will take into yourself what the world gives you, and you will return to the world bearing the best gift you have to give to mankind, which is whatever is best and truest of yourself. Because the only straight path you can pursue in this life is the path of self-exploration. And that path is a paradox, for the more you learn of yourself (which is the inward path) the farther you will journey in your knowledge of your fellow-man and of the world in which you live (which is the outward path). You see how clear and simple it is? But if you are caught in the circles you are lost."

Here the old man again saluted them gravely, and (because this is a folktale) blew them a thousand and one kisses. The young people went on their way, beautifully determined to live happily ever after. As for the old man, he hurried away as fast as his legs would carry him.

University of Manitoba's *Alumni Journal*, Summer 1972

The Table Talk of
Robertson Davies

The following pronouncements were recorded by Peter C. Newman in 1972. By giving Davies' responses and omitting his own questions, Newman created a flow of "table talk" similar, in many ways, to the collection Davies himself had published as *The Table Talk of Samuel Marchbanks*. (ed.)

If Britain had never been invaded by the Normans, it is quite likely that the position of women would be splendid now, and would have been splendid for the last 1,500 years. The Normans brought to England the Roman law and the attitude of the Roman Catholic Church toward women, which tended to downgrade them in one way while exalting them through the figure of the Virgin in another way. But under the old Celtic law that had prevailed in Britain and under old Saxon law, women inherited equally from their fathers. They could have divorce upon showing good reason, and good reason was cruelty, madness, sexual incapacity. They could, when they were divorced, take their property back from the marriage, and they could marry again without any difficulty whatever, and they had a well-recognized and honourable place in society. But as soon as they came under the dominance of Roman law and the Catholic Church, women had an awful time, that continued right up to 1882, when the Married Women's Property Act was passed. I have a very high regard for women. I am very fond of women.

I admire them, and think they have extraordinary qualities which are not at all like the predominant male qualities.

The world is burdened with young fogies. Old men with ossified minds are easily dealt with. But men who look young, act young and everlastingly harp on the fact that they are young, but who nevertheless think and act with a degree of caution that would be excessive in their grandfathers, are the curse of the world. Their very conservatism is secondhand, and they don't know what they are conserving.

I think of an author as somebody who goes into the marketplace and puts down his rug and says, "I will tell you a story," and then he passes the hat. And when he's taken up his collection, he tells his story, and just before the denouement he passes the hat again. If it's worth anything, fine. If not, he ceases to be an author. He does not apply for a Canada Council grant.

Because I am a Canadian, I couldn't really live anywhere else. I have had chances to do so and have never given it serious consideration. I belong here. To divorce yourself from your roots is spiritual suicide. The expatriate, unless he is really a rather special kind of person, is very unhappy. I just am a Canadian. It is not a thing which you can escape from. It is like having blue eyes.

I tell my class of graduate students, "Keep your ears open to the promptings of your destiny, and don't worry too much if you and your destiny do not agree about what you should have, and when you should have it. Happiness is always a by-product. It is probably a matter of temperament, and for anything I know it may be glandular. But it is not something that can be demanded from life, and if you are not happy you had better stop worrying about it and see what treasures you can pluck from your own brand of unhappiness."

I'm always urging architects to bring a whisper of magnificence, a shade of lightheartedness and a savour of drama into the setting of our daily lives. How long is it since any Canadian architect has included a secret passage in a new house? The building inspector would no doubt insist that it be equipped with electric light, drainage and an air-changing system.

I feel that people will eventually have to come back to getting their serious information from print. When you see TV and film, you're seeing what is primarily a work of art. It is calculated to catch and hold your attention by the arts of theatre. Now when you are reading a report or anything like that, you can stop, you can consider, you can contradict. You can check your information and you can make notes. You can't do any of these things with the theatrical arts, and it's wrong to be hoodwinked into taking them as information. They are entertainment.

I don't think I would ever write a book with what anybody could call pornography in it, because I feel that pornography is a cheat. It is an attempt to provide sexual experience by secondhand means. Now sex is a thing which has to be experienced firsthand, if you are really going to understand it, and pornography is rather like trying to find out about a Beethoven symphony by having somebody tell you about it and perhaps hum a few bars. It's not the same thing. Sex is primarily a question of relationships. Pornography is a do-it-yourself kit—a twenty-second best.

I am very interested in the condition of sainthood. It is just as interesting as evil. What makes a saint? You look at the lives of some of the very great saints and you find that they were fascinating people. Just as fascinating as great criminals or great conquerors. Most saints have been almost unbearable nuisances in life. Some were reformers, some were sages, some were visionaries, but all were intensely alive, and thus a living rebuke to people who were not. So many got martyred because nobody could stand them. Society hates exceptional people because such people make them feel inferior.

The English influence in Canada has not, I think, in general been a happy one. We have been patronized by the English and they have taken us for granted. No people in the world can make you feel so small as the English, and they have, I think without ever being conscious of it, made many of their dominions feel small. We are the good daughter who stayed at home to help Mother. We did it in 1776. We did it in 1812. The good daughter who stays home ends up by being taken for granted by Mother, and that is what happened to us. My background is not English, it is Welsh and Dutch, and I look at the English with a fairly cold eye. I am fascinated by them, because I want to see what makes them tick, but I am fascinated by them as a Spaniard in the third century might have been fascinated by Rome. England is on the slides, and I want to see what happens.

The American influence on Canada is again a strange and ambiguous one, but the Americans are much more influenced by England than they pretend. I don't believe in historical parallels, but when Rome was at its pinnacle the most prestige-lending possession a Roman could have was a Greek secretary. At this moment the most prestige-lending thing you can have in New York is an English secretary. Britain has reached the secretarial level of decline. You look at American magazines and their booze and their classic clothes and their shoes and all those things are still advertised in English terms; when they really want to build something up, there is a saddle, or Anne Hathaway's cottage, or a Guardsman plastered on it, to give it prestige. This is fascinating. But it is the sign of a country that is becoming a symbol of the past.

Canada demands a great deal from people and is not, as some countries are, quick to offer in return a pleasant atmosphere or easy kind of life. I mean, France demands an awful lot from her people, too, but France also offers gifts in the way of a genial, pleasant sort of life and many amenities that we don't regard as important here and have done little to create. Canada is not really a place where you are encouraged to have large spiritual adventures.

I don't think we're particularly eager to look for the Canadian identity, because many people are afraid of what they may find. They fear it will not be a very flattering picture. You have got to get rid of a lot of the Shadow side of your nature before you come to the reality of it. The Shadow is the inferior side, the unacknowledged evil. And Canada is scared of her Shadow.

A lot of people complain that my novels aren't about Canada. I think they are, because I see Canada as a country torn between a very northern, rather extraordinary, mystical spirit which it fears and its desire to present itself to the world as a Scotch banker. This makes for tension. Tension is the very stuff of art. Plays, novels—the whole lot.

Maclean's, September 1972

The Happy Intervention of Robertson Davies

On December 24 the Secretary of *Opera Canada* telephoned Robertson Davies, and the following is a transcript of their conversation that followed.

OPERA CANADA: *Is that Professor Davies?*

ROBERTSON DAVIES: As much of him as has survived the festive season until this moment. What do you want?

O.C.: *The article. You know—the one you promised to Ruby Mercer on December 15.*

R.D.: You speak of Dr. Ruby Mercer, the linchpin, the life and soul, the animating spirit of opera in Canada?

O.C.: *That's the one.*

R.D.: I yield to no one in my admiration of Dr. Mercer, but what's all this about an article?

O.C.: *She says you promised her one when you met at a cocktail party on December 15, and it is due now, and where is it?*

R.D.: It is lost, lovely child, somewhere in the ragbag that I laughingly refer to as my memory. What was it to be about?

O.C.: *About the opera you and Derek Holman are writing for the Canadian Children's Opera Chorus. Don't tell me you've forgotten that!*

R.D.: No such thing. But you are mistaken, you know. Dr. Holman is writing the opera. He is the composer. I am merely

349

the librettist. I am to him as Schikaneder was to Mozart, or Da Ponte to Mozart, or Hickenlooper to Rossini, or Meilhac and Halévy to Whoever-It-Was. A Librettist is a mere drudge in the world of opera. Why don't you get Dr. Holman to write something?

o.c.: *Dr. Holman says you are the man of words.*

R.D.: I see. And when is this piece expected at the palatial offices of *Opera Canada?*

o.c.: *Yesterday.*

R.D.: You rob me of speech.

o.c.: *Oh no I don't! You'd better tell me what you can on the phone, and I'll make the best of it I can.*

R.D.: May God reward you, as we librettists say.

o.c.: *How far is the opera toward being completed?*

R.D.: The libretto is completed, insofar as it can be while Dr. Holman is still working on it. But I am poised to make alterations, rewritings and excisions as he wishes. A librettist must be totally at the disposal of the composer. You know how Strauss used to kick Hofmannsthal around and demand new material? Even so between me and Dr. Holman.

o.c.: *Is he very cruel?*

R.D.: Not so far, but at times I see a red light in his eye.

o.c.: *Couldn't that be the light of inspiration?*

R.D.: The divine fire? I suppose it could. I never thought of that.

o.c.: *Enough of this trifling. What's the opera about?*

R.D.: Well, it's rather complicated, but essentially simple, like all noble creations.

o.c.: *Where is the setting?*

R.D.: In northern Italy. I see a charming roadway, beside an inn. In the background are splendid romantic mountains. Derek and I both hope the scene-painter is going to excel himself.

o.c.: *Sounds very pretty. But what happens in this charming spot?*

R.D.: Turbulence! Furious dispute! The innkeeper has just

expelled a travelling opera company from his inn because they can't pay their bills! He has seized all their orchestral instruments until the debt is paid. The opera company is torn between rage and despair!

o.c.: *Aha! What next?*

r.d.: The company cannot function without its orchestra. It has singers but no instruments. What are they to do? They think of various expedients, and try one or two, but they simply won't do. The innkeeper is adamant and they are on the rocks. Until—

o.c.: *Yes?—don't leave me in suspense! Until what?*

r.d.: Until a strange figure appears, an immensely tall, top-hatted man of demonic appearance, accompanied by his blind daughter. He asks what the trouble is; they tell him; and he laughs and says he can put everything right.

o.c.: *How?*

r.d.: The strange gentleman is the great Doctor Canon, friend of all the mighty musicians of the day, who has helped Mozart, Haydn and countless others out of difficulties. He says that the problem presented by the travelling company is duck soup.

o.c.: *Duck what?*

r.d.: It is a musical term meaning "simple of solution." He knows just what to do.

o.c.: *Yes, yes—and what is it?*

r.d.: Ah, that would be telling! You must wait and find out when Dr. Holman completes his score. But it *is* a solution, and a splendid one, and the company is able immediately to perform a new opera it has had in preparation. And that opera is a beauty.

o.c.: *What kind of beauty?*

r.d.: It is an opera suitable to the period of the piece, which is very early nineteenth-century Italian. It is about young lovers who are prevented from marrying by a tyrannical father. The hero, Harlequin, is a magnificent tenor, and the heroine, Columbine, is a coloratura of a sort to make Joan Sutherland decide to take up some other career. The Basso Buffo is just the sort of role that the late Salvatore Baccaloni delighted in. And of course there is a Chorus, which is very prominent, and there are some other characters.

o.c.: *Sounds as if it might be funny.*

r.d.: It *is* funny. And when it is over, the innkeeper is so moved that he restores the instruments to the opera company. But they no longer need them, because of the great secret Dr. Canon has imparted to them. The whole thing ends with a paean of praise to Dr. Canon, the Ingenious Virtuoso. That was to have been the title of the opera, you know.

o.c.: *Was it?*

r.d.: Yes, I wanted to call it *Il virtuoso ingegnoso,* or *The Happy Intervention of Doctor Canon.*

o.c.: *And isn't it being called that?*

r.d.: No. That is too long to go up in lights, and you know that an opera with a title too long to go up in lights works under a special disadvantage. So it is going to be called *Dr. Canon's Cure,* which will just fit on the front of La Scala, the Met., Covent Garden and other good houses, but especially Harbourfront.

o.c.: *You sound full of confidence.*

r.d.: I am. Confidence in Dr. Holman, in the Canadian Children's Opera Chorus, in the audience and in Dr. Ruby Mercer and all her assistants, among whom I rank you very high, my dear young friend.

o.c.: *Are there going to be lots of good tunes?*

r.d.: It is all tunes. Dr. Holman has hummed me some of his best—you know how well he hums in four parts—and I can assure you that it is a splendidly tuneful opera.

o.c.: *How long will it take to do?*

r.d.: We are aiming at forty to forty-five minutes. The audience will want it to go on all evening, but it is best to put great gifts in small parcels, as we say where I come from. And now do you think I might ring off? I hate to keep people waiting, and up on my roof I hear the pawing and prancing of many a little hoof. Reindeer, you understand. Christmas is very near.

o.c.: *Well—I can't think of any more questions at present. I must say you seem to have said a lot.*

R.D.: We librettists are professionally gabby. Good-bye.

Diary of a Writer
on the Escarpment

Sunday: Attend a brunch party given by a neighbour. Reflect for the hundredth time that my wife and I should give one of these affairs, and discharge our manifold social debts. Am reminded once again that I am supposed locally to be a hermit, by an Ample Lady who approaches me, saying: "Oh, Mr. Marchbanks, we see you so seldom. But everybody knows you are hard at work on Your Book. Don't you find the Escarpment the perfect place for your work?" I mumble something noncommittal. "Of course we know that's why you live on the Unfashionable Side," she continues, shimmering her eyelashes in a meaningful manner. "Unfashionable Side of what?" I ask. "Of Airport Road, of course," says the Ample Lady, and I divine by the intuition for which all writers are famous that she lives on the Fashionable Side, where the signs at the gates read PORTCULLIS ABOUT TO FALL, and SAVAGE DOGS ON THE PROWL, and SECURITY BY THE ZEUS AND GODS OF OLYMPUS PROTECTION CO.—PROCEED AT YOUR PERIL. I think of all the people who live on the same side of the dividing line as I do, and wonder if they know they are unfashionable, or if they care. "I can see you," the Ample Lady continues, "sitting in your study, looking out over the hills, the streams, the woodlands of the Escarpment, and just soaking up Inspiration. We shall expect very great things from you! You mustn't stop writing for a moment! Because the Niagara Escarpment is unquestionably a writer's Paradise!" Rolling my eyes furiously,

like an author full of Inspiration, I make my way to the bar
. . . Return home, weighed down by the Ample Lady's expectations, but after these Escarpment brunch parties I find that a
short nap—not more than two or three hours—is necessary,
and by then it is too late to begin any writing. However, such
naps are a kind of work, known to us literary folk as Creative
Lassitude.

Monday: Settle down to work bright and early, determined
to be worthy of the Ample Lady's expectations, but find my
attention distracted to the lively doings around my bird-feeding
station. My keen interest in birds is somewhat impeded by the
fact that owing to short sight and stupidity I have never been
able to tell one bird from another except in the most general
way. If I see a bird trying to knock its head off against a tree,
I give a cautious guess that it is a woodpecker. A blueish bird
is probably a jay, if it is not the Bluebird of Happiness, though
I suspect that this creature spends all its time on the Fashionable
Side, near the Forks of the Credit; over here, on the Knives of
the Hockley, we get an altogether commoner class of bird. My
feeder attracts small birds, and a few big birds. The one bird I
could recognize with a little effort is the Cardinal, but I have a
neighbour who is lavish with suet, and the Cardinals, being
high-livers, go to her. I have hawks, which I can tell because
they behave like aeroplanes but don't make a noise, and I have
owls, who occasionally scare the wits out of me by going—no,
not *Whoo!* which is what owls are supposed to go, but *Gruk-
Gruk!* when I walk in my woods. I have even—great student
of Nature that I am—found an owl-ball or two among the trees,
and when I dissected one of these I found quite a mess of mouse-
bones and fur, and a presumably inedible bit of a tail. Nature
is not really the nice old girl that people like the Ample Lady
suppose. Or maybe Nature reserves her nastiest manifestations
for the Unfashionable Side. . . . Some squirrels are under my
bird-feeder, devouring the seed that the birds (wasteful creatures! Do they think I am made of seed?) cast out upon the

ground, like Onan in the Bible. Perhaps Onan was really a bird. I must ask a clergyman.

Tuesday: Having written nothing yesterday, because of the excitement around the bird-feeder, I feel that I must put on steam today, so I get to my desk early, choose a nice clean sheet of paper, and type at the head of it *Chapter One . . .* Look at this for a while and decide that it is worthy of being underlined in red, so I get out a red pencil and my fine new metric ruler. My approach to the metric system has been gradual and suspicious, for I have romantic and legendary associations with the old system. A yard, I have been told and have always believed, was exactly the length from the end of Henry VIII's nose to the end of his outstretched hand. A foot was precisely the length of the foot of Mary, Queen of Scots, who had rather big feet, though as she was six feet tall, probably not disproportionate. When I was a boy my grandmother used to talk about a unit of measure called an ell, which I discover from the dictionary was 45 inches. (Or was *that* the length of Henry VIII's arm? A yard doesn't seem much for a big man.) Anyway, Grandmother was always saying of somebody that if you gave him an inch he'd take an ell, and if anybody had proposed a change to metric to Grandmother they would have received a Piece of Her Mind, which I never measured, but it was quite long. And there used to be all sorts of measurements like chains and rods and, of course, acres, which I suppose we shall now have to call hectares, except that a hectare is 2.471 acres, which is a very inconvenient size for it to be. I reflect that the old system, rooted as it was in history and full of romance, was a lot more fun than metric, which appears to have no history, and certainly no romance. After thinking about it all morning—for I never got around to underlining *Chapter One*—I decided that the metric system was a *tonne*—which is to say 1,000 kgs—of barnyard fertilizer.

Wednesday: Hear a lot of racket in the night and go to see what's up. There are three burglars clustered under my bird-feeder. I know they are burglars because they are wearing masks and convict stripes. They are gobbling up fallen seed, and also the suet I have put out in hopes of getting a little of the Cardinal trade. Whenever the supply fails one of the burglars leans heavily on the stem of the feeder and shakes down some more. Greatly worried, and as soon as it is dawn I call Tim Stewart, who is my advisor on all such matters. "Raccoons," he says, which he means to be reassuring, but for all I know the word may mean "dwarf burglar." So I look it up and find that it is an Algonquian word, and thus entirely appropriate to the Escarpment, and it means a greyish-brown, furry, bushy-tailed, sharp-snouted North American nocturnal carnivore. Carnivore my eye! A seed-eater, as I can attest by personal observation. The dictionary says nothing about stripes or masks, and my faith in it is shaken. So I look up raccoons in the Big Dictionary, which has never failed me, and learn nothing more that is helpful except that this creature used to be called the Jamaica Rat, which I like much better. I recall that a friend of mine once had Jamaica Rats under his roof, and regretted it very much, because one of them lived a full life and (my friend insists) organized games of football up there with his friends. It died, possibly of athletic heart, and as raccoons apparently do not bother about such niceties as funerals, it cost my friend a great deal of time and money and psychological anguish to get his house into living condition again. This, in its turn, reminds me of my mother-in-law, whose eaves in her Australian house were invaded by possums, and as possums are protected creatures and may not be shot or poisoned, she had to employ a very high-powered and brilliant barrister to argue them down. . . . All this looking-up of information and solemn reflection consumes the morning, and I get no writing done.

Thursday: No thought of work today, for the newscast speaks darkly of storm warnings. We are heading for a miserable week-end. I decide that if more snow falls over the snow that is already gathered in my drive I shall be snowbound, so I call the man who ploughs me out when necessary, and he has bad news. The Big Baby is down. He has two ploughs, one of which looks like a front-end loader, which shifts snow by various cunning tricks known to its owner, but it is not attuned to very heavy work. That is undertaken by the Big Baby, a huge affair with a device on the front that grabs up snow in a series of revolving gears and hurls it into a hopper, where some unseen force projects it upward through a curved chimney, spewing it to right and left and all over everything. To see the Big Baby at work on a large drift is to stand in awe of man's triumph over Nature. . . . The only thing is that the Big Baby is temperamental, and if it by chance grabs up a stone it gets mechanical colic and won't eat any more snow. It is then said to be *down*. When it is down, several clever men gather around it and sit on their hunkers and look at it and guess what ails it. These are occasions when a writer is simply a nuisance, and I keep out of the way. After a while they coax the Big Baby out of its sulks and it goes back to work. . . . I have long cherished a mad ambition to climb up into the cab of the Big Baby and see what I could make it do. I am not a mechanical man—indeed, I cannot even ride a bicycle—but the Big Baby arouses all the thwarted mechanic in me. . . . Today, however, the Big Baby was on the fritz (as we mechanics say in our technical jargon), so I shovelled quite a lot of snow by hand, reflecting that the coroner is always warning writers and other sedentary people to avoid just such exertion. But am I a man or a mouse? I am a man to begin with, but after an hour of shovelling I begin to be "wee, sleekit, timorous and cowerin'."

Friday: No snow yet. The CBC has deceived me, as it so often does. I do not believe it is intentional; it is simply that the CBC does not understand weather prediction. What it needs is a copy of *The Old Farmer's Almanac*, which every right-thinking person on the Unfashionable Side of the Escarpment possesses and trusts. (On the Fashionable Side they buy *The Mature Estate Owner's Almanac*, which is the same thing bound in leather.)

I look up the *Almanac* and find that tonight all hell will break loose. To console myself in the face of this news I read some of the *Almanac* jokes, but they only serve to depress me. Listen to this one: " 'Papa, didn't you once whip me for biting baby?' 'Yes, my child; you hurt him very much.' 'Then, Papa, you ought to whip that fellow who is in the parlour, for I saw him bite sister right on the lips; and I know it hurt her, for I saw her put her arms around his neck, and try to choke him.' " The Old Farmer must have heard that one in his boyhood from his grandfather. Nobody on the Escarpment has had a parlour for at least a century. Indeed, nobody has needed one since the invention of funeral parlours, which take care of the principal purpose of parlours very conveniently. . . . By the time I have read all the jokes in the *Almanac* I am too far sunk in gloom to do any work.

Saturday: Woke in the middle of the night to hear the howling of wind and the shattering of sleet on my windows. But that was not all; there are suspicious sounds in my house, which I suppose must be burglars, or perhaps raccoons. After some inner debate as to what I should do, I creep out and look down the stairs and there, in the darkness, is a mysterious form on a ladder, undoubtedly up to some mischief. I consider calling the Provincial Police, but years ago they told me not to do so, as they are far too busy to chase burglars. At this point something about the burglar seems familiar, and I perceive that it is my wife, stuffing long grey objects like snakes into walls. I watch for a while, admiring the skill with which she does this, and when she has finished I ask what is happening. "Draughts," she says. The snakes are some sort of highly recommended draught-defiers which we buy by the yard—or should I say metre? I join her and we creep about the house, almost like burglars ourselves, listening to it creak and groan, until at last we remember to test the taps, and find that one of them will not work. This is what strikes terror into the householder's heart, so we get to work at once with the hair-dryer, taking turns standing on a chair in the cellar, directing the hot breath of the machine at the suffering pipe, but without effect. While we are doing this, there is a terrible silence, and we know that the furnace has ceased to function. . . . After a night of terror, dawn comes at last, and by passionate pleadings over the telephone we secure the assistance of the furnace-psychiatrist, who diagnoses a dirty photoelectric cell, which he cleans with what looks like a handkerchief. Furnace starts again. Universal joy! We have coffee with the furnace-psychiatrist, who tells us that he does all the baking for his family and is an expert on apple pies. He leaves as we stand in the door, carolling our gratitude. And after that, am I expected to do any writing? Life on the Escarpment is too serious to permit such frivolity. I know the Ample Lady is going to be disappointed in me, but what am I to do?

Cuesta, Spring 1982

In a Welsh Border House, the Legacy of the Victorians

My father was a Welshman, and in 1950, when he retired, he bought Leighton Hall on the borderland between Wales and Shropshire. You will find Leighton on any good-size map, because it has been a manor for centuries and there used to be a fine half-timbered manor house that was already old in the reign of Henry VIII.

But somewhere around 1840 the property was bought by John and Jane Naylor of Liverpool; they were great ship-owners and certainly not Welsh. They tore down the old manor and employed an architect to create for them a house, congruous with their great wealth and self-esteem, in the extreme of Victorian Gothic style. This was the house my father bought and in which he lived for 17 years.

I shall not describe the house. It is enough to say that it was grandiose, pretentious, absurd and yet congenial, lovable and delightful, as so many Victorian things were. If you had come to one of my father's frequent, jolly parties, what would have met your eyes?

You would have entered directly from the driveway, passing through a vestibule of modest size, paneled in the style called linen fold—very hard to do, and the Naylors had demanded it by the furlong; on your left hand, a life-size statue of Mrs. Naylor, dressed as a Roman matron, at whose knee two small Naylor sons were obviously learning something edifying; and on your right, two small female Naylors, also in marble, reading the Lord's Prayer from a marble book; on the base of Mrs. N., under the tassels of her cushion, you might have read "B. E. Spence, fecit Roma, 1855." You would not linger with Mrs. Naylor but would press at once into the Great Hall, and great it indeed was, for though I cannot tell you its dimensions it held 125 people with plenty of room to move about, and it was three storeys high, mounting to an oak-timbered roof.

Beneath this roof was a clerestory of stained-glass windows in which were shown the arms of the royal tribes and the non-royal tribes of Wales, 20 in all, and splendid as ancient heraldry can be in that genealogically minded country. Genuine descendants of these worthies (and there were often many of them at parties) knew that the great chieftains were linked with the Naylors by money, rather than blood, but 10 centuries later there was no point in being pernickety.

My father had furnished the room to make it as comfortable as it is in the nature of so large a room to be, but there were Naylor associations that could not be altered. Wherever it was possible to carve a monogram in oak, linked J's and an N, in the most gnarled Gothic script, were to be seen.

Portraits of more than life size of John and Jane Naylor hung on the walls, she large and bonny, he slight and looking rather like Mendelssohn disguised as a wealthy ship-owner.

There were other pictures, huge in dimension, that remained in place until some unspecified time when the Naylor descendants would come and take them away. (But where? In what ordinary dwelling could such monsters hang?) *Napoleon Crossing the Alps,* and Napoleon meditating, obviously about something of a melancholy nature; *The Temptation of Christ,* the Fiend portrayed naked, but decently vague where the Victorians demanded vagueness; four huge paintings by Turner. But wait— not quite by Turner; the genuine Turners had been sold to the National Gallery in less prosperous Naylor times, and these were copies from the hand of a Miss Naylor, who was diligent, but not quite as talented as Turner.

When my father took over the house, two of these Turner copies fell from the wall and did quite a bit of damage. It is by no means uncommon for such things to happen when properties change hands, and perhaps my father's admiration for the genuine Turner played some psychic part in this downfall. It is a matter for Jungian speculation. Anyhow, there the four pseudo-Turners remained, happily too high for close inspection.

Until my father had it dismantled and removed to a stable, the Great Hall was dominated by what I can only call an altar to gluttony against the south wall. It was a German sideboard of monumental proportions that the Naylors had acquired at the Great Exhibition of 1851. Every fruit, flower, meat, game and edible was carved on it in life size, including four large hounds, chained to the understructure with wooden chains, so cunningly wrought that they could be moved, like real chains.

In addition there were fat, life-like wooden children, representing the seasons. I still have one of them, young Autumn, and I like to think of his bulging eyes fixed upon the crowd, including the Great Queen herself, at the 1851 exhibition. It was awesome; it was a triumph of the wood-carver's craft; it was monstrous.

The really fine thing, to me at least, was the hall clock, which occupied a tower over the entry. Only the face showed in the hall, but the works could be visited by way of a spiral staircase, and they were wondrous; they recorded the seconds, the hours, the days of the week, the months, the seasons, the signs of the zodiac and the phases of the moon, all in bronze and ormolu.

Not only did it strike the hours; it had three octaves of fine bells, and when a secret wire was pulled in the hall it would give out merrily with Welsh, English, Scottish and national airs, and of course some hymns. My father loved to astonish his grandchildren by leaning nonchalantly near the activating lever and saying, "Would you like to hear some fairy music?" Then a covert tug at the cord and—Astonishment! Wonder! Owen Glyndwr lives again! Isn't Grandfather amazing!

He was amazing, for he managed to make that extraordinary house a charming habitation, where he lived not quite like a Victorian, but almost. And it was there that I gained some glimpse of what Victorianism really was.

New York Times, 29 November 1984